The Search of Grace

A novel

by

James Gottesman

ISBN- 978-0-9911557-0-5
JayEddy Publishing

ACKNOWLEDGMENTS

Thanks go to many. Gloria Brown, my longtime co-conspirator, read it first and, like always, was brutally honest, but said that the story was solid.

My muses, Grace, Ellie and Sophie Gottesman continue to inspire me.

I need to thank the initial readers of the book, particularly Tony Wartnik, Chuck Caplan, Ruth Bunin, Karen Robertson, Greg Gottesman and Marsha Siegel, to name a few, gave valuable insights.

Aviva Layton, my editor, told me, "I loved the book but that's the last nice thing I'm going to say."

Also to Diane Mackay Richie, the first person to really teach me how to write. She may not remember, but I do.

Although I listened to everyone and everything, I didn't always follow all their suggestions.

Thanks to Grace Gottesman who shot the photos of Ellie Gottesman for the cover. So talented.

I am sure more will need to be thanked, but for now.........jeg

To no one else but Mrs. Brown's Lovely Daughter

Mrs. Brown, You've Got a Lovely Daughter, sung by Herman's Hermits, #1 on the U.S. Billboard Hot 100, May 1965

The Search of Grace

Prologue

1994, Seattle, Washington

Seattle Med School Library Archives – early morning

The immense, windowless archives were silent and dark, except for the soft rhythmic whooshing of overhead fans and a sliver of ambient light from the hallway.

Grace started most every weekday the same. She checked that housekeeping had not moved her chair behind the counter, and then closed the door.

Dead dark.

She shut down the fans.

Dead silent.

She felt her way around the counter and sat. She would not close her eyes.

Grace thought mostly of the orphanage, Sarah and Jodie, and Ezekiel Watkins.

She sat longer if her nightmares had been too vivid.

She sat until her thoughts weren't so heavy.

She sat until she didn't have to think about breathing.

Chapter 1

Seattle, Washington

God, I hate being used.

Alex Gordon entered the medical library at 8 a.m. and approached the main desk. Anger had changed his confident stride to a semi-stomp.

The reference librarian, a number two pencil going through her hair like an arrow that just missed, looked up from her computer screen and asked, "Doctor, how may I help you?"

"I'd like to find as many of these ancient references as possible."

The librarian scanned the list. Finishing only half, she stopped. "Good luck with any of these. They would all be in the archives, somewhere, but none are catalogued."

Alex asked, "Where are the archives? Hopefully not in Kansas."

The librarian smiled. "The archives are on the fifth floor, southwest elevator. Be prepared, the archives are bigger than the Kingdome and we have only one person up there. She's been with us a short time, and is a bit unusual. She'll help you."

Alex wasn't sure what 'unusual' meant. He rode to the fifth floor and exited to a long hallway which had a solitary door with a sign that read *'Medical Library Archives - Restricted to Authorized Users Only.'* He entered to find the room dark. He could see from the hallway's light that the room was huge, and standard 48-inch fluorescent fixtures, all off, lined the ceiling. Alex ran his hand up and down the wall near the door trying to locate a switch without luck. He then looked, unsuccessfully, outside the door for a switch. He re-entered the room and walked in a few steps, only to take a jab to the groin from a counter edge.

"Ouch. Damn it."

A soft voice from the darkness arose, "May I help you?"

Alex, startled, and seeing no one, queried to the dark and cavernous room, "Is someone here, or is there a camera and a speaker?"

A calm voice said, "I'm a few feet from you."

"This is freaking me out. Do you mind turning on the lights?"

At once, rows of fluorescent fixtures pinged and crackled like lightning popcorn, and there was light.

Alex was speechless. A woman occupied a small chair behind the counter, in left profile, not five feet from him. Alex thought she might be young. She wore a plain black one-piece sack dress, almost Amish in appearance. Her hair was in a tight bun except for one long loose strand down the left side of her face. She continued to look away, purposefully not trying to make eye contact, her hands clenched and folded in her lap.

She repeated, "May I help you?"

After a few seconds, trying to decide whether to run or stay, Alex spoke up, "You're the librarian?"

She replied, "I wish I were a librarian. I'm a file clerk."

Alex, confused, said, "I was told a librarian worked the archives. I need some old references pulled."

The woman, still frozen, said, "I'm the only one here. Do you have a list?"

"Sure, here." Alex extended the list in his hand over the counter towards the woman and held it for a moment. She made no attempt to move off her chair, so Alex circled the counter and handed the list to the woman/lady/girl. *Whatever she is.*

"Thanks." The woman, still making no attempt at eye contact with Alex, scanned the list. As she scanned, she twirled the loose strands of hair with her left hand and then slid down the strand to straighten her twirl. "Hmmm. Some easy, most not. When do you need them?"

"My chief wanted them yesterday." Alex smiled at the little bit of intended humor. He finally got a reasonable look at her face. *Definitely less than thirty. Nice features. Odd demeanor.*

The woman, sans smile, monotoned, "I'll work on it. You'll have to come back."

Alex, knowing the difficulty of the search, said, "Sure. I can come back, maybe a couple of hours."

"Maybe a couple of weeks. We'll see."

4

"I don't think my chief wants to wait that long. Do what you can. I'm curious, tell me, why were the lights off?"

"Habit."

This is one weird person. "I'll be back at 11 a.m."

"Suit yourself."

Alex, unamused, took on a sarcastic tone, said, "Will the lights be on when I get back?"

Ignoring the sarcasm, she said, "Don't know. Depends how many of these I've found."

Alex, realizing that being rude wasn't going to help locate any of his articles, retreated, with a modicum of sincerity, "Hopefully some. Thank you."

As Alex started to leave, the woman remained seated and said, "Please close the door."

Alex exited and closed the door. Approaching the elevator, Alex's curiosity got the best of him. He returned to the door and opened it just a crack.

A voice from inside returned immediately, "Yes, the lights are still on."

Alex closed the door. *I've got to stop drinking so much coffee in the morning.*

Alex Gordon was having a God-awful day. For the second time in his first week at Seattle General, the Chief Resident in Urology, Carleton Holland, his immediate boss for the next year, had not assigned him any surgical cases. Instead, Holland gave Alex a research assignment to find medical articles from the distant past on obsolete treatments for kidney stones. The chief was apparently writing an article or giving a talk.

Either this a test to see if I'll lose my cool, or he's decided he doesn't like me and doesn't give a shit how I react.

Alex ran into Art Siegel, another first year Urology resident, who was between cases.

"Hey, Alex. How's it going? Holland said something this morning during our first case that he hopes you'll dig up some references for him. Sounds like a bullshit job to me."

Alex said, "Ain't that the truth? I had forty references I'd hoped to find, most written before 1900 and more than half in German and some in French and Italian. I went up to the archives this morning and the librarian up there is a total whacko. I'll be lucky to find four or five of the articles. I'm on my way there now."

She's missing a screw. The lights were on but nobody's home. Three cards short of a full deck. Alex mused clichés, certain that the strange girl would find nothing on his list. He could sense Dr. Holland's vengeance awaiting him on patient rounds that evening. *'Gordon, you did shit all day. I'm keeping you on the patient floors and library duty for the rest of the year.'*

Alex re-entered the archives with his laptop in hand. The lights were on, but the area behind the counter was empty but he could hear what sounded like a copier whirring in a small office. He followed the sound and entered a small room. The sack-dressed young woman was facing the copy machine

6

trying to compress a large book down on the copy plate. She had not heard Alex enter.

Alex spoke over the din of the machine, "Hey, how are things going?"

The woman jumped and lost the book onto the floor. The old binding split and pages of fragile yellowed paper spilled everywhere around the room.

The woman, hands on her hips, had still not turned towards her intruder, but said, "Damn, you scared me. Look at this mess. And look at the book."

Alex couldn't tell whether she was angry or scared or both. Alex, realizing his abrupt intrusion, said, "I'm so sorry."

They both went down to the floor picking up loose pages.

Alex got his first close look at the woman. *She's younger than I thought, maybe twenty-three or twenty-four, at the most. She's stunning, but doing everything she can to hide it.* The loose strand of hair was still the only aspect of her appearance out of place. He stopped gathering papers and watched her. She glared at his stare and Alex's eyes and hands jumped back to the papers on the floor.

Alex repeated, "I'm sorry for startling you. I didn't mean it. Hey, we're even for the lights being off this morning and me running into the counter. I'm too young for a vasectomy."

She responded sourly, "Not funny."

Alex said, "Maybe a little funny."

"Not," she said, "if I had been holding a baseball bat instead of an old book, a vasectomy sounds better than a crushed skull."

"Ouch. Urologists and librarians must have strange senses of humor."

"Hmmm. I'll think about it," she said, as her posture softened. "I was so happy about finding the references and making copies that I wasn't listening for someone to enter. Not like me to be caught unaware. I'm madder at myself. By the way, I am not a librarian. I'm only a file clerk. I know because I am paid minimum wage."

Alex, not understanding the total gist of her comments, said, "You've said that before. To me, if you work in a library, you're a librarian. Did you find a few of the references?"

"You're a bit dense, but have it your way. You can call me anything you want. As to the articles, almost all. Turns out, someone must have done a similar search, three or four years ago. All the work just sat in a file. I thought I had seen something like your request when I started here full-time a few months ago, but I'd never gotten around to cleaning out those cabinets. Your lucky day. I would have thrown all this away," pointing the the neat stacks of copied articles. She continued, "Anyway, sure enough, thirty-five of the forty were there already. Found three more on the shelves. I was making three copies of everything. One for you, one for your chief and one for the library. I figure someone else will come in asking for them. Things happen in threes, so they say."

Alex, instantaneously in a better mood, asked, "I'd be impressed if you could tell me who 'they' are."

8

The woman, for the first time, smiled, "Touché."

After picking up the mess, she said, "Leave the loose pages on the counter. I'll put it all back together. Simple paste holds these old journals together. They fall apart if you look at them funny. Here are the folders for you."

Alex looked through the folders. "Incredible,... awesome.. I had a shit day until...," Alex hesitated, "Oh, excuse me, I didn't mean to swear."

"Fine by me."

"Anyway, I had a down day until now. If the chief doesn't like this, he's either plain mean or crazy. I need to do a little perusing of this stack. I can't read German or French but I'll try to muddle through."

The file clerk said, "I can read both. There are some Italian papers, too. I can muddle through Italian as long as it's technical jargon. There, we both used the word 'muddle.'"

"Really."

She said, "Really, what? Using 'muddle' in a sentence?"

"Really, can you read German and French?"

Still smiling, she said, "I lived with nuns. There's a table over there. I'm going to work mending this old journal but if you need some translating, let me know."

Alex sat down. *Nuns? Who lives with nuns? What did that have to do with speaking German or French?* He started reading the English papers, keying notes into his laptop as fast as he could. After finishing the English references, he was ready to tackle German.

"I'm done with the English, so I'd like to start on the German papers. Can you help?"

Without comment, the young woman sat in a chair beside Alex. He stared, again, at the eccentric file clerk-librarian, who was in the process of saving his ass, figuratively. She had large brown penetrating, expressive eyes, a strong, clefted chin and ebony colored hair. From her light olive complexion, he thought she might be Mediterranean, but doubted that she ever sat in the sun. She wore no makeup. As before, her glare back caused Alex to shift attention to his papers.

She said, "What do you need?"

"First, I need your name. I'm Alex Gordon, and I'm a third year resident, but in my first of four years in Urology."

"I'm Grace."

"Oh, like the charm and loveliness Grace, or the benediction or blessing Grace?"

"Just Grace...and I don't feel comfortable with you playing with me."

"No last name?"

"Grace is enough for now. You don't need to know my whole name."

With a slight shake of his head, Alex said, "Let's start with these German papers. Maybe you can tell me the title of the paper, and read the conclusion. It's too bad some of these old papers don't have abstracts at the beginning like modern articles do."

Grace read aloud all twenty-two titles and conclusions, in German followed by English. As she read, she returned to twirling the loose strands of hair with her left hand and then sliding down the strands to straighten the twirl. Alex tried hard to concentrate on the translations, although he was semi-fixated on her hair twirling. When he lost concentration watching her, he'd ask her to repeat what she had just read. If the article seemed relevant, Alex would place the paper in a separate pile. When done, Alex picked up the short pile and asked, "Any chance we could go through these 5 in depth? Maybe not today, if you don't have time, but soon."

Grace responded, "I'm okay for time. How long do you have?"

Alex thought for a moment and said, "The chief and two other residents started a five hour surgery at 10:00. They won't likely be done until 3:00, 3:30. Then we'll make rounds. So I've got until 3:00. I'll call down to the OR at 2:00 to see how things are going."

Grace wrinkled her mouth and nose, took the top paper and started to read in muted German, "*Überprüfung der Nierenstein Chirurgie*," and then followed in English in regular voice, "*Review of Kidney Stone Surgery*," twirling all the while.

Alex was able to help Grace understand some of the advanced technical medical jargon in the conclusions, which he could understand by the context of the article. She read and he keyed the information onto his laptop. From the German, they switched to the first of the four French papers.

"Examen de la chirurgie de la lithiase rénale. Review of Nephrolithiasis Surgery."

Alex Gordon couldn't help himself. This mysterious polyglot, hair-twirling librarian, who wasn't a librarian, fascinated him.

As 2 p.m. approached, Grace asked, "Don't you have to call and see how the surgery is going?"

Alex looked up at the clock and realized that he had lost all track of time. "Wow. Time flew."

Alex called the OR and talked for less than thirty seconds. "They'll be done at 3:15, rounds at 3:30. We have another hour or so. I'm sorry; did I make you miss your lunch break?"

Grace said, "No, not really," and turned back to the stack of papers and the two Italian articles. She looked at the title for a moment.

"I haven't read much Italian lately, but I'll get the hang of it. *Policlinico Universitario Agostino Gemelli - Recensione di nefrolitiasi chirurgia. Review of Nephrolithiasis Surgery at the Agostino Gemelli Teaching Hospital or University.*"

At 2:45, Grace had finished all the papers Alex needed.

Alex, again, found himself staring at this mysterious young woman. "You are amazing. How lucky was I to find you? Is there a way that I can print out what I've typed so far?"

"Sure." Grace rose and went to her desk and pulled out a formatted 3.5" floppy disk from the drawer. "Copy your stuff onto this and I'll print it here."

As the library printer was spewing out papers, he reiterated, "You are amazing. How lucky was I to find you?"

Grace responded, "I think you said that once already. You tend to repeat yourself. Is there anything else you need?"

Alex said, "Absolutely. I need to pay you back. I mean wasting a whole day, missing lunch, and doing all this, just for me. How about I buy you lunch?"

She responded quickly, "No. No. Not necessary."

Alex's curiosity didn't budge. He responded, "You're not getting off that easy. My treat in the hospital cafeteria." Alex, now smiling, continued, "The food's crap, but the location is to die for."

Grace responded emphatically, "No. I don't go to the cafeteria. I don't ever go there."

Alex, persisting, said, "Okay then, next time I have a free lunch hour, I'll bring up some food."

"I know for a fact that we're not supposed to eat in the archives," she responded.

"Grace, if that's your real name, we've been here all day and not one soul has come through that door. I don't think anyone will ever know if you eat something here."

She said nothing, which, he assumed, meant yes.

Alex said, "I've gotta go and get ready for rounds. I'll be back. I promise."

Grace said, "Call first. Dial the main library number and ask for the archives. I'm not always here. And my name is Grace."

"Grace, isn't there a direct number into here?"

"No, you have to go through the main library."

As Alex was leaving, he turned and asked, "Lights, on or off?"

Grace, turning away, said, "I'll take care of the lights."

As he exited, Alex noted a phone sitting on the counter. He saw a number above the key pad, 54003, and made a mental note. Alex knew that the main library's extension was 54000.

Alex walked to the elevator, laptop and papers in hand, in a much better mood.

He couldn't help thinking about the librarian or file clerk, whatever she was. *How lucky was I?*

When the elevator arrived, he put down his laptop and added *Grace the Librarian*, and *54003*, to his contact list.

The next morning, Alex dialed the main library number and then asked for the archives. After four rings, it jumped to voice mail.

The message, in Grace's voice, was of no help. *"The archives are open from 9 to 5, Monday to Friday and closed on weekends. If you have a list of articles, then fax the list to 206 – 232 – 8207, or email the list to archives@seattlemed.edu. Voicemail is not available for the archives."* The line disconnected.

Alex tried the direct number and got the same message. He emailed Grace at archives@seattlemed.edu. 'Grace. Just wanted to thank you again for yesterday's help. Would like to bring you lunch as a thank you. Alex Gordon, MD.'

Twenty-four hours later, Alex had received no response. *I don't think she'll ever respond.*

Alex's last surgical case of the day finished at 3:30 p.m. Rounds were at 4:15. He had scut work to do, but decided to complete his tasks after rounds. He dialed the archives one more time but received the same canned message. He wrote and sent a cryptic email. *Grace, I don't know if you're there. It's 3:35 and I'll be there in five minutes.* He headed up to the archives. As he approached the door, he wondered, *lights on or off?*

The lights were off as Alex entered. "Hello? Anyone here?" Without an answer, he stepped, carefully, into the room and found the light switch behind the counter.

Ping, crackle.

Grace was sitting in her chair, back against the counter, softly crying. She said, between sobs, "Why can't you leave me alone... I don't want any friends... I don't need any friends... Friends hurt you, every time."

Alex found a chair and slid it to face the crying Grace.

Alex sat for a moment. When Grace stopped crying, he said, "Grace, please, listen to me. I am new here. I don't know anyone in the medical center. My chief resident admitted that he didn't like me at first. The stuff you did for me blew him away. Anyway, he's been nice to me since, and unless I screw it up, my first year here will be good. I owe that to you."

Grace responded, "I did nothing and I don't want or need accolades from you or anyone."

"That's not true. You did something; you helped me. I will be here for four more years and was hoping to do some research and paper writing. To me, you're the greatest resource I could have ever found. I don't need to be social friends with you but... but I'd like to be able to work with you. That's it. Business friends. Yep, just business friends."

Grace hesitated, then said, "...Okay. Business friends."

"Great. I still owe you for your help. It's the way I work. I have to be able to pay you back. Tomorrow at noon, I will be here with lunch. No locked doors. No *'Sorry I Missed You. Back at 2:30'* signs."

Grace nodded yes.

"I've got clinic at 1, so I'll need to leave by 12:45."

The following day, Alex entered the archives at noon. He placed a tray on the counter with a chicken Caesar salad, a plate of macaroni and cheese, a Diet and a regular Coke, and a bottle of water.

Alex, nodding hello to Grace, started, "Sorry, I didn't ask if you had any dietary hang-ups. I asked the cafeteria staff and they said these were the two most common dishes served. If you are a vegan, I'm in trouble."

Smiling, Grace said, "I'm not."

"Great, you can have one or the other or we can share both."

"Uh, well..." Grace said, pointing to the right side of the counter with her thumb.

Posted on the wall, a new sign, in big bold red letters, that read, 'No Food in Archives.'

Alex realized that inside the veneer of seeming indifference, a sense of humor did exist. He said, "We're safe. If Mac and Cheese on a Styrofoam plate is food, our society is in big trouble."

Grace smiled and said, "Je suis d'accord. I'll have the salad."

Eating at the worktable, Alex watched Grace approach her salad. Both arms semi-surrounded the salad, as if she was protecting it from wolves. *She has to have a story.*

"Grace, I've already seen a case that's worthy of reporting. Have you ever heard of Ehlers–Danlos syndrome?"

"No. I'm not a doctor." But Grace's eyes and tone were not dismissive. "What is 'Air...uh,. whatever?"

"Ehlers–Danlos. There are many different types. The most common is Type III, which causes joint hypermobility or what's called being 'double jointed.' I've seen a few, and it's astonishing to see someone put their leg behind their neck. But that's not what I saw today. Type IV causes disintegration of the blood vessels in young adults..."

Alex droned on for another five minutes.

"...From what I could gather, the patient will likely close off all his large vessels in the next few days or weeks and will die. Anyway, I'd like some information on Ehlers–Danlos syndrome so I can present something at Saturday's grand rounds."

"How do you spell Ehlers–Danlos?"

"E-H-L-E-R-S, Dash, D-A-N-L-O-S."

18

Grace wrote but said nothing.

Alex asked, "Can I come back at six, after clinic, and pick up what you've found?"

"We close at five."

"Uh oh. So what do we do? I'll call if I can't get up here before five."

"Don't call. I won't answer the phone," Grace said. She hesitated and thought for a second, then continued, "If it's after five, I'll lock up and leave the papers under the door. Housekeeping doesn't get here til ten p.m. or so. That's all I can do. My bus leaves at five fifteen, so I can't stay."

As Alex left for clinic, Grace, said, "Please close the door on the way out."

And thank you for lunch, but Alex kept that thought to himself.

At six p.m., Alex returned to the archives to find the door locked and a treasure trove of printed information on Ehlers–Danlos syndrome in a folder peaking out under the door. Inside the folder was a 3.5" floppy disk with pictures, references and articles, already in PowerPoint format.

After his presentation at grand rounds the following morning, the Chairman of the Department of Urology, Harold Kauffman, approached Alex. "Wonderful presentation, Alex. That case came in two days ago. Impressive amount of research. Great work."

Alex emailed Grace's library account, *'You are gold! Thank you. Lunch Tuesday noon.'*

Over a hamburger and Cobb Salad, Alex again told Grace how valuable she had been. Again, she refused to accept any credit.

As they sat and ate, Alex tried his best to get Grace to open up.

"So where'd you learn to speak all those languages?"

"Just around. The nuns."

"What's that mean?"

"Just here and there."

"Grace, that isn't an answer."

"I don't like talking about myself."

"Most people don't speak multiple languages. It's unusual. Where'd you learn to speak?"

"You're not going to stop asking are you?"

"Nope."

"Growing up. Two nuns. One spoke German, one French. Happy?"

"No. You're not even finishing the sentences. Where were the nuns? At school?"

"In an orphanage. I grew up in an orphanage. Sister Greta spoke German; Sister Claudette spoke French. I showed interest and they taught me to speak and read. I read everything they gave me. I

20

rarely talked to them in English. I took a few free courses in Italian in Missoula. I can't tell you why, languages come easily to me."

"Missoula, that's in Montana, right? How'd you get to be a librarian?"

"You're prying. I'm not a librarian; my title is 'file clerk.' I'd need a college degree to be an actual librarian. It was a job. And, yes, Missoula is in Montana."

"I'm not prying. I'm being inquisitive. How'd you end up here in the archives?"

"God, you're nosy. I started filing in the main library. When people would want something pulled from the archives, I seemed to be the only one who could find things. Actually, most of the librarians hated coming up here. They thought it creepy. The head librarian, Mrs. McPherson, asked if I wanted to work up here full time and I said yes. I liked the quietness. I liked not having people poke into my life." Grace stopped for a moment to let her statement sink in. "I learned how to re-bind broken journals, so I spend a good deal of time up here doing that."

"Grace, you're not going to tell me much about yourself, are you?"

"No. I don't talk about myself...to anyone. I did tell you how I learned German and French and how I ended up in the archives. Be happy that I told you that."

"Grace, I have clinic every Tuesday at one p.m. and we seldom have significant cases on Tuesday mornings. How 'bout we say that I'll bring lunch next Tuesday, unless I call and say I can't make it."

"That's not necessary. Besides, I may have things to do on Tuesday."

"Grace, uh, uh, I don't buy it. You've had nothing to do on the last two Tuesdays. You can call me if you're busy; otherwise, I'm coming up with lunch. You're worth every Styrofoam container."

"Now there's a compliment."

"That didn't come out right. Sorry."

Something about Grace piqued Alex's curiosity. He'd see a chicken burrito. *Would Grace like that?* He'd hear about an interesting diagnosis like xanthogranulomatous pyelonephritis. *Could Grace help me research that? I may never understand her, but she's like no one I've ever met.*

Alex had his third and fourth lunches with Grace on consecutive Tuesdays. Alex talked about his education, Lowell High School in San Francisco, UCLA undergrad, UCSF med school and two years of General Surgery back at UCLA before coming to Seattle Med for Urology. Grace wouldn't bite when Alex asked, "How about you?"

"Here and there," was all Grace could offer.

After lunch, Alex threw a curveball to Grace, with a huge smile and a Clark Gable voice, an octave lower than normal. "Grace, we can't go on like this anymore. I can't take it."

Grace's eyes widened, but she said nothing, waiting for the next sentence.

"You have to let me take you out of the hospital for a meal."

"No, I don't think so. I don't do those things."

"Please. If I have to go back to Mac and Cheese again, I'll hang myself. You'd be responsible."

Grace said, "Go for it. I doubt you'll hang yourself."

Alex repeated, "Please."

"I'll have to think about it. That's all I can do right now."

"Grace, I'm going to go out on a limb right now. I'm guessing you don't have any friends here, for whatever reason. I think you are unique and I'd like to be friends. I'm still not sure what you have against being friends with me. So I'm going to ask you again, and this time I'd like you to say 'Sure, I'd love to go.'"

Grace was twirling her hair strand in double time. A bead of sweat balanced between her brows as Alex asked her to dinner and waited for an answer.

Grace said nothing, but nodded 'yes.'

Alex, trying to push his luck, said, "There's not enough time to go out anywhere for lunch, so why don't we do dinner. Tuesday after clinic and evening rounds. You'll have to wait a little but I should be done before six, six thirty, at the latest. We'll go out to eat and then I'll drive you back to your place."

"No. No. You can bring me back here to the hospital. I'll take a bus. They run every hour after seven p.m. Last bus is at ten fifteen. I can't have you taking me home."

Alex acquiesced with a nod. *If I push her, she'll back out.* "A deal. But if I have to reach you, for whatever reason, what do I do?"

"Why would you need to reach me?"

"I'm a resident and stuff happens."

"Just leave a message on the archive voice mail."

Alex said, "You don't have voice mail, I've tried. I've been emailing you."

Grace hesitated to think and said, "Okay, email me if you have an issue. See you next Tuesday night." Grace nodded but, as before, didn't say thanks for the meal. After throwing away her empty salad container, Grace sat in her chair by the counter and twirled and pulled on her strand of hair.

Chapter 2

October 1970 - Outside Chappaqua, Westchester County, New York State

22 years earlier

Katy Harris entered her father's study.

"Katy, sit down."

When Culver Harris said 'sit and listen', people, including his wife and children, his employees, friends, judges or politicians sat and listened. He was that powerful. Culver had the looks, smarts, education, personality, demeanor, pedigree and money to back up his authority. Culver was over 6 feet tall, broad in the shoulders and solidly toned. His full head of hair had been snow white since his late thirties. Steel blue eyes, given to each of his four children, were laser set in a full face.

Culver Harris had learned from the best, his father, Ambrose Harris. Ambrose Harris had built a fortune before he was forty in railroads, steel, and a good percentage of real estate in Manhattan and Chicago. Ambrose lamented often that America had no royalty and, if they had, he surely would have been king. Ambrose groomed his oldest son, Culver, to continue the Harris fortunes and legacy. Culver did not disappoint.

Ambrose's best advice to his son when making demands to anyone was letting it be known at the beginning of a dialogue that his word was rule and that his demands were not negotiable. "Son, that way, it keeps the discussions to a minimum. Any change would be in direct opposition to my word, and I don't let that happen. Ever.

As soon as Katy had taken a seat across from Culver's massive, and purposefully intimidating, twelve-foot desk, he said, "I will tell you once, I don't want you screaming at me again, or running out of the room. It won't do any good. I am going to do all the talking. Do you understand? This is my house and I make the rules, plain and simple."

Katy nodded.

"First, I wasn't happy about you going away this summer to a mixed prep school. Your mother admits she made a mistake. You've been in private girls schools your whole life and I wasn't sure that you were ready to make decisions on your own. By your behavior, I erred in letting you go. However, that is done now. In my view, your sinning went way past any level of depravity. You slept with a young man. You slept with him and got pregnant. We've known for three weeks now. Time enough for me and you to reflect on what you've done, what you've done to this family, and your mother and me.

"I have talked to my attorneys, and spent an afternoon in New York in the counsel of Cardinal O'Bryan. I have examined all my options. Having an abortion is not an option in the eyes of God and the Church, but neither is keeping this child an option, in my eyes."

Katy raised her hands in protest but before she spoke her father yelled, "I am talking. You have nothing that I want to hear."

Lowering his voice, he continued, "I don't really care who the father of this child is, but I will certainly not have Jewish blood mingled with ours. I have thought about disowning you, literally and figuratively, throwing you out on the street. However, you are still young and the damage to the family, publicly, from that could be worse."

"Here is how this is going to play out for all of us, if you want to remain a member of this family.

"One, you will never try to contact this boy, Ben Kaplan, ever. I have let none of your letters leave our estate or the local post office. I have not let you talk to this Jew or received any of his letters. Nor will I ever."

Katy's eyes opened widely, unaware that her father had been intercepting her mail, inbound and outbound. "Father, that's not..."

Culver Harris shouted again, "I am doing the talking. Keep your mouth shut. My house, my rules."

He waited a moment to make sure no further interruptions would occur. Harris said, "And if your diary is ever located, I will destroy it. I don't believe that you lost it."

Katy said, "I did. I was sure I packed it when I left Andover, but it wasn't there when I got home."

Harris grimaced and then said, "Under no circumstances will this boy or his family ever find out that you bore this bastard child.

"Two, we will cancel your admission to Smith College.

"Three, we will arrange a home for you to stay in throughout your pregnancy. This home will be far away, in another state. You will have no opportunity to talk or write to anyone during this time.

"Four, you will have this illegitimate child, privately. You will never see it, not for a second. The child will be given to an orphanage, unnamed, and even I won't know where it will be placed." *Better she not know that I will follow this bastard for the rest of its life.*

"Five, after the pregnancy and your recovery, we will arrange for you to go to a private girls college out of the country, probably Switzerland. You will not have access to outside mail or phone privileges. You will not return to New York until I say so.

"Six, you will try to put all of these sinful events behind you, as if they never happened. Your mother knows and your brothers and sister know. It will stay that way. We are not going to discuss this. You will be getting therapy to help you re-align your life as a Harris.

28

"Seven, if you break any of these rules, I will disown you, utterly and completely. There will be no second chances.

"Allowing your sister, Holly, to be dragged into this fiasco, as your ally, is unconscionable. She is only thirteen years old and still a baby and understands nothing. She is meeting with Father Kiffers today and will see him weekly so that she may understand how you have gone astray.

"Katy, you have been a disgrace to me, to this family and to your religion. While I won't forget what has transpired, I will try to forgive you and I hope God forgives you. You are not to talk to your brothers or Holly about these arrangements, or go behind my back to anyone. Your mother agrees with my decision, but I do not want you discussing our arrangement with her. There will be no arguments. Am I understood?"

Tears streaming down her face, "Yes, sir." was the only response Katy could give.

"Tomorrow at 8 am, you will be driven to the house we have set up to take care of you for the pregnancy. I'd pack toiletries and whatever reading material you want. You will not be coming back to Chappaqua for the next nine months."

* * * *

"Mr. LeVite, your two o'clock appointment is here. A Mr. Kelly. He's here with another man who is apparently an attorney. Mr. Kelly assured me that no one is angry or in trouble. Purely a business opportunity."

As LeVite buttoned his collar and tightened his tie, he said, "Show them in, Rose."

Two men entered the modest office of Richard LeVite, Director of the Lost Souls Orphanage of Mt. Nazareth, Virginia.

"Mr. LeVite, I am John Kelly. To be clear, John Kelly is not my real name. You don't need to know my real name." Culver Harris waited a few moments for what he had just said to register.

LeVite said, "I don't understand."

Harris continued, "You will in a moment. This is my attorney, Henry Farley, and that is his real name." The two visitors shook hands with LeVite and Farley gave LeVite a business card with a New York City address.

LeVite pointed to two worn Naugahyde seats facing his desk. Harris looked at Farley, then nodded towards the two chairs and waited while Farley's hand-swiped both seats to remove dust. The men sat. The visitors, both with New England-like accents, were well dressed; three piece suits with expensive ties. Too well dressed for LeVite's usual visitors.

Uh oh, this is going to cost me money. LeVite said, "What can I do for you fine gentlemen?"

The fictitious Mr. Kelly, with traces of perspiration on his forehead, leaned over to his attorney and whispered something.

Mr. Farley, his dark hair slicked down and parted neatly, 1930s style, spoke, "There are no recording devices in this room are there?"

LeVite replied, "No. None."

Farley continued, "My client, Mr. Kelly, has a delicate issue that we hope you can help us with. If you cannot help us, you need only to tell us and we will leave."

"I'm not sure that I understand yet, but go ahead."

"Mr. Kelly is a wealthy and important man in a different part of the country. You don't need to know where he comes from. He is happily married and has children. One of his daughters, let's assume her name is Mary, which it is not, now eighteen years old, went to a summer program at a prestigious prep school last June. Mary returned from this school in mid August. In late September, the family discovered Mary was pregnant. Mary, of course, initially denied having sex, but finally admitted having a relationship with another student. Not unexpectedly, the boy deceived Mr. Kelly's daughter with promises that she could not become pregnant. This young man has no idea that he fathered a child, nor will he ever know. Mr. Kelly is a devout Catholic and, of course, aborting this bastard was not an option."

LeVite said, "I see. How far along in the pregnancy is Mary now?"

"Mary is one month from her due date and she has been sequestered at a safe house, which has been turned into an obstetric clinic, the location of which you do not need to know. A board certified obstetrician will deliver the baby. Mary will never see this child, not for a moment, ever. She has agreed to this and we, and she, hope that she can resume her life, afterwards, without this blemish. It will be as if it never happened. Mary will return home immediately after delivering the child." Farley hesitated so that the information given to LeVite could set in.

LeVite said, "Am I to assume that you want Lost Souls to take the child?"

Farley said, "Yes, but more than that. You will receive the child without information about who the mother, father, or family are, or where the bastard was born. You will never know that information and you are not to look for it."

LeVite interrupted, "Wait a minute. In all fairness, don't you believe the child's father has some rights to know the baby exists? Maybe he or his family will want to raise it."

Harris aka Kelly, tensed his jaw, pointed his shaking finger at LeVite, and said, "No one will ever know who the parents of this child are. Am I clear? In time, I'll want my daughter to forget she even had it. And there's no way that fucking Jew bastard that raped my daughter will ever know either."

Farley, grabbed Harris aka Kelly's forearm and said, "Please, Cul... Mr. Kelly, let me do the talking."

LeVite was shaking his head, "I don't know about this. Seems illegal and I don't need the

32

trouble. Are you crossing state lines with this baby? That complicates things even more."

"Essentially, Mr. LeVite, it will be as if the baby was left on your doorstep. It is important to us that you try not to locate Mr. Kelly or his daughter afterwards."

LeVite crossed his arms and sat back. He said, "Why should I be doing this for you, at great risk to me, I might add?"

Farley responded, "Because we are willing to pay you handsomely for your services. We know that you make fifty-one thousand four hundred dollars a year."

LeVite's eyes widened with the realization that Farley knew information few others knew.

Farley continued, "You owe money on your house and cars, and have educational expenses for your children coming up. To help us in this endeavor, to protect the child that is not wanted by Mr. Kelly or his family, we are willing to pay you twenty thousand dollars a year in untraceable funds, tax free, for five years. When the child is eighteen months old, we will move it to another state and another facility, with the same nameless status. Even though the baby will leave Lost Souls, you will receive your money through year five. When the baby leaves Lost Souls, it will be as if he or she did not exist. We will leave the details of erasing the child's existence to you. To help you ensure that Lost Souls forgets about the child's existence, the orphanage will also receive an anonymous gift of ten thousand dollars when you receive the child and another ten thousand dollars when the child is removed."

"Why should I trust you? I don't know either of you from Adam."

"Let's just say, Mr. LeVite, that we are trustworthy," said Farley, bringing his briefcase up to his lap, "and if you do this for us, we will make it worth your while immediately." Farley opened the briefcase loaded with twenty-dollar bills, placed it on the desk and spun it around towards LeVite's gaping mouth. "Here is your first year's twenty thousand dollars. If you agree, I will leave this briefcase on your desk and walk out. You will receive a similar briefcase every year for four more years."

Farley pushed the top of the briefcase down and the closing pop made LeVite jump. LeVite was shaking while sweat rolled down his face, staining his starched blue shirt. He used a handkerchief from his suit pocket to wipe his face. Levite said, "What's...What's next? Do I have to sign something?"

Farley smiled to himself. *We've got him.* Farley said, "Nothing to sign. Every penny is untraceable and is not to be reported to the IRS. You keep your side of the bargain, we'll keep ours."

LeVite nodded assent.

Farley said, "When the baby is about three weeks old, we will notify you at noon to expect a package from Chicago. That evening at midnight, you, personally and alone, will receive the baby at the back entrance to Lost Souls.

Why you happened to be here at that time is up to you. You'll have a month to create an alibi."

LeVite, rolling his tongue around his mouth, said, "Yes, very clear. That might raise suspicions."

Harris aka Kelly interjected, "You'll have to fix that, now won't you?"

Farley said, "There is more. You will not try to contact us for any reason. If you do try, you will not receive any additional money. I might add that we know where your family and your children are. Need I say more?"

"Uh. No. Is that a threat?"

"Take it how you will, Mr. Levite."

LeVite opened his desk and removed another handkerchief to wipe his face and neck. He then placed his hands in his lap to conceal the shaking.

Farley continued, "Lastly, once situated at Lost Souls, under no circumstances will you allow the child to be adopted or placed in foster care. When the child is about eighteen months old, we will return using the same phone call message, that you are to 'expect a package from Chicago.' We will arrive at midnight and take the child at that time. Where we go with the child will be none of your business. She will not be hurt but we are taking every precaution that her origins will never be found. Am I understood?"

"Yes."

"Mr. LeVite, if for any reason you lose your job or change jobs, the money will stop coming. So don't do anything stupid."

"Yes. Yes, sir." LeVite's hand was shaking as he subconsciously inched his fingers towards the closed briefcase. Levite saw the two visitors watching him and he pulled his hand back to rub his chin, as if that was his intent from the beginning.

Farley smiled and said, "We will take our leave now, Mr. LeVite. I hope you will not disappoint us. We will not disappoint you. You will be getting a phone call sometime in the next four weeks. If the baby, for some reason, does not survive the delivery, you will receive no phone call, but you may keep the money. You will never hear from us again.

"If the baby, once in your hands, for any reason, does not survive until eighteen months, you may call me at the phone number on the card. You must talk only to me. Do not leave a message or talk to anyone at my office or tell anyone why you are calling. In any event, you will still be paid the money promised you."

LeVite said, "I understand."

Farley said, "I hope you do." Farley turned to Mr. Harris aka Kelly and said, "Mr. Kelly, I don't think we'll have any problems with Mr. LeVite. I believe we are done with our business."

The two men then stood, turned and walked out of the office. The closed briefcase remained on LeVite's desk. Levite stood at the window and as soon as he saw the two men get into a car and drive away, he reopened the briefcase.

* * * *

Culver Harris had created a state of the art delivery center in a house in central Virginia and hired, at great expense, an elderly retired obstetrician, two nurses and an anesthesiologist to live nearby until the baby was born. Katy Harris delivered a baby girl by Caesarian, four weeks later on May 1st, 1971. On the third day, post C-section, Katy transferred back to the family estate in Chappaqua, Westchester County, New York. From that point on, her medical records reflected that she had suffered a ruptured ovarian cyst, which required surgical exploration. Her two brothers and younger sister knew why Katy had been gone for eight months, but never spoke of it. Many of Harris's personal house staff knew, but discussion of Katy, and her plight, would never occur in the Harris household. Strict directives, such as this, from Katy's father were followed to the letter, always.

Immediately post-delivery, a team of nurses transferred the baby girl, unseen by Katy, to a safe house four miles away. When the baby was twenty-one days old, Mr. LeVite, at the Lost Souls Orphanage, received a call that a *'package from Chicago'* would be delivered.

Chapter 3

Cambridge, Massachusetts

Late May 1971

"Hey, Ben, phone's for you. It's a collect call."

Ben Kaplan, unshaven, unshowered, his curly black hair uncombed, said, "Really. Who is it? I need to get on the road if I'm going to make it back to Detroit by midnight."

Brad Hahn, Ben's first-year roommate at Harvard, shrugged his shoulders, "Dunno. Operator said her name is Katy."

"Stop shitting me Brad. You know who Katy is, or was. Christ, you drove with me to Westchester County looking for her."

"Ben, I dunno know who it is. The operator just said Katy."

Ben, curious, eyes widened, wiggled his tongue against his upper lip and walked to the phone. "Operator, this is Ben Kaplan."

"Mr. Kaplan, will you accept a collect call from Katy?"

"Yes, operator, yes, of course."

"Ben, it's me Katy Harris."

"Is it really you?"

"Yes, yes, I've been unable to call or write anyone for the past year and I'll be leaving for private school in Switzerland in four days. I've had no way to reach you. You never called me after the summer."

"Katy, that's not true. I tried. I swear. I starting calling your home every day and wrote letters every day for three weeks."

"Ben, I'm so sorry. My family intercepted all the mail from you. I never saw any of it. All the letters that I wrote to you were never mailed."

Ben said, "Why Katy? What happened? After school started, I called Smith College every day. They told me that you never came. They wouldn't tell me anymore than that. I called a friend from high school who was going to Smith and she confirmed that you never arrived."

"I didn't make it to Smith, or any college."

"Why?"

"I need to talk to you, Ben."

"Then, my roommate, Brad, drove with me to Westchester to see if I could find you at the address you gave me. We never got past the front gate. We were told you weren't there anymore and that if we came back, they would call the local police."

"Oh my God. Ben. I've got so much to tell you."

"I didn't stop calling. Finally, some man got on the phone and told me that I was never to call or try to reach you again or he'd call the police and have me arrested for stalking. He told me that you didn't want to talk to me. So I gave up."

"Ben, you have to believe me that I never knew that you called and never received any mail and didn't know that you had come to Westchester. I told my parents about you the day I got home. They went berserk when I told them your name. They weren't happy that I even talked to someone who was Jewish. After that, I was guarded day and night. I wrote you every day as well. I now know that my parents intercepted everything."

"Katy, I've missed you so much. How did you find me?"

"My parents had a big party three nights ago. My parent's friends, the Gratts, were there with their daughter, Mora. She has been a close friend of mine forever and I was hopeful that I could trust her. Anyway, she's at Radcliffe and I told her almost the whole story and asked her to find you. Mora asked my parents if she could return and visit me before I left for school and they said 'yes.' She gave me this phone number. I didn't tell her everything and there's stuff you don't know either. I snuck out of our estate into town and I'm using a payphone. They'll be looking for me soon if I don't come back."

"Are you in danger?"

"A little. I mean no one going to kill me, but if my parents knew I was talking to you, I'd be in trouble. Ben, I need to talk to you. No, I want to see you, but I don't know how or when. I know the school in Switzerland will open my mail and I'm not allowed to make calls out."

"Katy, that's appalling. You did nothing wrong."

"Not to my father."

"Katy, I'm driving back to Detroit as soon as we hang up. Can you call me tomorrow? My number is 313-862-0434. Call collect. I promise to stay home all day waiting for your call."

"I'll try. Ben, I have so much to tell you. Uh oh, I think I see Liam, my father's chauffer, slowly driving down the street. He's looking for me, which means there'll be others doing the same. Listen. Ben, we had a child, born six weeks ago, May 1st, you and me."

"Katy, we what? I don't think I heard you correctly."

"Ben, I never got to see it, the baby. I don't even know if it was a boy or a girl. My parents gave it away. Uh oh, that is Liam, I gotta go. I'll call tomorrow, somehow." The line went dead.

Ben raised his voice into the phone, "Katy, Katy, Katy..."

The dial tone caused Ben to drop the receiver on the table. He fumbled to pick it up and placed it on the phone cradle. He collapsed on the bed onto his neatly folded clothes and then sat up and put his head between his knees.

Brad said, "What's with you? Looks like you've had double helpings of dorm food." Brad waited for the laugh.

Ben, not laughing, sat up and said, "Oh nothing. I have to get home, that's all. Brad, do you mind giving me a few minutes alone? I need to talk to my parents about something private."

"Sure. I'll be back in ten minutes." At the door, Brad turned and said, "Ben, was that *the* Katy?"

"Yes."

"That's it, yes?"

"Where was she, Ben? Hell, you looked all over the original thirteen colonies for her."

"I can't talk about it. I need to talk to my parents." Brad closed the door.

Ben dialed and waited. "Hi, Mom, I hope to be in my car heading west in about thirty minutes and should be back to Bloomfield Hills by midnight, no later. I'm going the northern route through Ontario."

"Ben, you drive carefully. Don't hurry. Your bedroom is all made up and you know where the key is."

"Thanks, Mom, but it's important that I talk to you and dad when I get home about something big. I know it'll be late, but we need to talk."

"Ben, are you in trouble?"

"Uhhh No. I'm in no trouble, but something's happened and I need your advice."

"Ben, the suspense is killing me. Give me a clue."

"Mom, we'll talk tonight. I love you."

* * * *

Jerome Kaplan said, "Helen, Helen. The phone's ringing. What time is it?"

Helen Kaplan looked at her nightstand and said, "It's one thirty in the morning. We went to sleep. Ben should have been here, or he's here and didn't wake us."

"Hello, Ben, is that you?"

"No, this is John Flaherty of the Ontario Provincial Police. Is this Jerome Kaplan?"

"Yes, it is, officer. What can I do for you?" Jerome Kaplan gripped the receiver with two hands and pressed it tightly to his ear. Jerome knew this conversation was going to be bad. *Good news doesn't come after midnight.* His heart and stomach had traded places, one heading south the other north.

"Mr. Kaplan, your son, Ben Kaplan, was involved in a motor vehicle accident tonight at 9:30 p.m. outside London, Ontario. A semi hauling lumber turned over on Highway 401 and it resulted in a multicar accident."

Jerome said, "Oh, my God. Is Ben...?"

Officer Flaherty, realizing the question to follow, interrupted, "I am so sorry to tell you that your son was killed, as were four other people."

Jerome said only, "Oh..oh..No. No. Not our Ben."

Flaherty waited a moment. "Mr. Kaplan, are you there?"

Jerome, unable to inhale, unable to feel his lips, unable to understand, said, "Yes. I'm here."

"We will need you to come to London's Provincial Police office as soon as possible. Again, my condolences to you and your family. I will hold for a second so you can get a pencil and paper."

Jerome Kaplan cradled the phone to his chest and sat. He couldn't speak or move.

Helen cried, "Jerry what's happening? Who's on the phone?"

"Helen, Ben was killed in a car accident a few hours ago in Canada."

* * * *

More than six hundred people came to Temple Beth El in Bloomfield Hills, Michigan, for Ben Kaplan's funeral. By Jewish custom, the burial took place a mere thirty-six hours after his death, delayed only by the transfer of the body from Canada. Ben Kaplan had been a bright star in the eyes of his parents, his family, his school and the Jewish communities northwest of Detroit. All who knew him came to pay their respects.

Ben's death, so incomprehensible, incapacitated Jerome and Helen Kaplan. Ben's older brother, Phillip, released from University of Michigan Hospital after fainting and hitting his head on a bedpost, was no better. Max Kaplan, Jerome's older brother, directed the funeral proceedings including the retrieval of his nephew's body from Ontario, naming the pallbearers, and selecting those who were to speak on Ben's behalf.

Max's daughter, Melissa, the same age as Ben, had taken the loss of her first cousin, and closest male friend, as hard as Ben's parents had. Melissa sat listlessly in the synagogue, away from her friends and family trying to gather the strength to proceed. As she sat, she twirled the loose strands of hair with her left hand and then slid down the strand to straighten her twirling. Melissa's strange habit had been with her as early as anyone could remember and reminded the family of her maternal grandmother, Rose Cohen, who had the same habit her entire life.

Harry Glickman, a family friend of both Jerome and Max Kaplan, approached Max.

"Max, what happened? How could this happen? Did the Ontario police give you any insight into this craziness?"

"Harry, it was a total freak of nature. A semi loaded with lumber blew a front tire The driver lost control and the whole rig turned over, throwing two ton logs in every direction. Ben was two cars behind, going with the flow of traffic. He crashed into the semi and then was rear ended by another four cars behind him. Four people died other than Ben, including a young woman and her small child in a Chevy Yukon. The semi driver walked away. The tire was two months old and full of tread. The police haven't figured out why it failed. God was not on our side that day. Not at all. God should have never taken the life of someone so precious and so talented."

Harry said, "I agree. Such a waste. Our prayers and thoughts are with Jerome, Helen, and your family today. I only hope that they will be able to find some peace."

A young man then approached Max Kaplan.

"Mr. Kaplan, I was Ben's roommate, Brad Hahn, from Spokane, Washington. I guess I was the last one to see him before he headed home. Something strange occurred just as Ben left. It's got nothing to do with Ben's accident and I'm not sure I should even tell Ben's parents about it."

"Tell me, Brad. I'll approach Jerry and Helen when the time is right, if that ever happens."

"Brad was his usual self, that last day, as he was packing up for home, I mean, in a great mood. He had done well in school and was already psyched for next year. Anyway, as we were packing up, he received a collect call from a person named Katy. The operator gave no last name, just Katy. Ben took the call and accepted the charges. He talked for no more than three minutes. The only thing I heard was "Is it really you?" or something like that. Then I tuned out. When the call was over, Ben seemed stunned. He dropped the phone and slumped on his bed. He then asked if I would step out of the room for a moment so he could have a private phone conversation with his parents. I left the room and returned fifteen minutes later. I assume he talked to them, or somebody, but I don't know for sure. He seemed distracted and unusually quiet. Ben was never quiet. He finished packing quickly, almost too quickly and said, "I've got to get home. I'll call you from Detroit. Send me the bill for the collect call when it arrives." He left soon after that."

Max said, "Brad, I don't know what to do with that information. I'll have to ask Helen or Jerry if they got the call. I do remember them saying that

46

Helen had talked to him just before he left. Ben had said that he had something to discuss when he got home that couldn't wait for morning."

"One other thing, Mr. Kaplan. At the beginning of the year, Ben talked incessantly about a girl he met last summer at Andover, the prep school in Massachusetts. The girl's name was Katy. I don't remember her last name. She was his 'ten' on the Richter scale. He did everything possible to contact her during the first three months of the school year. We even drove to Westchester County, north of New York, trying to see her. He was mystified that she was unreachable. By December, he gave up. Every so often, he'd say 'I can't believe Katy dumped me without a call or a note.' I specifically asked Ben if the collect call was from the Katy that he'd been trying to find. He said yes."

"Thanks for the information. You might send me the number of the originating phone from the collect call when you get the bill. Not sure what I'm to do with what you've told me."

"Mr. Kaplan, I'm sorry for your family's loss. Ben was a good friend and a great roommate. He will be missed and I won't forget him. I will talk to Ben's mom and dad, but I'm not going to bring up the phone call."

"Thank you for your kind words. I agree that bringing up the call with them now would not help."

* * * *

Chappaqua, Westchester County, New York

"Mora, thanks for coming back to visit. You've been a godsend. I am heading back to Switzerland tomorrow morning." Katy stood, opened a drawer and rifled through the contents. She then opened her closet and went through her dresses, selecting none. "I tried calling Ben twice the day after he called and then once yesterday, but no one answered. I was afraid to leave a message. Can you try to reach him and tell him that I tried calling and not to give up on me?"

"Katy, I'll do what I can. Is there anyone at your school that I can send mail to? Mail that won't be screened?"

"Yes, great idea. I do know someone who is already there." Katy spoke as she wrote, *Elise Marteen. Institut Le Rouge, Chateau Le Rouge, Switzerland*."

As Mora was reviewing the information, Katy added, "I don't want to be there, but my parents, at least my dad, does not want me here in the US."

"Katy, it was great seeing you again. Everything will be all right, in time. I promise that I'll find Ben and when I do, I will write Elise. We'll use the code name Bob Knight, instead of Ben Kaplan. Got it. Obviously, you'll have to tell Elise what's up."

"Thanks, Mora."

Laughing, Mora said, "Katy, make sure my parents don't hear about Bob Knight."

* * * *

Elise Marteen walked into Katy's room at Institut Le Rouge with a book in her hand. She sat next to Katy, opened the book and removed a folded, opened envelope. "Katy, I received this letter today from your friend, Mora, from Boston. Actually, there was only a clipping from a newspaper article from Detroit about an automobile accident in Ontario, Canada. Anyway, here it is."

Katy read the clipping twice and waited for Mora to leave her room. She laid down in bed, clutching the clipping to her chest, and cried. *Oh, Ben..... Oh, Ben..... Oh, Ben......*

* * * *

Cully Harris sat comfortably at his desk overlooking the New York skyline.

"Mr. Harris, your attorney, Mr. Farley is on the phone. Says it's important."

"Hello, Henry, what did you find out?"

"Mr. Harris, I just faxed over an article from the Detroit Free Press. It seems that half our problem has been taken care of."

"Hold on a moment Henry." H. Culver 'Cully' Harris, punched a few buttons on his phone and asked his secretary to bring in the fax. His eyes narrowed upon seeing the headline. After finishing Ben Kaplan's obituary, Cully didn't smile and stared out his window for a few moments. *Tragic, not a bad child. Couldn't he have stayed away from my daughter?.*

"Mr. Harris, you there?"

Cully spoke into the phone, "Henry, do you think he knew anything or told anyone?"

"Cully, I don't know how he'd know. I assume that if he or his family knew, and if they cared about it, they would have approached you already. My guess is that they know nothing and never will."

Harris ended the call and spun slowly in his chair to view the New York skyline. *Makes things easier for me. He or his family would have never known anyway.*

Chapter 4

St. Joseph's Orphanage, Missoula, Montana

November 1972, - Eighteen months later

Agnes Brown, Head Night Nurse, dialed, and waited.

"Hello. What time is it? Who's calling?"

"Miss Carmichael, it's Agnes and it's one in the morning. I think you're going to have to come back to St. Joe's tonight. Someone, somehow, opened the back door to the orphanage and left a small child, a girl, maybe two years old, maybe younger, in the downstairs playroom."

Carol Carmichael, Director of St. Joseph's Orphanage, said, "You're not joking?"

Agnes said, "I'm not joking. No note, nothing. Just a child. The child is not talking but seems happy and well nourished. I've talked to everyone here at St. Joe's on the night shift and called all the staff from the afternoon shift and no one has any idea where the child came from."

Carmichael said, "Okay, Agnes. This is strange. I'll call the police and let them know what you've told me. If they are going to come out tonight, and I suspect they will, then I'll come back in. For what it's worth, I have no idea what's going on."

Carol Carmichael sat at her desk and shook her head. "Agnes, It's been six weeks and we've still got no information on Baby Jane. The police are stumped. They've put queries out to every police department in the Northwest and northern Midwest. We have to assume that we're not going to get any additional information. We'll need to register the child, give her a name and a birth date. You have any other ideas?"

Agnes, agreeing, said, "Such a shame. Seems like a nice child and obviously well taken care of, by somebody. I've polled the staff and we've come up with a name. Grace. Good name for a girl. We thought Helena as a middle name for the state capital. The Montana State flower is the bitterroot, so that won't work for a last name. The state bird is the meadowlark. That's even worse. The state tree is the Ponderosa pine. That said, we think Grace Helena Pine. Sound okay?

"Fine with me. How about January 1st as a birth date?"

"Montana's admission date is November 8th, so we thought that should be her birthday. That would make her two years and two months. Seems appropriate. She's probably a bit younger, but we'll never know."

"Fine, Agnes. I'll draw up the papers and have the orphanage attorney send the papers to Helena and get a Certificate of Birth Registration."

"She's a smart little girl. I can tell already. She should be adopted out easily, don't you think?"

"Yes. I already have a family in mind. Bill and Henrietta Ostergard are schoolteachers. I'm guessing he's thirty and she's about twenty-eight. My son is in Henrietta's third grade class at Franklin, so I've met her. When I told her that I run the orphanage, she told me that she's been trying to have children for four years without luck. The doctors have told her there's nothing wrong with either of them, but she doesn't think she'll ever get pregnant. I'm going to give them a call. The farmers and ranchers around here who want to adopt, want boys. Schoolteachers and a girl make great sense. I think I remember that her mother lives in town and might be able to help take care of the baby."

* * * *

"Mom, guess what?"

Elsa Nordquist, Henrietta's mother and a widow of two years, said, "Henrietta, you are always making me guess. Let's see, you've won the Nobel Prize?"

"Funny. Nope, Bill and I are adopting a baby girl. Mrs. Carmichael, the lady that runs the orphanage, called us last week. Her son is in my class and I mentioned to her that we were thinking about adoption. The baby is already two years old and was abandoned at the orphanage six weeks ago. They, the police and the orphanage, don't have even a sliver of information where she came from. Seems that God put her there for us."

"You've seen the child, Henrietta?"

"No, just some color photographs, she appears lovely. Black hair and bewitching olive eyes that are so alert. I know she's smart."

"Well, my blonde daughter with a blue-eyed, blond husband, no one will ever think you bore this child. Where does she come from? Does she have a name?"

"Mom, I'm not getting pregnant and we've tried for four years. This opportunity may never come along again. Please support me. As I said, Mrs. Carmichael says that they have no family information on her at all. She was left at the orphanage one night. The police did everything they could to try to find the parents without success."

"Does she have a name?"

"Yes, the orphanage had to give her one and a birth date as well. Grace Helena Pine. Her birth date is November 8, 1970.

"November 8th, that's the Montana's state admission day. A coincidence?"

"Mom, they had to give her a birth date and that's what they chose. We'll never know her birth date for real. The orphanage doctor said she could be a little younger but that the date was not inappropriate for her size."

"Henrietta, what do you want me to do?"

"If we go through with this, you'll need to help me out with her during the day. Bill and I can't afford for me to quit teaching, just yet."

Elsa said, "Of course. You didn't need to ask."

Forty-eight hours later, the Ostergards were ushered into Mrs. Carmichael's office. Accompanying them was an older, heavyset woman.

"Mrs. Carmichael, this is my mother, Elsa Nordquist. She's agreed to help with child care so that I don't have to give up my job. Mom is a retired elementary school teacher."

"Sensational, Henrietta. Not that I was concerned too much, as I knew you'd figure things out. The way this works is you and Bill will take custody of little Grace today. We will have an agent of the orphanage and the state come to visit you in a few days and then at regular intervals. If all goes well, meaning that you want Grace and the agent says the home environment is stable, then you may formally adopt her after two years. As you must know, I am not worried about the environment for Grace. I think this is the perfect fit. Once adopted, she will be your daughter in every sense of the word legally, and, hopefully, emotionally. Her last name will change, officially, from Pine to Ostergard."

Bill Ostergard said, "We can't thank you enough, Mrs. Carmichael. We know how difficult it can be to adopt a child, a good child."

Mrs. Carmichael looked to Henrietta and then back to Bill and then to Mrs. Nordquist, tears running down the faces of the entire family. Carmichael, tearing herself, said, "I am so happy for your family."

Time passed quickly as the Ostergards and Elsa Norquist adjusted to their abrupt change of life.

Elsa Nordquist said to her daughter, "Henrietta, I am so sorry I ever doubted your adoption of little Grace. It's been fifteen months and I love every second of being with her. I had given up hope of ever hearing the word Grandma and then, poof, there she was. She devours books like no child I've ever seen, including you, and you were a book nut."

"Mom, I couldn't have done this without your help. Bill and I are so thankful that everything has worked out so well. Pinch me, but I know I'm the luckiest person in the world. I know we're supposed to wait until the two year mark but I'd sign the adoption papers today if they'd let me."

"Anyway, I think Grace is incredibly smart. She's not yet four and recognizes most books by their side cover and asks me to read them. I'll ask her to get "Biscuit and the Farmer" off the shelf and she knows what to do. She loves to handle books, as if she's reading them and then tries to scribble letters. I'll point to a word like pig and say to her, "Grace, does this spell horse?", and she'll say, "No gwamma, p – i – g is *peeg*. You know dat.""

Henrietta and her mother laughed together.

Elsa said, "I've even come to loving her habit of twirling and straightening her hair when she reads. I've asked her to stop twirling and she does, only to start up again. I'm sure she does it subconsciously."

"Mom, Bob and I see her doing it all the time and we've given up trying to stop it as well. We are blessed. How lucky were we? Why would anyone ever want to give up a child as special as Grace? I'll never be able to figure it out. Actually, I hope I don't. What if the true parents show up some day."

"Did you talk to Mrs. Carmichael about that happening?"

"Yes, but she said once the adoption goes through, there's nothing the real parents can do until Grace is eighteen years old at which time Grace can seek them out. Mom, I swear, we'll make sure that she's so loved that she'll never look. You and us, I mean, we'll make her so loved."

Chapter 5

New York City April 1974

H. Culver Harris was sitting as his desk in downtown Manhattan, feet up on the desk, and whistling. He had purchased a distressed lumber mill in Arkansas eighteen months earlier for seven and one-half million dollars, dropped one and one-half million into renovations, and had just sold it to Weyerhaeuser Lumber for just over fourteen million.

His private phone rang, the only phone that didn't go through the switchboard or secretaries.

"Cully, Farley here."

"Yes, Henry. What have you got?"

"Our Montana investment, as you know, was leased out fifteen months ago. Apparently, the new owners are content and are willing to exercise their right to purchase the business, which they will do at the end of the twenty-four month lease."

Cully Harris smiled at Farley's use of jargon. He was close to certain that his phone lines were not bugged but he liked Farley's anal approach to all his dealings. As Farley had put it once, "Some things are black and some are white, I enjoy working in shades of gray."

"Henry, thanks again for taking care of my western investments. As always, I'll have a cashier's check for your services. Let me know when the deal goes through."

* * * *

Henrietta, preparing dinner while humming a Norwegian folk tune, watched with wonder at Grace reading at the kitchen table while twirling and straightening a strand of hair. She looked up at the kitchen clock and stopped humming. Bill was late coming home. *He didn't say he'd be late. Not like him. I'll give him another thirty minutes and then call the high school.*

Twenty minutes later, Bill Ostergard silently walked into the kitchen, picked up Grace, gave her a kiss and then sat down. Normally upon entering the house, Bill would yell, 'I'm home', expecting Grace to run to the door. Today, Bill had said nothing.

"Henrietta, I had a problem today at school. I'm afraid that it will become a big issue."

Henrietta, not certain that Bill wasn't kidding, said, "What could be a big issue. Tenth grade English in Missoula doesn't create issues."

"Don't be funny, I'm serious. Do you remember I told you that I was likely to flunk a new girl that had moved here from Las Vegas? She's been late with every assignment and the ones turned in have been incomplete and incomprehensible. She's smart, I know it, but she doesn't care."

"So?"

"Last week, I told her to come to my room after school to discuss her schoolwork. I told her that she was going to flunk if she didn't take her studies more seriously. She then laughed at me and said, "I don't give a shit about this class or this school. But you'd better not flunk me. I swear I'll do something that you won't like." Anyway, her paper due

58

yesterday came in today. The five hundred word essay had 'fuck you' repeated over and over."

"Why didn't you tell me, or somebody, about this?"

"I should have but I didn't want her to get into more trouble than just flunking. I gave her an "F" on the paper and wrote her a note to come back after school so we could talk again. I was going to try to counsel her and see if I couldn't get her back on track. Remember that Petersen boy last year. I talked to him a time or two after school and he's turned around so well that his dad came in to thank me twice and brought us those apricot preserves."

"So?"

"So this girl, her name is Cher Benoit, came back to my office as I was leaving. Before I could get a word out, she demanded that I change her grade. I declined and told her that she needed to work harder. She started screaming and then started tearing off her clothes."

"What?"

"She removed her blouse and then tore it and did the same with her bra. I tried to stop her but couldn't and then she ran half-naked, holding her torn bra and blouse down the hallway. She was screaming 'Help, Help me.' She claimed that I tried to rape her."

"Oh my God. This is terrible."

"The police came and I told them what had happened. I even showed them her paper. Then she fabricated the most outrageous lie. She showed them the note that said, 'come back after school', as evidence that I trapped her. Worse, this little tramp has two male students who are willing to say that I had been hitting on her."

"Oh, Bill. Now what?"

"Principal Cartwright suspended me, pending a full investigation. He had no choice. The mother of the girl is a piece of work and wanted me arrested and the father told me that if he ever saw me on the street, he'd shoot first and explain later. Cartwright said there would be a hearing in two weeks, after they can gather and evaluate the evidence. She's been in trouble in every class but nothing like this."

"Bill, I'm scared. I trust you, but I don't know what to say. Is our adoption of Grace going to be in jeopardy?"

"Henrietta, I hadn't even thought about that. I don't know. Cartwright told me to hire an attorney. What's that going to cost? We can't afford for this to go on for a long time."

The following morning, Bill Ostergard hired a local attorney, Sam Bell. Bell was honest enough to say that defending Bill, if the case went to trial, would cost more than twenty thousand dollars, which was more than either Ostergard made in a year. They had little savings. Bell took a thousand dollar retainer, gathered information, and told the Ostergards that he'd meet with the County Attorney, Ralph Porter, to see if he couldn't work out a deal that was palatable. Bell told the Ostergards to say nothing to anyone. As a result, the newspapers in Missoula and much of Montana had already crucified Bill Ostergard, without getting his side of the story. Forty-eight hours later, succumbing to

local pressure, Henrietta's principal demanded
Henrietta take a paid leave of absence for her own
safety.

Bell called the Ostergards, sequestered at home,
eleven days after the incident.

"Bill, I've met with the County Attorney, Ralph
Porter, yesterday and we spent an hour looking at
options. I must be honest and tell you that no
option was perfect. Porter was going meet with the
other attorneys in his office and and see what he
could come up with. The three of us need to be there
at one p.m. tomorrow to talk. Rather than get your
hopes up or down, let's wait and see what the
County proposes. I hate to guess on these things
and be way off base. I'll meet you at Missoula
County Courthouse, Fourth Floor in Courthouse
Annex Building, 200 West Broadway. Don't be late."

The door sign read, 'Ralph Porter, Missoula
County Attorney.' The Ostergards and Sam Bell were
ushered into the office and sat in front of Ralph
Porter. Henrietta had a packet of Kleenex in her lap.
She had been crying continuously for twelve days
and knew that she would start crying again as soon
as the conversation with the county attorney
commenced.

Sam Bell started, "Ralph, what did you come up
with. My client did nothing wrong, has had no
complaints of any kind against him. This is a total
farce and you know it."

Porter leaned forward and put his hands on his
desk, "If it were only that simple, Sam. In almost
every type of case I handle, the burden of proof is on
me, as prosecutor. With this stuff, kids, schools,

parents and PTAs all shouting, your client is guilty until proven innocent in the eyes of the public. If I don't take this seriously, I will never be re-elected, and you know that. I made a call to Las Vegas and her prior school. I suspect that Miss Benoit had similar issues there, but under a plea bargain, the records are sealed. The only thing I could get from the president of their School Board to say was something like, 'It's your problem now. Good luck.' For what it's worth, I don't think Mr. Ostergard did do anything wrong, except use poor judgment in asking the girl to come back to his classroom after hours without another student present. It's a different time than when you and I went to school. But that's what it is."

"Mr. Porter," Bill Ostergard asked, "what do you suggest? What can we do?"

Porter replied, "If you want to fight this, we will need a hearing and then possibly a formal trial. The parents of this girl are adamant that they want you prosecuted to the full extent of the law. They know their daughter has some issues and a couple of misdemeanor priors. However, she's a juvenile and none of that is admissible. The trial will be a 'he said, she said.' Trust me when I say the young lady will come to court looking - and acting - like a nun. Regardless of the trial outcome, no one comes out unscathed. 'He said, she said.' Even if you win, and I suspect you would have a reasonable chance to beat this, the public will judge you guilty. Shit, regardless of the evidence, the papers will judge me incompetent if I lose. If you win and even if the girl admits she concocted the whole story, the parents in this town will still not want Mr. Ostergard teaching their children, plain and simple. Even if you win the criminal trial, I can't stop the family from suing you in civil court. This is a nightmare, a total nightmare."

Henrietta had already used most of her Kleenex.

Ralph Porter punched the button on his intercom and said, "Phyllis, bring me a box of Kleenex and some water." He then turned to Sam Bell and said, "The cost of the trial would be substantial, right Sam?"

"Yep. I told the Ostergards that defending him would cost more than twenty thou."

Porter nodded his agreement with the dollar amount and started, "I've talked to the Benoit parents three times. I told them that I couldn't predict the outcome of the hearing or trial. Mr. Ostergard has been a model teacher and no one has ever made a complaint about him. Nevertheless, their daughter's story isn't going away, so we have to proceed. The Benoits are willing to settle for Mr. Ostergard to quit. I realize that is tantamount to quitting teaching, likely forever, and leaving Montana. If you agree to quit teaching, the Benoits will drop all charges. Your teaching records, however, will reflect the settlement, so getting a teaching job in Montana will be almost impossible. Out of state, I can't speculate, but not good. Even if we could seal the records, any school district that finds out you deserted, and for no apparent reason, is unlikely to hire you."

Porter stopped to let things settle in.

Sam Bell restating the obvious, turned to the Ostergards, "Option one is to stay and fight, possibly... probably win, but spend all your savings plus take out a loan, that no one will give you. Option two is to quietly leave Missoula and Montana and start over. Ralph, is there an option three?"

"Not that I can see."

Bell said, "Ralph, I'd agree. I need to speak to my clients alone and I'll give you a call later today."

The Ostergards and their attorney left the Missoula County Attorney office and went to a small coffee shop nearby.

After ordering some coffee, Bell got to the point, "What are you two thinking?"

Bill Ostergard, gripping his fork as if he was trying to strangle a snake, said, "This isn't fair. I want to clear my name. I did nothing wrong. I was trying to help. What do I have if I don't have a good name?"

Henrietta, still crying on and off, held her husband's hand and added, "Bill, we have each other and my mom and Gracie. We can start over somewhere. It will be hard but we can do it."

Bell's posture changed. "I'm afraid there's more to all this. If we take the plea bargain and you leave Missoula, Grace will have to go back to the orphanage. I didn't want to bring this up until we were out of the county office. The orphanage attorney, Jeff Howard, called me eight days ago to tell me that until this mess is cleared up, they'll have to take Grace back."

Henrietta interrupted, "I will never let you take my daughter."

Bell, hesitated and then said, "I pleaded with Mr. Howard to let Grace be. I suggested that he ask the orphanage inspectors about their visits to your home. He called back and told me what you know already; Grace is loved and is thriving.

64

Unfortunately, this isn't something Porter, or Howard, can change. Honestly, the State isn't going to let you keep Grace. Even if we go to a hearing or a trial, they will retake her until the trial is over. When it comes to children, the burden of proof is on us to show that you've done nothing wrong."

Bill clenched his fist even tighter, and the veins on his forehead were bulging. He had bent the fork in half and had small amounts of blood on his thumb. He said, "We'll,...we'll leave the state tonight and take Grace with us. Your mother can send us our stuff when we get settled."

Bell, shaking his head, said, "Bill, Henrietta, I didn't hear that. Leaving the state, with or without Grace, until we've agreed on a bargain, implies that you were guilty. Taking Grace is kidnapping and once you cross state lines, the federal government will get involved. Need I say more? You will stay here until we've worked out a deal with the county attorneys. I'm afraid that Grace will need to return to St. Joseph's tomorrow. That was the only deal I could work out with the state and the orphanage."

The waitress came to the table to see if something was wrong as Henrietta started wailing. Bill held her tightly and kept repeating, "I did nothing wrong. Grace will stay with us."

Mrs. Carmichael called the Ostergards that night. "Henrietta, I can't tell you how sorry I am about all this. I know you and Bill to be good people and I don't believe a word of what he's charged with. Nonetheless, we are bound by state and county laws. The orphanage attorney, Mr. Howard, and I will be at your house at 8 a.m. to pick up Grace. Department procedures require that we have a police escort. Don't take it the wrong way. Grace will not need any clothes but she's welcome to bring all the books that you will let her have. They will be put in our library and she'll have access to them any time she wants. Again, I am so sincerely sorry."

Henrietta had run out of tears and she hung the phone up gently.

The next morning, when the doorbell rang, Grace, unaware of what was transpiring, thought nothing until Henrietta started wailing again. Hugging her little daughter, she moaned, "Grace, my poor little Grace, they are taking you away from me. I am so sorry." Henrietta handed Grace's little hand to Mrs. Carmichael.

Grace looked back and forth between Henrietta, Mrs. Carmichael and the police officers. She started to fight back against Mrs. Carmichael, broke her grip, and ran to Henrietta screaming, "Mommy, mommy, don't cry. I won't go."

Henrietta sobbing, said, "I don't want you to go."

"Then I won't go. Make these bad people leave. Make Daddy make them leave. I don't like them."

One of the police officers snatched Grace, her little arms flailing, and carried her out of the house.

The Ostergards accepted the plea bargain from the county attorney. Four days later, Bill and Henrietta Ostergard left Missoula. They told no one where they would be going, including their lawyer. Elsa Nordquist, Henrietta's mother, would handle all correspondence.

Elsa attempted to see Grace on two occasions. The orphanage denied visitation each time. Mrs.

Carmichael reckoned that Elsa's visits would be disruptive. Grace was not informed of the attempted visits. Over the next two months, Elsa would tell anyone that would listen how unfair the legal system had been to her daughter and son-in-law. In time, no one in Missoula seemed to care. Elsa left Missoula to parts unknown, other than to say, 'she was going *home.'* Most people assumed she would be going back to Norway.

Back at St. Joseph's the reality of the abandonment by the Ostergards set in quickly. The snickering stares by the orphans felt like mosquito bites, unrelieved by the random hugs and 'I'm so sorrys' by the nuns. Grace stopped talking other than the occasional yes or no. She would find solace in the dark, dead dark, going missing whenever the nuns weren't watching. Broom closets, storage sheds and even cupboards were rotated to sequester herself into complete darkness. Initially the nuns would scour the orphanage looking for her, but after a few weeks of wasted time and effort they left Grace alone. She would return to her room when she was ready. State-appointed psychiatrists examined her twice. Grace refused to talk to them and, in the end, the doctors offered no suggestions. Grace continued to read voraciously and attended class while remaining largely mute.

Four months after the Ostergards left, Grace started talking and gave no reason for her return to normality.

* * * *

Henry Farley's call to Cully Harris was short, and painful.

" The Montana business fell through eight weeks before the closing. A teenage troublemaker set up one of the new intended buyers. Total bullshit. The original owners, 'Saint what's his name', reclaimed the business. Shit. I'll get back to you."

"You do that." Harris slammed the phone hard enough that the earpiece shattered.

Chapter 6

Kennedy International Airport, New York, June 1975

Katy Harris deplaned Air France Flight #3453 from Paris. She had not been on American soil for three years.

At the exclusive, and prison-like, Institut le Rouge, Katy had undergone almost constant counseling from a team of therapists, hired by Culver Harris. Their solitary goal was to repress the memory of the child Katy bore. Harris had been told, much to his dismay, that the reprogramming approaches made famous during the early fifties, were too harsh and had little chance of being successful. Harris told the lead therapist, "Then, you do whatever you have to do to repress the memory of her eighteenth year and I'll match that with threats of being thrown out of the family to suppress those memories. Between us, she'll never bring it up."

No mention of the pregnancy, the baby or Ben were picked up by secret voice recorders in Katy's room over the next three years.

Cully Harris allowed Katy's return to the US after Harris had been given assurances by the therapy team that she would likely not bring up the pregnancy.

"Does she remember anything?"

"Mr. Harris. It's in there, somewhere, but deep," the lead therapist said, "I'm sure she'll repress it unless something big were to happen."

"Like what?"

"We never know for sure. Maybe a pregnancy."

"We don't need to worry about that, if I can help it."

Katy's studies in Switzerland had given her enough credits to transfer to Colby College in Waterville, Maine, as a junior. Colby was a small, but prestigious private school, with a student population of eighteen hundred. Katy would live off campus in a house purchased by her father and be chauffeured to school each day. Katy had twice-a-week therapy sessions in Bangor, an hour away from Waterville on US 95. For the first time in four years, she could socialize with whomever she wanted.

Robert Ralston, a pre-med senior from Portland, Maine, first saw Katy Harris in their Psychology 203A class. Robert's father, Peter, was a pediatrician and his mother, Ruth, a social worker. Robert's family was not wealthy enough to afford Colby without assistance. Fortunately, Robert's academic successes qualified him for grants and scholarships to cover seventy percent of his college costs. Educational loans made up the difference.

The tall, quiet and introspective girl, with long auburn hair and deep blue eyes, enraptured the pediatrician's son. Robert approached Katy the second week of school on a Wednesday after class.

"Excuse me. I see you're new here at Colby. I'm Robert Ralston."

70

Katy, unused to male advances, said, "I'm Katy. Katy Harris. I just transferred to Colby."

Never confident that any girl, on any level, would say yes to him, Robert took a shot, "Any chance you'd like to go to an off-campus party on Friday. The pre-meds in the senior class are getting together at a local pub called the Silver Street Tavern."

"Sure, I'd love to," Katy said, "but I'd need to make a few calls first to make sure it's okay. I'll let you know Friday morning in class. If I am able to go, I'd meet you at the tavern."

Robert thought it strange that Katy would need to check with someone about whether she could go out. However, Katy knew the rules. Her stay at Colby was conditional on disclosing all social interactions. Upon return that evening, Katy told the housekeeper/cook/chauffeur/spy about her intended plans. The housekeeper called her contact at the Harris household. Twenty-four hours later, after Harris's lawyers had vetted the Ralston family, Katy received permission to date Robert.

Katy arrived at the pub, a fashionable twenty minutes late. After the obligatory introductions, the couple retreated to a corner table.

Robert asked, "Okay, Katy Harris, who are you? Where did you come from? No one just shows up at Colby, junior year. Over your shoulder are twenty drooling pre-med students, most way cooler than I am, but here you are with me. I need answers."

"Robert, you're funny. I've been in Switzerland the last three years at Institut le Rouge."

"Switzerland, private school. I thought that stuff was from the 1930s. I didn't know people still actually got sent to private schools in Switzerland."

"Here I am. I wasn't happy being there, but my family demanded it."

"Why?"

"Why not. My mother went to school in Europe."

"What did you study?"

"Mostly languages and the arts."

"You speak English, what else?"

"I'm fluent in French, German and Italian. Picked up some Dutch from a fellow student and was learning Chinese before I left. Mom also speaks French, German and Italian. Languages seem to come easily to the two of us."

"I don't believe your story for a minute," Robert guffawed. "There's a suspected Commie spy on the faculty of the Department of Art History and you're a CIA operative dropped in here to discover his contacts."

Katy, looking faux-stunned, replied, "How'd you figure that out so fast? I'm really 008, working for MI6. Bond was busy. Actually, that's not true. James picked up a venereal disease on assignment in Paris and will be out of commission for six weeks. So they called me."

Both smiled at each other, an equal match.

Robert said, "So I looked at the roster and your name is there, but no address or phone number. Why?"

"I'm staying in a house my father bought, off campus. I get driven and picked up every day."

"Joke?"

"No joke."

"Then I'm guessing you're not getting any financial assistance from Uncle Sam or the school, and you've got no loans."

"That would be true."

"So who's your dad?"

"H. Culver Harris, III."

"That doesn't mean anything to me."

"My family owns banks, railroads, steel mills and property. A good deal of Manhattan, too."

"Why would you go out with the likes of me? Poor son of a poor pediatrician."

"One, you asked. Two, I think you're handsome and smart. I guess I never worry about your family's money because I have enough."

Katy and Robert melded back into the group of pre-meds. Katy watched Robert circulate effortlessly amongst his peers. Katy's driver picked her up at 11 p.m.

Two more dates followed.

Katy told Robert as she was being picked up, "My father is coming to Waterville on Sunday. He wants to meet you."

Eyebrows raised, Robert said, "Is that good or bad?"

"Good. I told him that I really like you. That was all he needed to come. I guess I scared him."

"Hey, you're scaring me."

The meeting with Cully Harris was benign. Cully approved of Robert....for Katy.

On his return home, Cully described Robert Ralston to Katy's mother, Lillian, "He's perfect for Katy. He's smart, but not too smart. He's poor and can be manipulated, won't ask questions and has not an ounce of motivation. He's perfect.

Robert and Katy continued to date for the rest of the school year.

Robert continued to excel in school, and gained admission to medical school at Tufts University, in Boston, as part of 'Maine Track.' Tufts had partnered with the State of Maine to provide medical education to residents of that state. Robert qualified for a twenty-five thousand dollar yearly stipend.

With his future mapped out, Robert called Cully Harris and asked if could propose to Katy.

"If she accepts me, sir, I think we could get married after she graduates from Colby."

Harris said, "Yes," without hesitation. "Robert, we'd be thrilled to have you as a son-in-law."

Robert said, "Thank you, sir."

Harris added, "Young man, keep your Johnson holstered. I do not want my daughter getting pregnant before she's married. Understood?"

"Perfectly understood, sir."

Harris continued, "I think you'll understand that a pre-nuptial agreement will be needed."

Caught off guard, Robert replied, "Uh...I understand."

Harris said, "The pre-nup will be written by my attorneys and is mandatory and non-negotiable. I will point out that every son-in-law or daughter-in-law will sign the exact same agreement. I am not singling you out."

Cully paused to let the comment sink in, then said, "Robert, if Katy agrees, and I'm sure she will because she's already told me she wants to marry you, then after the wedding, I will take care of your education debts. Don't argue with me about it." Cully smiled to himself. *That ought to prevent him from having second thoughts.*

Katy agreed to marry Robert. Without asking or considering Katy, Robert or Robert's parents, Cully and Lillian Harris selected the Harris Estate in August 1976 for the nuptials, fifteen months away.

Katy, now over twenty-one years old, without permission, sought out a physician in Waterville and started herself on oral contraceptives. She paid cash for the consultation and pills. She confided her moment of freedom with Robert but explained that her parents would be upset if they knew. From that point on, Robert paid for the pills. Their sex life was good, with neither having much experience.

Katy, often after sex, would be a bit sullen. *Ben, I'm sorry. Ben, I'm sorry.*

Robert told Katy every time they saw each other, "I am so in love. I have got to be the luckiest person on the earth. My fiancé is drop dead gorgeous, smart, and witty." Robert would add, silently, *and rich beyond belief.* His new in-laws to be seemed to care for him, and were happy to have a physician in the family, even one without great ambition. Robert continued to hope to join his father, practicing pediatrics in Portland, Maine.

With an arm tightly around Robert's shoulder, Cully would say, "Robert, my boy, Jay Buford's pediatric group in Manhattan is holding a spot for you. They are the leading pediatric group in the New York area. What a fabulous opportunity for you. And you and Katy will be in the city, only an hour away from Chappaqua." As usual, Cully and Lillian Harris left no doubt that their options were not optional.

Cully would say to Lillian with each step closer to Katy's nuptials, "I am so relieved by this marriage. I truly believed that all my manipulations were for naught and Katy would sully our family name for a hundred years. I am certain that Robert suspects nothing. That bastard is sequestered somewhere in the US. Only Henry Farley knows where that might be and you and I aren't asking." Cully thought, *fucking Missoula, Montana,* but would keep that tidbit of information to himself.

For the summer between her junior and senior years at Colby, Katy enrolled in a fine arts camp in Adirondack Park to learn painting and sculpture. Henry Farley, on Cully Harris's instructions, hired a professional actress to enroll in the camp to befriend Katy. Her job was to ascertain, if possible, whether Katy had any memory of her pregnancy and delivery. By summer's end, the actress/informer said, emphatically, that, no mention of any pregnancy had surfaced.

That summer, Robert had lined up a nickel and dime job drawing blood at a medical clinic in Portland. Cully Harris made two phone calls and Robert found himself working in the research labs at Pfizer, Inc. in Rye Brook, NY., twenty minutes from the Harris estate, and earned a thousand dollars a week, eight hundred more than sucking blood in Portland. Robert saw his parents only once that summer.

After the summer, Robert moved into an apartment in Boston to begin his medical education at Tufts and Katy returned to Colby for senior year. Cully Harris owned Robert's building and was rent-free. Robert made the commute up to Waterville every weekend that he could.

Cully Harris arranged to meet Katy, Robert, Robert's father and any lawyer of Robert's choosing in New York at the offices of Henry Farley to go over the pre-nuptial agreement. Harris demanded to pay travel costs and lawyer fees. Robert's attorney was Harry Fields, the son of a family friend who had recently passed the Maine bar.

At that meeting, Farley, read the entire pre-nuptial agreement to the group. Farley pointed out that all of Katy's assets would remain in a special trust fund, managed by Cully Harris's bankers. The trust, once established, could only be passed to 'legal naturally born children.' If Katy and Robert divorced, for any reason, Robert would have no rights to any portion of the trust, nor would any adoptive children. If Katy died from natural causes, childless, Robert would have no rights of inheritance and all moneys would transfer back to the Harris estate.

Harry Fields reread the agreement and asked to speak to Mr. Farley alone.

"Mr. Harris will demand to be in any meeting," said Farley. Fields consented.

Fields, Farley and Cully Harris removed themselves to another suite.

"What's up, Fields. We're not changing anything," Farley said, as he thought, *country bumpkin rookie lawyer.*

Fields said, "I need a clarification, without embarrassing the young couple. This clause here, Article IX, section 2, says 'legal naturally born children.' Is the word 'legal' a typo? Otherwise, I have to ask if Mr. Harris's daughter has had an illegal child, a child out of wedlock, and one that my client does not know exists?"

The shrewd pickup, by the neophyte attorney, tongue-tied Farley.

Cully Harris watched the interaction between the two lawyers. *Shit. Shit. Farley's been caught, and surprised. If the dimwit hesitates too long, Fields would know that something was amiss. Worse, Fields could push Ralston to ask some delicate questions. Lying to Fields or Ralston could nullify the pre-nup.*

Without hesitation, Cully Harris said, "Take the word 'legal' out. It makes no sense. Once these two fine people are married, every child born is legal." Farley's secretary printed out another page, deleting the word, legal.

Robert, after talking to Mr. Fields, consented and signed the documents. Katy said nothing throughout the meetings.

After all had signed, Cully told the assemblage that he wanted to have lunch, alone, with his daughter.

After ordering, Cully unloaded five years of anxiety on Katy, "I am going to say something that has been on my mind for a long time. You don't need to comment, in fact, I don't want you to comment, as what I am going to say is as non-negotiable as the pre nup we just signed. I don't know how much you remember about what happened years ago at Andover, then back home, and at that house in Virginia. I know you've said nothing, or at least, nothing has gotten back to me. You want to tell me?"

Cully hesitated for a moment to watch his daughter's face. She had no expression, good, bad or indifferent. *Could she really have been forced to wipe this from her memory?* After moments of silence, Cully said, "If what happened then is ever revealed by your doing, so help me God, you will never get a penny from me. That is a promise and is non-negotiable."

Katy remained still, didn't blink, nod, shrug, or smile. She was as bland as the first sheet out of new ream of cream-colored paper.

Cully watched his daughter, and then said, "Good. Let's get on with your life and my life and your mother's life. I like Robert. You'll be happy and, in time, I hope to see some grandchildren."

Katy continued to show not a trace of emotion and her apparent lack of reaction was duly noted by her father.

Katy graduated from Colby College in May with a Bachelor of Fine Arts degree. The Robert Ralston and Katy Harris wedding proceeded as planned by Lillian and Cully Harris. The wedding would become the highlight of Westchester's summer social calendar. Twelve hundred people received invitations and the Harrises expected all twelve hundred to come. Eleven hundred ninety-nine attended. The lone non-arriving guest was in the ICU at Sloan Kettering Medical Center after colon surgery. He was barely forgiven. Robert's student loans disappeared the week after the wedding.

While Robert toiled in medical school, Katy entered the masters program at Boston's School of the Museum of Fine Arts.

24 months after marrying, Katy stopped her oral contraceptives and was pregnant within four months. Cully Harris's New York physician, Dr. Joseph Mullen, recommended an obstetrician, Dr. Dana Richie, at the Boston Hospital for Women. At Katy's initial physical examination Dr. Richie asked about the lower abdominal incision, which, according to the records forwarded by Dr. Mullen was the result of a twisted ovarian cyst.

Dr. Richie commented that Katy's breast enlargement and areola pigmentation was a bit unusual so early in a first time pregnancy, but made no note about it when Katy shrugged her shoulders. Katy began on pre-natal vitamins and revisited Dr. Richie monthly.

Dr. Richie had offered to tell Robert and Katy the sex of the child, but they wished not to know. At thirty-eight weeks, Dr. Richie performed a routine ultrasound and told the couple the baby appeared healthy and large, perhaps eight and a half or nine pounds. Katy's pregnancy remained uncomplicated and she went into labor at 3:00 p.m. in her forty-first week, five days after her estimated due date.

By 6:00 p.m., Katy's contractions were coming every 4 minutes and strong. As Robert drove Katy to the Boston Hospital for Women, her water broke. Good fortune put Dr. Richie in the hospital as she finished her evening rounds. She saw Katy, and then went home, expecting to return to the hospital in the next few hours for the delivery. Richie mandated Lamaze for her patients and spouses, so Katy and Robert expected a natural childbirth.

By midnight, and after three hours of variable and ineffective labor, Dr. Richie ordered a prostaglandin E2 pessary to stimulate uterine contractions. Katy's labor contractions increased dramatically within fifteen minutes. Thirty-five minutes later, the nurses reported to Dr. Richie that Katy's cervix was still only half dilated. Dr. Richie told Helen Fremont, the OB nurse assigned to Katy that she would be back to the hospital in fifteen to twenty minutes.

Nurse Fremont said, "Don't hurry too much. I'm guessing we're fifty minutes to an hour before she crowns." Helen Fremont had been an OB nurse for thirty-two years, and was rarely off in her guesses by more than ten minutes, give or take.

The monitor at the nurses' station started beeping an alert from Katy's room moments after Fremont hung up. The baby was in distress with severe slowing of the heart rate.

At the same time, Robert appeared at the nurses' station yelling, "Katy is having difficulty breathing. In the middle of a contraction, she began having abdominal pain and chest pain. She says it's hard to breathe.

"Get Dr. Richie, now and tell her to hurry." Helen Fremont yelled to the secretary as she was running down the hallway, "Mrs. Ralston is in trouble."

A quick assessment by Nurse Fremont told her that something terrible had occurred. Katy was nonresponsive, her skin, clammy, cool and white, with rapid heart rate, barely discernible blood pressure, and shallow, painful breathing. Katy's abdomen, instead of smooth and round, was irregular and misshapen. Fremont put her hands on the belly and her eyes widened.

Robert was yelling, "What's going on? Please tell me."

Fremont yelled, "Katy's uterus has ruptured. The baby is outside the uterus. This is bad. I'll stay here. You go out and get me another nurse. NOW. And tell them to get Dr. Richie here, stat."

Robert ran to the front desk, "I need another nurse for my wife. Nurse Fremont says her uterus has ruptured. Call Dr. Richie. Where can I find another nurse?"

The secretary, a young girl with no nursing experience, sat paralyzed, not knowing what to do or whom to call.

Robert ran down the hallway until he found a nurse in another room and yelled, "Please help. My wife's uterus has ruptured. Please help me."

The second nurse ran with Robert to Katy's room where Helen Fremont was working to lower the head of Katy's bed in an attempt to move blood back to her heart.

"Call the OR, tell them we have an emergency C-section coming," Fremont, in control amidst chaos, barked to the second nurse, "and let anesthesia know. She'll need a ten-minute type and cross her for six units of O negative blood as soon as we've wheeled her to the OR. Have the lab ready to draw blood, stat. Move."

Fremont turned to Robert, "Help me push Katy to the OR. We can't wait for the orderlies."

Robert, almost as pale as Katy, let go of Katy's limp hand and started to push the hospital bed towards and out the door and down the hallway to the OR suite for Obstetrics, repeating, the whole way, "Katy, hold on, You'll be okay."

Dr. Richie scrubbed into the OR within twenty-five minutes of the rupture. Using her previous scar, Richie quickly opened the abdomen. Floating free in the abdominal cavity was a dead male fetus, fully developed, weighing eight pounds fourteen ounces. The bleeding was profuse and arose from a huge longitudinal tear of Katy's uterus. All attempts to stem the bleeding were unsuccessful and Dr. Richie made the only decision she could and removed Katy's uterus.

Sixteen hours later, and ninety minutes after being extubated and removed from a breathing machine, Katy, in and out of profound shock, and after 11 units of blood, awoke briefly. Robert remained at Katy's side through the entire ordeal and was alone with Katy when she regained a blurry consciousness.

"Robert. Robert. I... am...so...sorry."

"Katy, I love you. You need to be strong and we'll pull through this."

"Is...the...baby...okay?"

Robert was conflicted. He didn't know if telling the truth at this point made sense but lying, particularly to Katy, wasn't in his nature. He bowed his head and said, "I am so tired."

"Robert,...please,...is...the...baby...okay? Was...it...a...boy...or...girl?"

"It was a boy."

"Is...he...okay?"

"The baby is fine." Tears welled up and Robert started to cry and rested his face on Katy's free hand.

Katy's eyes were fluttering open and closed as she used all her strength to focus. Speaking barely above a whisper, she said, "Thank..you,...Robert...Thank...you."

Robert picked his head off of Katy's hand, "Katy,..."

Katy, eyes scanning the ceiling, looking for wisdom, said, "Robert, I have to say something. He has a sister or brother, I don't know which, somewhere. Oh, Ben. Oh, Ben... Oh, Robert,...I'm...scared. I'm...so...scared."

Robert heard exactly what she had said and responded, "I don't understand what you're saying, Katy. You rest. You need your strength. Please rest."

Katy closed her eyes and slipped back into a semi-conscious state. Within the next 45 minutes, her oxygen levels fell precipitously as she labored to breathe. The ICU specialists re-intubated Katy and put back on the respirator. The ICU team of lung, kidney and heart specialists worked with Dr. Richie for the next twelve hours. Katy's kidneys had stopped functioning in the middle of the crisis and despite adequate hydration, she was making only a few drops of urine an hour. She required hemodialysis forty-eight hours post rupture. Stabilization of her blood pressure required a myriad of potent cardiac stimulating drugs. Every attempt to remove the drugs resulted in pressure so low that her brain would not receive adequate oxygen.

Katy Harris never regained consciousness and her heart and lungs gave out three days, fourteen hours, seven minutes and twelve seconds from the time her uterus had ruptured. Twenty-four minutes of CPR was fruitless and after eight minutes of flatline EKG, Dr. Richie stopped the resuscitation and pronounced Katy Harris Ralston dead.

A preliminary pathology report on the uterus returned ninety minutes after her demise. The Chairman of the Department of Pathology called Dr. Richie and told her of the findings.

Dr. Richie was beside herself with anger. She approached Robert first. Robert was sitting alone in Katy's room, crying, and waiting for Katy's family to return to the hospital.

Richie, shaking as she spoke, "Robert, you are in medical school but if it were my decision, I'd throw your ass out now before you kill someone. Your wife had a longitudinal scar of her uterus, which caused the rupture, killed your son and killed your wife. The solitary explanation for a longitudinal uterine scar is a prior classic Caesarian section. I know of no other answers. None, by God. By withholding the fact that Katy had a prior pregnancy and Caesarian delivery, you put a patient's life, my patient's life in jeopardy. I am not sure that you couldn't be held culpable for accessory to murder of your wife and son. How dare you withhold information. The coroner and medical examiner will review this case."

Robert, unprepared for the verbal barrage, replied, "I swear on my life, my mother and father's life, that I had no idea that Katy had ever been pregnant. I had no idea. I swear that I had no idea." Robert then remembered Katy's strange comment during her ten minutes of semi-lucidity. *He has a sister or brother, I don't know which. Then Oh something and then Oh, Robert, I'm scared. I'm so scared.* He kept that information to himself.

Dr. Richie, undaunted, said, "Someone knew. Somebody, God damn well, knew. I don't know how far to go with this. If it's true that you didn't know, then you've suffered enough in my estimation. You've lost a wife and a child. That may be punishment enough. But somebody knew and I'd strangle them if it were legal. I am going to call the coroner's office and ask for a full investigation." Dr. Richie stormed out of the room.

Katy's body was covered and transferred to the morgue. The nurse told Robert that if he, or any of Katy's family, wanted to view her body one last time, that she would provide an escort to the morgue. Robert sat next to Katy's now empty bed, confused, and unsure what he should do next. He continued to sit, and think, and as he did, he became angrier and angrier. A nurse came into the room to tell Robert that Cully and Lillian Harris would arrive shortly.

Twenty minutes later, Cully Harris entered Katy's room.

"Hello, Robert. Lillian will be here in a second, she's in the washroom. I am so sorry."

Robert stood up from the chair, walked to the solitary window in the room to peer out. The morning sun shone so bright, that death seemed impossible. After a moment of reflection, he said, "We lost her. I don't know what to do."

Cully sat in the chair Robert had vacated, the only chair in the room. "We'll just have to go on, Robert. She was our daughter. How could something so crazy happen?"

Robert talked to the open window, "Dr. Richie talked to me an hour ago. The uterine rupture was caused by a scar running the length of Katy's uterus."

"Really. A scar?"

"Yes, a scar." Robert, trying to be steady, spun to confront Cully Harris, "She, I mean Dr. Richie, said that the only thing that could cause a scar like Katy had was a previous Caesarian section from a prior pregnancy."

Cully Harris's eyes narrowed and gave a laser intense look into Robert's eyes.

Robert could barely breathe, but continued, "Dr. Richie said by withholding the knowledge that Katy had a prior Caesarian delivery, you put Katy's and the baby's life in jeopardy. If the doctors had only known, they would have treated Katy differently, and Katy and my son would be alive now."

Robert pointed his finger at Cully Harris, a physical act that few had ever done, and said, "How could you? Dr. Richie told me that anyone who knew this information and didn't reveal it could be held culpable for accessory to murder of your daughter and grandson. How could you not tell someone? I didn't need to know, but the doctors did. How could you?"

Cully Harris remained silent, stood, brushed by Robert and left the room. Cully grabbed his wife by the arm as she was entering and said, "We're leaving."

Lillian Harris, pleaded, "Ouch. Cully, that hurts. Please, I want to see my daughter's body, I want to say good-bye."

He turned her around saying, "It's too late. She's gone and you can't see her."

As Cully forced his wife down the hallway, she kept looking over her shoulder at the entrance to Katy's room and at Robert standing in the doorway. Cully Harris left the room intending to never speak to his son-in-law again. Three days later in Boston, the Harris family attended the funeral, en masse, in a row of black limousines, and left, en masse, immediately after the ceremony. Given no instructions, nor asking for any, Robert had Katy Harris Ralston's body cremated and the ashes strewn in the Charles River.

By the terms of the pre-nuptial agreement, all of Katy's trust returned to the Harris estate.

Fourteen hours after Katy's death, and three hours after Cully Harris left Robert Ralston standing in the doorway, the Boston coroner's office decided, without an inquiry or an autopsy, that no filing of charges would be forthcoming regarding the death of Katy. The President of the Board of Trustees of Boston Hospital for Women called Dr. Richie and told her not to pursue the investigation further, if she wished to continue to practice in the State of Massachussetts.

A week later, Robert called Harry Fields, the attorney who had helped review the pre-nuptial agreement a few years earlier.

Harry, after hearing the story of Katy's death, said, "The Harrises could say that you knew as much as they did. 'They said, you said.' That makes you as much an accessory as the Harrises. How are you going to prove you didn't know? Furthermore, as a medical student, you would be held to a higher standard that disclosure was important. Finally, going after them would be expensive. They can afford it, you cannot. Lastly, what's to be gained, Katy's dead and you are excluded from the trust. That's not going to change, even if they were found guilty. Only her child, if the child is alive, would have a chance to regain the money. Not a penny to you. Moreover, with all you've told me, I wouldn't be surprised if Bedouins were raising that child in the Sahara desert. You also don't know who the father is. Robert, drop it. Get on with your life and walk away from the Harris family. Trust me."

Ralston moved out of the apartment that he and Katy had shared. He sold the unused and unneeded baby furniture and anything else that reminded him of his temporary silver-spooned life with Katy. Robert moved in with two other medical students near Tufts Medical Center, borrowed money from his father and Uncle Sam and finished medical school. He did his residency in pediatrics at the Maine Medical Center in Portland and lived at home. He met Gwen Charles, a nurse working in pediatrics at the medical center. They married as Robert finished his residency and joined his father, practicing general pediatrics. Gwen Charles Ralston delivered a healthy boy two years later and then a second healthy son two years after that.

Chapter 7

Seattle, Washington, October 1994

Absent any other form of communication, Alex left an email message to Grace that he would meet her outside the main library at 6:15 p.m. He arrived at 6:10.

Alex thought *I give her a fifty percent chance of showing up. No more.* He looked around the foyer of the library, without success. *I am a little early, I hope.* Alex then walked into the main reading room, bustling with medical, dental, nursing and other health science students. Alex scanned the room quickly.

Grace was unmistakable. She was reading. Her right arm was surrounding the book, exactly as she surrounded her food, protecting it from marauding book thieves, rapscallions and scoundrels. Her left hand was twirling and straightening a strand of hair. She looked at her watch, closed her book and looked up. She spotted Alex, and smiled. The warm smile caught Alex unprepared. He was transfixed, velcroed to the floor, as she stood and walked towards him. She looked no different, same plain dress, tight hair in a bun, no makeup, but the smile with her warm, penetrating brown eyes, made all the difference.

Alex smiled back, hoping his smile was as warm as hers. "Hey. You're here." Alex was disgusted with himself for the lame comment.

"Yep. Here. Where are we going to go?"

Alex said, "There's an Italian place near Seattle Center, Buco de Beppo. Sound okay?"

"Sure. I don't know many restaurants. On my budget, going out to eat is...in fact, I never go out to eat."

Alex smiled. *She's so brutally honest and unpretentious. I've never known anyone who would have ever given that response.* "It's not super fancy, but the food is good and everyone seems to enjoy it."

Alex's four-year-old Honda Accord sat in the hospital's garage. Alex's mom had used it for two years before giving it to Alex on a lend-lease program. Alex and mom knew that she'd never use the car again. Alex opened the passenger side for her, much to her surprise.

"You didn't have to do that."

"Yes, I did. I was raised corny. I will open car doors and pull out your chair."

"No, really?"

"I do it to make other guys look bad. It's effective in pissing them off on double dates."

"Funny."

Tuesday night and Buco de Beppo wasn't busy. The hostess sat Alex and Grace in the back in a small booth. The room was quiet enough. The waiter came quickly, handed over two menus, and asked if they wanted something to drink first.

Grace said, "I'll just have some water."

The waiter responded, "Perrier? Pellegrino?"

Grace appeared mystified and looked at Alex and whispered, "I merely wanted a glass of water."

Alex rescued her, "Some of Seattle's finest with ice, for both of us. You could bring a wine list."

The waiter, handed over the wine list, already under his arm, turned and walked away.

"I didn't know that water didn't mean water."

"I never thought about it. I guess it doesn't. Do you drink wine?"

"No, not really. It's so expensive."

"I'll tell you what. I'll get a glass of wine and we'll share it," Alex said, as he perused the list. "White wines are a little easier on your palate if you're not used to wines in general. A glass of Stella Pinot Grigio. It's somewhat fruity. I think you'll enjoy it."

"Okay." She left no doubt that she was treading in new territory.

Alex said, "You came. I wasn't sure if you'd even show up. I'm glad you did."

"I thought about what you said about having no friends and all. You're right. I don't."

"That's a shame, Grace, you are very unique."

"So was Genghis Khan. I'm guessing he didn't have lots of close friends."

"Grace, that wasn't an answer."

"My life has been different than yours."

Alex responded quickly, "Hey, how do you know? You don't know mine yet."

"True, but I know mine and I don't think we're going to be saying 'me-too' often."

Alex said, "Okay, let's try. Where were you born?"

Grace said, "I don't know. No one does. My name and birthday were given to me around the age of two at an orphanage in Missoula, Montana. I was literally dropped there one night. Where were you born?"

Alex responded, "San Francisco. Mt. Zion Hospital. OB was Judith Braun. seven pounds six ounces."

"See, there's a bunch of 'me-toos' out of the way."

"You don't know, or have any clue, who your parents were? Any brothers or sisters?"

"None. Not a clue. You?"

"Aaron and Beverly Gordon. Dad's a urologist. Mom's a retired schoolteacher. I have a sister, Samantha, who's a junior at the University of Michigan in Ann Arbor."

"Another 'me-too' out of the way."

"I'm sorry. I didn't know. That's not easy."

Grace said, "I started off, I guess, not so lucky. Then, it seemed that my luck didn't improve."

Alex chuckled, "That's not true. You met me."

Grace retorted, "We'll see, in time, how lucky I am."

"What's that supposed to mean?"

"In the orphanage I was able to make two close friends. Both times I felt that I had someone to share the misery of the orphanage." Grace started spinning and straightening her hair. "Those two brief periods, maybe six or seven months each, when I was seven and then when I was fifteen, I felt happy and secure. Well, maybe not happy, but happier. Sarah was first. I was just seven and she was almost eight. I remember Mrs. Carmichael banging a spoon on her plate to introduce Sarah....."

* * * *

"She banged until everyone was quiet. "Everyone. Josies. Everyone. Listen up. Today we have a new person joining the Josies." Carmichael never used the word orphan if she could help it, instead, 'children' or 'Josies' for the orphans at St. Josephs.

"This is Sarah. Sarah will be eight years old in a few months. She's very nice and enjoys reading. So everyone give a big welcome."

In unison, all the Josies said, "Hello, Sarah. We're glad you're here."

In unison, all the Josies, except Grace, forgot about Sarah and went back to eating and talking. Grace had no friends her age. Her period of silence after returning from the Ostergards keyholed her into the 'untouchables.' When she resumed talking, the established cliques kept her from joining, even to the point of hostility and bullying.

As soon as lunch was over, Grace sought out Sarah.

"Hello, Sarah. I'm Grace."

Sarah nodded that she understood but said nothing.

Grace continued talking in rapid sequences. "I didn't talk for months when I came back here... But, I got tired of not talking...I don't have any friends...I read a lot...Books make me feel good...Do you like to read?"

Looking at her toes, Sarah nodded again.

"We have free time one hour before dinner. I'll take you to the library and show you how to get books. Okay?"

Sarah didn't nod assent.

"Sarah, please, please, say yes."

Sarah, still counting her shoelaces, nodded.

That afternoon, Grace found Sarah, or they found each other, in the same reading class. Mrs. Carmichael escorted Sarah into a classroom and spoke softly to the teacher, Sister Evelyn. Hiding to the side of her escort, Sarah scanned the room, sure that no friendly faces would surface. Upon seeing the familiar face of Grace, smiling and waving, Sarah smiled back.

The class was reading *Charlotte's Web*. Grace had read it twice. Apparently, Sarah had as well. Each of the thirty-three students, almost all older than Grace and Sarah, read a small portion. However, none of the students read with the ease and animation of the two girls. Sister Evelyn told both girls they had done a superb job.

As they left the room, Grace said, "I hope you'll be my friend. You really read well," as she took Sarah's hand.

Sarah, accepting the hand, gladly, said, "I think we'll be best friends."

Grace asked, "What happened? Why did you come here?"

Sarah responded, "My mom and dad and brother were killed in a car crash three weeks ago. In some ways, I wish I had were in the car too."

Grace said, "Don't say that. You're here and I'm here."

Sarah continued, "My dad has a sister. I don't remember ever meeting her. When they couldn't find her, they moved me here."

For the next seven months, Sarah and Grace were inseparable. They pleaded to Mrs. Carmichael daily for three weeks to have their bunks next to each other. Carmichael finally acquiesced.

Eight months after Sarah arrived, Grace had her yearly state-mandated health checkup in downtown Missoula. She returned two hours later to find all of Sarah's belongings gone.

Seeing the empty bed and shelves of her soulmate, Grace was frantic and started to run to Mrs. Carmichael's office.

Henry Buford, a ten-year old bully, who didn't like Grace or Sarah, stopped Grace en route.

"Grace, you should have been here," said Buford, in a rare fit of compassion. "It was terrible awful. Some lady showed up to take Sarah away. Sarah didn't wanna go. The lady was real mean. Sarah held onto her bed so tight that the nurses couldn't pull her off. The lady came to Sarah's bed and used bad language, but Sarah wouldn't let go. I heard Sarah say, 'I don't want to go with you. You're mean. I want to stay here with Grace.'"

Grace's hands went up to cover her mouth as Buford continued. "The lady slapped Sarah across the face so hard that she started bleeding from her lip. No kidding, that hard. Sarah started crying. The mean lady was gonna hit Sarah again, so Sarah let go of the bed."

Grace kept her hand over her mouth as she gasped for breath.

"The nurse told this lady that hitting children wasn't allowed. The lady said awful bad things to the nurse and told her to mind her business or she'd hit her too. We'd have our mouths washed with soap if we said any of those words. The mean lady grabbed Sarah and walked out. Sarah pleaded to the lady to let her say good-bye to you or write a note, but the lady wouldn't listen and yanked Sarah out to a car."

Grace ran to Mrs. Carmichael. "Where did Sarah go?"

"Grace, I don't know for sure. Sarah's aunt took her. She is a wicked, wicked person. She said she would sell all of Sarah's family's belongings and then move to St. Louis. That's in Missouri. Her address had been in New York. I don't know where Sarah will be. Hopefully, she'll write you."

Sarah never wrote. Grace returned to another period of self-imposed silence and broom closet darkness.

* * * *

Alex said, "Not even a good-bye. That's terrible. I'm sure wherever Sarah is, she remembers you. She has to."

The waiter returned and Alex asked for a glass of Stella Pinot Grigio, with two glasses. Alex knew he wanted lasagna and a Caesar salad. Grace looked at the menu as if written in Sanskrit. She had no idea what to do.

"Grace, the lasagna is why we're here, and the portions are huge."

"I don't know. It's so expensive. I do like lasagna."

Alex looked into bewildered eyes and placed his hand on Grace's. She made a fist but didn't remove her hand. "I'll tell you what. I'll order for us." Removing his hand and looking at the waiter, he said, "We're going to split an order of lasagna and bring each of us a small dinner Caesar salad and a cup of minestrone soup."

The waiter retreated. *Small order, split a glass of wine, my tip will be shit.*

Grace looked at Alex and said "Thank you."

"Plus, if we don't eat too much, there'll be room for dessert. I know an ice cream place on Capitol Hill, not too far, that has salted caramel ice cream."

"Really? Someone makes salted caramel ice cream?" Grace was smiling but, moreover, she kept her eyes on Alex, waiting for him to talk.

"Yep, and you haven't lived until you've tasted it." *She's looking at me. Not her glare, the one she uses to make me look away, but a warmth that asks me to keep looking. Those eyes would melt granite. I wonder how I look to her?*

Alex never thought about his looks. He remembered a line from some article he had read about Howard Hughes telling Katherine Hepburn *'You don't worry about money, if you have it.'* Alex was good looking enough. He was a bit over six-feet tall, fair, with light brown hair that was thinning a bit. Baldness ran through his mother's side of the family, so he knew his days with a full head of hair could be numbered. Large and expressive brown eyes sat against a nose, while Romanesque, was a bit too large. Alex played basketball in high school. He had reached his adult height as a ninth grader and he had started as center on the freshman team. The varsity coach was excited at the prospects of Alex reaching six-foot, four-inches, or more, until he met Alex's parents at the beginning of the year introductions. Aaron Gordon, Alex's father was five-foot, nine, maybe, and his mother, Beverly, was under five, two. Alex wasn't getting any taller and he didn't. He played seldom his senior year.

While Alex wondering how he looked to Grace, Grace solved the puzzle and said, "You're handsome, you know."

Taken aback, Alex said, "You're an expert on those things? You've done research? What papers have you published? Have they been peer reviewed?"

"Whoa there, I was trying to be nice."

"I know, but I was giving you a taste of what it's like giving an opinion when one is a resident, a lowly one at that, in an academic surgical program."

"I still think you're handsome and a simple 'thank you' would have been nice."

"Thank you. Am I supposed to say you are beautiful now?"

"No. That would be a prevarication and I could get upset and leave."

"I'll take my chances. You haven't eaten and I know you're hungry. Grace, you are beautiful."

Grace glared and the waiter with a glass of Pinot Grigio saved Alex. He poured half into the second wine glass. "To friendship."

Grace smiled, said, "Friendship," and took a small sip. "Hmm. This is kind of fruity."

The soup, salad, and the split lasagna came in order. Grace surrounded her dishes with both arms.

The salted caramel ice cream, later that evening, met its promise.

Alex said, "I've had a super evening. Can I take you home?"

"NO, Alex, no. That wasn't part of our deal. You need to take me back to the hospital and I'll take a bus. Or take me downtown and I'll catch a bus there."

As they sat in Alex's car, waiting to go to a place to be determined, Alex said, "Grace, let's make a deal, as friends. We need to be truthful with each other, without filtering, editing and manipulating. Just be truthful. I'm guessing that the place you live is not nice; in fact, I'll bet it's awful. I get it. You don't make much money. I'm guessing just over the minimum wage for the position you have, but with some benefits. I don't care what kind of hovel you live in. It's late, it's dark and I'm not letting you get on a bus and then walk wherever. Either I drive you home or we go back to the hospital or downtown and I take the bus with you and then take a cab back. If you don't want to speak to me again, it's your prerogative."

"That wasn't the bargain."

"Bargain, schmargin. I don't care. I'm not letting you go home alone. I've had a great time tonight and I'd like to hear more about trying to tread through the orphanage. Please don't fight me on this."

Grace folded arms and her lower lip pouted a bit.

"So where do we go?"

"First and Yesler."

Grace's boarding house did not disappoint. A shithole. A small neon sign crackled on and off over the front door. The sign would have read 'Rooms to Let', but with two of the Os broken, 'Ro ms t Let' summed up the conditions. The building had no name. A small hand painted 9 x 12 inch sign on the front stoop read, 'Rooms by day, week or month. $4/night, $25/week, $95/month.' Two hookers stood twenty feet from the front door and a '59 pink Cadillac cradled the curb just down the street past the girls.

"Grace, can I walk you up?"

"No, this is good. I'm okay from here. I know most people around here. LaValle and Misty must not be busy tonight," nodding towards the girls down the street. As Grace exited Alex's Honda, she turned back and said, "I had a nice time. Thank you. Maybe I'll see you this week at the hospital." Grace turned quickly and walked up two small, cracked cement stairs into the 'Shithole' Hotel.

At five forty-five a.m. the next morning, Alex slid a note under the archive doorway and then hurried off for rounds. 'Had a great time last night ?Saturday again? Pager 4353 AG'

Alex finished his last surgical case at three forty-five p.m., wrote orders and rushed up to the archives before rounds were to start at four thirty. The door was ajar, unusual in itself, the lights were on which was a fifty-fifty proposition, but Alex heard voices from the copy room. He circled the desk and found Grace holding down the side of a huge book while a man, wearing a white lab coat, held down the opposite side. Alex couldn't help notice that the intruder, to his heretofore-private domain, was well over six feet, muscular, fit and handsome.

"Knock, knock," was the least cool thing that Alex could have said, yet it came out.

Grace and the unknown resident turned to face Alex, but kept pressure on the book as the copier rode back and forth on its trolley. Grace's hair was in a ponytail, the first time he'd ever seen her without a tight, controlled, safe, and unyielding bun.

"I'll wait here," Alex proclaimed.

"She'll be with you in a few minutes, buddy. We're halfway done with these copies and I have rounds in fifteen minutes," the stranger said.

Dripping with sarcasm, Alex retorted, "It's nice to meet you, too...buddy," then turned and walked out to sit by the counter. While Alex sat and stewed, Grace and the resident continued talking. The din from the copier prevented Alex from garnering any of their conversation.

Five minutes later the man came out to the counter to confront Alex. His lapel ID tag, now visible, read, A. Thomas Arnett, M.D., Chief Resident, Internal Medicine. Arnett, the left side of his mouth curled up, looked at Alex and snarled, "You're somewhat rude, aren't you?"

"What. For saying 'knock-knock.' Asshole?"

Alex stood. He was about the same height and weight of his counterpart. Grace interrupted the obligatory *mano a mano* posturing.

"Would you two settle down. Alex, this is Tom Arnett, he's a chief resident in Internal Medicine and I just printed out some old articles on arrhythmias. Tom, this is Alex Gordon, an R3 in Urology."

Arnett said, "So you know this asshole. I assumed that he walked in and was being pushy."

Alex said, "I may be dense, but was that an apology?"

Arnett shot back, "I don't apologize to residents, particularly to surgical types."

Alex said, "Fuck you, asshole."

Grace put herself between the two men and said, "Anyone listening, you two bozos take it down a notch, now, or I'll see that neither of you comes in here again. Capisce?"

The two men backed away from each other.

Grace faced Alex and said, "Dr. Gordon. I have about twenty minutes before I'm done with Dr. Arnett. Why don't you come back tomorrow? I assume you have rounds and I won't be here when you're done."

Alex turned at walked out of the archives. *Shit, I can't believe I acted like that.*

Thursday was busy from 6:00 a.m. to 6:00 p.m. and Alex didn't have time to return to the archives until Friday morning. No phone and no direct email made communications with Grace annoying.

As Alex entered, Grace was at the counter sorting paper, but didn't look up. Her hair was back in a tight bun. She said, "So what was that about on Wednesday? And before you say something, I will quote someone you know well... 'We need to be truthful with each other, without filtering, editing and manipulating. Just be truthful.'

Alex hesitated, "I was jealous."

"Of what?"

"I've gotten used to having you to myself here in the archives. I had a great time on Tuesday and was anxious to see you. Your hair was in a ponytail and you looked...you looked great. I didn't know Dr. Arnett, and... and, I acted like a seven year old."

"That was truly honest. I'm not sure I would have admitted as much." Smiling she added, "You've set the bar way too high on not lying. I don't know if even I can match it."

Alex curled his nose and waited.

"Alex, where are we going on Saturday?"

"Really? Cool."

"Really, Alex. Dr. Arnett will sit in the back of your car."

"You are such a shit."

Grace was laughing and said, "Where we going?

Alex said, "I'm not sure, I wasn't positive that you'd go, so I couldn't confirm plans. How about a surprise?"

"I'm not big on surprises."

"Tough, that's for making me jealous. I'm going to pick you up at 5:00 p.m."

"For obvious reasons, I don't stand around the front door of my place, so I'll come out when I see your car."

"Deal."

Alex drove up to the front door of Grace's rooming house at exactly 5:00 p.m. During the daylight hours, the look wasn't improved. Grace came out immediately. Her hair was in a ponytail but she wore her usual drab, one-piece dress, although in royal blue. Grace got into the car before Alex could circle around and let her in.

"Grace, remember that I need to open the door for you."

"Sorry. I'll try to remember."

"First, we go to dinner, eat light, and then do something I'm guessing you've never done."

"Tell me. I hate surprises. I'm getting out if you don't tell me."

"I doubt it, but we're going to a play, a musical actually."

"Really? A live theater. We tried to put on plays at the orphanage but we had no one with talent, including Mrs. Carmichael, who thought she was a director. My best part was playing a tree. We did it every year to raise money, I guess. Not that I ever saw any of it."

"There's a new theater in Issaquah that just opened. *Cabaret* is playing, a musical about the seedy side of Germany between the world wars. Dr.

Kauffman, our chairman, offered the seats and I jumped at them. Play's at 7:30. I thought we'd have dinner in Issaquah. Dr. Kauffman suggested a Chinese restaurant near the theater.

Beaming from ear to ear, Grace said, "I'm excited. Truly, I'm excited. Lots of firsts for me, being picked up in a car, going out for a pre theater dinner, going to a play. If I didn't know better, I'm reading a book about a New York socialite."

Alex, smiling, said, "Chinese dinner and a musical in Issaquah may be a stretch for that, but I'm happy you're excited."

Cascade Garden was a revelation. Too many choices and Grace was again overwhelmed. Alex ordered hot and sour soup, Kung Pao chicken, sweet and sour pork, and fried rice.

The theater was a few blocks away and as they walked, Grace, smiling, said, "I don't think I'll order that soup again but everything else was incredible."

Dr. Kauffman's seats were fourth row, center. Alex spent a good part of the evening watching Grace watch the play, which was excellent. Grace's eyes sparkled and a smile was glued to her face.

"Alex, thank you so much. I had the best time. I don't know how I'm going to sleep tonight."

Alex pulled off I-90 on Mercer Island on the way back to Seattle. Denny's was open until 2 a.m. He ordered two coffees and an apple pie a la mode slice to share.

Alex said, "You left your story after your friend Sarah was snatched by the wicked witch of the east. What happened next?"

"Do you care?"

"Yes, I care."

"Lots of the story isn't nice. I still have nightmares about the next part of my life. The more I try to not think about it, the more I seem to do just that."

"Have you ever tried to talk to someone, professionally, about your nightmares?"

"No. I was least of the orphanage's problem. They had few resources and once I was let go at eighteen, I never had the money to spend on help."

"I'm no psychologist, Grace," said Alex, "but maybe if you did share your thoughts, the burden might be lighter."

"I'll have to give that some thought. I've always thought that by keeping my fears secret, I would protect myself. There would be two of me, the one that knows and the one that everyone else knows."

"That's too much to bear for the rest of your life.

"Alex, if I were to tell you what happened to me, I would worry that you'd judge me. You wouldn't be able to help it. Our relationship would change. I'd always be wondering what you are thinking."

"That's a risk, I suppose, but keeping the evil genie in the bottle isn't good for you either. It'll keep eating at you. Think about it; think about getting some professional help."

Grace nodded tacit approval.

Alex continued, "Besides, I didn't know we had a relationship. I thought we were mere business partners."

"Alex, you're being coy with me. I know we're not having a 'business relationship.' This is all so new to me. I've spent the last ten years trying not to be noticed.

Alex drove back to Grace's rooming house and parked in front.

Alex said, "I had another really great time."

Grace said, "Me too."

Alex remained still. He could see that Grace had something to say.

"Alex, honestly, what do you see in me?"

"Grace, honestly, I think I see in you what everyone else doesn't."

Grace smiled. "Thanks. I guess."

"No guess." Alex bent over and kissed Grace on the lips and then pulled back to see Grace's reaction. As if ordering from the menu at the Chinese restaurant, Grace seemed confused.

Alex said, "I had a really great time."

Grace smiled, knowing that Alex knew that he had repeated himself. She turned, got out of the car, and ran up the stairs to her rooming house.

As Alex drove away, he saw only one of the two hookers. *Business is up fifty percent.*

The following Tuesday, Alex brought two subway sandwiches to the archives for lunch. He unwrapped the sandwiches as Grace pulled up two stools.

"I just found out that I am rotating to Portland next week for three months," Alex started.

Grace's eyebrows went up as she waited for more information.

"The resident that was supposed to go had a family emergency and Dr. Kauffman switched me from next April. I leave on Saturday. They keep a condo for the rotating resident near the University of Oregon Medical School. Funny, as soon as I heard, I thought about you and how people keep leaving you without notice."

Grace said, "How long will you gone?"

"Three months, I'll be back January 1st."

Alex wiped a small smear of mustardy mayonnaise from Grace's lip. "Maybe you can come down and visit me, unless Portland is too provincial for you."

"What?" Stunned by the offer, Grace slowly nodded her head side to side and pursed her lips. "I don't know when I'd come, where I'd stay, or what it would cost."

"When? I'd say Thanksgiving. I am assuming you get a four-day holiday. You can stay in the condo which has two separate bedrooms and I'll pay for the flight or bus or train, however, you'd like to travel. The train would be the easiest. Leaves from the King Street station which is a few blocks from your rooming house."

"I don't know, Alex."

"Grace, I want you to come."

Grace remained silent, her eyes widened, and face frozen, like a deer caught in the headlights.

"Grace, I want you to come."

"I heard you. You do tend to repeat yourself. What will we do there?"

"Dunno yet. I haven't been to Portland myself, but I'll have six weeks to scout the terrain. Maybe we'll go out and we can look for a Christmas gift for you."

"Alex, that's not fair. I don't have the money to buy you a decent Christmas gift."

"Not to worry. I don't celebrate Christmas."

"What does that mean? Everyone celebrates Christmas."

"I don't. I'm Jewish."

"You're kidding?"

"Grace, why would anyone kid that they're Jewish?"

"I've never had a friend that was Jewish."

"I'm guessing there weren't many Jewish orphans in Montana, one. And two, you haven't

112

made many friends since leaving. So not having many Jewish friends is expected, right?"

"I suppose. I assumed you were some Christian faith, not that it matters much to me. We were raised Catholic in the orphanage. The overseers of the orphanage were the Sisters of Mercy. I guessed early that God or Jesus wasn't listening to me, so I gave up on religion. Are you observant?"

"I was raised as a reform Jew. I had a Bar Mitzvah when I was thirteen. Our family celebrates the major Jewish holidays together, Passover, Rosh Hashanah and Yom Kippur. I don't have any dietary restrictions. I'll eat anything and I'm sure you'll vouch for me after our dinners and lunches. I go to a synagogue maybe three to four times a year, depending on the event. Mostly weddings these days."

"Alex, I didn't understand three-quarters of what you said. There's so much I don't know about you. Now this."

"Grace, there's little to know and you'll pick up the rest in time. I haven't eaten a Christian liver in three months...I'm kidding. Ballpark figure, I'd guess about half my friends are Jewish. My best friend growing up was Bobby Sullivan. Still is. We played every sport together from third grade on. He's just finished law school at Hastings and is working for a medium sized law firm in Oakland."

Grace sat silent, taking in Alex's revelation.

"Grace, I want you to come."

"Six weeks is a long time. How do I know that you'll still want me to come? You may meet someone, a nurse or somebody."

"Same goes for you. Remember, we're being honest with each other. If I meet someone, I'll tell you."

"My batting average isn't so hot. One friend, one date in five, six years since leaving St. Joes. Not likely my luck's going to change."

Alex said, "It has nothing to do with luck. It's all fate."

Grace said, "I'll come."

"Now another problem. I have no easy way to get hold of you."

"GracePine11870@gmail.com"

"You couldn't have told that me before?"

"I've never given it to anyone. Ever. I don't have a phone, way too expensive, and until now no one ever calls me."

"I have an idea. Long distance is expensive, but from the hospital, you can call the University of Oregon Medical Center through Seattle General's operators. They'll never question a call going to another hospital. They won't even ask what it's about. When I get down there, I'll find a phone in a sleep room or the clinic and then we'll set up a time to talk."

Chapter 8

One week later - Seattle and Portland, Oregon

Grace's first email from Alex arrived the following Monday. 'Here in Portland. The condo is 600 yards from OHSU, up a hill. Walk down easy. Walk up, not so easy. 3404 SW 13th Ave. Portland, OR 97239. Phone number in unit is 509-232-8288. Phone number in Urology Clinic resident's office is 509 494-8311, ext. 5402. Call me tonight at 4. I'll be in clinic but tell the secretary to interrupt me if I'm in with a patient. You need to say you're Dr. Pine or she'll tell you to call back. You will not be arrested, I promise. AG '

* * * *

"Urology Clinic. Amy Peterson speaking. How may I direct your call?"

"This is ...uh...This is Dr. Pine from Seattle General. I need to speak with Dr. Alex Gordon."

"He's in with a patient, Dr. Pine. Can you call back?"

"It is important. He told me to say that he should be interrupted."

"Hold on, Dr. Pine."

"Dr. Gordon, here. Is this Dr. Pine?"

"You know it is," Grace bemoaned, "I hate lying."

Alex said, "Amy, can you transfer this call into the office."

"Grace, how you doing? Worked like a charm, no?"

"If charm relies on lying, then it worked perfectly. But for some strange reason, as I see it, charm and lying don't fit together."

"Understood. Hey, I miss you."

"Me, too. I took you up on your recommendation. I made an appointment to see the local mental health clinic people about my issues. It's a free service. I have no idea who I'll see. The next open appointment isn't for three weeks and they need a doctor's referral."

"Grace, I'll take care of that for you. Email me the address of clinic and the phone number. I may call and try to see if they can see you earlier. I've got to get back to work, first week here and all."

Alex received an email the next day, Tuesday, with the contact information for the public health mental health clinic. She ended with 'Oh, BTW, fate struck again. Grace.'

Alex replied, 'What's that supposed to mean about fate????.'

Back came Grace's response, 'I got asked out by Dr. Arnett. Is that okay with you??'

Alex didn't respond, and didn't hear from Grace for three days, until Friday night. Grace emailed Alex, with an 'URGENT' tag. 'Please call me. Please.

Don't be mad. There's a payphone in the restaurant across from my rooming house. I will be there at 10 p.m. tonight. 206 929 6488. I don't want to wait until Monday when I'm at the library. Please call. Grace'

A nine fifty-five p.m., Alex had no intention of calling. At ten p.m. plus fifteen seconds, he dialed.

"Alex is that you?"

"Yes, it's me. What's the big emergency?"

"I need to talk to you. I'm scared. I went out with Dr. Arnett tonight and he frightened me."

"Grace, why would you go out with that asshole in the first place. I was so pissed when you told me?"

Talking in a rambling, but hesitant voice, Grace said, "I don't know... It was a mistake... Don't be mad at me... I thought it would be okay...ya know... to go out with other people. I thought that you'd probably meet someone in Portland... and I didn't see the harm in trying to date."

Alex could hear the hurt in her voice, "Grace calm down. Jerks like him are.... Oh forget it, Grace. Why him?"

She said, "I had so much fun with you that I thought that I could handle dating, but I wasn't ready. I'm scared."

"Hold on a minute, Grace. Did he hurt or threaten you? Did he even touch you?"

"No, not physically. Maybe emotionally. I'm almost certain now that he didn't find me attractive. He asked me out because he thought you and I were seeing each other and I guess that irked him."

"I'm sorry, Grace, what an asshole."

"He said we were going out to dinner, but '*dinner*' turned out to be at his apartment. When we stopped, I thought maybe he had to pick up something. But..but, when we got there, he had no intention of leaving," Grace's stuttering was interrupted by soft sobs.

The pay phone was on a wall near the entrance to the restaurant. The cashier came up to Grace and interrupted her.

"Hey..Hey, lady, you okay? Your crying is upsetting some of the customers, so keep it down. You need help?"

Grace said to the woman, "I'm sorry. I'll try to keep it down."

Grace, trying to continue, said, "Alex, the restaurant wants me not to be so emotional. I can't help it. Hold on for a second so I can try to get hold of myself."

After a few moments, Grace continued, "I told Dr. Arnett that I was uncomfortable being alone in his apartment. His response was something like, 'What do you see in that loser urology resident.' I told him that we were friends and we had gone out for a couple of dinners. He said, "I know you're sleeping with him. You can do better." I yelled, "That's a lie." He said you had bragged to everyone how we were having sex in the archives and at your apartment. I said, "You're lying, Alex wouldn't say that." I told him that I've never seen your apartment and I didn't even know where it was."

Alex interrupted, "Grace, you know I've never said anything to anyone about you. I swear."

"I know, Alex. At least, I think I know."

"Don't doubt me, Grace. I've said nothing. Are you okay now?"

"Wait, there's more. Then, I said, "I don't want to be here. I want to go home." He then said, "I've got some marijuana. Let's smoke a little dope. That'll put you in a better frame of mind." I panicked when he said that. I told him I can't be around marijuana and I pleaded with him, again, to take me home. He got angry and told me to 'get the fuck out of his apartment and go find that Jew.' I ran out and walked from Capitol Hill back to my rooming house. On the way, I went to an internet café and emailed you. I knew the number of the payphone across from the rooming house because I've used it before. I so wanted you to call." Grace stopped and took a few deep breaths.

Alex said, "Are you okay now?"

Grace resumed her frenetic speech, "Alex, I didn't really like him but I thought that I needed to be a little more worldly, not so naïve about everything, so that you'd like me. I didn't expect him to act the way he did. I was so scared, I'm still afraid."

"Grace, he's not coming to your rooming house to find you. He doesn't know where you live."

"I know, but I'll be alone in the archives all week and I'm scared."

"Grace, you'll have to trust me on this one. He's a lowlife braggart and you embarrassed him. He's no more likely to show up again at the archives than Elvis or Jimmy Hoffa. I'm proud of you for walking out."

"Alex, I miss you. I want to see you."

"Grace, I've got to be here. I'm presenting a case at grand rounds tomorrow. I can't come home right now."

Grace said, "I'm scared. I'm so scared."

"Scared of what?"

"I don't know. I'm so frightened. I had no one to turn to....except you."

Alex paused to answer, "Grace, I have an idea, if you want. One of the senior residents at Seattle Med told me there's an early train to Portland in the morning that gets in before noon. His wife used to take it. I think it leaves around seven, seven thirty. If you want to come down tomorrow morning, we could spend the weekend and you could take the six p.m. train back on Sunday night."

"Really. Could I?"

"Sure. You'll have to pay for the train down. I think it's twenty-five bucks or so. I'll reimburse you. I'll be at the train station as soon as rounds are over. If I'm late, just wait. Go up to your room now, lock the door and try to sleep. You'll be okay. If you need to call me, my beeper is 509 772-8280, then dial in the number you're calling from and I'll call you back."

"Okay. But I'm scared."

"Grace, I know you are. I can hear it in your voice. You'll be fine. I'll see you at noon, tomorrow. Another adventure, that's it."

"Thanks, Alex. Just talking makes me feel better."

Grace went back to her room, locked the door, bolted the chain, and moved a dresser in front of the door. She got into bed, fully clothed, and turned off all the lights. But she found no peace in the darkness as she usually did. *I am so scared.* Grace turned on an incandescent forty-watt bulb over the small reading desk in a corner of the room. The bare fixture hung down from the ceiling on a solitary black cord and dangled back and forth over the desk, like a noose trying to strangle the energy from the flickering bulb. The crying started as soon as she tried to close her eyes. She didn't sleep.

The next morning, Grace took the toiletries she needed and one change of clothes. She put all into two small thin plastic Safeway shopping bags and headed to the King Street Station, three blocks away at 5:30 a.m. She had thirty-seven dollars and change in her purse. She purchased a one-way ticket to Portland on the 7:30 a.m. train for $24.75. Bottled water was a dollar, so she went into the woman's bathroom and drank out of the sink. All the breakfast options were over seven dollars. Frustrated, she walked the three blocks back to her rooming house and made herself two peanut butter sandwiches for the trip, put them in the already crowded plastic bags, and returned to the station.

After finding her seat, she hoped she might find sleep. She saw the other passengers putting their travel bags in the overhead compartments. Grace reasoned that if she fell asleep someone could take her bags and she'd never know. She placed both plastic bags on the floor under her feet. The conductor nudged her twenty minutes later to collect her ticket.

"Sir. I haven't slept for a day and I'm afraid that I'll fall asleep and miss Portland. Can you remember to get me up? Please."

"Miss, I get off in Vancouver, Washington. I'll try to tell the next conductor, but I ain't promising."

Grace fought sleep until Centralia, just after 9:00 a.m.

At 11:50 am, a conductor kept poking Grace's right shoulder until she awoke.

Confused, Grace said, "What, what. Where are we?"

A different man in a blue conductor's uniform said, "We're in Portland. Been here 'bout twenty-five minutes. You've been asleep and everyone's off, that wants off. There's a guy outside saying that he's sure his friend is on the train and must have fallen asleep. I figure it's gotta be you."

"Oh my God. Did he leave?"

"Nope, don't think so. I said I'd check the train and he said that he'd wait."

As the conductor continued down the aisle, Grace went under her seat to grab her two plastic shopping bags. Both were gone.

Grace shouted, "Excuse me. Excuse me, mister. I had two plastic shopping bags here with my stuff. They're gone."

The conductor turned and walked back, head shaking, saying, "If you had them on the floor they may have slid under an unoccupied seat and the cleaning crew may have picked them up as trash. Why didn't you put them up above? They'd have been safe there. People use plastic bags as trash containers."

Grace, close to hysteria, said, "Please, where's the cleaning crew now? Where can I find them?"

With twenty-two years of experience, the conductor had heard this all before, "Miss, I got nothing to say to you. The cleaning crew's come and gone and you can wallow through the trash outside the train depot at your leisure, far as I'm concerned."

"But those were my clothes and toiletries. I need them."

"Miss, this here train is about to pull out of the station," the conductor said, looking at his watch, "in exactly one minute and thirty seconds. If you want to stay, pay, and then get off in Salem in thirty minutes, that's your business. Otherwise, you're gonna have to get off. The train don't wait for nobody."

Grace knelt, looked again under rows, two and three ahead and behind, stood and exited the train. She looked up and saw a myriad of signs until she lit on the 'Exit This Way' sign. As she headed towards the exit, she kept rubbing the left side of her face. An indent stretched from under her eye all the way to her chin. She had been sleeping, without moving, against the seat stitching for the past two hours. The train whistle blew and before she got halfway to the terminal, the train started to move.

The dimly lit station, all in smoky gray and mostly shielded by the lazily rolling train, appeared empty, ghost town empty, and devoid of movement. Grace, angry at losing her belongings, and frightened at the thought that Alex had left, started to shake. When she got to the end of the platform, sitting on a bench, arms folded, and asleep, was Alex Gordon.

She sat next to him. *Look at the two of us. What would the casual observer think? Two worthless, pieces of shit, dead beats.* "Alex, wake up."

Alex, startled, perked up quickly. "Grace. Where were you? I was here by 11:15 when the train was pulling in. People got off the train and then there was nobody. I pleaded with a conductor to look for you. He wasn't happy."

"I fell asleep. Someone took all of my belongings. My toiletry stuff and a change of clothes for tomorrow are gone. I didn't know what to do. The conductor thought the cleaning crew picked it up as trash."

"Grace, the cleaning crew wouldn't throw away a travel bag."

"I didn't have a travel bag or suitcase. I put all my stuff in two small plastic bags from the grocery store. I was afraid to put them up above, so I left them on the floor under my feet. When I fell asleep, they must have slid back, or something. I've got nothing."

Alex, stood, pulled Grace up, hugged her, and said, "To add to your misery, you look like shit. What'd you do, sleep on the floor grating?" as he rubbed the indent line along her face.

Tears flowing, lips trembling, shoulders sagging, she replied, "Hey, you don't look so hot either. You were sleeping on this bench. I could have taken your wallet and walked off."

"I was up all night with a complicated kidney stone patient with sepsis and then we had grand rounds this morning. I'm beat."

The two stood, toe to toe, and said nothing.

"Grace, you hungry?"

"More tired than hungry. I had a peanut butter sandwich three hours ago. Alex, I'm more scared than tired."

"Okay, I get it. First, we're going to go back to the condominium. You're going to take a shower and I'm going to fix you a light lunch. I've got extra toothbrushes. The condo has two bedrooms and we're both going to take a nap for a couple of hours. After that, we get up and talk. You're safe here. We're not going to let losing your bags upset us."

The car ride to the condo was fifteen minutes. Grace was asleep before Alex exited the parking lot.

He nudged her gently until she opened her eyes. "We're here. Let's get you upstairs."

"That's the second bedroom. Has its own bathroom. There's an extra new toothbrush in the drawer next to the sink."

The laundry room was off the front door and as Alex talked, he walked in, opened the dryer, rifled through the wash and was out in seconds.

"Here's a clean T-shirt and some boxer shorts that'll have to do as pajamas. There's a robe in the bathroom."

Grace disappeared behind the closed the door as Alex went to the kitchen to make a sliced turkey sandwich with Provolone. He cut it in half, added a few potato chips to each plate and poured two glasses of cold water. He could hear the shower running.

Grace, clad in a robe and Alex's makeshift pajamas, came into the kitchen, face reddened from the hot water, twirling the loose strand of hair with her left hand. She said, "Thanks for doing all this. I didn't know what to do. I didn't know whom to turn to."

Alex smiled, "Eat. I'm as tired as you are. Long night." They both ate quickly and quietly.

Grace sat as Alex put their dishes into the sink and left them. "Let's try to get a couple hours of shut-eye."

Grace nodded and walked into the second bedroom as Alex went into his room. He jumped into the shower but was too tired to shave. He put on an old T-shirt and boxers and got into bed. As he turned toward the nightstand to turn off the room lights, he saw Grace silhouetted in his doorway, wrapped in the blanket from the guest bed,.

"Grace, what's up? You need something?"

"I don't want to be alone, I'm scared. I'm scared of being alone." Grace said, twirling her hair in double time.

Chapter 9

Alex said nothing and pulled back the sheets of his double bed. Grace hesitated in the doorway looking at the floor at the foot of Alex's bed and then back to Alex.

Alex beckoned Grace by smoothing the sheets on the empty side of the bed. Grace, blanket and all, got onto the bed, face up, as far to the side as she could be in a small double bed. Tears were flowing again and she opened the blanket and used the bottom of her T-shirt to wipe her face.

Alex said, "Grace, you're safe here."

"I know. I know I'm safe. Thank you." She rolled towards him and kissed him on the lips, softly, and rolled back.

"Grace, what are you thinking?"

Grace turned again towards Alex and caressed his face with the back of her hand, as the tears continued to roll down the side of her face, "As I rode on the train, I didn't know what to expect or how I would feel when I saw you. I didn't even know what to hope for. I even thought that I would have to turn around and take the train back to Seattle. But as soon as I saw you on the bench, sleeping, a strange sensation of peace came over me. I was so relieved to see you. I've never felt that before. Right now, I'm exhausted, I'm unsure of myself, I'm conflicted, but for the first time in two days, maybe two months or two years or ten years, I feel safe."

Alex held her face and kissed her on the lips.

Before he could say anything, Grace said, "Let me talk. I have done nothing wrong, nothing. Maybe I've used bad judgment, but I didn't do anything wrong. Why do bad things always seem to happen to me, my whole life?"

"Grace, you're safe...."

Grace said, "Please be gentle...Please...Please be gentle," as Alex got the message and kissed her softly on the lips, then her eyes, nose, lips again and then her ears, her forehead and back to her lips.

"Alex, I've never done this, anything like this, I've never been here...in bed with anyone... when I wanted to. I never thought that I'd want anyone to touch me again. I need you to talk to me and be gentle." Grace sat up, removed the blanket still wrapped around her waist and laid back down facing Alex..

Alex paused a second to digest what she had said, or more importantly, what she hadn't said. *I had figured on the mental abuse, I wasn't sure about sexual abuse until now.* "I will," Alex murmured, as he continued to explore her face and neck with soft caresses.

In time, Alex sensed that Grace's pulse and breathing had slowed. As he continued to explore and caress, kiss and stroke, in no specific order, she would emit the tiniest of purrs of either escape or comfort.

Alex moved down in the bed as he slid his hand under Grace's shirt and massaged her tummy with slow circular motions using his palms and then the back of his fingers. Her breathing was slow and deep.

Perhaps it was the softness with which his hands moved up and down her body, or the sympathy she thought she could read in his eyes, or possibly, she was exhausted by the sense of foreboding, or all of these together. Sensing the heat from his body and the strength in his hands, she felt safe.

"Grace, help me take off my shirt." She turned and he followed, both kneeling, facing each other. Grace pulled Alex's shirt over his head. His chest was muscular and bare, save a small patch of light brown hair between his nipples. She kissed his chest and then held her arms up allowing Alex to remove her T-shirt.

With his fingertips and then with kisses and then with his tongue, Alex circled her breasts slowly, over and over. Her nipples tautened.

"Grace, please don't diminish what I am going to say. I want to tell you something that you don't realize and I'd like you to not to moderate or reduce what I know to be true."

Grace shook her head, no. But not the 'no' of no, but the 'no' of I don't know what you are going to say.

"Grace, you are enchanting... You are exquisite... You are so beautiful."

As she started to protest, he put his index finger over her lips, and said, "Grace, please don't diminish what I have just said. Just think on it a second, then say nothing. You are beautiful."

Alex removed his finger and again she tried to talk and he replaced the finger. "You are beautiful."

Grace said, "Please," under Alex's finger and he removed it once again.

Grace said, "No one has ever told me that."

Alex repeated, "You are so beautiful."

Grace pulled Alex down on top of her and wrapped her legs around his waist, while he resumed kissing as he held her hands over her head against the headboard. "You are beautiful."

He moved slowly down, licking her neck and breasts and tummy with his tongue and wet lips. He ran his fingers under the waistband of her boxers and sat up. She, without hesitation, raised her back and legs and allowed Alex to slip off her boxers. He resumed caressing her body with his lips, heading lower as he gently spread her legs and continued down. Grace's purring was now constant and deep throated. She pulled him back to accept deep kisses as he kicked his boxer shorts off the bed.

Alex said, "You are so beautiful."

Grace smiled, as she placed her hands on his buttocks and glided him into her, filling her lungs with air through pursed lips.

At 5:00 p.m., Grace woke up first. She felt good, painfully good. She rolled Alex onto his back, sat on top of him, bent forward and tickled his lips with hers. His eyes fluttered, then opened.

She said, "What's for dinner, Dr. Gordon?"

Alex surprised her by rolling her back over and got up on his elbows. "You, you're for dinner. You are so beautiful," he said, pressing forward.

Grace said, "Oh, that's a little sore... Don't stop. Don't stop."

They showered together and dried each other as the clock passed 6 p.m.

Looking at herself in the mirror as she combed her hair, Grace said, "I'm not so beautiful, but thank you."

Alex moved behind Grace and wrapped his arms around her chest to force both of them to look into the mirror together. "You are beautiful and if you don't think so, I'll have to get a better mirror." He kissed her on the neck. "You surprised me last night. I wasn't expecting what happened. I loved it, but didn't see it coming. A little out of character for 'Miss Montana Protection of 1995'"

Grace said, "I surprised myself. I had been in a steady state of panic until I saw you on the bench at the station, then not at all. I felt safe. When I shut the door to your guest bedroom, got into bed and turned off the lamp, within seconds, I could feel the fear crawling up the sides and the foot of the bed like wild ivy strangling a tree trunk. I turned the lamp back on, sat up against the back wall and waited. The fear wouldn't go away. You can't know how I feel when I'm scared. It's so deep, so black, so hollow inside me. I am exhausted but I would have never slept. I wrapped myself in the blanket and hoped that you would let me sleep on the floor of your room. I thought I'd be safe there. I guess that wasn't realistic but when I'm frightened, my reasoning doesn't work so well. I don't know what happened, but when you pulled the sheets back, inviting me, it felt right. Thank you."

Alex said, "You're welcome and thank you, too."

"Thanks for what?"

"Thanks for letting me help you," Alex said as he kissed her ear and then nestled his face in her semi-dry hair. Alex pulled away suddenly and said, "Oh, by the way, we need to get some clothes for tomorrow."

"Why, I can wash my stuff here tonight?"

"Didn't tell you. We're going to one of the professor's house for brunch at noon. Dr. Hildebrand. After grand rounds this morning, he invited all the foreign fellows, both chief residents and me. I told him I had an important guest coming for the weekend. He said, "Bring her, if it's a her. I guess he's old school."

Grace frowned.

"Anyway, we've got to get you some clothes. He said shorts, and a light shirt, and bring a bathing suit. Apparently, he has a swimming pool. I couldn't say no. He's the one in charge of me for the next three months."

"I can't have you buying me stuff."

"Grace, we're not going to argue about this, or even discuss it," Alex pleaded. "I've got money. My dad's a doc and I'm comfortable. You're here with nothing and it's not your fault. If you like, we can keep track of what we get and you can pay me back." *She would have looked out of place with anything she had brought.*

"I will pay you back," Grace demanded.

Alex said, "How much do you charge for services rendered. Sorry, that didn't come out right."

"What services," Grace replied tartly.

"Researching topics and putting together PowerPoint presentations," said Alex, trying to save himself.

"One million dollars an hour for you, buster."

"That's fair, and here I thought you were going to gouge me."

He kissed her on the lips and said, "Let's go. We'll shop and get something to eat."

At Macy's on West 5th Street, Grace and Alex fortunately found a sales woman who had some free time. The young woman's lapel button read, 'Jeannette – How may I help you.'

 Grace explained that her luggage had been lost and she needed to find something to wear for an informal brunch.

Jeannette said, "I'm so sorry. I guess it happens all the time, not that I fly much."

Grace and Alex saw no reason to correct her about the train.

Jeannette looked Grace up and down. "Poor girl. Follow me. I'm guessing you're a size 4. With your looks and body, I could put you in the Tin Man's get up and you'd look great. Where did you find that outfit you're wearing? In your boyfriend's dumpster? I'm sorry you had to wear that in here."

Alex kept his mouth shut.

Ninety minutes and three hundred fifty-seven dollars later Grace had Calvin Klein jeans, an Alfani print blouse, a cardigan sweater for the evening, a pair of sandals and a small travel bag.

Jeannette encouraged Alex to push Grace towards a Guess animal print bikini. The master of sales clichés, Jeanette, said, "If you got it, you flaunt it." Grace was dumbstruck and said little as the purchases mounted.

As Grace returned to the dressing room to grab her old dress and shoes, Jeannette commented to Alex, "Your friend is a looker, but sure doesn't say much."

Alex responded, in defense, "She was traumatized by the loss of her bag. You know how it is."

As they exited Macy's on their way to the Veritable Quandry restaurant, Alex said, "Four hundred seventy-seven dollars are on your account. You're going to owe me every single penny. Happy?"

As they sat facing each other, Alex, holding Grace's hands, said, "Your life is out of control. I'm going to make some calls Monday to get the names of therapists at the med center who can help you and will take your insurance. You can't do this by yourself and I'm not the one with experience. You need to talk to someone."

"You're right, I suppose. I've tried to do this by myself by hiding. But, for the moment, I feel good. Thank you again for everything. I don't know how I'm going to repay you."

"We'll find a way, if I have to sell your body parts on the internet."

After dinner, they made a quick stop at a twenty-four hour Walgreens and grabbed shampoo, conditioner and a hairbrush. By the time they returned to Alex's apartment it was well after midnight.

"I don't think I've ever been this tired," Grace said.

"Me neither, and I've some two-day all night stints as an intern."

They shed their clothes and got into bed. Alex curled around Grace and both were asleep in minutes. When Grace awoke at nine thirty the next morning, she was alone, naked, in bed. She searched the room and could find only a T-shirt, which she put on, and walked out of the bedroom. Alex was making coffee, wearing the missing boxer bottoms.

"Morning," Grace said.

Alex said, "Did you sleep well?"

"Yes. I don't remember getting into bed. Where are my clothes?"

"I hung them up this morning. We had clothes strewn over the bedroom and living room. Here's a cup of coffee. Black, right?" Alex went into the laundry room and brought out another pair of boxers.

"Thank you. I don't think anyone's ever made me a cup of morning coffee. I know that no one has ever given me a second pair of men's boxers to wear."

Alex laughed. "You're fabulous."

"Alex, you hungry?"

"I'm guessing that lunch is going to be huge, so I'm going to hold off. I can still taste the veal from last night."

"Come back to bed. I like your boxers better. These clash."

Alex picked her up and carried her back to bed. The got up at 11 am to get ready for lunch and showered together.

Grace said, "I may stay in the pool to cool things off."

Alex, again, had the good sense to say nothing.

Grace put on her new purchases and looked at herself in the hallway mirror. "This is the way people live in fairy tales. It can't be real. I feel so good, I know it can't last."

Alex responded, "It could last."

"Thank you again for calling. You saved my life."

Alex said, "On that note, were you talking literally or figuratively?"

"I don't know. I was scared."

"Seriously, Grace, I want an honest answer. Have you ever thought of hurting yourself?"

"Not since I saw you at the train depot yesterday. Before that, every day since I was twelve."

"I am so sorry. We need to get you to see someone."

The party at Professor Hildebrand's house was pleasant. A foreign fellow from Stuttgart found common ground with Grace, speaking to her in German. Professor Hildegard overheard them and came over.

"Excuse me, Miss, Miss..I'm sorry, I forgot your name."

"It's Grace Pine, Doctor Hildebrand."

"Yes. Yes. Grace. How many languages do you know besides German?"

"French and some Italian. A little Spanish."

"Grace, maybe you can help me. Alex tells me you're a medical librarian and I'm scheduled to give lectures this December in Paris and Munich. Is there any chance that I could hire you to translate slides into French and German? I can then put the translations side to side with the English in my PowerPoint presentations."

Grace didn't correct Dr. Hildebrand on the medical librarian designation and would deal with

Alex later. "Dr. Hildebrand, I can use PowerPoint, and I can format the slides for you. I could do both translations, French and German, simultaneously and give you two files."

"Do you know urological jargon?"

"If I don't know it, I do have a friend," nodding towards Alex, returning with drinks in hand.

Hildebrand replied, "The drug company sponsoring the talk said they would give me a thousand dollars to have the talks translated. I couldn't find a service to do both for less than fifteen hundred dollars. Will you take a thousand dollars?"

Trying to not act dumbfounded, but failing, she said, "Sure. When would you need them?"

"Three, four weeks. Possible? There's not a conflict with your current position. I don't want to jeopardize your job."

"No. It'll be okay." *Oh my God, a thousand dollars is six weeks pay.*

"I can email the presentation to you. I'll need your email address."

"GracePine11870@gmail.com, I'll write it down for you. Thank you so much."

"If this works out, I know lots of professors who will pay for your services."

Alex watched as Grace's fortunes kept improving. Hildebrand turned and went to get a piece of paper and pencil. Grace turned to Alex, her eyes widened and she smiled.

"Grace, you are beautiful."

At the train station that evening, Alex said, "We'll need to do this again. Soon."

Grace said, "I don't know that I can wait until Thanksgiving. I'm afraid that I'll start to believe that this weekend was a figment of my cluttered imagination."

Alex said, "Let's talk when you get home. We need to get you to see a counselor. Also, I'm thinking of coming back to Seattle weekend after next for some important business."

Grace, not knowing of any business, frowned, "What business is that?"

"Oh, there's a girl I know. I have an idea, if it goes well."

Grace smiled, "You're sweet."

"Oh, one other suggestion. Go to Planned Parenthood on Madison Street and get started on birth control pills. They're expensive, but I can get all the samples you need once I know what you're taking."

When Grace returned to Seattle, this time with her new travel bag intact, her room seemed one-tenth the size. Worse yet, it triggered all her negative feelings about herself. *Was the weekend real? Will Alex call? Will he come home in two weekends? Will it be the same? Could he meet someone else?* Grace got into bed and cried tears of happiness and fear. The light bulb cord swaying over her small desk still looked like a noose.

Grace still didn't have a phone but Alex emailed every day.

Twelve days couldn't come fast enough. Alex drove north to Seattle as soon as Friday night rounds were over. His car pulled up outside Grace's rooming house at 10:00 p.m. Grace ran down the stairs and got in.

Alex's kiss dispelled any thoughts that the Portland trip was imaginary. He said, "Can we go to my place?"

"I was hoping you'd say so. My hotel manager wouldn't be supportive, so to speak," Grace chuckled, "and he'd charge me an hourly rate."

"Do you have a bag of stuff for the weekend?"

"Yes, it's packed up in my room. I didn't want to be presumptuous, so I didn't bring it down."

Alex said, "Go."

Grace ran up three flights and back, proudly showing Alex her new travel bag. The ride to Alex's Capitol Hill apartment was less than ten minutes. Grace slapped Alex's meandering hand twice. "Just wait."

Alex said, "Too difficult to wait."

Grace said, "Try. It's not any easier for me. I finished Dr. Hildebrand's slides last week and emailed them back. I stayed at the library to use their computer after hours. Thanks for the help on some of the meanings. I think he'll like it. He emailed me that he'd send a check in the next week. I am so excited. One thousand dollars. I've never seen that much on a check."

Walking into Alex's second floor, one bedroom unit, she said, "Wow, nice to be rich."

"I thought you were working on trying to be worldly. You could have stopped at nice. I'll give you a tour later," Alex said, as he unbuttoned Grace's cardigan and started on her blouse.

Not wanting a tour either, Grace undid Alex's belt.

* * * *

Alex's apartment was as nice as the one in Portland, but with no second bedroom. Alex's king bed was like a playground. Grace was getting used to the T-shirts and boxers, although she wasn't wearing them most of the weekend.

Holding Grace tightly, lying side to side, at 4 am, Alex, turning on the bedside lamp, said, "We need to talk a little, okay?"

"Sure. About what?"

"About you. Grace, I've not had much luck getting you in to see someone, but I'll keep trying. I may ask Dr. Kauffman, my chairman, to help. If that's okay with you?"

"What do you think?"

"I think it's important. Have you had any bad thoughts since you were in Portland?"

"Only really bad the first night I got back. The room was so small and dark and I thought I imagined Portland and you. I guess I didn't. I was scared and sad, but I didn't want to hurt myself."

"In the meantime, I think you need to keep talking to me. Tell me a little more each time. I won't judge you, I promise. I know you need to vent some of this shit stored inside you. Grace, it's not going away by itself.

Grace bit her lower lip softly, then said, "Okay. We'll talk. You and I."

Alex said, "What happened after..."

Grace interrupted Alex and said, "So you know. I feel so vulnerable, so naked, so unprotected, when I have to think about my past. I don't know how I'll feel after I've actually told someone. I expect that I'll have more nightmares for a while. And there are some things that I can't talk about, ever."

Alex said, "I understand. What happened after your friend Sarah was snatched away by her aunt?"

"It took me a year to get over Sarah and then another six or seven years until Jodie, my next friend, came to the orphanage. I was about fifteen. She, like Sarah, told me stories of family life and happiness that I could only find in books. We would read together, laugh, and talk about boys. Nevertheless, like Sarah, Jodie just upped and left. I think her mom got out of jail, showed up, took her, and left the state. As if, I never existed. As if, I was so unimportant. After that, I made sure that I never got close to anyone at the orphanage. I didn't want to have that emptiness feeling ever again. That's why I didn't want to be friends with you."

Alex said, "But you did in the end, make friends with me. Why?"

"I guess because you had figured me out. You know, about having no one. Maybe I wasn't ready before. People had tried to engage me but I wouldn't let them get close, so they gave up. You didn't seem to go away."

"There were a bunch of years between Sarah and Jodie. What happened then?"

"I lived with a family but I'm not able to talk openly about it. I won't even say their names. At least, not yet. I spend most of my nightmare time reliving those few years. They never adopted me, thank God, but they tried. Every so often, I'll get a trigger to remind me. Marijuana, a food smell, a comment, a flannel shirt, the smell of chewing tobacco, a certain intonation when someone says 'Grace', whatever.

"After leaving the orphanage at eighteen, I got used to being alone, not depending on others. In fact, that ability to find solace in being alone kept me going. Then you came along and questioned my thinking."

"Didn't you ever get adopted out when you were real young?"

"Yes, once for two years. I was two or three. I think I remember being happy all the time or I was told I was happy. I called those parents, Mommy and Daddy, right away. I remember a Grandma too. Then, all of a sudden, I was back in the orphanage. Years later, one of the sisters told me about the

Ostergards, that was their name, Bill and Henrietta Ostergard. They were both teachers. A student had accused Mr. Ostergard of attempted rape. Even though most people didn't believe the charges, the newspapers and public opinion forced them to leave Missoula and Montana, without me. The orphanage took me back. Years later, the same girl was arrested for drug dealing. She admitted her claims against the Ostergards were all lies. By that time, the Ostergards were long gone and untraceable, or the orphanage didn't look."

Alex said, "Unbelievable, Grace. I am so sorry."

"Still no 'me-too' moments?"

"None, not even close. I'd be embarrassed to tell you how easy my life has been, comparatively."

"I thought so. It's not you see tons of bumper stickers that say 'I'd rather be raised in an orphanage.'"

"Yeah, but I'm not going to abandon you like those others."

"We'll see, won't we?"

"A trace of optimism would be nice about now. Your luck was bound to change."

Frozen pizza, frozen waffles and peanut butter on Ritz crackers provided all the sustenance Alex and Grace needed for dinner, breakfast and lunch. Sunday afternoon came too quickly.

Grace, twirling her hair, sat in a corner of the bedroom watching him pack. She said, "Alex, I wish you didn't have to go."

"I wish I could I stay, but we both know I can't."

Grace said, "I'm still afraid that I'll lose you."

"Grace, I'm going to make you an offer. This apartment is unused while I'm in Portland. I want you to stay here while I'm gone. That way someone is watching my stuff. Not that there's that much here to steal. I do have internet, a telephone, and my desktop computer, so you won't have to stay late if any more translating jobs come your way, and we can talk at night."

"I don't know that I could do that to you. What if we stop liking each other or you meet someone else."

"Possible, but unlikely. I worry about you staying alone at that rooming house. Here, it's safer. Please say yes."

"I'll be alone here, too."

"We both know it's safer here."

Grace nodded acceptance and said, "How will I get my belongings here?"

"I'm going to have Mr. Mendoza help you. Hector and his wife, Rosa, live below me here in unit A1. He'll take you back to the rooming house tomorrow after work and help you bring your stuff. He said he's got boxes, if you need them."

"How do you know he'll do it?"

"I asked him last Wednesday and he said yes."

146

"Kind of presumptuous that I'd agree, weren't you?"

"Yes. Very presumptuous. I was thinking about me, not you. I didn't want to worry." *That's not true but what the hell, it sounded good.*

"When will I see you again?"

"I'm busy the next two weekends, then free. We can decide later whether I'll come up or you'll come down. I have grand rounds on Saturdays so it would be easier for you to come Friday night. Mr. Mendoza has been forwarding my mail, but you can take over that job. I have nothing to hide. Plus, we get to talk every night, if you want."

The next night after work, with Hector Mendoza's help, Grace moved in to Alex's apartment.

Grace called back to the rooming house every day until her check arrived from Dr. Hildebrand. Alex persuaded Grace to open her first checking account at a nearby Wells Fargo and use his address.

Grace now had money and was no longer paying rent. She kept looking at her checkbook. She hadn't written a check yet, but seeing a thousand dollars in the balance line made her feel rich. Grace and Alex talked every night at ten p.m.

Grace returned to Portland for Alex's free weekend. After three weeks apart, sightseeing was still not on either's agenda. Grace returned to Seattle on Sunday night knowing that she'd be back in Portland for four full days for Thanksgiving only three weeks away.

Chapter 10

Grace received an email on the Monday morning, ten days before Thanksgiving from Alex. 'OMG. Parents coming Portland 4 Thanksgiving. We need 2 talk tonite. AG.'

The phone rang at 10 p.m.

Grace started with, "What's this mean? Your parents coming??"

Alex said, "They called two weeks ago and asked if I was coming home for Thanksgiving. I told them I couldn't, which was a little white lie. Anyway, my mom called yesterday. I guess my sister isn't coming home from Ann Arbor and my parents hadn't been to Portland for years, so they want to visit and see me. I told them that I had a guest from Seattle coming to stay for the weekend. That didn't go over real well."

"Oh, I'm a guest."

"What did'ya want me to say?"

"I dunno, 'guest' plays wrong with me."

"I agree, now. My mom didn't appreciate the word either. She wanted to know more. I told them that I was seeing someone and that she was the 'guest.' Of course, she wanted more information. I told her a little about you. Now they really want to come."

"Alex, what do you want to do?"

"Grace, I don't know. You know parents will have a thousand questions to ask about you."

"Nope, didn't know that. I don't have parents."

"Sorry, that just came out. I look at it this way, if we keep seeing each other, then you'd have to meet them sometime. Might as well do it now."

"If they don't approve of me, could they make you stop seeing me?"

"Absolutely. My mother has only to say 'she's not for you' and we're done. Mom is going to say that to anyone who's not Jewish, hasn't finished college, doesn't have a strong and stable family life, and comes from Montana or Wyoming. I could go on, but you get the gist. You have no chance of making it through the weekend unscathed."

"You're kidding with me, right?"

"Not completely. You've been telling me all along how much you missed having a family. The downside is that family is going to have opinions, occasionally, strong opinions, about everything, including who a family member can or cannot see. I don't have to follow their suggestions, but I have to listen."

Grace said, "So you don't want me to come?"

"Absolutely....wrong. I want you to come. Where my parents are going to stay and where you're going to stay is still in the clouds. They thought they'd take the master bedroom, but I told them that there are only double beds here and they can't sleep in anything smaller than a football field. In the end, I'm sure they'll stay at the Heathman Hotel, downtown. That means you can stay here."

"I don't know about this, Alex."

"Neither do I. But it will be a test of courage."

"Oh, shit."

"Yep, oh, shit."

"Anything I can do?"

"Sure, convert to Judaism, find a bogus family who raised you, get a degree in astrophysics from CalTech. I'll find more for you to do."

"Alex, help me out, please. Is there anything I can do?"

"My parents will speak Yiddish when they don't want someone else to know what they're talking about, including me and my sister. Yiddish is a variant of German, which you already speak. I just know a few words. Get some books on Yiddish. It'll scare them."

* * * *

The evening before Thanksgiving, Alex entered his parent's room at the Heathman Hotel in downtown Portland. They had flown in earlier that day and taken a cab to the hotel. Alex got off work at 6 p.m. and went directly to the hotel. They ate dinner at the hotel's five-star restaurant.

"Mom, Dad, I'm glad you're here. Grace comes in on the ten thirty train tonight from Seattle.

Tomorrow morning, we'll meet for breakfast here at the hotel and then go to the Japanese Gardens. I know you are curious."

Aaron Gordon chimed in with, "I could care less about the Gardens."

"Funny, Dad. Grace is different from anyone I've ever met and you've ever known. She is captivating, kind and smarter than I am and..."

Beverly Gordon, herself a graduate of UCLA and a teacher, stopped Alex, "Please, honey, don't be so dramatic. Few people are smarter than you, except me. I'm sure she's a nice girl and we'll judge for ourselves. Right, Aaron?"

Aaron said, "Agreed. We'll decide."

Alex said, "Grace has issues, many of which I've not told you about. She is disarmingly honest and will answer most questions without a filter. Honestly, she doesn't know any other way of answering. We had some funny discussions when we first met called 'me-too moments.' When I asked her about her past, she said she would never say 'me-too' to any of my life events. I thought she was kidding but as we delved deeper, she was right. She appeared mysteriously at an orphanage in Missoula, Montana at the age of two. The orphanage gave her a name and an estimated birth date. She has no idea who she is or where she's from. Her life has been one trial after another with things she can't talk about, yet. We have no clue what she's been through. Just give her the benefit of the doubt. She needs help emotionally, but we've not been able to find a therapist to see her. A free-clinic visit a few weeks ago got her to some bozo that made her feel worse and I won't let her go back. I can't seem to get through to anyone in the Psych department at

Seattle Med yet. I guess first-year urology residents don't get much traction."

Alex's dad shook his head, "Alex, why do you need this aggravation. You know she's going to have problems her whole life. You don't know what you're getting into. Why can't you find a nice Jewish girl, from a good family, and settle down to a peaceful life. This girl sounds like *tsuris,* big trouble.*"

"Dad, I agree, I would have never looked for a partner with all these problems. We met when she did some work for me at the medical library. She did everything she could to make me go away. Really, she wanted no friends. That was her defense mechanism, or so I've come to understand. But something about her intrigued me. Her way, her demeanor. She was so different. It made me want to find out more."

"Alex, we'll see for ourselves," said Beverly Gordon.

Alex continued, "I'm not wedded to her and I've not proposed. I've never even mentioned marriage and I'm sure it's the farthest thing from her mind."

Beverly interjected, "I'm sure it's not the farthest thing from her mind, but believe what you want to believe."

"I love being around her." Alex, turned and spoke directly to his mother, "I know that I am acting like a rescuer and you've always said the rescuer becomes the victim. Maybe. But try to be fair, that's all. She comes from nothing, she has nothing, and, at the moment, the only thing she wants is me. And that makes me feel good."

* * * *

Grace, having money in the bank for the first time in her life, and knowing that she was to meet Alex's parents, had gone to a beauty salon before leaving Seattle to have a professional haircut and learn a little more about applying make-up. At Ross Dress-For-Less, she found a simple black dress and a pair of black patent leather shoes with 4" heels. She practiced walking around with the heels for an hour each night before leaving.

Alex met her at the station. He said immediately, "Grace, I love your hair. Nice."

Grace said, "Alex, do you notice anything else different about me?"

Alex said, "No." After a slight pause, Alex added, "Except you got off the train on time."

"I have some makeup on. You don't see it?"

"My mother and sister would have known in a second. My dad and I are makeup blind. It's genetic. I can tell if your kidneys are working, but I haven't the slightest idea about makeup. It's a defect of mine and it's permanent. That said, you look great."

Grace said, "It would be so easy to hate you on so many levels. When are we meeting your parents?"

"But you do love me, and tomorrow at ten for breakfast. Then a quick trip to the Japanese Gardens for my mom, the aesthete. Then back to the condo to cook Thanksgiving dinner. I've already bought the turkey."

Grace said, "Whoa, whoa. We're cooking dinner? I'm not cooking dinner for your parents. No way. I didn't know about that."

"No, my mom is going to cook and you're going to help while my dad and I watch football on TV. It's a tradition."

"Me cooking anything is not a tradition. I'm lost in a kitchen."

"No, football is the tradition, Cowboys and Lions. I could eat Chinese and be happy. Mom enjoys making Thanksgiving dinner. Let's get back to my place first. We've got other more important things to do tonight."

"What things?"

"T- shirt and boxer things, or lack thereof."

* * * *

"Mom, Dad, this is Grace Pine. Grace, this is my mom, Beverly, and my dad, Aaron."

Beverly said, "It's nice to meet you Grace. Alex said you were attractive. He lied. You are stunning. I love your hair."

Grace said "Thanks," and squeezed Alex's hand with the hair comment.

At breakfast, despite Alex's attempts at teaching Grace table manners, she would unconsciously put her arms on the table and surround her food. Alex's unsaid message was a tug on his ear and when she'd see the ear pull, her hands would go back into her lap.

After the third or fourth time, the entire table was aware of the Emily Post faux pas.'

Grace turned to Alex's mother and said, "I'm sorry about my table manners. At the orphanage, if I didn't protect my food, someone would take it. By the time I was big enough to protect myself, it became habit. Alex's doing all he can, but all I can do is try."

Alex's father mumbled, "*Oy, a scheina shiksa mit tsuris.*" Beverly nodded and Alex smiled.

Grace said, "Dr. Gordon, thanks for the 'pretty' compliment, I guess. I hope you'll have some *rachmones* for me until I learn better manners."

Aaron Gordon's mouth fell open, as Beverly asked, "You understand Yiddish?"

"*Ich bin gut in sprachen,*" Grace said. She looked at Alex and translated, "I'm good at languages." Then back to the table, she said, "They just come easy. Alex told me to learn some Yiddish a week ago. It wasn't so hard because I already speak German."

Alex, looking to his mother, added, "You can still speak Yiddish around me, I don't understand a word. Hey, now you three can talk about me and I won't have a clue." The laughter from all four was genuine.

After breakfast, they headed to the Japanese Gardens. As father and son talked medicine, Beverly and Grace walked behind.

"Mrs. Gordon, I don't know how much Alex has told you about me, but if you have any questions, ask."

"You really don't know who your parents are? Not even an inkling?"

"None. Just abandoned. No name and no clues. The police and the orphanage made calls to every police station and orphanage in ten states. They found nothing as to where I came from. I do know that I'm not from Krypton because I have no superpowers."

Bev laughed, "If you got Alex to fall for you, you must have some kind of powers."

Beverly Gordon and Grace sat on a bench while Alex and his dad continued to walk and talk.

Grace said, "Mrs. Gordon, I know a lot about you from Alex. I know that I am being scrutinized this weekend. I suppose if I were a mother, I'd do the same."

Beverly said, "Alex said you didn't filter things. He was right; you do get to the point. I like that. I'm not sure I can be as honest as you. It's not in my nature. Hell, it's not in the nature of most people I know."

Grace nodded.

Beverly said, "Grace, what are you plans in life? What do you want with Alex?"

"Three months ago, I could have answered that easily. I wanted to be alone, I needed to be alone.

Every relationship I've ever had ended in disaster. Every friend I had abandoned me. Every family I lived with caused me pain. I decided that my only refuge was insulating myself from others. For some reason, and I'm not sure why, Alex refused to let me be. And I changed and I feel better about myself. Now, I look in mirror and like what I see." Grace paused for a second. "Actually, that's not correct, I look in the mirror and I don't hate what I see. That would be more honest."

"Grace, you didn't answer my question. What are you plans in life? What do you want with Alex?"

"I'm sorry, Mrs. Gordon. I get a little self-involved sometimes. In my new fairy tale life of seeing possibilities, I dream of going to college, more than anything, and get a degree and maybe teach. I'm good at languages. I could teach that. It's been five years since I left the orphanage. Maybe I have enough credits from classes in Missoula and Spokane to equal a half-year in college. I've never had enough time or money to do more. I'd like to be able to go to college."

"And Alex and you?"

"Right now, I love being with Alex. He's given me strength, compassion, opportunity, hope, a place to stay, and what I think is love. But, I have to be honest with myself. I don't know what he sees in me. I know that he could do better, so I'm afraid I'll lose him when he meets someone else who is worth more, is more stable, has a more complete background, or has any background. Even has a family. Would I hope that he'd want to marry me? Maybe. I hope. I first need to get some help sorting out some of my issues. After that, if I'm strong, then I can only pray that he'll see that I may be a person of merit."

Beverly sat for a while without answering. Tears hung from her eyelids, waiting for the right or the wrong moment. She took Grace's hands in hers. "You are one of the bravest people I have ever met."

Grace leaned over, gave Beverly Gordon a hug, and said, "Thank you. Thank you so much. I can only hope."

After a few moments of silence amidst the incredible beauty of the gardens and after feeling the weight of Grace's story, Beverly stood. "Come on, you and me, we'll make a turkey."

Grace said, "I'd enjoy that."

As mealtime approached that evening, Beverly Gordon looked at her kitchen assistant. "Grace, you are unique."

"Really, why so?"

"I have never met anyone, over the age of 8, with so few kitchen skills."

Grace smiled, "Ouch. I thought I was doing okay. I didn't cut off any fingers."

"It's not that you didn't try though." Beverly came around the dining table as Grace was setting places. "Forks and napkins on the left, knives and spoons on the right, bread plates on the left, water glasses on the right."

Looking like a hurt puppy, Grace said, "Does it really make any difference?"

"Yes, Grace. It does to me."

Grace twirled and pulled on her hair for a bit, then stood and put the place settings in their proper place.

Dinner conversation had nothing to do with Grace. Seattle weather, Reagan's Alzheimers diagnosis, Alex's apartment in Seattle, where Alex expected to go after his training, problems with medical delivery in the US, Republicans taking control of both houses, all received sound bites. Grace, the voracious reader, had something to add to every conversation.

With her hands moving rhythmically, like a conductor's baton when emphasizing a point, she relished being 'in' the conversation.

"Seattle's cloudy days are better than Montana's snow." "Alex's apartment is fabulous, roomy and best of all, his neighbors are nice and caring." "He's said a few times that if he chooses academics, he may not be able to pick where he goes." Alex's parents could not help watching Alex focus on Grace when she spoke.

As soon as the Gordons were dropped at their hotel by Alex and Grace, Aaron Gordon said to his wife, "We better be accepting of this girl because 'your' son isn't letting her go. I've never seen him act this way."

Beverly said, "Absolutely. He's cooked."

On Sunday morning, prior to Aaron and Beverly's return to the Bay Area, the four took a walk along the Willamette River waterfront.

Beverly Aaron held Grace back so they could talk.

"Grace, I've enjoyed meeting you."

"But, what?" Grace said without hesitation.

"No buts."

"Mrs. Gordon, I was so afraid that this weekend would be the last I see of Alex. I am so used to having things I care about snatched away. Why would Alex be any different? I don't come from anything that you'd understand. I have no money. I've had no education to speak of. I'm not worldly or sophisticated. I'm certainly not Jewish. I don't really know how to cook, how to dress, wear makeup, or do my hair. I'm still mystified that he wants to be with me."

"I know my son, and the way he looks at you, tells me he's smitten."

Grace said, "Maybe it's the sex. That's been really good. I don't know how it could be better. He's my first boyfriend, heck, he's my first friend. I can't get enough of Alex. Last night,...."

Beverly was quick to stop the dialog, "Jesus, Grace, you really don't filter anything, do you?"

"Oh, I'm sorry."

"Don't be sorry. I truly love your honesty. Grace, I really do like you. I do, and no buts. Your honesty is more than I could ever expect from any human. From what you've been through, you are already a person of merit and distinction, at least to me. You are worthy of a happy and full life. Whether that life is with my son, I can't answer. That's up to you two.

I won't stand in the way and neither will Alex's father."

Grace gave Beverly a hug that lasted long enough to know that Grace needed a hug back.

Alex, with Grace, drove his parents to the airport. After dropping of his parents, Alex said, "I thought this weekend went spectacularly. My parents liked you, I think."

Grace said, "When will they call you to talk about me. I'm not going to stop worrying about that call until I hear from you."

Alex took Grace to the train station.

Back at Alex's Seattle apartment, Grace's email contained a request from a friend of Dr. Hildebrand at OHSU. An orthopedic professor needed to translate slides for a talk in German. The talk was sixty minutes long and he offered Grace seven hundred fifty dollars. She accepted and emailed Alex the good news, but also asked if he had talked to his parents.

The next evening when Alex called, he started the conversation with, "Please don't ask me what my parents thought of you. We can talk about anything else."

"Alex, that's so unfair. You know how worried I am."

"Little Miss Optimism, let me put it this way. If I said they hated you, you'd be devastated. If I said they loved you, you wouldn't believe me. If I said they said nothing, you'd think I was lying. So what should I do?"

"Please, Alex, tell me the truth."

"They said they loved you."

"I don't believe you."

"See."

"No, really."

"I didn't talk to my dad. My mom says you are the most honest person she's ever met. You were, also, much prettier than I told her you'd be. My bad. My mom said she was glad that you realized you needed some professional help to get through some of your issues. She felt that most people with your life situation would fold like a cheap lawn chair if given severe obstacles. But then she said, 'I think Grace has something to prove to the world. I don't see her folding, if given the opportunity.'"

"I already love your mom."

"On that note, did you tell her something about our sex life?"

"Uh, yeah. That did come out."

"Thanks, actually. She has a whole new image of her stud son."

"Don't let it go to your head, Romeo."

"Actually, that's not where it was going. God, I miss you already. I am so in love."

"Me too. When can I see you again?"

"My last day in Portland is December 27th. The faculty delights in putting the Jewish guy on-call for Christmas week. It's obligatory and a tradition. Then, I've got to be at work in Seattle on January 2nd. My parents invited me to Cabo for Christmas, if I can get a flight."

"Just you."

"Just me. My sister is coming from Ann Arbor, too. They've rented a three-bedroom condo in San Jose del Cabo. They're not sure it works with you, me and my little sister being there."

"Are you going?"

"No. I said I have to move back to Seattle and get some other things done before returning to work on the 2nd. I've decided to take in another person to co-rent my unit. I'm expecting that they'll pay a fair share of the rent."

Grace said, "What? Who's that?"

"It's this woman who does translating for professors. She's making a killing and she's richer than Croesus."

"You're funny. So when are you coming back?"

"If you can get a few days off after Christmas, I thought you'd take the train down, help me pack, and then we'd spend a few days on the Washington coast before coming back to Seattle."

"I've got three weeks of sick leave coming to me. I can feel the flu coming on already."

A week later, Grace's email started with a happy face icon. "I finished another translating job from

Oregon and made another five hundred fifty dollars. I'm able to check my balance online and I have nineteen hundred thirty-seven dollars and fifty-three cents."

Alex's response, "Are you sure about the fifty-three cents?"

"Don't make fun of me. U r such an a..hole. I am flush with cash and feel so rich. I've been thinking about my life and trying to make plans for the future."

Alex quickly came back with, "It's Doctor A..hole to u. I miss you so much. Luv, and I mean it, AG."

At two am, two days before New Year's, with a whistling, window-rattling, coastal storm howling outside, Alex and Grace lay facing each other in bed in a rented condo in Westport, Washington. They each had two days of freedom before returning to work in Seattle. In the aura and warmth of great sex, Grace took a big leap, or a big chance, depending on how one looked at it.

"Alex, I want to discuss something that's been on my mind."

"Go for it."

"I want you to know how much what you've done for me over the past three months has meant. I look forward to every day. I feel good about myself. But, I want to be more than I am now. I want to be someone you can be proud of. I want…"

"Grace, you're rambling."

Grace said, "I'm sorry. I can't help it. I've been thinking about this for three weeks, thinking about it so hard that I can't sleep at night. I may never have another chance to get this done."

"Grace, you're rambling again. What the hell is 'this' and 'it'? When do you start college?"

Grace was dumbstruck, and blinked to clear her head. "Alex, I haven't told anyone. How did you know?" Grace rolled on top of Alex and covered his face with kisses. The hardness between her legs was now familiar and welcome.

Alex, coming up for air, said, "You told my mom that more than anything, you dream of going to school. I think I'd like to see you do it, too. It's never too late to do what you dream to do. When do you start?"

"I want to see if I can get a few more translating jobs from Oregon, maybe in Seattle too." The now giddy Grace spoke in triple time, trying to get as many thoughts out as quickly as she could, as if they had been stored in a Jack-in-the-box toy waiting to burst out. "I'd like to take as many credits as possible, so working will be difficult, anyway, I want to start spring quarter in April, I think I can get enough done in a year to then transfer to the University of Washington."

"Hold on. Hold on. You're talking too fast."

Grace slowed, "Alex, you know I can't do this without you, but I'll try to understand whatever happens, if you find someone else."

"Grace. For that to happen, I'd have to be looking. I'm not looking."

166

Grace sat up and guided the hardness in.

On January 14th, Grace Pine emptied more than half of her bank account, eight hundred forty-three dollars, to pay for sixteen credits at Seattle Central Community College. She was going to school, full time.

Chapter 11

New York January 1995

"Cully, Henry here."

"Of course it's you. No one else calls me on this line."

"Through your contact at the IRS, we've known for a while that our Seattle project was working for minimum wage as a file clerk in a medical library. She had been holed up in a rooming house, a real shithole, in downtown Seattle."

"We knew all that."

"Yeah, but I had her followed for the first time in six months. I got wind of a change of direction," Henry Farley said, in jargon, with an air of caution.

"Henry, this phone isn't bugged, so what's on your mind?"

"She's got a boyfriend."

"That was always a possibility. So?"

"He's a resident at the medical school in Seattle. She's moved in with him fulltime, apparently, because she's not at the flophouse anymore."

"Why's that concern you?"

"Doesn't really. But then everything concerns me. That's what you pay me to do, worry, right."

Cully Harris said, without emotion, "No, I pay you so I don't have to worry. I don't give a shit how you feel."

"I liked it better when she was as poor as a church mouse. She had no options. If she was seeing a low life, I'd feel better. This guy, being a doc, and all, makes me a little uneasy."

"Can you fix it?"

"I thought about it and I don't know if we should. She has no idea we've been trailing her. If we do something and it doesn't work, it raises the possibility that she'll know we're watching and manipulating her. I don't want that to happen. But, if we do nothing, and she gets out of the pits, so to speak, she could start to look for you."

Cully, now irritated, said, "You've told me a thousand times, Henry, even if she looks, there's no way she could find us. Right?"

"Ninety-nine point ninety-nine percent true. However, I hate those hundredths-of-a-percent risks. Anyway, I'll break this duo up if you want, or we can watch."

After a brief silence on the line, Cully said, "Break it up."

* * * *

Henry Farley sat in his office as his secretary led in a large swarthy man in an ill-fitting suit. He'd been in the office before, always with the door closed. The secretary knew to say nothing. Not her kind of guy.

Rico Carpetti, Henry's dirty work, go-to guy, sat, and said, "What's up, Henry?"

"Rico, I've got a job for you to do in Seattle. Yourself, or farm it out, but soon. I need to get a girl in a little trouble. Maybe a little jail time. Nobody gets hurt. That's all you need to know."

Rico said, "No biggie. We could plant some drugs, tip off the cops, and let them do all the work."

"That's kind of what I thought. She's living with her boyfriend. He's clean as a baby's ass. I don't want him involved, or anywhere near this, when it goes down. She works alone as a file clerk in the library archives, I'd do it there."

"What the fuck is a library archive?"

Shaking his head, Farley said, "It's a storage place for old books that no one gives a shit about."

"Oh. I've got some contacts in Seattle. We'll plant some shit, call the cops, badda bing, badda boom. Been to Seattle before, no fuckin' sun and dreary as my mother-in-law's face. Don't know how people live there and not kill themselves."

"Rico, I don't need commentary. It's a job. Here's a briefcase. Thirty thou in untraceable twenties. It'll cover you for the whole job. I don't want to hear back from you, other than when it goes down. There's info and a picture of the girl in the side pocket. Can you get this done in the next month?"

Rico, opening the suitcase, eyes widened, "For this, I'll do it yesterday."

Both were smiling as Rico exited Henry Farley's office, briefcase in hand. The secretary didn't bother to look up. Not her kind of guy.

* * * *

Jaime Montez, Rico's Seattle connection, answered the phone, "Hey, Rico, waz' up, amigo, long time no hear, no see."

"Been a while, Jaime, I'm flying into Seattle day after tomorrow. Got a little work to do. No risk. I like no-risk jobs, especially with the bread I'm getting for it. Don't need no guns either."

"And where do I come in."

"I need some drugs, little recon, and maybe some back up."

"I'm listening."

"My source wants me to set up some girl for a fall, maybe get her arrested. Nobody gets hurt and nobody sees us. Girl's got a boyfriend but my source wants us to fuck the girl up, only her, and get the limp dick to dump her. The boyfriend's gotta stay out of trouble. That's alls I know and I don't ask no questions. I just take the money."

"I'm still listening."

"I figure I need about two pounds of weed. Don't even need good stuff. Then we plant the weed at her job and tip off the cops that she's dealing."

"Why not put it where she lives. Might be easier."

"Nah. Can't do that. She lives in the boyfriend's apartment. We need to keep the boyfriend clean. Not sure why, but those were my instructions."

"Where's the bitch work?"

"At Seattle Med Center, in the library."

"Whoa, Rico, lotsa people there. That's not such a good idea."

"My thoughts, too. Except she don't work in no library exactly. They got a storage thing called an archive. She works there, and alone. Should be piece of cake."

"What's in it for me?"

Rico said, "I've always been square with you. I'm getting fifteen big ones. I figure 5 for the drugs, 5 for you and 5 for me. If you can get the drugs cheaper, you keep the difference."

"I'm listening," Jaime said, and thinking, *He's getting twenty-five. Asshole.*

"I figure you case this 'archive' place, see how I get in and get out. Check out surveillance shit. You knows what to do. Then you get me some weed. I'll do the drop and leave town that day. You give the tip to the cops through someone that don't know nothing about me."

"When's this gonna happen, Rico?"

"Soon as we can. I hate Seattle's shitty weather. Makes my back and hands hurt. Gotta be a weekday, 'cause the bitch don't work no weekends."

"That's a lot of weed, but I can get the shit in 48 hours, but I need the money first for the buy. They don't give me no credit. You give me the location of this archive place and I'll check it out."

"I got the money, three feet from me. I can meet you at your place morning after I get in. Okay?"

"Sure."

Rico, looking at his own writing on half of matchbook cover from a shoebox he uses as a file cabinet , said, "You still living in the same shithole you were before on 30th South."

"Yep. If you'd get me more work, I'd have a nicer place, asshole."

"I'll be there at seven a.m., Friday."

* * * *

Jaime said, "Rico. You were right. This is gonna be easy. Been there three times already."

"Whatcha got."

"The girl works alone as you said, and no one else ever seems to go in this archive place much. Fifth floor, southwest elevator. Elevators to the south after you enter the main lobby of the hospital. Only one door on the floor other than the two doors to the stairs. Elevator close, and the stairways fifty feet each way from the door. No cameras. No alarms. I figure they don't give a shit if anyone steals stuff there."

"Jaime, I can't do it when the bitch is in there."

"I gets it. She goes out twice a day to make deliveries and pickups from the main library. Usually at ten in the morning and three in the afternoon, and she's gone at least fifteen minutes, but back within thirty. She always locks the door and always uses the elevator. She doesn't leave for lunch. The one door in has a cheap, ten year-old Schlage self-locking entry lever. No deadbolt. My four year-old son could pick it in thirty seconds. I'd get off a floor above, wait in the stairwell with the door ajar. When she leaves, you move. I never saw anyone in the stairway. I'd exit a floor below after the drop, or better yet, stay out of the elevator and walk down the five to the lobby. I went in pretending I was lost. I could see a small room behind the counter with a copy machine and some cabinets. I'd drop the stuff in the cabinets and get your ass out. I'll have the tipster call thirty minutes after you text me."

Rico, happy with the setup, asked Jaime, "You got the stuff?"

"Yep. You come to my place and give me the rest of my five thou."

"Be there in twenty."

"Rico, when you gonna do this?"

"It rains every fucking day here, I gotta get home. You don't get no fucking sun. Three days from now. I got a flight booked March 15th. That day means something, but I don't remember what."

Jaime, disregarding the dig at Seattle, said, "Your compadres should be happy. The DA here in Seattle has a bug up his ass about drug dealers and wants to run for Governor. This poor bitch is gonna do some time, even if she's a first timer."

Rico shrugged, "I give a shit whether she's in the slammer or not, though I don't have a clue what the bitch did or didn't do to have us mess with her. She's a poor fuckin' file clerk, far as I know. Maybe they're trying to get back at her boyfriend."

* * * *

Janice Jones ran into the archives looking for Grace. Grace had already given notice that she'd be quitting to attend college in early April. Janice was going to take over Grace's archive position. She was twenty years old and had been a student at Bellevue Community College. She had run out of money and was going to work two jobs and then try to go back to school.

Grace chuckled at the comment by the head librarian, Helen McPherson, that Grace was 'returning to school', when Grace felt she had never started.

Janice, excited, said, "Grace, Grace. Your friend Alex is trying to reach you. He's at extension 44303 and will be there for five minutes. He says it's important."

Grace dialed. "What's up, that's so important."

"Bad news, my mom fell and hurt her shoulder."

"That's terrible, what happened?"

"She was walking their dog, Otis, and fell. Otis is a big chocolate lab and he saw a squirrel and bolted, pulling mom over. She tried to protect herself and fell on her right shoulder and tore her rotator cuff. She's going to have it repaired on Friday when the swelling is down, but right now, she's in a ton of pain. After the surgery she won't feel any better for a few weeks, and will need three to four months of rehab. Why does it always have to be the dominant hand?"

Grace said, "I'm so sorry. What can we do?"

"I don't know. My dad's at wits end. He's trying to find a nurse or someone to stay with her. He's busy and doesn't have time for this. Anyway, I thought you should know. Maybe send an email or something. They'd like that."

"I'll call your dad now."

"He's home. 415-789-5555."

* * * *

"Dr. Gordon, it's me, Grace, Grace Pine, Alex's friend."

"Grace, all you had to do was say Grace. I know who you are."

"I'm so sorry about Mrs. Gordon. I talked to Alex and he thought I should send a card or something, but I wanted to see if there's anything I can do? Is she there so I can talk to her?"

"That's so nice of you. She's here, but sleeping. She's taking heavy doses of narcotics, Oxycontin, to be exact, to control the pain. She can't get comfortable. Unfortunately, it's her right arm and even with the surgery, she's going to be uncomfortable for a few weeks. I don't know what I'm going to do."

Grace hesitated a moment and said, "Dr. Gordon, I have an idea. I've worked here at the library for almost two years and I have more than two weeks of sick leave unused. And they have my replacement already. If you, and Mrs. Gordon, would allow me, I'll come down and help out for a couple of weeks, then return for my last two weeks here."

Aaron Gordon said, "You'd do that?"

"Sure. I'd need to tell the library that I have a family emergency. I think Mrs. McPherson, my boss, will understand, and they do have a replacement. I could come down tonight if I can get a flight."

"Have you talked to Alex about this?"

"No. He was rushing off to surgery, but he'll get along fine without me."

"Hold on, Grace. Let me talk to Beverly." Grace put the phone on speaker and went back to copying.

"Grace. Beverly said you'd be her prayers answered. She would be so appreciative if you could help, at least until we could find someone else."

"I could stay twelve days, until March 24th. By that time, she may not need anyone, hopefully."

Aaron Gordon, excited, said, "I'll see if I can get you a flight tonight. I'm reluctant to leave her, so can you rent a car and drive here?"

"Umm.. I don't know how to drive yet. I could figure out a bus. Luckily, Alex made me get some Washington State ID, in case I had to fly. I've never been on an airplane. This will be all so new to me. I could take a cab."

"Grace, I don't want you to worry. I will have a limo pick you up. The limo service will have a man holding up a placard with your name as soon as you exit security on the way out. He'll bring you straight to our house. Call back in twenty minutes and I'll give you the flight information. Grace, what's your birth date, in case they need that information?"

"November, 8th, 1970. Eleven eight seventy. Pine is spelled like the tree."

"Got it. I can't tell you how relieved I am, Beverly, too."

* * * *

Grace found Beverly propped up in a new Barcalounger in the den. She would likely spend most of the next four weeks in the lounger.

"Grace, Beverly and I are so appreciative that you are doing this."

"Dr. Gordon, this is nowhere near what your son has done for me. It's the least I can do."

Beverly Gordon, slurring her speech and half-awake, said, "Thank you so much, Grace... I don't know how I can ever repay you."

"For starters, you'll have to teach me how to cook so you won't starve. Dr. Gordon, is it possible to move a bed or mattress into the den, so I can be near Mrs. Gordon?"

"Sure, we can do that. On another note, this 'Dr. Gordon' and 'Mrs. Gordon' will need to stop. How about Aaron and Beverly?"

"I wouldn't be comfortable calling you by your first names. I'm okay with Dr. and Mrs."

"How about AG and BG, our initials? Or just A and B. Alex and Samantha call us that, sometimes."

"I could do that, or try. For a while, we might have to wait for eye contact to start a conversation."

Aaron laughed at Grace's unabashed honesty. "By the way, Samantha decided to come home tomorrow night and see her mom before the surgery and then return to school on Sunday. You'll get to meet her."

"Oh," Grace said, with an air of trepidation.

Aaron, sensing that Grace would be nervous about being judged again, smiled and said, "Yes. She's coming home to see what her brother sees in you."

"Oh," Grace responded, as the hair spinning and straightening started. From the short Thanksgiving visit, the Gordons were already used to her unusual habit.

Aaron laughed and said, "Don't worry. She'll adore you. She has to, because her brother, mother and I already do."

Grace said, "Thanks. But, she'll have to decide for herself."

Grace called Alex as soon as Beverly Gordon was comfortable.

"How are things going with my mom?"

"Your mom's so grateful that I'm here. She's in a lot of pain, but your dad convinced her that being a hero won't work, so she's taking Oxycontin around the clock. Her surgery is day after tomorrow. Did you know that your sister is coming in tomorrow?"

"I guess I did know, but didn't think much of it. She'll only be there for a couple of days. I'm glad Sam is coming in, it'll give mom a boost."

"You could have told me she was coming."

"Grace, you have nothing to be afraid of. Sam's not going to bite. She's coming in to see her mother."

"I can't help it. I always think people are going to judge me."

"What's wrong with that? You're fine, in addition to being paranoid."

"You're not helping. I made your mom scrambled eggs and toast this morning, but the coffee was too strong for her. I told her that Seattle people need it strong to get through the dark days of winter. Your mom asked if I wanted to stay in your room, but I said I'd stay on a rollaway with her for a while."

Alex said, "Here's a tip. My mom loves omelets with spinach, cheese and mushrooms. She hates scrambled eggs but was too nice to tell you. Call me when you're free tonight and I'll walk you through it. Alternatively, plan B, is to have Sam show you how

180

to make them. My dad doesn't have a clue. He thinks hens lay spinach, cheese and mushroom omelets."

Grace, with Alex's instructions over the phone, mastered the spinach, mushroom and cheese omelet late that night while Beverly and Aaron slept.

The next night, Aaron Gordon went to the airport to pick up Samantha. Grace sat with Beverly, who was having good days and terrible nights, unable to sleep or find a comfortable position.

Beverly, lucid and twenty minutes from her next Oxycontin dose, said, "I'm excited to see Sam, but I'm not excited for her to see me like this."

Grace said, "I'm nervous. Almost as bad as when you and AG came to Portland for Thanksgiving."

"What did you have to be nervous about?"

"You weren't nervous whenever you met your boyfriend's parents?"

"Aaron and I started dating in junior high. Our parents were social friends. The Gordons knew me as well as they knew their own kids."

"Oh. That was convenient, assuming they liked you."

"They loved me."

"I think our meeting in Portland went well?"

"Yes, it did, Grace. You do like to cut to the chase. So now you're worried about Sam?"

"Yes. Samantha is three years younger than I am, but more educated and sophisticated. I worry that I won't measure up, to her, and then to you and Alex."

"Samantha has grown up with a silver spoon in her mouth. That's our doing. She wants for nothing. How well she'd survive if all that was taken away, your guess is as good as mine. You, on the other hand, have been tested your whole life. You found ways to adapt."

* * * *

"Shit," Rico yelled into the phone, "Jaime, where the fuck is the bitch? Some old lady and a young blonde were the only ones in the archive today."

Jaime said, "Where are you right now, Rico?"

"I'm outside the medical school trying to figure out what happened. I been up there three times already."

"Get outta there and I'll go back and see what's up. Last thing you needs, asshole, is to get ID'd."

Jaime hustled back to the medical school. He entered the library archives and acted as if he were lost.

"Scuse me, ladies. Where is the Department of Medicine office, it's supposed to be on the fifth floor?"

Jaime had made certain that he knew of an office on the fifth floor in another part of the medical school.

"And whom might you be?" an older woman said.

Jaime guessed the woman was in her late fifties or early sixties. "I'm just a delivery guy. Name's Roberto. I works for Northwest Delivery Service." Looking at a bogus envelope, he added, "I got an envelope that I'm 'sposed to deliver to the Department of Medicine."

The woman, held her hand out to look at the envelope, "Let me see. Usually deliveries are made only to the mail department in the basement off the east elevators."

Jaime kept the envelope and said, "This one's private and I needs a signature."

Pointing down the hallway to the elevator, the exasperated older woman said, "Okay, Roberto, have it your way. The Department of Medicine office is on the fifth floor on the east wing. You'll have to go down to the main floor and then walk across the lobby to the East Elevators, and then go up to five."

"Thanks. I think I was here a couple of weeks ago and I did the same thing and entered this same room. A nice girl helped me. In fact, she walked me to the elevator and across the lobby. Where's she now? I was going to say thanks."

"Oh, that must have been Grace. She had a family emergency and is in San Francisco for two weeks. That's all I know. She's leaving us in mid-April to return to school."

"Thanks for the info. I hope I don't get lost again, next time I come. This place is huge."

"Yes it is, but you can ask the people at the information desk next time."

"You bet. Thanks, lady."

Jaime exited the archives, entered an empty elevator down and called Rico.

"Rico. The bitch left for some kind of emergency with her family. She'll be back in two weeks. That's alls I know. You're gonna have to wait until she gets back, unless you want to go down to San Francisco. The old witch that was there told me she's only working a couple of weeks after she comes back. Goin' back to school."

Rico said, "Asshole, I'm not getting on a plane with two pounds of weed. You dumb or something. I'll have to wait here. Fuck, I hate this weather. You're gonna have to start going back to the medical school and let me know when she's back. I can't be sniffing around there every day."

"Sure, Rico, but time is money. You're gonna have to give me a little more. Not my problem the bitch split."

"Fuck you. You got enough for this shit-ass job. If you ever want me to call you again, you'll say 'Thanks again for the job and, of course, I'll go back for you.'"

"Fuck you, cabrón. And thanks again for the job and, of course, I'll go back for you, asshole."

* * * *

Aaron Gordon made the introductions in the kitchen as Grace was making Beverly lunch. "Sam, this is Grace Pine. Grace, this is Samantha."

After a moment of silence while the two sized each other up, Grace spoke first, "Nice to meet you."

Samantha Gordon retorted, "Back at you. Can't imagine you with my brother."

Grace blinked hard. "What?"

"You're much too attractive for him. He likes dumpy."

"You're kidding me, right?"

"Dad told me you take everything literally. In this family, nuance and innuendo are the only ways to communicate. It's going to be rough for you, until you get the gist of it."

Aaron, listened, then interrupted, "Sam, Grace, before you scratch each other's eyes out, let's go say hello to mom. She's waiting, I'm sure."

"Dad, we're not going to scratch each other's eyes out. You've been reading too many romance novels." Looking back to Grace, Sam continued, "First, I want to thank you for helping my mom. She didn't want a new strange person every eight hours for the next couple of weeks. She said she likes you, and that, in itself, is not an easy accomplishment. Under all that honesty, has to be some tiny bit of conniving and opportunism. We'll find it yet."

"Sam, be nice," Aaron pleaded, "and I don't read romance novels."

"Dad, I am being nice," Sam said. Nice, for me. Grace and I are going to get along great, as long as she makes my brother happy." Turning to Grace with a smile and two thumbs up, "Mom tells me you make him *verrrrrry* happy."

Grace smiled back, "C'mon, I'll show you where we've stored your mom. She's semi-permanently parked in the den on a lounge chair."

Beverly Gordon's surgery was planned for the next morning. She was to spend that night in the hospital and come home the following day.

The next morning, after Beverly was rolled off to surgery, Aaron Gordon parked Samantha and Grace in the hospital surgical waiting area.

"Girls, the OR will call me at my office when the surgery is over. Then I'll meet you here to talk to Dr. Hollande, her surgeon."

Grace and Samantha spent the next three hours in the waiting area talking. Grace wanted to know what being a full time college student was like, a topic about which Grace had only dreamt.

Dr. Hollande reported to Aaron and the girls that Beverly's surgery went well. Hollande added, "She's going to be heavily sedated until tomorrow morning. I promise she'll have a good night. Home, tomorrow morning if all goes well. For the next ten days or so, it'll be tough for her to get comfortable."

"Girls," Aaron said, "I'm exhausted. I'm going to finish some work in the office and then head home to sleep. You two can go out if you like. Mom'll be fine here. The nurses know to call me. There's no reason that you two have to stay while she's sedated. I'll come back later tonight."

Sam said to Grace, "Some old friends of mine are having a get together in honor of my three day visit. No guys. Would you like to come?"

"Was I invited? I don't want to feel out of place."

"I told Kathleen about you. She said it's cool. I'm sure it's some girl talk. We'll be back before midnight, hopefully, unless I run out of steam. For me, it's three hours later."

Grace replied, "I can't drive us home. I've never driven a car and I don't have a license."

"No, really."

"Really."

"We may have to make it an early evening. You really were raised under a rock...Oops, Grace, that didn't come out right. Sorry."

Grace said, "No innuendo or nuance there, just truth."

Grace and Sam entered Kathleen Cline's apartment near the University of San Francisco. "Kathleen, Amanda, Melissa, this is my brother's girlfriend, Grace Pine."

A chorus of 'nice to meet you' followed.

Kathleen, Samantha's best friend, said, "Grace, Sam tells me you grew up in an orphanage. Jesus, that had to be tough. What was it like."

Grace gave the four a quick synopsis of her life. The fact that she had no clue as to the identity of her parents was, to them, the most disturbing part of Grace's life.

Amanda asked, "Doesn't that bother you every day? Not knowing anything about where you come from or why you were dumped in the orphanage."

"Honestly, some, but I've never known any differently. Most of the kids at the orphanage knew something about their parents that wasn't so nice. In some ways, knowing that your parents were in jail, or died, or were too poor to raise you, was as bad as not knowing."

Kathleen got up saying, "This is heavy conversation. I think we need to lighten the load a bit." She walked into her bedroom and was gone only a few minutes.

Grace listened to Sam talk about the University of Michigan when she smelled something that caused her to stand quickly and wrap her arms around herself. Stuttering, she said, "I don't like that..that.. smell."

Kathleen, unaware of Grace's reaction, walked into the room smoking a joint. She held three more joints and a pack of matches in her hand and announced, "Party time."

Grace panicked. She looked to Sam and said, "I'm sorry. I'm going to be ill. I have to leave here now."

Sam, unprepared for Grace's reaction, was looking back and forth between Kathleen and Grace, "Why, what's going on Grace. It's just a little marijuana."

Wobbling towards the door, Grace, panic on her face, said, "Sam, I have go. I can't be around that smell. I'm going to be ill. Please, we have to go. Or, you can stay and I'll go."

Grace ran out the door and down the stairs of Kathleen's apartment house. Sam followed.

"Grace, Grace. Wait. Wait up."

Grace leaned over the railing in the stairway and vomited.

Sam reached her, but stood back, until the retching was over. Grace was pale, sweaty and had the color of skim milk. The smell of vomit caused Grace to dry heave but then she had the wherewithal to move away from the odor, with Sam's assistance, down the stairs and out into the chilly San Francisco night.

"Grace, you've got to tell me what happened. Are you allergic to weed? I've never heard of anyone allergic to it. What happened?"

Grace slid down against the wall of the building until she thumped to the ground and put her head between her legs. "I'm so sorry Sam. I didn't know Kathleen was going to bring out marijuana. I'm not allergic but I can't be around it. It triggers an emotion that I can't explain. I don't know what to do when I smell it, other than run."

"Kathleen will put the weed away. Let's go back upstairs and get you cleaned up."

"No, Sam, no. I can't go back in there," Grace cried, tears flowing down her cheeks. The color had still not returned to her face. "The smell will be around for hours, even if you opened all the windows. I can't go back there. Can you call me a cab? I have money. I don't want to spoil your evening with your friends."

"Grace, my dad entrusted you to me. Besides, I'm exhausted because of the time change. I'll go back up and say good-bye. Will you be okay if I leave you here?"

"I'll be fine in a few minutes. I can't go back there, please."

"I won't be a minute," Sam said as she re-entered the building.

Kathleen, Amanda and Melissa returned with Sam.

Kathleen approached Grace first, "Grace. I am so sorry. I've seen people not want to smoke, but never have I seen or heard of a reaction like yours. I couldn't have known. I am so sorry."

"It's not your fault. It's mine. I know why it happens, but I can't talk about it without getting ill." Turning to Samantha, Grace continued, "Please, Sam, I'd like to go back to your house."

Kathleen and Sam helped Grace to her feet and, without assistance, she walked to Sam's car."

Arriving back at the Gordon's, Grace said, "Thank you for letting me come with you. I'm going to take a little walk. I don't feel like coming inside yet."

"Sure, Grace. Do you want me to go with you?"

"No, I'll be fine alone."

Samantha went to her father's bedroom. He was still awake and reading the Journal of Urology.

"Dad, you're up."

"Home early, eh?"

"The weirdest thing happened at Kathleen's. Grace got violently ill when Kathleen brought out some marijuana. Don't say it, I know."

Aaron Gordon said, "So."

"Grace became sick as soon as the smell entered the room. She puked her head off. It was awful. She said it was an emotional deal, not an allergy."

"Honey, Alex says she has some emotional issues from the orphanage years that she hasn't sorted out. She's been trying to get in to see a therapist but hasn't been able to connect. I'm guessing that the smell triggered off an emotional response. What happened to her, I don't know? But it must have been deeply traumatic. You better make sure she's okay."

"She said she wasn't ready to come inside. She wanted to walk around for a bit."

"Samantha, that's not a good idea. Get out there and look for her."

Samantha put on a coat and walked up and down a two block radius and could not find Grace. She returned home.

Aaron Gordon said, "Shit, Sam, it's after 10. She can't be walking around at night. I'll get in the car and search for her. You stay here and see if she calls or shows up. Call Alex to see if he's heard from her."

Samantha's call to her brother's apartment went to voice mail and Sam left a message. "Alex, Grace and I were at Kat's apartment near USF this evening and Grace panicked when Kat brought out some weed. She went out for a walk after we got home and I can't find her. She's been gone about thirty minutes. Dad's driving around looking for her but if she calls you, call me or Dad at home."

Aaron returned thirty minutes later without finding Grace.

Sam said, "I'm sorry I let her go. Should we call the police?"

Aaron said, "She's an adult. The police won't respond until she's been gone a day. Hopefully she'll call us or call Alex. Damn it, Sam. Mom is coming home tomorrow morning and I've got no one to take care of her. I'm thinking that Grace may be a huge liability."

At 11:30 p.m., Alex called Aaron.

"Dad, I've found Grace. She's in a 24 hour laundromat across from the Safeway on 7th Ave and Cabrillo in the Richmond. She'll stay there until one of you picks her up."

Aaron said, "Alex, what the hell is going on? Mom's coming home tomorrow and Grace is supposed to help take care of her. Sam and I have been going crazy, not knowing what's happening. If she's got a screw loose, I can't rely on her watching mom."

Alex said, "Dad, Grace'll be fine. She panicked when Sam's friend brought out some marijuana. It triggers a panic and run response. She's okay now. She needed to collect herself. I promise, she'll be okay."

Aaron said, "Anything Sam or I need to do?"

Alex said, "First, don't ask her about why she panics. She won't tell you and she hasn't told me either. You and I and Grace know she needs professional help. We've not found the right people, yet. Anyway, you or Sam have to pick her up. I promise she'll be okay and mom will be okay."

Aaron and Sam drove to the laundromat together to retrieve Grace.

As they approached Cabrillo and 7th, Aaron and Sam agreed not to say anything and let Grace explain.

Grace was standing in the doorway of the laundromat as they arrived and sat in the back seat. For the first minute, the only noise in the car was the thumping of the tires on pavement.

Grace said, "I suppose you need an explanation. I don't know that I can talk about it."

Sam wasn't satisfied and said, "Grace, you scared the holy daylights out of us. You just disappeared. I walked around and then Dad drove all over looking for you. Didn't you think we'd be worried?"

Grace said, "I'm sorry. I couldn't help myself. I had to get away and be alone. I'm so sorry. I tried calling Alex but he wasn't at our apartment and I called his pager and the hospital. He finally got the page and called the payphone on the wall in the laundromat."

Sam said, "Grace, you were just thinking about yourself. How do you think I felt? You weren't being fair and...."

Aaron Gordon interrupted Sam, "Sam, that's enough. I'm certain Grace knows that she scared us, but I'm certain she's got good cause. Let's leave it at that."

The silence and the thumping of tires resumed.

Aaron said, "Grace, are you going to be able to take care of Beverly tomorrow? I can't have you bolting."

Grace said, "I'll be okay. I promise I won't run, no matter what happens. I promise."

Thump...thump...thump...thump, until the garage door open and closed. Aaron walked into the house.

As Sam exited the car, Grace remained seated in the back. Sam opened her door and said, "C'mon, let's get inside. It's freezing out here." Sam extending her hand. Grace, shaking and cold, took Sam's hand.

Sam said, "You look like shit." Then embraced Grace tightly and said, "You'll be fine. You're safe here."

Grace held the embrace and said, "You sound like Alex."

"I'll take that as a compliment."

"Yes, it was. Thank you. I'll be better in the morning, I promise. We've got to pick up your mom. Again, I'm so sorry to spoil your evening. I'll call Kathleen and your friends and apologize if you'd like."

"Not necessary. I'll deal with it. After mom comes home tomorrow, I'm going out to lunch with them. They'll understand."

"Sam. I'm not sure I understand why I get so sick. It's been thirteen years and it happens so quickly."

Sam did a quick calculation. *Grace was eleven or twelve.*

Grace continued, "Tomorrow will be a big day. Alex taught me how to make omelets with spinach, mushroom and cheese for your mom. I should try it on you, before killing your mother in her weakened condition."

Sam said, "It's a deal."

Grace said, "I've got to get to bed."

Samantha went to her dad's room.

Aaron asked, "She okay?"

Sam said, "Yeah. I think so. She's nice, but she's had so many strikes against her and has so many issues. What's the attraction for Alex?"

Aaron Gordon said, "Good question. But Grace knows that she has issues that need to be dealt with, which is half the battle. Alex says that Grace is an extraordinary person, incredibly smart, with so many good traits. When mom needed help, Grace wasn't even on my radar. She stepped up without hesitation and used her sick leave. That tells you a little of her character. We're going to give her, and Alex, the benefit of the doubt for now."

Grace called Alex early the next morning. "I wanted you to hear this from me first. I went to a friend of Sam's apartment. A girl named Kathleen had a few friends of Sam's over."

"I know her. Nice and one of Sam's best friends. She's going to USF, if I remember."

"Right. Anyway, Kathleen brought out some marijuana and the smell caused me to panic. You know I mentioned my aversion to the smell. I became hysterical and ill and ran out of Kathleen's apartment. After we got back to your parent's house, I couldn't go inside. I wanted to walk, but I guess I lost track of time. It was so embarrassing. I'm fine now."

"Grace, are you sure you don't want to talk about it?"

"Yes. I don't want to talk about *it*. Please understand."

Alex was about to say '*Sometime you'll have to face this issue',* but let it drop. "So when's my mom coming home?"

Beverly returned home that morning to the care of Samantha and Grace together. Beverly Gordon, despite pain and the inability to find a comfortable position, loved the doting from two temporary young nurse-wannabes.

Samantha left for Ann Arbor the next morning. Grace stayed by Beverly's side for the next 12 days and nights, spelled by Aaron for thirty minutes in the morning before he went to work and a couple of hours in the evening.

Alex and Grace would talk on the phone every evening after Beverly found comfort and a short bit of sleep.

Alex called Samantha a few days later in Ann Arbor and she described the events at Kathleen's apartment.

"Alex, she scared the shit out of me. She was totally out of control."

"Sam, Grace has crevices, cracks and holes that no one has explored yet. She needs help and she knows it but we haven't found the right person, at least, yet."

"Do you need all this aggravation? As Aunt Fannie would say," Sam then switched into a heavy Yiddish accent, "Honey, find a nice Jewish girl *mit* a good family and lots of *gelt* and you'll be happy forever. That's a promise."

Alex laughed. "That was perfect Aunt Fannie. Sam, you're going to have to trust me. Grace is worth whatever aggravation she causes. You'll see. As for her family, we'll never know. As for money, she's never put two nickels together, ever."

Beverly and Grace spent each day in pursuit of trying to get Beverly comfortable, or trying to divert her attention away from the discomfort. Beverly could not hold a book in one hand, so a good deal of their time spent together involved Grace reading books aloud.

Beverly asked Grace every day, "If reading to me is an ordeal, I'm sure we might be able to buy books on tape."

Beverly was wrong. Grace's prime escape from her life's travails was to read, and before meeting Alex, she would often read aloud to herself.

Grace would say, "I'm good. Really, I enjoy doing this."

At first, Beverly's bathing and bodily functions were tricky, but once modesty was forsaken, the two worked out routines like Marine drill sergeants. For the short periods that Beverly was comfortable standing, she would teach Grace how to work the kitchen. Slowly, Beverly's pain levels subsided, and by day ten, she was comfortable for long stretches without narcotics. She returned to her own bed with Aaron the night before Grace was to return to Seattle.

On the morning of Grace's departure, a Sunday, Aaron and Beverly sat down with Grace.

Aaron, holding Beverly's hand, said, "Grace, we cannot tell you how grateful we are that you were able to help Beverly through a painful recovery. While you may want to diminish your presence, we cannot. We would have needed three daily shifts of nurses, all strangers, for two weeks. It was never the cost. I can afford the nurses. Honestly, I would have worried all day about the care. With you here, I never worried for a second. Anyway, Beverly and I need to be able to repay you for your kindness."

"AG and BG, that's not necessary. I had the sick leave accrued and it would have gone unused. Alex has done so much for......."

"Grace," Aaron interrupted, "that's what I meant by diminishing your value. Don't even go there. Anyway, we've decided that Beverly and I would pay your school tuition, books and course fees for the year. Think of it as a merit based scholarship."

Grace began to speak. Beverly put her finger over her own mouth to quiet Grace's protestation. Beverly said, "Don't argue. You will need to learn how to accept gifts graciously. Rather than continuing with 'it's too much', 'I don't need it', whatever, you need to just learn to say, 'Thank you so much. This means the world to me', or something to that effect. Am I clear?"

Tears were dropping slowly down Grace's cheeks as she said, "Thank you, thank you, thank you." She gave Aaron and Beverly big hugs as the tears continued.

Aaron said, "Alex gave us an idea of the first year costs based on your April quarter. Here's a check for thirty-three hundred dollars. Keep track of your expenses and we can work out the details later. This will allow you to go to summer school and hopefully be ready for the UW by fall quarter next year."

Grace continued to hug Beverly until she said, "Okay, my arm hurts."

Aaron, smiling broadly, then said, "One more thing that I hope is okay with you. I was referred a patient from Oakland by an old med school classmate, Harvey Grant. After seeing the patient, I called Harvey to discuss some issues and afterwards we chatted about friends from school. Harvey had dated another student and common friend, Marilyn Crayman, and I asked what had happened to her. I knew she had headed off to the Menninger Clinic in Topeka to do a psych residency after med school. Anyway, Harvey had stayed in touch with her and it turns out that she's in private practice in Seattle specializing in traumatized adults. I called her and she'd be glad to take you on as a patient. She is on the clinical faculty at the med school, so she's confident she can get your insurance to cover your visits. If your insurance doesn't cover her costs, Beverly and I will take care of things for a while."

Grace, stunned, sat quietly, and nodded up and down for a bit and then said, "Thank you."

Alex picked Grace up at Sea-Tac at seven twenty-five p.m.

Coming through security, Grace saw Alex first and broke into a run, letting go of her rolling travel bag, and jumped into Alex's arms.

"Grace, you don't know how much I missed you."

"Yes, I do, because I missed you more."

The ride home kept Alex smiling as Grace, as always when excited, talked in triple time. He already knew about the tuition coverage and the psychiatrist find from his parents but said nothing.

Grace was rapid firing her visit, "Your mom was this... Your dad did that... Samantha told me...Your house is... Your dad found a psychiatrist..."

Knowing everything about her trip already, Alex, smiling, said, "I'm glad things went well. You hungry?"

Grace said quickly, "No. I had four bags of nuts on the plane. Go home. We'll find something to eat in the refrigerator. If there's nothing in the fridge, we'll starve until morning. Go home."

Alex said, "No arguments here."

Grace said, "Alex, I missed you and I need you. That's all you need to know."

They found sleep at two a.m. Left until morning was a trail of clothes from the front door to the bedroom.

Chapter 12

"Rico, she's back. She was there today, and alone."

Rico said, "Then I'm doing the drop tomorrow morning, around ten. I gotta get out of this town. There ain't enough Advil in the world to make me come back."

Jaime, laughing, said, "For enough money, asshole, you'd live here."

Rico countered with, "I'd marry my first wife again, before I'd come back here."

"That bad, eh. Rico, you're funny. You take care. Call me after the drop and you're outta the place."

At nine forty-five am, Rico Carpetti found himself in the stairwell outside the archives. He had exited the elevator on the sixth floor and walked down a flight in the stairwell. With the door ajar, he had a clear view of the archive entrance. He waited.

At nine fifty-nine, Grace exited the archives holding a short stack of books and papers. She checked that the door locked and headed to the elevator. As soon as the elevator door closed, Rico entered the hallway, looking back and forth. The hallway was empty.

Using a hook pick and a tension wrench, even with rubber gloves, Rico had the door open in less than twenty seconds. With a penlight for guidance, he averted the counter edge, entered the copy room, opened his backpack, and placed four half-pound packages of marijuana on the top shelf of the cupboard. He closed the cupboard, set the exit door lock, and went back to the stairwell. The entire time from stairwell to archives and back was less than 4 minutes. He walked down five flights, took off his rubber gloves, and exited the medical school through the main lobby. As Rico walked to the parking lot, he called Jaime, who would call his tipster buddy, who would lay the tip with the Seattle PD narcotics squad. Rico, satisfied with himself, and ecstatic about leaving Seattle and the cloudless sky, headed to the airport. He would try to make the two p.m. United flight to Newark.

* * * *

Grace would have been back earlier but stopped to chat with Mrs. McPherson.

"Grace, we're going to miss you. You will have been here two years and, admittedly, I didn't get to know you until these past six months. You seemed to come alive. Anyway, you will be missed. If you ever need a recommendation, let me know."

The new Grace gave her boss a hug and headed back to the archives at ten forty-five a.m. She unlocked the door and switched on the lights. Within seconds, a strange sense of foreboding came over Grace but not strong enough to panic. She had no reason to fear anything. But Grace could sense something different. She walked to the entrance to each aisle thinking someone might have gotten in and was searching for an old journal. *I know I turned off the lights and checked the door was locked. I know I did. And the lights were off when I came into the room.* Nonetheless, she searched each aisle. *Something's wrong, I know it.* Seeing no one, she entered the copy room. In an instant, her foreboding morphed into abject fear. *Oh, my God. Oh, my God. I can't breathe. I've got to get away.*

Get out. Grace ran past the telephone. *Get out.* She slammed the door and ran down the hallway to the elevator. When the elevator didn't come immediately, she ran to the stairwell and down a flight of stairs to the fourth floor to the Department of Surgery office.

A young woman, sitting at the reception desk, asked, "Honey, are you okay. You look like you've seen a ghost."

"My name is Grace Pine and I work upstairs in the library archives. I smell something in the archives and I need to call campus security."

"Is there a fire?"

"No, no."

"Gas?"

"No, I'm sure it's marijuana."

"Hell. Go back up and enjoy, as far as I'm concerned."

Grace was too scared to pick up the humor. "Please. Can you dial security for me?"

The young woman dialed 'O' and handed the receiver to Grace. "Here, it's the operator, I don't have a clue what the security number is, and I'm sure as hell am not going to call 911 for marijuana."

Grace held for a recorded message until the hospital operator came on.

"Seattle Med. How may I direct your call?"

"I need to speak to security, quickly."

"Is someone in trouble? Do I need to call a code Black?"

"What exactly is code Black?"

"It means there is a violent or dangerous patient or someone that is armed."

Grace, rapid firing, said, "No, not that. Please connect me to security."

"Hold on."

"Security. Officer Mayeda speaking."

Grace spoke as fast as she could, "Please, I need help. I work in the library archives on five southwest. I went out to deliver books to the main library and when I returned I could smell marijuana in the archives. I need help. I can't go back in the archives while that smell is present. Can you come right away?"

"Slow down. Your name, please?"

"Grace Pine."

"Miss Pine, is anyone with you now?"

"I'm calling from the Department of Surgery office on the floor below the archives. I had to leave. I didn't see anyone else in the archives. Just me."

"How are you in danger?"

"I get panicked when I smell marijuana. I can't go back in the archives while the smell is there."

"Do you know who put the marijuana in the room?"

"No, that's the issue. No one has been in there that I know of. I went out at ten a.m. and everything was fine. I returned at ten forty or ten forty-five, no more than thirty or forty minutes. As soon as I walked in the smell was there. I ran out. I think it's in the copy room," Grace's voice became more pleading, "Can you come? I can't go back in there. Please come."

Mayeda said, "Okay. We'll be there. I'm the lone officer in security now, so I can't leave. I'm waiting for another officer to return and then I'll come. Maybe ten or fifteen minutes. I need you to go back up to the archives and wait. Can you do that?"

"I can wait outside in the hallway. I can't go back in. If I smell anything near the door, I'll move away. There's only one door."

"Okay, Miss Pine, I'll be there as soon as I can."

Seattle Med security officer Joe Mayeda hung up. Mumbling to the wall with a picture of President Clinton, "You happy now, Bill. Another crazy."

Grace gave the phone back to the secretary. "Thank you. Are you busy right now?"

The young woman, not wearing a name badge, said, "Not particularly, why?"

Grace said, "I was wondering if you could come and sit with me until the police come. I'm scared."

"Wish I could. I've got to stay here and answer phones. From the sounds of it, you'll be fine. Just take a deep breath. I'll get you a bottle of water to take with you. You come back if you have a problem. Okay?"

"'Okay. I'll try."

Grace took the elevator up one flight. Her hands were shaking and her lips were dry. The hallway was empty and quiet. *I don't remember it being this quiet.* She approached the archive door quietly, not knowing why. *So far, so good.* Outside the door of the archives, she smelled around the edges of the door. *Nothing.* Grace got to her knees and smelled under the door. *Nothing. Was I dreaming all this?* The door was self-locking and she had run out so quickly she had forgotten her key. *Stupid me. Now what? I hope security has a key.* Halfway between the archive door and the elevator, Grace slid to the floor, and waited for security.

Within minutes, two identically clad, Kevlar armored, Seattle Police officers burst into the hallway from each stairwell with automatic rifles drawn. One officer, a male, was huge, the other a woman, but big. As the female officer, closest to Grace, approached, she motioned Grace to remain silent by raising her index finger to her lips. Then raising her hand from low to high, the officer had Grace stand up and turn around. She was a head taller than Grace. Her name tag, just below Grace's eye level, said, 'MORGAN.' Officer Morgan whispered, "Are you carrying a weapon? Don't lie to me, or my partner will kill you before you move."

Grace looked behind her at the other officer, his rifle aimed at Grace's head. He was sweating and appeared nervous.

Grace responded, "No. No. I don't own a gun."

Morgan shouldered her rifle, patted Grace down from chest to ankles, and whispered, "She's clean." The other officer said something into his walkie-talkie. Within seconds, the elevator opened and two men in street dress, khakis, half-buttoned cotton shirts, and white sneakers, exited. Both were unshaven, but armed with handguns, drawn and ready.

The two clad officers moved to stand opposite the entrance to the archives, eyes and guns pointed at the door. Neither looked away, even for a second. If something or somebody exited the door, they were prepared to shoot.

One of the disheveled men came up to Grace. "I'm Lieutenant Tim Harkins, Seattle PD Narcotics. Anybody in there?" His thumb pointed at the archive door.

Grace said, "I'm almost certain no one is in there."

Harkins said, "How come you're so sure?"

Grace said, "I left there ten minutes ago. I searched the place and could see no one. No one much comes in there except me. The door is locked and I left the key inside. Security is coming."

Harkins, obviously in charge, turned to the biggest officer and said, "Kick the door in."

Grace pleaded, "Don't do that. Nobody's in there."

The large officer looked at Harkins, who nodded towards the door. Almost with glee, the officer held his rifle over his head and with one kick from the heel of his right shoe, the door flew open, shattering the lock and the doorframe. With guns drawn, the officers rushed into the archives, screaming repeatedly, "Police. This is a raid." Within a few minutes, the officers exited. The large, door-kicking, officer said, "All clear, Lieutenant. Nobody's in there."

Grace said, "I told you that. Now the door is shattered. Why couldn't you wait?"'

Harkins said, "I don't need to wait for some make-believe gumshoe security guard with a limp dick, who may or may not show up. Tell me again what you know."

Grace, annoyed, said, "I told this all to Officer Mayeda. You're not nice."

Before Grace could go further, Harkins turned to the other officers and said, "Put your weapons away and search the place. I hope the fuck this hasn't been a wild goose chase."

Grace added, "You might as well look in the copier room. That's where I could smell marijuana."

Harkins came back, "Miss, I don't know no fucking 'My Eda', or whatever his name is. You might be in trouble here, so tell me what you know."

Grace, having no idea why she would be in trouble, said, "Sure. I work alone in there. I went out at ten a.m. and everything was fine, normal, whatever. I went down to the main library with books. I returned at ten forty or ten forty-five, no more than thirty, forty minutes. As soon as I walked in, the smell was there. Marijuana. I know the smell. I ran out. I think it's in the copy room. That's where the smell was strongest."

"Then what, you got my attention?"

"Okay," Grace continued, "when I smelled the marijuana, I left immediately, closed the door, ran downstairs to the Department of Surgery office and called security. The officer who answered, I'm almost certain he said his name was Mayeda, said he'd come in ten or fifteen minutes."

"Who'd you talk to?"

Annoyed, Grace said, "Jesus, you're dense. I said I talked to a Seattle Med security officer. I think he said his name was Mayeda, but I don't remember for sure. He said he'd be up here shortly. I thought Seattle Med security called you, instead of coming themselves. I guess they didn't. Anyway, Officer Mayeda told me to stay up here until he came. I couldn't smell anything in the hallway, so I wondered if I was dreaming all this up. But I left my key inside, so I was unable to go in and recheck the smell."

The other disheveled police officer, Harkin's partner, came out into the hallway toting four bags, wrapped in cellophane. "Hark, here it is. I'm guessing about two pounds. Looks like good stuff to me. It was as the lady said, in the copier room."

Grace's eyes widened and she started to back away. "Please get that away from me. I'll get sick. Take it back inside, please."

"The officer walked back into the archives with the bags, but stayed close enough to the door that Grace started backing up. Harkins grabbed her arm and said, "Where d 'ya think you're going?""

"I'm sorry. I can't be near that smell. I'll get ill."

"I don't know shit about the security department here. We got a tip that someone received a large shipment of drugs and was going to start selling marijuana from here in the library archives. The tip, which came from a reliable police informant, said the buyer, a woman, had purchased two pounds of marijuana to distribute. I got a warrant to search the archives from Judge Spencer. If you're the only one that uses this space, then I'd figure you to be the one we're looking for."

"That's crazy. I no more would be near marijuana than...than...the Pope."

"How do you know the Pope doesn't do a joint every day? Let me get this straight. You're the only one with access to this room?"

"No, all the security and housekeeping people have keys. The library staff has keys, too. However, none of them, to my knowledge, has been here. But at ten a.m., there was no marijuana. At ten forty-five it was definitely there."

"And you're the only one that's here, right?"

"Yes."

"I'd like you to turn around."

Grace complied and before she knew what was happening, Harkins had her handcuffed.

"Miss Pine, you are under arrest for attempting to distribute drugs, in this case, two pounds of marijuana. You have the right to an attorney.." Harkins finished giving Grace her Miranda rights.

"Miss Pine, you are going to come with us to central booking. At that point, you can call an attorney or whomever you'd like. Within forty-eight hours you can make a plea in front of a judge."

Grace, stupefied, said, "You have to be kidding. This is a joke, right?"

"Not a joke. This much marijuana, in a public institution, so you've gotta be distributing it. This is a felony and you're going to do some time. I've still not seen any security people, so that was all bullshit."

Grace, too stunned to speak, found herself pushed to the elevator. Once inside, the elevator doors closed and she pleaded, "Please. You're making a mistake. I don't know how the drugs got there."

The lobby of the hospital came to a freeze-frame stop watching four Seattle Police officers force march a handcuffed Grace from the elevator and out of the building to the waiting police cars.

Grace pleaded with Harkins as they entered his unmarked cruiser, "Please. Please put the drugs in another car."

Harkins said, "Shut up. I could care less what you want."

Harkins shoved Grace, head down, into the back of the patrol car, separated from the front seat with a wire screen. Morgan, the female officer, now free of her Kevlar vest, drove and Harkins sat in the shotgun seat with the drugs between them. Within a minute of leaving Seattle Med, Grace leaned to the opposite side and vomited on the floor of the car, doing her best to miss her pants and shoes.

She pleaded, "Please move the marijuana to another car. Please. I'm so sick."

Harkins said, "What, you so sick you're going to jail. Shouldn't have been dealing."

Grace dry heaved and pled again to move the drug. Harkins didn't even turn around. Morgan spoke up, "Harkins, you a mean motherfucker. Who gives a shit if the drugs are in Bucklin's car? Fuck you, I'm calling him. You gonna clean up the mess in the back, asshole." Morgan picked up her mike, told the trailing police car to pull over and Morgan then transferred the marijuana. The floor mat, full of vomit, found its way into a nearby trash barrel.

Harkins, turning to Grace, said, "Hope you're happy, bitch. That was a waste of time."

Grace, looking at the back of the female officer's head, said, "Thank you for doing that. Could you open the windows to let the smell out?" She did.

Grace was booked, fingerprinted, and placed into a holding cell with two other women, one in for petty theft, the other for soliciting prostitution.

Closing the cell door, the booking officer said, "We'll be in to get you your phone calls. About thirty minutes. We're busy right now."

The hooker spoke first, "What you in for, honey? You looks like shit. What they do to you, I don't see no beating marks?"

Grace sat in the corner of the cell, said nothing, wrapped her arms around her chest, closed her eyes and wept. After a bit, she started rocking while her left hand went up to her hair and she started to twirl and pull. *Why? Why? Why me?* In a flash, in the blink of an eye, her old life was back.

An hour later, a uniformed female officer clanged on the cell door. All three occupants looked up. "Miss Pine, you wanna make some telephone calls? Now's the time."

As they walked to a small room near the cell, the officer, said, "You got a lawyer. Sounds like you're gonna need one."

Grace said, "No. I don't have a lawyer and I don't have any money for a lawyer."

"You got any family you need to call?"

"Nope, I don't have a family."

"C'mon. Everybody's got family. Yours ain't talking to you?"

"Nope. Raised in an orphanage. Never adopted. I've got nobody."

"Shiiiiieeeeet. You ain't ever caught a break."

"I do have a boyfriend. After this, I hope he'll even talk to me."

"It's a start. You call him."

Grace looked at the officer's name badge which read 'Hards.' Grace smiled and said, "By the way, you're the first one that seems human in this place. Thanks."

"No problem. Colleen's my first name. You don't seem to belong here."

"I don't, but life doesn't always put you where you belong."

"Amen, Miss Pine."

"Colleen, is there a number my friend can call back to? I may not get him."

"He can try 206-476-5555. That's the main number. You may not be able to talk to him if he calls, but they'll tell him where you are."

Grace sat at the desk in the barren room and dialed Seattle Med's main number.

"Operator, can you page Dr. Alex Gordon. He's a urology resident. I'll hold."

Grace held for two minutes and the operator returned. "Dr. Gordon is scrubbed in OR 4 with Dr. Kauffman. He said to leave a message."

"I'm Grace Pine. He needs to call 206-476-5555. It's the county jail. Just put the word, 'Help' on the note."

Grace returned to her cell, her corner, her rocking and twirling, and waited, and waited. Other than a drink of water and the open toilet in the cell, Grace stayed in the corner. The digital clock on the wall outside the cell, said '19:15.'

Officer Hards clanged on the cell wall, "Grace, there's someone to see you. You can have fifteen minutes. By the way, since you don't have a lawyer, a public defender will be assigned to you tomorrow when you make a plea."

"Thanks, Colleen," said Grace, as the door to her cell opened. Colleen put on ankle cuffs and then she escorted Grace to a modest size room with cubicles and chairs. On one side were prisoners, the other guests. When Grace walked through the door, Alex, grim-faced, stood up in the cubicle.

Grace started crying as soon as she sat down. She said to a mystified Alex, "We only have fifteen minutes. I've got to stop crying so we can talk."

Alex's mouth was moving but Grace couldn't hear him. She realized that he hadn't heard her either. She then saw a sliding door that was blocking the sound transmission. Grace slid the door to the right.

Alex was repeating, louder and louder, "What happened?"

Wiping the tears, Grace said, "I can hear you now. We've got to be quick. We have only fifteen minutes."

"What happened?"

Grace recounted the story. "That's all I can remember. I don't have a clue who put the marijuana in the archives. Not a clue. No one was ever mad at me, except for Dr. Arnett, but I don't think he'd do this to me. The Seattle Police officers never checked with the Seattle Med Security. Hopefully, that officer will be able to help. Maybe Mrs. McPherson in the library. Alex, what happened? My life had changed for the good. I did nothing. Who would do this to me?"

"Grace, I don't know. I know you had nothing to do with this. I will try to see what I can find out."

"I have school starting in two weeks. I've already paid for tuition. Your parents gave me the money but if I don't make it to class and have to drop out, I'm afraid they'll want their money back."

"Grace, that's not what's important, now. You did nothing wrong. I'd stake my life on it. Hell, that whole episode with my sister and her friends tells me this is a hoax, or something."

"Alex, I need to get out of here so I can go to school."

Officer Hards came over to Grace and said, "Time's up. Your friend here will have to go."

Grace smiled at Hards, "Okay, thank you." Turning back to Alex, "Please try to get hold of the Seattle Med security people. An Officer Mayeda, or something like that."

"Grace, I've got to work tomorrow, but as soon as I can get free, I'll do what I can. Be brave."

"Alex, I need you so much."

Grace returned to the cell. The hooker made bail when her pimp showed up with one thousand dollars. The shoplifter's mother bailed her out with fifteen hundred dollars. Twenty minutes later two large police officers carried in a semi-awake girl and dropped her, face down, on a cot opposite Grace. She tried to kick one of the officers as they attempted to remove the handcuffs. The dodging officer, laughed at the lame attempt and planted his knee, hard into her back, to immobilize her. The cuffs came off as she screamed, "Fuck you," over and over. Once the officers exited the cell, the girl quieted.

Grace, buoyed by seeing Alex earlier, said, "Hello. I'm Grace."

The girl, stood, holding onto the jail cell bars for support. She wobbled to a corner, put her back to the bars and slid to the cold cell cement floor. She had a shiner around her right eye, a small cut over her left eye and a bruise on her left shoulder. She wore only a flimsy knee-length nightshirt, which hid little. She opened her good eye as Grace was staring. Speaking haltingly between deep sighs, she said to Grace, "Fuck you, bitch. You a spy for the cops? I ain't telling you shit. You ask me a question and I kill you with my bare hands." The druggy bared her teeth, like a wolf eyeing a meal.

Grace retreated to the far side of the cell, sat and waited. *I don't even know what I'm waiting for.* Grace was given a dinner in the cell, found an empty cot and fell asleep.

At two a.m., her cellmate started screaming. "Help me. Help me. I needs a fix, bad. Help me." Grace awoke to find her cellmate kneeling in front of Grace's cot, shaking and crying, "Help me, please, God help me."

Grace, now fully awake, came to the cell door and shouted to the night crew, "Can't anyone come and help this poor person. She's in a bad way."

A new female officer walked, as slow as a human could move, towards the cell. Arriving finally, she looked, with a sneer and a shake of her head, "That's Freddie. She's in here every three months. Goes through the same antics. She be okay in the morning, but none of us are getting much shut-eye tonight. She probably gonna have one of her seizures. Hope she chokes on her tongue." Looking at Grace, she added, "What do you drug dealers want from us. You're either buying, selling or using, or all of the above. Mostly using. You shut up now and lcarn to live with the life you're makin' for yourself. And that's a shit life." She turned and walked out of the cellblock, closed a steel door, and flipped Grace a middle finger as the door thudded closed.

Freddie stopped screaming about 4 a.m. Grace thought Freddie had a seizure, but at least it brought some peace and quiet.

At seven thirty a.m., after a cold, stale sweet roll, colder runny eggs and a warm carton of milk for breakfast, Grace returned to her corner and closed her eyes.

At nine fifteen a.m., Officer Hards had returned and surveyed the cell. "Shit, Grace. You got Freddie as a roommate. You get any rest?"

Grace responded, "Quiet after four thirty. I'm certain she had a seizure and then shut up. Been sleeping ever since, except breakfast. It's nice to see you back."

Hards said, "You're lucky. Sometimes Freddie goes on all night. Anyway, your assigned public defender is outside looking at your report. I told him you were nice and probably don't belong here. Name's Snyder."

"Thanks, Colleen."

"Unfortunately for you, he's new, because I've not seen him before, and I know about everyone that comes in here, on both sides of the bars. Too bad. A good PD can get you out of here lots quicker. If the DA owes the PD something, they can do business. This guy's not going to have any credit built up, if you know what I mean. More bad is that the Prosecutor, Chet Kreel, is supposedly running for Governor at the next election. He wants to make a big deal of everything. Dealing drugs at the med school. That's going to get him a ton of free airtime. You got a tough road to hoe."

Grace listened, trying to take one bad piece of news after another.

Colleen continued, "But in the end, they mostly get it right. I don't see you being a dealer. If it don't smell like a rat and don't look like a rat, you know, probably ain't a rat. You're going to beat this."

Grace said, "I wish I had your optimism. I was doing so well, too. I just don't understand."

Officer Hards turned around when she heard a thump at the cellblock door and saw the PD waving. Hards opened the cell, cuffed Grace's ankles, and walked her to an interrogation room. "Sit here, Grace. He'll be in shortly."

"Hello Miss Pine. My name is Paul Snyder." He handed Grace a card. Snyder had handwritten his name on the card above the Seattle Public Defender Department information. "I'm a public defender and I've been assigned to defend you. I've read your file. It seems that the prosecutor has a solid case. They found two pounds of marijuana in a room that you admitted being the only one that could have put it there. Dealing drugs is a serious offense, particularly using a public institution as a distribution center. My boss says that the courts don't go easy with dealing drugs in public institutions. Since this your first offense, we might get the prosecutor to go light on you. Maybe plea for a reduced sentence. Couple of years maybe...if we're lucky."

"Mr. Snyder, I did nothing wrong. This is all a terrible mistake."

"Miss Pine, or would you like me to call you Grace?"

"Grace is fine."

"Grace, everyone in here says they did nothing wrong. The evidence against you is solid. Best if you fess up and our office will see what we can do for you. Maybe some kind of bargain with the prosecutor. If you continue to deny everything, and, worse, if this goes to a trial, the penalties are much stiffer. Best if you tell me the truth."

"Mr. Snyder, are you on my side?"

"Yes, of course. I'm here to help."

"The officer that let you in said you are new in the Public Defender's office. That true?"

"Yes, I started forty-five days ago. Anyway, I'm assigned to your case, like it or not."

"How long have you been a lawyer?"

"Finished law school at UPS last June. I passed the Washington bar in March."

"Why so long, June to March."

Snyder said, "I didn't' pass the bar the first time. So, I had to take it again. I was law review and the top of my class. I got cocky and didn't study hard enough for the bar. I missed out on a good job. I learned a lesson."

Grace said, "I hope so, for my sake and yours. I will say this to you as clear as I can make it. I did nothing wrong. I did not buy, put, or use the marijuana that they discovered in the archives. I have no idea how it got there."

"There's a shit load of evidence against you, Grace. Denial isn't going to help. The quicker you get to accept your situation, the better we'll be."

Grace shook her head. "Snyder, you're missing the key stages of Kubler-Ross's steps after denial. Namely, anger, bargaining, depression and, then, acceptance. I will never have acceptance, ever. I will get angry, soon, although anger isn't in my nature. I'm already depressed. I will not bargain."

Snyder interjected, "You seem a bit angry now."

"I'll tone it down, sorry. I thought things were getting better and then this happened and I don't understand it."

Snyder said, "You're obviously smart, or at least, well read."

Grace nodded acceptance of the quasi-compliment.

He continued, "Okay, start from the beginning and tell me your side of this." From a shiny new briefcase, he took out a new yellow legal pad and a cheap BIC pen and said, "Shoot."

Grace told her story from the time she left the archives for the library.

She continued, "I've been sitting in the cell for twenty-four hours and I've tried to pinpoint the important parts of my story. One, I am intolerant of the smell of marijuana. I've had some things happen to me as a young girl that triggers a terrible reaction. I would no more use, or be around, marijuana than you'd sleep with a nest of rattlesnakes. Two, as soon as I smelled the marijuana, I rushed out of the archives, ran down the stairs to another office and called campus security. I talked to an Officer Mayeda, or something like that, and I told him there was marijuana in the archives and that he needed to get up there. He said he would come, but never did, and the arresting officers didn't bother to contact him."

Snyder interrupted, "That's strange. It's not in the report either."

"The secretary at the Department of Surgery was a witness to the call. In fact, I asked her to come with me back to the archives because I was afraid, but she couldn't leave her desk."

"Do you have her name?"

"No, but I can't imagine more than two people at that desk and she'll remember. Department of Surgery office is on the fourth floor, just under the archives."

"Third. I am an orphan and have no family that I know of. I've been penniless for six years since leaving the orphanage at eighteen. At times, I've lived in shelters, been homeless, had no warm clothing, and gone hungry. I found a minimum wage job two years ago here, working in the archives, and eked out a living. I got lucky four months ago and met a urology resident, Alex Gordon, who's helped turn my life around. I finally made a little money doing some translating and, with his help, I am scheduled to start college in two weeks. More to the point, I've never had enough money, ever, to be able to buy drugs, even if I wanted to. I'm guessing that the two or three pounds of marijuana they found are worth thousands. Nobody is giving that away for free and I could have never afforded it."

Snyder said, "That does shed some light on this. I'll have to corroborate your story. Do you have anyone who's out to get you? Jealous of your relationship with..uh," looking at his notes, "this, Dr. Gordon?"

Grace responded, "I've been a loner since leaving the orphanage and don't have any real friends or enemies. I mean it, none. I did have a run in with another resident at Seattle Med last October. A Dr. Arnett, Thomas Arnett, Department of Medicine, who was jealous of Dr. Gordon. He is a bigoted asshole, and Arnett didn't like the fact that Alex is Jewish. Arnett asked me out while Alex was out of town and I accepted. I wasn't going with Alex at the time, just some lunches and dinners. Arnett got me up to his apartment under false pretenses. I would have never gone there. He made some racial slurs about Dr. Gordon. I'm sure he thought I was sexually involved with Alex, and he wanted the same. I refused."

"Did you report all this?"

"No. I was scared out of my mind, but had enough wherewithal to run out of the apartment and walked back to my rooming house. Never heard from him again, and never want to."

"I'll check it out, but, you're right, not likely he'd come up with five thou for drugs to get you in trouble."

"Anyone in your family mad at you?"

"I don't have a family. I was orphaned at age two. I know of no relatives, don't know where I was born or where I was before age two. The Montana police and the orphanage looked for a while and never came up with any information. I was dumped at the orphanage, no note, no good-bye, and no thank you."

"Never adopted out?"

"Couple of times. Once, when I was two or three years old, but I was returned to the orphanage when my family got in legal trouble that later turned out to be bogus. The second time I was about twelve or thirteen, and that lasted a couple of years. I was abused and don't like to talk about it. Actually, I won't talk about it, so don't ask me."

"Grace, what if we need you to explain that...."

Grace interrupted Snyder, "I will not talk about that time in my life. It took me two years before I could trust anyone after returning to the orphanage. The nightmares kept me up almost every night and I still have them. The smell of marijuana triggers the most dreadful feeling. I become hysterical with fear."

"Okay, Grace. What happened to the man that abused you?"

"They never prosecuted him, that man, that I know of. They took me back to the orphanage. No one tried to adopt me after that because I didn't want to be adopted. I don't want to talk about it, please."

Snyder continued, "What happened then?"

"After I was eighteen, they let me go and I slowly made my way to Seattle. I never had any money, would do odd jobs, stay in shelters, took a few classes here and there. Then I got my first real job at Seattle Med. I lived in a cheap rooming house down on Yesler and scraped by. Then I met Dr. Gordon and things have been better. Anyway, I'm supposed to be starting school on Monday, April 17th.

"Okay, Grace, from what you've told me, I think, or at least, I hope, the other witnesses will be strong enough that you won't have to testify. I'm liking what I hear. Let's go over the police raid one more time. They came down the hallway, you were sitting outside the archives because you locked yourself out."

"Yes."

"Okay. The lady officer," Snyder was looking at the report, "...Morgan, walked towards you with gun drawn, frisked you. Then the narcotics lieutenant, a

Lieutenant Harkins, exited the elevator and questioned you."

"Yep. I told him what I told you, but I don't think he believed me. I told him that no one was in the archives, that I was the only person usually in there, and I told him the marijuana was in the copier room. They busted the door down, found the marijuana where I said it was, and then arrested me."

"When did they read your rights to you, you know the Miranda rights."

"When they arrested me, just as we were leaving."

"Interesting, Grace, interesting."

Snyder called for the guard to escort Grace back to her cell. "Grace, I've got to make some calls. At least to the security officer, the secretary and Dr. Arnett. If you think of anything else, let me know. I'll be back," he smiled and said, 'don't go anywhere."

Snyder came back two hours later and had Grace re-escorted to the interrogation room.

"Grace, I've got some good news and some not so good news."

"Give me the bad, first."

"The Deputy Prosecutor himself, Chris Callo, is going against you and me. He's supposed to be smart and good. Three other public defenders have told me, 'we're both fucked.' He doesn't take cases he's likely to lose. My hope is that he's only read the same report I've read, which means he doesn't know about Mayeda or the secretary."

"What's the good news?"

"Mayeda, and that is his name, Joe Mayeda, has been at Seattle Med Security for eighteen years, and he's pissed big time at the Seattle PD. He was a US Army MP before Seattle Med and knows police procedures. Seattle PD never called him to say they were coming to Seattle Med and they should have. He knew nothing when you made your call to him. He said you should have never been arrested. After your call, he didn't think you had an emergency and he needed to wait for an officer to return before he could leave the office. Better than that, when he heard about the raid and arrest, he made sure that he had copies of the conversation you and he had. Seems that they tape everything that comes in and hold it for a week. In addition, the secretary at the Department of Surgery, a Polly Harper, told me the same story you told me. She felt bad she hadn't gone up with you."

"So now what?"

"We are going in front of a judge in thirty minutes so you can enter a plea. I'll be there. The courthouse is across the street. I've heard that the Prosecutor and Deputy Prosecutor are giving a press conference after your plea."

The courthouse was a zoo. A large male officer escorted Grace into court, cuffed at the ankles. Paul Snyder was waiting off to the side, shaking hands with two older men in suits.

As soon as Grace entered, the guard whispered something to the bailiff who whispered something to the judge.

The judge, a handsome older man with thinning hair and a smile that seemed genuine, at least to Grace, sat at the bench. In front of him was a wooden nameplate that read, Anthony Wallnik, Judge, Superior Court.

Judge Wallnik banged his gavel and said, "In view of our distinguished guests from the prosecutor's office, we'll let them get out of here quickly so they can call tell their loving public how safe we are. Bailiff."

The bailiff stood and announced. "State versus Pine."

Grace, her guard and Snyder walked to a stand facing the judge, and the two prosecutors, Chris Callo and Chet Kreel moved to a stand to the right of Grace and Snyder.

Judge Wallnik started, "Are the parties ready? Mr. Kreel, Mr. Callo?"

"The state is ready, your honor."

"Mr. Kreel, you know you didn't need to be here for the plea?"

Kreel said, "Of course, your honor. But this case is important and we need to show the public that King County is taking no prisoners with regards to drug dealing, particularly when that occurs in a public institution of education, and....."

Wallnik interrupted, "Chet, this isn't a political soap box, it's a court. Pity the defendant, eh?"

Kreel and Callo knew enough to shut up and smile.

Wallnik then looked to Snyder. "You're new?"

"Yes, your honor. I'm new. I started with the Public Defender's Office forty-five days ago."

"Welcome to my court, Mr. Snyder. You're going against two seasoned veterans. I'm not going to have any mistrials here because you're a novice and make a bonehead mistake. Tell that to your boss. He should know better than to send a rookie against these two barracudas. Are you ready to make a plea?"

Snyder said, "Yes, we are, your honor."

Wallnik said, "Miss Pine, you are charged with possession of two pounds of marijuana with intent to distribute. You are also charged with intent to sell an illegal drug at a public educational institution. Do you understand the charges?"

Grace looked at Snyder. He whispered back, "Say, yes."

Grace said, "Yes, I understand the charges....which are all false."

Wallnik, now frowning, and not appreciating the ad-lib, said, "Mr. Snyder, tell your client that a yes or no answer was all that was called for."

Snyder leaned over to Grace and said, "Don't fuck around, yes or no."

Grace repeated, "Yes, I understand the charges."

"Thank you, Miss Pine," said the now smiling judge.

"And Miss Pine, how do you plea, guilty or not guilty."

"Not guilty, your honor."

Grace's response caught Wallnik off guard. Earlier, Kreel's office had informed Wallnik that their case was rock solid. Six inches of granite solid. Wallnik said, "Miss Pine did you say, not guilty?"

Grace said, "I did your honor. I did not do the things they said I did."

The judge looked at Snyder, "Mr. Snyder, you're new here. We can't have all our cases going to trial. Does your client know she's unlikely to win a trial, if it goes to trial? Moreover, that the penalties, when she loses, and Mr. Kreel tells me she will lose, are much more severe? Does she know that? Do you know that?"

Snyder, stone faced, said, "Your honor, we are aware of the consequences of a trial and my client has already declared that she's going to plead not guilty. I agree with her plea."

The judge, silent for a second, said, "Fine, we need to set a court date. Mr. Kreel, Mr. Callo, when will the state be ready for a trial?"

"Your honor," said Callo, snickering, chest expanded rooster-like, "we can proceed with the trial anytime the defense wants to go."

"And my good Mr. Snyder, who has no idea, not a clue, what he's up against, when might you be ready to go?"

Snyder said, "I need to talk to my chief and..."

Wallnik, interrupted, "I'd hope so. And after you talk to him, you may want to call Mr. Callo and my bailiff and we'll see if the plea is going to stand. Anyway, if you don't change your client's mind, when might you be ready?"

"Your honor, my client has paid for tuition to college which is non-refundable at this late date. School starts in two weeks. I'd say we would be ready next week, if our witnesses are available and if your honor permits. I've asked my client and she trusts your judgment. We don't need a jury. You can decide."

Wallnik said, "Jesus. Excuse me, folks, didn't' mean to say that. Okay. I have a case that cancelled that was to start Monday. See you men, and lady, in court, on Monday, nine a.m. If your witnesses are not available, or your chief talks some sense into you and your client, call Mr. Callo and call my bailiff and we'll see whether we can re-plea this mess. If you do proceed next week, against my better judgment, there will be no retrial because you f..., uh, messed up. God help us."

Grace's guard turned her towards the exit when she saw Alex at the back of the courtroom. "Can I say hello to my friend over there?" she asked the guard.

"No way, you're going back to your cell."

Grace, pointing to Alex, said to Snyder, "That's my boyfriend, Dr. Gordon, over there."

Snyder finger waved to Alex to meet him outside the courtroom.

"Dr. Gordon, I'm Paul Snyder, Grace's attorney. We need to talk, but the Prosecutor, Chet Kreel, and the Deputy Prosecutor, Chris Callo, are going to give a press conference. I want to hear what they have to say. Then, we can talk and afterwards, you can go across the street to see Grace."

Alex and Snyder walked to the front steps, outside the lobby of the courthouse. Three microphones and ten reporters were present as Kreel's administrative aide stepped to the mike.

He said, "Thank you for coming. I am Timothy Knapp, administrator for the King County Prosecutor's Office. Prosecutor Kreel will give a short talk about his plans to take a 'no-holds barred' attitude towards drugs in King County. Afterwards, you are free to ask questions. Today is Day number one in his overall plan. We are hoping by Day number three hundred sixty-five, one year from now, drug dealing, buying, and use will have their legs cut out from underneath them. I give you Prosecutor... Chet Kreel."

Kreel stepped to the mike, "Thank you, Tim. Hello to all those out there in our beautiful King County that want to see drug dealing, and use, a thing of the past. Tim said we were going to cut the legs out from drug use. Not enough. Not enough for me to be happy. I will not stop until we have cut the arms, heads and hearts out of drug use as well. Today's first case involves distributing drugs in a school, albeit, our fine medical school. Nonetheless, drugs do not belong in any place of education where students from kindergarten to graduate school are trying to get ahead in the world. Today marks the end of bargaining with drug dealers, the purveyors of this heinous crime, drug use, which affects us all. I'm here to tell the fine people of King County that we're not going to let any drug dealer get any less, not a penny or an ounce less, than the full weight of the law. I was glad to hear that the public defender's office has agreed to move swiftly. I am all for getting drug cases quickly in front of a judge, and jury, if need be, to get these scum suckers off our streets."

Timothy Knapp retook the microphone and said, "Prosecutor Kreel and Deputy Prosecutor Callo will be glad to answer questions......"

Snyder and Alex stayed for ten minutes of questions, all related to whether Kreel was going to run for governor of Washington State in fourteen months. He answered the questions with the skill of the consummate politician...with no answer. As the crowd started to disperse, one of the reporters pointed at Snyder and announced, "There's the perp's lawyer." The group moved toward Snyder and Alex, en masse, like four-year olds playing soccer.

"Excuse me, Mr. Schneider, what did you think about Prosecutor Kreel's remark."

Snyder had never been in front of a microphone at a legal press conference. He was afraid to say anything that could hurt the case against Grace. Taking a deep breath, he figured a way to start, "Thank you, everyone. My name is Paul Snyder," emphasizing the correct pronunciation, "and I am an attorney in the public defender's office. I agree with the prosecutor that a reduction of drug dealing and use in King County will be a good thing. The only thing I have to say at this point is that my client is innocent of all charges and her plea of 'not guilty, was appropriate. Gentlemen, we will see you in court." Snyder turned and waved for Alex to follow and they re-entered the courthouse, leaving the reporters at the door.

"Snyder, a bit cocky there. Good for you," said Alex.

The two sat and exchanged what they knew. Alex told Snyder what Grace had already said. "She can't be near marijuana, she gets seriously ill, and quickly." He related the story of Grace, Samantha and her friends, as told to Alex by Grace, and then by Sam independently.

Alex added, "Their descriptions of the events were identical. My sister also said that Grace had alluded to the fact that her fear of marijuana dated back to age twelve or thirteen. I haven't discussed this fact with Grace, figuring that the psychiatrist she is scheduled to see in a couple of weeks would handle those delicate situations that Grace had specifically said she couldn't and wouldn't discuss."

"Dr. Gordon...."

"Shit, Snyder, we're about the same age. Call me Alex or call me Gordon."

"Alex, any chance you can get any of those friends of your sister up here for one day in the middle of the week. Your sister won't make as credible a witness, unless we're stuck."

"I don't know. I can try."

"Try hard. I'd hate to ask the judge to move the trial date. Their testimony might be crucial."

"I'll try."

"The county can't pay for their transportation. Sorry. No budget for that, just so you know."

"I figured as much."

* * * *

Henry Farley sent Cully Harris a video tape of Kreel's speech on the courthouse steps and clippings from the Seattle Post-Intelligencer and the Seattle Times.

Cully left a message on Farley's phone. "Henry, Cully here. Good work."

Farley left a message on Rico Carpetti's phone. "Rico, Henry here. Good work."

Rico didn't call Jaime in Seattle. His bones ached even thinking about calling Seattle.

Chapter 13

On the advice of his boss, Snyder called Deputy Prosecutor Callo the next day to arrange a meeting and present him the new information, not in the police report. Snyder hoped to have the charges against Grace withdrawn.

Tim Knapp, chief administrator for Kreel and Callo, took the call. "What can I do for you, Mr. Snidler?"

"It's Snyder. S-N-Y-D-E-R. I think we need to talk about the case against Grace Pine. There is stuff you don't know, and I don't believe Grace Pine is guilty."

"Mr. Snidler, one, this case is cut and dry, and we have all the information we need. There will be no bargaining. Your client is going to spend at least four to five years at the Purdy Washington Corrections Center for Women, and Callo will ask for more. Even if she had pled guilty, we would have asked for the maximum sentence. Additionally, because she was dealing in a public institution, the sentence will likely be enhanced by another two to three years. Only difference, I see, is a two, three-day trial and the same result. This way, we get two or three extra press conferences."

Snyder knew enough not to get mad over the intended mispronunciation of his name. "Mr. Knapp, I need to meet with Mr. Callo. Grace Pine's case should not go to trial."

"Snidler, you're new. You don't get to make appointments with Callo or Kreel. Hell, for this case, even your boss wouldn't get a meeting. Sorry Charley."

Snyder visited Grace and told her that a trial was inevitable. He also called Alex Gordon, Joe Mayeda and Polly Harper. The next day he received the phone numbers of Samantha's friends, Kathleen, Amanda and Melissa. Samantha had already talked to them. They weren't sure if they could make it to Seattle on short notice and the flights were expensive.

Alex Gordon called Snyder on Friday morning.

"Paul, Alex Gordon. Good news. My parents will send Samantha's friends up, if you need them."

"Great. I've sent the prosecutor the witness list. You, Mayeda, Hopper, your sister's friends, and the head librarian, McPherson. Doubtful that I'll call you and I haven't even talked to the librarian, who would be only a character witness. The prosecution has only the arresting officers. They probably think that our list is only character witnesses and, in your case, a boyfriend. I sent over a cassette tape of the conversation with Grace and Mayeda in a plain envelope and I've got a signature from the prosecutor's receptionist that they received it. I haven't heard back but I'm guessing no one's going to listen to it. They're so fucking cocky. I have one other trick up my sleeve. I'm going to hold on to it until the end of the case as a last gap measure. If the judge is waffling, I'll use it."

"And what's that?"

"I'm going to keep it to myself. Ran it past my boss and he says it's a desperation play. If I try to use it early, the judge will think our case is weak."

Alex said, "You know that Grace won't allow herself to be questioned about certain parts of her life?"

Snyder said, "She's made that abundantly clear. I pray we don't need it."

Alex said, "You better do more than pray."

Alex went to the jail every night to see Grace. Her arrest for drug dealing went viral amongst the hospital employees. Only the library staff was in disbelief. The rest of the medical center, given the tone of the Kreel and Callo, already had Grace in chains. A few people in the Urology Department knew of Alex's relationship with Grace. Alex's stock response was, "Let's wait for the trial. Grace's attorney told me not to talk to anyone, in case the defense calls me to testify. Grace is innocent."

Snyder's entire office worked to get him up to speed on trial work. A more senior defender would be second chair, but Paul was anxious to try the case himself. He had won the UPS Law School moot court competition and felt comfortable in court. He visited Grace on Sunday night.

Officer Hards, Grace's sole friend in the jail, moved Grace to a single cell to insure that she'd get some rest before the trial.

Hards told Snyder "Good thing the trial was right away. Grace is going to crack. She spends another week here and she'll be of no use to anyone. Poor kid. You make sure you get her off."

Snyder and Grace spent the last evening going over expected trial proceedings. The prosecution would present their evidence first and would take two days.

Monday, just past nine a.m., Judge Wallnik banged his gavel and the trial started. Deputy Prosecutor Callo called Lieutenant Tim Harkins, Seattle PD narcotics, and Elizabeth Morgan, the female arresting officer, and Johan Minkof, the huge officer that had kicked in the door.

Before the case started, Snyder stood.

Wallnik said, "Yes, Mr. Snyder. It's too late to change the plea."

"Yes, your honor, I know. The defense will stipulate that the cellophane bags on the prosecutor desk are two pounds of marijuana. My client is severely affected by the smell of the drug and we'd like to see it removed from the courtroom."

"Mr. Snyder, that's an unusual request."

"Ask the arresting officers, my client destroyed a floor mat in their squad car."

Wallnik looked over to the prosecution witnesses. Only Elizabeth Morgan nodded yes. Wallnik said, "So moved."

Chris Callo called Lieutenant Harnick first.

After being sworn in, Harnick told the story, as he saw it. "I received a tip from an informant that had been a reliable source of information to me for the past three years. I then presented the information to Judge Spencer and obtained a search warrant. Using due care and caution, and following the guidelines for the Seattle PD for drug arrests, my men and I would take no chances and be prepared for a firefight at all times. We have the layout of the hospital on computers, so we were aware of all the exits and entrances. Once the hallway was secure by armored police, my partner and I, without Kevlar, exited the elevator.

"We found the perp.., uh... defendant, sitting in the hallway outside the archives. She said she had locked herself out and that no one was in the archives. I remember her saying that hospital security was coming to let her in. By this time, she must have realized that she'd been caught and told us where to find the stash. Having no idea when or if anyone from security was coming, and whether there might still be people of interest in the archives, I had Officer Minkof kick the door down. The lock was a simple non-commercial grade knob, without a deadbolt. Offhand, I'd say their security was below par. After finding the marijuana, we read her her rights, and here we are. Case closed."

Snyder asked Harkins, "Did the defendant tell you that she had called security because she had smelled marijuana."

Harkins said flatly, "No, she said she had been locked out. The lock was set and she exited and was waiting to be let in."

"Officer Harkins, I'll repeat the question. Did the defendant tell you that she had left the archives because she had smelled marijuana, became ill, and called for help?"

Harkins replied, "That didn't come up. By that time, if she said anything like that, I would have thought she was trying to create an alibi. We were there, she was alone, she admitted that no one enters the archives but her, and we found the drugs. She concocted a story about where she was hiding the marijuana. That suggested to me that she knew she'd been had. Obviously, we would have found the drug. Her telling us where it was didn't create even a hint of her innocence to me."

Snyder said, "I have no further questions, but reserve the right to recall Officer Harkins. I would ask the court that the defense would like to hear testimony from the informant."

Callo responded quickly, "Your Honor, I object. The informant could not testify, or even be questioned, without divulging his identity, and thereby putting himself, or herself, in jeopardy. The tip had been only that marijuana was in the archives and a woman was dealing. The tip proved to be true."

Wallnik agreed with Callo's objection.

As the clock struck two p.m., Judge Wallnik said he had motions to hear from other pending cases. Trial would resume in the morning.

The next day, Elizabeth Morgan, the female officer, Johan Minkof, the large door-kicking officer and Harkin's partner, Buster Koe, testified. The three corroborated Harkin's testimony.

Morgan did add, "As we drove to the county jail, the defendant became ill in the car and vomited. Whether it was from marijuana or not, I have no idea. Could be 'cause she'd been caught."

Snyder asked, "After the drug was transferred, did the defendant feel better?"

"After the marijuana was removed, she thanked me, asked me to open the window, and didn't vomit again. I have no idea why she was sick....."

Snyder interrupted, "You've answered my question, thank you."

Callo, in re-cross, said, "Officer Morgan, finish your thought."

"I had no idea why she was sick and why she got better."

Snyder, then asked, "But you believed her about the marijuana and transferred the drugs."

"Yes, I did. Whether it was..."

Snyder interrupted, "You've answered my question, thank you."

Callo, in re-cross, said, "Officer Morgan, finish your thought."

Morgan said, "Whether the defendant's aversion to marijuana was real or she was lying, I don't know, but I didn't see any harm in moving the drugs to the other car."

Callo said, "So, Officer Morgan, you have no proof that the defendant is intolerant of marijuana."

Morgan said, "No proof."

Snyder then asked, "But, you have no proof that she's not."

Morgan said, "No proof, either way. I'm not a doctor."

Callo rose and said, "The prosecution has no further questions for this witness, your honor. The prosecution rests."

Court ended at three p.m.

Snyder, Alex and Grace met afterwards at the jail to discuss strategy. Snyder said, "I feel confident that we have a strong case. Nothing is certain, but we have some credible witnesses. Thanks again to your family, Alex, for getting your sister's friends up here."

The next morning, Snyder called his first witness, Kathleen Cline.

Snyder started, "Ms. Cline, are you a personal friend of the defendant?"

Kathleen responded, "I've met her. We're not friends, at least yet. She was the guest of a friend of mine, Samantha Gordon, at a party in San Francisco last month, on a Friday night. Grace was in town to help take care of Samantha's mother who had shoulder surgery that morning. Her mother was coming home the next day."

"Miss Cline, would you tell the court, in your own words, the events of that evening."

"There were five of us. Me, Samantha, Grace and two other friends, Melissa Morton and Amanda Newell. We were having a good time and were discussing Grace's life in the orphanage. One of the

244

people in the party went into a bedroom and came out with a lit marijuana cigarette. Within seconds, Grace panicked, berserk almost, and fled the apartment. Outside the apartment, she vomited over the railing. She was apologetic and said that she couldn't be around marijuana. I'd never seen anything like it before. She wouldn't even go back into the apartment after extinguishing the marijuana because she said the smell would linger. She also said that the problem with her and marijuana went back twelve or thirteen years. Later, Melissa, Amanda and I commented that she was twelve or thirteen when it started and we wondered what had brought this on."

Callo's cross was simple, "Are you a doctor?"

"No."

"So you don't know why the defendant reacted the way she did?"

"No."

Snyder said, "Did you believe the defendant's action were real or made up?"

"I believe they were real."

"Isn't it possible that she acted this out, so that if she was ever arrested, she could use this as an alibi?"

Kathleen said, "This was not an act. I may not know reasons for being sick or allergic to things. I'm not a doctor. But Grace was scared, and I can tell when someone is scared. She was afraid to death of the smell, plain and simple."

Snyder then called Amanda Newell. Her testimony and cross-examination was identical to Kathleen's.

Polly Hopper, the Department of Surgery's secretary, testified next.

Ms. Hopper testified that the defendant, whom she did not know, ran into the Department of Surgery office. "I asked if she had seen a ghost, she looked that scared. Or maybe I asked if there was a fire. Anyway, she said she smelled marijuana. I'm no prude, so I told her that she should go back and have some fun, or something like that. She remained agitated and asked if I would call campus security, which I did. She talked to someone on the phone and told that person exactly what she had told me. She smelled marijuana and was scared. I guess whoever was on the phone told her to go back to the archives and wait. She then asked if I would come with her because she was frightened. I told her I couldn't leave the desk and that she'd be okay. She left and I didn't hear anything about it until the next day when I heard that the Seattle Police arrested a file clerk for drug dealing in the archives. I would have bet the ranch it was not the defendant."

Callo's cross asked a simple question to Hopper, "Isn't it possible that the defendant knew she was about to get arrested, had nowhere to hide the drugs she had brought into the archives, and then came down to your office as a subterfuge, or alibi, to claim the drugs weren't hers."

"I suppose anything is possible."

Snyder asked, "Did you think it was an act."

Hopper said, "No. I'd have given her an academy award. She was agitated and frightened."

Callo said, "If you knew you were to be arrested, and you had no way out, wouldn't you be agitated and frightened?"

"I suppose I would."

Snyder and his second chair, Jon Rambler, talked quietly.

"Jon, I'm a little concerned that the judge isn't buying the stories. I'm not sure that I wouldn't have some doubt."

Rambler, a veteran in the defender's office, said, "The biggest issue you still have is who else, if not Miss Pinc, would have brought the drugs in there. No one ever used the archives except for Grace; she admitted that to the officers. If she didn't put the *MaryJane* there, then who did and why? We have nothing to offer as an alternative. Let's hope the tapes this afternoon seal the deal. Honestly, I'm worried. I don't want you to put Grace on the stand. We have no idea what she'll say or do. But you might have to."

At lunch, Snyder made a call to a classmate from law school to ask a favor. Grant Barton said he'd do what he could. If he could locate the information, he'd have it Fedexed overnight to the defender's office.

After lunch, Joe Mayeda, the Seattle Med security officer took the stand.

After being sworn in, and asked by Snyder to tell the events, as they transpired, Mayeda said, "I can tell you what I remember from memory, but we tape all calls into the security center. The defendant's call was taped and I think that playing it back makes more sense than trusting my memory."

Snyder stood and said, "With the court's permission, I'd like to play the tape."

Callo jumped to his feet and objected, "We did not receive this evidence before the trial. Therefore, it is not admissible, and I'd like to exclude it, your honor."

Snyder, still standing, fought the urge to smile, "Your honor, I have a signed receipt of delivery from the prosecutor's office dated last Friday. I received the tapes from the security department at Seattle Med that morning, and once I heard the tapes, I called Mr. Callo's office to schedule an appointment to discuss settlement of this case. I talked to Mr. Timothy Knapp, the administrative aide to Mr. Kreel and Mr. Callo. Mr. Knapp told me that the prosecutors had all they needed and were not going to negotiate. You are welcome to swear in Mr. Knapp and ask him what he said. Anyway, I sent the tape to their office and have a receipt of acceptance here."

Wallnik looked at the receipt and then looked at Callo. "Shame on the prosecutor's office. Thank you, Mr. Snyder. Let's hear the tape."

"Security. Office Mayeda speaking."

"Excuse me, I need help. I work in the library archives on five southwest. I went out to deliver books to the main library and when I returned I could smell marijuana in the archives. I need help. I can't go back in the archives while that smell is present. Can you come right away.......

When the tape was finished, the courtroom remained silent for a moment.

Snyder asked Mayeda what happened next.

"I was alone in the office; all the other officers were out on patrol around the medical center. I couldn't leave unless there was an immediate threat and I felt there was no immediate threat to anyone. The other officers returned twenty minutes later and I headed up to the archives. As I was heading over, I received a radio message that the Seattle PD had arrested a woman and was leading her, in handcuffs, out of the hospital. We, none of us in security, had any knowledge of an impending arrest, which is in clear violation of the agreements between the medical center and the Seattle Police. When I got to the archives, fifth floor southwest, the hallway was empty, a door had been shattered and the archives were open. No notes, no message, no nothing. Didn't take rocket science to put the broken door, Miss Pine not waiting in front of the archive like she was told, and the Seattle PD leading someone out, to put it all together. I was angry, really steamed, but I thought I'd give the Seattle PD the benefit of the doubt and waited to hear from them. That call never came. Someone's gonna pay for this, I can promise you that."

They, the Seattle PD," Mayeda pointed at Harkins, "had no right not to get us involved at the onset, and, at least, let us know what happened afterwards. If I were to take three security officers from my office and raid an apartment off campus, not in our jurisdiction, do you know what the Seattle PD would do?"

Callo was stunned, but regained his composure quickly. He took the same line of reasoning with Mayeda.

"First, Officer Mayeda, you are right. The Seattle PD needed to get you involved. Our office is separate from theirs, but be rest assured that we will make sure this lack of cooperation will not be tolerated."

Mayeda, now smug and smiling, and glaring at Lieutenant Harkins, who was sitting in the gallery, said, "Thank you."

Callo looked at his notes and reviewed his question to Miss Hopper. "Isn't it possible, Officer, that the defendant knew she was about to get arrested, had nowhere to hide the drugs she had brought into the archives, and then called your office as a subterfuge, or alibi, to claim the drugs weren't hers."

Mayeda, now calmed after Callo's declaration that he'd fix the relationship with the Seattle PD, said, "It's possible."

Snyder asked, as before, "Did you think the defendant was putting on an act."

Mayeda said, "No, but I didn't have any idea what was going on. She seemed excited, that's all. I even thought it might have been a crank call. Marijuana in the archives? Didn't make sense to me."

Rambler turned to Snyder and whispered, "We're in trouble. We don't have the judge believing the 'fear of marijuana' story. Moreover, we don't have an alternative as to why the drugs were there. I don't like this."

Snyder whispered back, "Jon, I'm new at this. We could try to say that they *Mirandized* her after they interviewed her and found out she was the only one in there. "

Rambler pondered the statement, "Slippery slope. If you use it, you weaken the merits of your own case. In any event, I don't think Wallnik will allow it. Grace never admitted doing anything before being given her rights. If you were going to use it, I would have done it at the beginning."

Snyder said, "I suppose you're right. We'll need to put her on the stand tomorrow morning and make them believe in her story."

Rambler agreed.

Wallnik asked, "Counselor, is the defense finished or do you have any other witnesses?"

"We will put the defendant on the stand in the morning, your honor. That will be our last witness," said Snyder.

Callo snickered. He knew that putting the defendant on the stand was a sign that the defense thought they were losing.

Wallnik announced to the courtroom, "Excellent. One witness and then closing arguments tomorrow. Court is dismissed."

Snyder, Alex and Grace met at the jail to discuss the next day's proceedings. For the first time, Snyder sounded cautious, "I admit that the impact of Sam's friends, Polly Hopper and Officer Mayeda was less than I had hoped for. Grace, Alex, I'll ask again, is there anyone you can think of who would have done this to Grace? Our biggest problem is that we have no other credible answer as to why the marijuana was in the archives. None. We need something."

Grace said, "I have absolutely no idea who or why. Honestly, it makes no sense to me."

Snyder, worry lines across his brow, said, "Grace, I think we're going to have to put you on the stand so you can tell your story. Can you handle it? It may be rough. No, it will be excruciatingly rough. Callo is an expert at grinding witnesses to a pulp. Can you handle it?"

Grace said, "Do I have a choice?"

"Yes, you always have a choice. However, your next six to eight years may depend on you testifying."

Grace and Alex sat quiet. Alex held her hand and squeezed.

Alex said, "I've gotten off for the last three days. I'm needed back at the hospital tomorrow, sometime. They know about all the trial and will hold off beeping me until it's necessary. I'll stay as long as I can. I'm so sorry, but they need me."

Grace said, "I understand." Turning to Snyder, she asked, "After the close, when might the judge decide?"

"Any time. Right after the case closes but usually not for a few days."

"I have school Monday."

"Nothing would make me happier than to say, 'Enjoy school.' At this point, I can't make a promise that we're going to win this case. I will do everything I can, I promise. Your testimony is going to have to be compelling. The judge needs to believe you. I'm going to stay here for a while and go over your testimony."

At nine ten a.m., the next morning, Snyder stood and said, "The defense calls Grace Helena Pine."

After Grace was sworn in, Snyder said, "Please tell the court, in your own words, a little of your background. Start with how your name came about."

"In November, 1972, I was mysteriously deposited in an orphanage in Missoula, Montana, in the middle of the night. I was about two years old. Despite a ten state scarch, police and orphanages in the northwest could not find any trace of who I was, or where I came from. The state of Montana named me Grace, because it was a beautiful name, Helena, the capital of Montana, and Pine, for the Ponderosa Pine, which is the Montana state tree."

As she finished her opening testimony, a courier entered the court and handed a large soft package to Jon Rambler. He opened it, wrote a small note and slipped the note in front of Snyder.

Snyder, nodded, pushed the note aside and asked, "Miss Pine, may I call you Grace?"

"Yes, of course."

"Grace, have you ever been arrested?"

"No."

"Have you ever smoked marijuana?"

"No, never. I cannot be near the smell of marijuana without getting violently ill. I cannot help myself."

"Grace, can you tell the court, how and why you became so sensitive to marijuana?"

The question caught Grace off guard and her hands started to shake. She said, "No, you promised me you wouldn't ask me about that."

Snyder, approached Grace, held her shaking hand, and said, "Grace. I think it's important that you tell the court why you can't be around marijuana. The judge needs to know so that he can make a just decision. It is important."

Grace turned to look at the judge. *He has a kind face and must understand my situation.* Wallnik smiled, but then, unmistakably, gave a head nod of acquiescence, Snyder was right. The judge wasn't convinced.

Grace looked back to the court and her hands grabbed the witness stand railing hard enough that her knuckles looked as white and brittle as bone china. Tears slid down her face, dropping onto her lap and she seemed unable to move to grab a tissue offered by the bailiff. She scanned the room until she found Alex sitting in the second to last row.

Grace shouted, "Alex, what do I do? I don't want you to hear this. I don't want to hear myself say it...What..."

Wallnik pounded his gavel until Grace quieted and said, "Miss Pine, stop, now."

Snyder looked at Grace and then to Alex. He approached the judge. "May we have a ten minute recess, so that the defendant and I can talk?" Snyder stood by Grace who remained on the witness stand.

Wallnik said, "Ten minutes, that's it. The witness stays in the chair. Counselor, talk some sense into your client. She can't be yelling to people in the courtroom."

Wallnik went into his chambers behind the bench. Snyder curled his finger at Alex and he came to the witness stand.

Snyder said, "Alex, she needs to tell her story." Snyder walked back to his table and sat.

Alex turned to Grace, "Grace, you've got to tell what happened."

"I can't. I know if I do, it will rekindle all my nightmares. I've thought about this for the past two weeks. I know that you will be so repulsed that you won't love me anymore. You'll try, but the weight of what happened is too great for me to handle and for you to know about it. Why don't they just believe me?"

Alex said, slowly, "They don't, I guess. I do. But the judge needs convincing, not me. I don't care what you say or what terrible things happened to you more than a decade ago. I'm here and I'm not leaving you. The stars and the sun and the moon will leave you before I do. I swear."

"Alex, I'm so scared."

"Grace, I'm scared that I'll lose you to jail for something you didn't do."

Judge Wallnik was back at the bench in exactly ten minutes. "Mr. Snyder, court is back in session."

Snyder approached Grace and said, "Grace, tell us what happened."

Grace drew a deep breath through her nose and exhaled it through her mouth, twice.

"It was 1980; I was eleven and a half, almost twelve, when the Watkins came to the orphanage. They owned a wheat farm ten miles out of Victor, Montana, which was forty miles from Missoula. Zeke and Margaret. I think his full name was Ezekiel. They were in their late thirties. Margaret gave birth to three children. One died at birth, one died at two of pneumonia. Their oldest remaining child, Susan, was fourteen when she ran away from home, two years before I came. She was never found, to my knowledge. Mrs. Watkins had arthritis, the kind that makes your hands look funny and bent. She couldn't hold heavy pots and had difficulty walking. She spent a lot of time in bed and was always in pain. The Watkins told the orphanage they missed having children, and said that God had tested them by taking away all three.

"Mrs. Carmichael, she was the head of the orphanage, told me that the Watkins were God-fearing and kind and wanted children. She told me that their farm was in a remote area and that books would bide my time.

"When I met them, I asked if I would be able to read books. I asked if there was a library nearby. They told me that after finishing my daily chores, I could do all the reading I wanted. There was a small school and library in Victor, and after settling in, I would go to school there.

"I wasn't happy about leaving the orphanage but I had no real friends and I kept busy with my books. Mrs. Carmichael said I should try it, living with the Watkins, and if didn't work out, I could come back to the orphanage. Mrs. Carmichael said the state had already visited their farm and the orphanage would send a social worker out in a couple of weeks and then every four months. If I was happy and the social workers were satisfied, the Watkins could adopt me.

"Their home was ten hard miles from Victor. I never went to school or saw the library. Mr. Watkins would bring me books to read to Mrs. Watkins. The reason they wanted me, as best I could tell, was to take care of Mrs. Watkins, so that Mr. Watkins could work. Mrs. Watkins loved books as much as me, but she wasn't a good reader. So I started reading to her. She was nice and I know she loved me. At least, I thought she did in the beginning.

"Mrs. Watkins had some pain syrup given to her by the doctors for when she was suffering, which was often, every day. *Dem-a-roll* was the name of the syrup, or something like that. She was supposed to take only a teaspoon, but she often took two or three teaspoons at a time. Within thirty minutes, she would be asleep and would stay that way for two to three hours. She always took a dose an hour after dinner. I would go to bed then, because she'd wake up in the middle of the night and I'd have to tend to her.

I had been there two or three months when things changed. I would smell this strange odor in the house every so often. I later found out that the smell was marijuana. I didn't know it then, I do now. It was always after Mrs. Watkins had been given her *Dem-a-Roll* and was sleeping, sleeping hard. One night, I snuck back into the living room and I saw Mr. Watkins smoking a funny shaped cigarette. Mr. Watkins was sitting there naked and was playing with his penis and reading a magazine. I was frightened, not knowing what was going on. I snuck back into my room and closed the door, but the smell didn't leave the house or me for hours. I am not sure why I was frightened at that point, but I was. I figured out for myself that when I smelled that sweet sickly odor, I should stay in my room.

"Two months or so after that, things changed again. One night, after I could smell the odor, and Mrs. Watkins was dead to the world after her *Dem-a-Roll,* Mr. Watkins came into my room. I kept my door locked but it was the kind of lock that opens easily from the outside with a small screwdriver. Mr. Watkin's face was flushed and he talked funny. He was bare-chested and wearing only his underpants.

"Grace. Do you like me?" he asked.

"Yes." That's all I said. I liked Mrs. Watkins. I didn't think Mr. Watkins was nice to her. I lied.

"I was nervous. I didn't understand why he was there. He then took a big breath with the sickly smelling cigarette, the marijuana."

He sat on my bed and said, "Would you like to have some fun with me?"

I said, "What kind of fun. Like reading?"

"'No...,' he said, 'Kind of like tag. I touch you and you touch me. Does that sound like fun?'"

"I told him, 'I don't know. There's nowhere to run, so tag is too easy.'"

"'Not tag like that,' he said. I'll ask you to touch parts of my body and I'll touch parts of yours.'"

"I knew enough from the orphanage that his game was evil, was bad. Touching certain areas was forbidden. So I said, 'No, I don't want to play that game.'"

"He said, 'You don't have a choice. It's my house and I get to choose the games.'"

"I was crying by this time and said, 'I'm scared. I don't like that game and I don't want to play.'"

"He then inhaled from his cigarette, a huge breath in, then held it, then blew it out. Then his face changed. He was angry. He said, 'Grace, we're going to play this game whether you want to or not.'"

"I said, 'I'm going to tell Mrs. Watkins and she won't let you play this game.'"

"He then grabbed me by the neck with one hand and squeezed. His hands were huge, at least to me. I couldn't breathe for a moment. I thought I was going to die. Then he relaxed a little, but didn't let go of my neck."

"Mr. Watkins said, 'Grace, we're out here all alone. You love Mrs. Watkins, don't you?'"

"I said, 'Yes, she's nice. We read together.'"

"He squeezed my neck a little tighter and said, 'If you tell her anything about what we do, I will hurt her. She's already frail but I'll make it so she's even sicker, so sick she could die. You don't want that, do you?'"

"'No. No,' I said, 'don't hurt her. She wouldn't be able to stand it.'"

"'That's my girl,' he said and he loosened the grip on my neck. 'You're not going to tell anyone, right?'"

"I said, 'Yes. I won't tell if you don't hurt Mrs. Watkins.'"

"'Good,' he said, and then he stood and removed his underwear. I started to scream but he blocked my mouth. He said, 'If you ever scream, Mrs. Watkins could wake up and that would be the same as telling her and then I'd have to hurt her.'"

"He then took my hand and started rubbing his already erect penis. He said, 'Keep rubbing,' as he smoked the cigarette. I kept this up until he had an orgasm. Of course, I didn't understand that then. He made me clean up my floor and left. His last words that night were, 'You can't tell this to anyone, or else.'"

"Mrs. Watkins asked me the next day why I was so anxious. I lied and told her I didn't feel well, but I knew why. I was too upset to read to her. Two days passed and I hoped, stupidly, that Mr. Watkins wouldn't want to play his kind of tag again. I restarted reading to Mrs. Watkins. I thought maybe it was all a nightmare. It wasn't. He came back on the third night. I knew it would happen because I smelled the odor – the marijuana."

"After a few more times coming into my room, he told me, 'I'm tired of this game. We need to play different games.'"

"I said, 'I don't like these games. I don't like them at all...' Before I could finish the sentence, he grabbed me by the neck again, and this time he held on longer. I felt dizzy and wet my pajamas. I thought I was going to die, but he let go and said, 'We play what I want to play. You don't tell anyone. You don't want me to hurt Mrs. Watkins, do you?'"

"I nodded no. I couldn't talk."

"Over the next few months, the games progressed, always preceded by the marijuana. First, he had me put his penis in my mouth. One time he got mad and choked me when he thought I had tried to bite him. I hadn't, I was gagging. Finally, he tried to have sex with me. I didn't understand intercourse at all then, or had a vague idea. He promised it would be fun. More fun than the other games. He tried a few times to penetrate but I was too small and too tight. He never gave up. Finally, he coated my vagina with Vaseline and despite my pleas that it hurt, he entered me. He kept his hand over my mouth so I wouldn't scream. I bled for a couple of hours and was so sore that I was afraid to pee for a day.

"Anyway, he waited for a week and then returned. After that, he always ended up penetrating me. It didn't hurt as much as it did the first time, but I never, ever, stopped crying, the entire time he would be in my room. He also never stopped smoking marijuana, before and during his visits.

"After almost a year of this, one night, he was so drugged with the marijuana, he forgot to hold my mouth and I screamed. He ignored it, but it awoke Mrs. Watkins who walked into the room with him inside me. He didn't see her face, but I did. I can't explain what outright disgust looks like, but that's what Mrs. Watkins had on her face.

"She walked to the kitchen and came back with a large carving knife. He was still on top of me but I turned my head so I could see her. She stabbed him in the back. He jumped off the bed screaming. He was hurt, but not so bad that he couldn't hit Mrs. Watkins. He hit her with a full fist across the jaw and knocked out a bunch of teeth and split her lip. They were both screaming. I tried to run to her but she called me a whore and refused to let me touch her. I pleaded that I didn't want to play his games but she wouldn't believe me. With gurgling from a bleeding mouth, she turned to Mr. Watkins and said, "You drove away our daughter. You promised you'd never do this again. You are the devil. Grace is a devil, too. I want to kill you, both. I want my daughter back."

"The yelling and screaming lasted for what seemed a long time until Mr. Watkins said, "I don't feel so good. I can't breathe. I've got to go to the doctor."

"Mrs. Watkins said, 'Take her with you,' pointing to me with a crooked finger attached to a shaking hand. 'I can't stand the sight of either of you. Ezekiel, you can come back and pick up your things in the morning and leave forever. Keep your whore with you. I never want to see her again.'"

"Mr. Watkins put on his shirt and pants and I dressed in pajamas. We drove forty minutes to the doctor in Victor. The doctor's house was the clinic. As his wife, who was his nurse, was drawing blood and taking his blood pressure, Dr. Kennedy, that was his name, asked what happened. I didn't think Mr. Watkins could hurt Mrs. Watkins any further, so I told the doctor everything. He then went into see Mr. Watkins and after only a few moments of talking, they both started yelling at each other. Mr. Watkins, even though he was weak, got up and left.

I heard his truck start and he drove away. I think he was going to try to drive to Missoula and see the doctors there.

"Dr. Kennedy examined me, while Mrs. Kennedy held my hands and washed my face. She cried the entire time I was being examined. Dr. Kennedy called Mrs. Watkins to see if I could return there. She said she didn't want me back, ever. She said that I was evil and the devil, and that she would send all my belongings to the orphanage. I slept at the Kennedy's house that night and returned to the orphanage the next day. I had been there, at the Watkins house, over a year and a half, and I figure I had been raped fifty or sixty times, each one preceded by the smell of marijuana. You might ask why the state hadn't been out to check on us every four months like they said. Mrs. McPherson said the orphanage called and that Mrs. Watkins always told them that everything was perfect and they were looking forward to adopting me. I never knew about these calls and when the visits never happened, I gave up hope. I never got to go to school in Victor. If I had, I probably would have told someone what was happening. I guess Mr. Watkins figured that out, so I stayed at their farm."

"Am I allergic to marijuana? No. Not in the classic way. But the smell sets off a response in me that I can't explain to anyone. I want to hide. I want to not be seen. I want to die, or wish I were dead. Eventually, the vomiting would start and last until I had nothing left to give up. That's what happened to me. I was twelve and thirteen. Why me? Why did this happen to me? What did I do to anyone to deserve that? What?"

Grace hesitated, and turned towards the judge and said, "Judge. Do you think I would sell marijuana?"

Grace looked around the room. The faces of the courtroom were pale and still, colorless, like a faded photograph that had been in the sun too long. Women were clearing the tears from their eyes with sets of Kleenex. Some of the men, too. Some of the men used their shirtsleeves. As Grace scanned the room looking for Alex, everyone looked away, unable to meet Grace eye to eye.

Grace felt alone. She said to the courtroom, "I know how you all feel. You fear that the devil will come out and snatch you and your loved ones. That's how I feel, whenever I remember." The judge did not stop her from talking.

She finally found Alex. He had also been crying, but Alex didn't look away. He stood and mouthed, "I will be there for you." The judge was as immobile as the rest of the spectators and said nothing.

Finally, Mr. Callo rose and said, "Good story, lady. I don't buy it. You should have been an actress...."

The judge held up his hand, wiped a tear from his eye and said, "Sit down, Mr. Callo, now!"

Snyder stood and held up a large folder. The front was marked 'Property of the State of Montana.' He said, "I have here the official records of Grace Pine from the orphanage in Missoula. I received this today after calling a classmate that is clerking for the Chief Justice of the State of Montana. He rushed it to me overnight. Every word that Grace has said is documented in these records."

After Snyder handed the records to the judge, the courtroom was silent. Wallnik looked through Grace's records at the tabbed pages. After he was satisfied, he asked the bailiff to hand the folder to Mr. Callo.

Snyder said, "The defense rests, I don't think that I need to make a closing statement, do I your Honor?"

"No, Mr. Snyder, I think not. Mr. Callo, are you of the mind to withdraw these charges."

Callo, pit bull that he was, would never quit. He said, "No. I still think it's an act. It says here in these records that Grace Pine was charged with assault when she was fifteen."

Snyder jumped up, "Those are juvenile records and should not be admissible."

The judge said, "Sorry, Mr. Snyder, can't have it both ways. You've introduced the records. Did you not know about the assault charge?"

"No, your Honor."

"Well, counselor, let's all learn about it," Wallnik said.

Snyder approached Grace, still sitting in the witness box. "You want to tell us about the assault."

Grace said, "Sure. I was charged with assault but the judge dismissed it."

Snyder said, "Tell us what happened, in your own words."

"I was fifteen years old and mostly stayed to myself. In the orphanage there were maybe ten boys older than I was at that time. I paid them no attention, which irked them. One night, after dinner, an eight-year old, Bobby Hunt, came up to me and asked if I would read to him that night. Bobby had dyslexia, and, at least once a week, I'd spend time reading to him. I know he cared for me. Anyway, he didn't want to hear me read, he wanted to tell me that two of the boys, Corky Jorgeson and Justin Wall, had bragged at the dinner table that they were going to sneak into the older girl's sleep room that night to bother me. Bobby never said exactly what bother meant, but it usually had something to do with holding me down and removing my underwear. I thanked Bobby and then went down to the gymnasium and borrowed a baseball bat and took it back to my room, and waited.

"The two boys came in at ten p.m., an hour after lights-out. As soon as they entered the sleep room, I hit Justin in the back with the bat. I broke a couple of his ribs and he was in the infirmary for three days and was spitting up blood for two weeks. The police came and made a report.

"A week later, we went in front of a judge. I told him exactly what I told you, except I didn't mention who the snitch had been. He asked the boys if the story was true. They said yes.

"The judge asked me why I didn't go beforehand to the Sisters and tell them what I had heard. I said that if I had told the nuns, the boys would have denied planning anything. They would wait and come up another night.

"Corky and Justin weren't the sharpest pencils in the drawer. The judge asked them if that was true and Corky said, "Probably. We told the boys we was gonna do it and we'd look like pussies if we didn't."

"The judge dismissed the charges. He told the boys they were lucky I didn't kill them and they had no business in the girl's wing."

Snyder said, "No further questions. And again, the defense rests."

"Mr. Callo?"

Meekly, Callo mumbled, "The prosecution rests, as well."

The judge said, "I will deliberate over this for a bit. I do want to look at the Montana records again. I will likely be back in a short while, so I'd like the prosecution and defense to stay around." Wallnik, shaking his head, got up as the bailiff handed him Grace's records, and retired to his office.

Grace sat in her chair next to Snyder. She looked around and could not find Alex. She then sat erect, frozen, looking straight ahead, and didn't move or talk. She started twirling and straightening her hair. The door guard came behind Snyder and whispered something in his ear. Grace took no note.

Wallnik returned in seventeen minutes.

Judge Wallnik said, "I have never heard testimony that moved me as much as Miss Pine's. Thirty-seven years on the bench and nothing like that. We still don't know who put the marijuana in the archives, but I would bet my soul that it wasn't the defendant. Miss Pine, please stand."

Snyder stood and helped Grace up.

Judge Wallnik said, "I find for the defendant in this case. You are not guilty on all charges and are free to go." He banged his gavel, stood, and left for his chambers behind the bench.

The courtroom was bereft of noise. Eerie silence. No cheering, no booing, no moans. The room emptied quietly leaving only Snyder, the bailiff, Grace and her jail guard. Grace then turned, expecting to find Alex smiling in the back of the courtroom. He was gone.

Grace said, "What now?"

"You go home. The guard will undo your ankle cuffs and you'll go back with him to the jail, pick up your belongings and sign out."

Grace said, "I don't feel well. I don't see Alex."

Snyder said, "Oh, the door guard told me that he had to go back to the hospital. He apparently said he'd see you tonight, either at home or at the jail. He couldn't wait for the decision. He'll be happy."

"Mr. Snyder, I doubt it. I don't know that he'll even come back," Grace started to speak quickly, "I'm not sure that he'll want to see me. I'm not sure that I can face him. I don't..."

"Grace, stop, I suspect he'll be there for you tonight. If I had to be honest, your relationship could change, but I do think he cares for you."

As Snyder talked, Grace went back to her frozen state.

Once Snyder realized Grace was not listening, he said, "Grace, you need to get up and go with the guard back to the jail and check out. Then you can go home."

Without turning her head, she mumbled, "Where's home. I don't know."

Snyder said, "Do you have a way to Dr. Gordon's apartment, that's your current home?"

"No. I could wait for Alex to come tonight, if he comes, or I could walk home."

Snyder said, "Okay. I'll be over to the jail in thirty minutes and drive you home. Okay?"

When Snyder picked up Grace he said, "Judge Wallnik asked if you would come back to his chambers on Monday morning so we can all talk. He's still concerned about who could have left the drugs. I told him you have school on Monday afternoon. He'd like to see you at seven thirty a.m."

Grace said, "I don't know who left them. I think I should have Alex with me if we talk, don't you think so?"

Snyder replied, "I'll ask if that's okay. But Alex isn't a party to all this."

Grace said, "I think he could be a big part of this, Paul," switching to Snyder's first name for the first time, "I want to go home and wait for Alex. I only hope he shows up."

Snyder nodded and drove Grace to Alex's apartment. Nothing was said in the car as Grace looked out the passenger window and twirled her hair.

Grace let herself in to the dark apartment at six thirty p.m. The darkness was comforting and she chose not to turn on the lights. She found her way to the large chair in the living area, and sat. *I'm going to stay here until he comes back. If I close my eyes, Ezekiel Watkins will appear.* Grace focused on a sliver of light coming around the drawn shades, kept her eyes open, sat, twirled hair and waited.

The phone rang twice until it went to the answering machine. Grace didn't move, look, or change her focus.

At eight fifteen p.m., Alex walked into a dark apartment. On his way home from the hospital he thought about how Grace could be faring. She had told him more than once, "If I have to re-live that terrible time I won't talk about, I don't know how long before I'll be able to function."

When Alex's calls to the apartment, twice, went unanswered, he knew. He thought, *When I open the door, be prepared for anything.* The darkness didn't surprise him at all. "Grace. Grace. I know you're here. Let me help you." Alex turned on the light. The déjà vu of their first encounter came to him immediately. "Grace. I'm here to listen and help you. On the bright side, I didn't run into the counter."

Grace couldn't help but crack the slightest of smiles, but she remained silent.

Alex said, "Did you think I wouldn't return?"

"I didn't know. I don't even know when you left the courtroom. I'm used to people leaving me."

"I told you that I'd be here for you."

"But you left after hearing me talk about that disgusting, awful time. I knew you said you might have to leave, but leaving after I finished, I thought...I thought you wouldn't be able to keep your promise."

"I did hear everything. But we have to trust each other. After Paul Snyer dropped you off, he left a message for me to call him. We talked when I was out of the OR at seven fifteen. He told me that the judge dismissed all the charges. He also told me that you were fragile."

"Alex. Why did you come home? How can you look at me?"

"Did you think for one minute that I haven't known that terrible things had happened to you? I see people all the time with horrendous stresses, emotional, physical, sexual, and combinations of all three. In my mind, I could have envisioned things worse than yours, although not much. Your testimony was riveting. I wasn't repulsed by it. In fact, I was so proud that you had been so brave. Your life has been one trial after another, and yet, each time you've survived. I'm only asking that you do it one more time. One more time for me. No, one more time for you and me. If you'll do that, then I'll do whatever I can to try to make sure that no one ever hurts you again. One more time, Grace. One more time."

As Alex pleaded, tears covered Grace's face, hanging on her upper lip and chin. Alex stood and retrieved a small washcloth and wiped her face.

Grace said, "I'll try. I was so scared you wouldn't want me back."

That night, Grace lay on her right side with her knees drawn tightly. She twirled and straightened a hair strand with her left hand. Alex surrounded her and said , "I'm here, Grace." He didn't move or let go until sleep found Grace. After the turmoil and angst of the past two weeks, the thought of intimacy was leagues away from Alex, light years from Grace.

They awoke at five thirty a.m. and spent awhile in the warmth and safety of the bed.

"Alex, I wish you didn't have to go in for work. I don't want to be alone."

Alex said, "Understood. Why don't you come and make rounds with me and stick around the hospital?"

She smiled, "That's okay, I'll come, but I'll sit in the library. I don't want to be alone. I'll go up and see what a mess they made of the archive door. By the way, Judge Wallnik wants to see me on Monday morning early. If possible, I'd like you to come with me."

Alex thought for a second and said, "I don't know that I can take any more time off. I missed most of last week. I'll have to see if someone can cover for me one more time. I don't think it's going to work out."

Grace said, "I'll understand if you can't. It was more important to me that you were with me this weekend."

Repair of the archive door hadn't begun. A large plywood sheet covered the old doorframe and a sign over the plywood entry read *'Archives Closed. Call Main Library for access.'*

Grace went down a flight, thanked Polly Hopper for her testimony and then went to the Security office to thank Officer Mayeda. In the library, she spent time with Mrs. McPherson, apologizing for the mess made in the archives.

McPherson said, "Grace, how could this happen? Who could be so mean?"

Grace said, "I don't know. I just don't know."

Grace found a comfortable cubicle and she wrote handwritten thank-you notes to Kathleen Cline and Amanda Newell. Next, she wrote, and rewrote, a long note to Beverly and Aaron Gordon, apologizing for putting their son through the arrest and trial, and for paying to fly Kathleen and Amanda to Seattle to testify. She ended with 'I start school on Monday. I hope to make you proud of me', and signed it 'Love, Grace.' Before writing the word, 'love' she hesitated, thinking what other word would work. She added 'P.S. I hope the 'love' doesn't sound obsequious but that's how I feel and I want you to know that I couldn't have done this without you.'

Alex appeared at five thirty p.m., as she was finishing up. "Ready to go. I'm off 'til Monday."

"I wrote a note to your parents, thanking them for sending up the girls to testify."

"That was nice. They'll appreciate that."

"Not as much as I appreciate them."

"Oh, I can't come to the meeting with the judge on Monday. I've missed too much work already. You'll be okay? Say, yes."

"I dunno. I guess, yes."

Alex said, "You know, let's get out of town for the rest of the weekend. If we veg in our apartment, acute radical moping will develop and it's almost incurable. Let's grab some clothes and a toothbrush and drive out to Port Angeles. It's supposed to rain like crazy until Tuesday. Port Angeles will be deserted; we'll get a room overlooking the Straits, light a fire, and put all this behind us. Monday, you start school and we re-invent Grace Pine."

Grace asked, "How will we know where to stay?"

Alex said, "Easy. We drive up there, cruise the main drag until we look at each other and say, 'Stop.'"

Forty-five mile per hour winds and penetrating rain made driving over the Hood Canal Bridge treacherous. Alex, in a death grip with the steering wheel, said, "I don't like driving in this weather. It's scary. Port Townsend is closer; we need to get off the road."

As soon as they entered the town of Port Townsend, a half hour closer than Port Angeles, Grace saw a sign that read 'Bungalows to Rent' with a phone number. Alex made the call.

Twenty minutes later Alex and Grace walked into a one-bedroom bungalow, on a bluff overlooking Puget Sound and the Straits of Juan de Fuca. The bungalow's only windows faced the water. The owner had started a fire in a potbelly stove after the phone call and before the two arrived. The simple room was already comfortable.

As Alex locked the door, Grace took off her coat, threw it on the chair, and said, "Thank you for getting me out of Seattle."

Alex smiled.

Grace started to unzip Alex's coat and he gently held her wrist, stopping her. "Grace, are you ready for this now?" he said. "I'll understand."

Grace said, "Alex, you've stood by me. You promised you would. I've spent my whole life expecting people to disappoint me. You haven't, ever. I'm going to spend this weekend trying to play catch up. I don't want you to be disappointed."

"Grace, you know that I only want you to feel safe and comfortable first. You won't disappoint me."

"Damn right," she said as she pushed Alex's wrist away and unzipped his coat.

Alex, already aroused, started on Grace's blouse.

Grace was frenetic. She couldn't get Alex's shirt unbuttoned fast enough. The faster she tried to undress Alex, the more crazed she became. Her breathing was rapid and deep while her hands and lips trembled in unison. Large beads of sweat were forming on her brow.

Alex grabbed Grace's hands. "Grace, stop. Let me do it. Are you okay? Don't get me wrong, I'm ecstatic...and I want you so badly. But after what you went through these past two weeks, I thought you might want some slow time."

Grace, wobbling forward onto Alex's chest, said, "I don't feel so good. I need to lie down."

Alex helped her to the bungalow's solitary bed with an immense down comforter. He picked her up, coat half on, both shoes, and laid her on the bed. "There you go. Let's talk for a while."

Grace mumbled, "I'm so hot."

Alex said, "I think the room temperature is fine. You've got on too much clothes and you've been sweating and hyperventilating." Alex stood and opened a small paper bag and removed one of the bottles of water they had purchased on the way to the bungalow. "Here, try this."

Alex picked up Grace's head as she sipped on the water and closed her eyes, "Thank you."

Alex said, "Let's get you undressed. You'll feel better. The weight of the world has been on your shoulders your whole life. First, you need to trust me. I'm not going to leave you. Second, let me help you, now, while you need help. I have not one shred of doubt that in time you won't need my help."

Alex had her overcoat, shoes and socks off quickly. "Better?"

Grace nodded.

Alex sat beside Grace and held her hand to his lips and then wiped her brow and face with a cool washcloth. He asked, "Grace, will you have nightmares?"

Grace nodded a bit harder.

"How long?"

"Forever. I've had them, forever. They will always be there. They'll be worse for a while. Please, Alex, don't stop. Help me."

Alex slowly removed her blouse and jeans, then hesitated.

"Please, Alex, don't stop."

He removed her bra, kissed each breast, her lips, nose, each eye and ear and her forehead, and stopped again.

"Please, Alex, don't stop."

"I'm not going to stop, but I want to absorb the beauty that surrounds me." Alex stood and shed his clothes and then slid Grace's panties off. He said, "I know that you are wounded but I see something so special in you. So many mountains we need to conquer, together, if you'll let me help."

"Please, Alex, don't stop. Try to help me forget."

* * * *

On the way back to Seattle on Sunday night, Alex asked, "What do you think the judge wants with you?"

Grace said, "I'm guessing that he wants my thoughts on who put the drugs there?"

"What are you are you going to say."

"I've always assumed that whoever put me in the orphanage, wanted nothing to do with me ever again. I guess I was wrong. But why now?"

Alex said, "It doesn't make sense that they don't want you happy or successful."

Grace, looking out at a calm Hood Canal from the floating bridge, said, "Alex, you are so naïve. I don't think my happiness was ever a concern or they wouldn't have put me in an orphanage in Montana. Maybe it's a warning that they don't want me to look for them. That's scary."

Alex said, "It is scary. Have you ever felt as if you were being followed?"

Grace hesitated, "Not for certain, but a time or two in Missoula and then a day about a week after I started working in the library. Just a sense."

Alex, shaking his head as if angry, bemoaned, "Grace..., Jesus..., you might have said something to me about this."

"It was nothing more than a sense of being followed. Nothing concrete. It would last for a day. If I had told you before, you'd have said I was paranoid."

Alex said, "Perhaps. Are you really scared?"

Grace said, "A little. After the past two weeks, I don't know what to expect or when."

Alex saw Grace's hand clenched in her lap and said, "I dunno. I don't think they want to hurt you, physically, or they could have done that a thousand times in the past two decades."

Grace continued to look out the window as the rain started. "I hope so. I truly hope so."

On Monday morning, Grace and Paul Snyder entered Judge Wallnik's chambers and sat.

Wallnik told Grace how sorry he was about the arrest and trial. Continuing he said, "But, we still don't know why. Have you given it any thought? You must have some idea why someone would do this."

Grace responded, "Of course I have. I don't know who or why. In hindsight, when I left the orphanage and stayed in Missoula for two years, I was certain someone followed me for a day or two, about a year apart. After I left Montana and went to Spokane and then Yakima, I never felt followed at any time, but I had no job and lived in and out of shelters. When I came to Seattle, and I got the job at the med center working in the library, I thought I might have been followed immediately and then about a year later. I even thought the Med Center had called someone to say that *'they found me.'*"

Snyder snickered, "Who would 'they' have called?"

"That's it, I don't know. The only forms I filled out were tax forms."

"So the IRS is following you?"

"Hardly," Grace said, "I never made any money until I got to Seattle, except for the rare odd job that paid me cash."

Wallnik said, "Let's start from the beginning. What do we know for certain? One, you were dropped off at the orphanage mysteriously. Two, despite a ten state search no one found a clue as to your origins. Three, you were possibly followed but not bothered after you left the orphanage, until you met Dr. Gordon and seemed to have your life turned around. Four, the drugs were left in the archives with the express purpose to get you in trouble."

Grace said, "I'd agree. So we know I am being followed."

Snyder added, "That means the people who left you, followed you, and then tried to get you arrested, must be wealthy, in fact, stinking rich. No one drops four to five thousand dollars of marijuana, done by a professional, or a group of professionals, unless they're loaded. Plus, having someone follow you every year or so must have cost money as well."

Wallnik said, "Grace, I'll ask you again. You had to have thought about this. How would you put this all together?"

Grace hesitated and then started playing with her hair, twirling and straightening, "Here's my best guess. Either my father was a man who got a girl pregnant, not his wife, and either, or both, didn't believe in abortion. They've been following me, or more likely, having me followed, to make sure I don't show up one day and embarrass them."

Wallnik interrupted, "Grace, you showing up could be embarrassing, but the reality is that you could have a claim on their estate. Money can never be underestimated."

Grace continued, "Possibility two would be a family who has a daughter that gets pregnant out of wedlock, they don't believe in abortion and they, again, don't want me to show up. From what you've said about the cost of the drug plant, I'd surmise that these are wealthy people."

Snyder interjected, "In both instances, by keeping you poor, you're not likely to find them. Your relationship with Alex changed that."

Grace said, "I was never sure that whoever left me at the orphanage didn't care who I was, what I became, or where I ended up, until now. I'm not sure it's fair to Alex to put him in the position of being hurt, if he stays with me. But Alex said that if they wanted to physically hurt me, they would have done it already."

Snyder said, "I agree, not likely that they'll hurt you. They've had ample opportunity."

Wallnik said, "I'm guessing that you'll never find these people unless they want to be found. But your existence scares them for some reason. To me, that means that money is involved. They know who you are; you don't know who they are. Tough situation. One thing they don't know is how much you know. We could try a little offense to see if they'll back off. We could make a statement to the newspapers. Something similar to, "I know that I have been followed. Whoever you are, I will stop looking for you, if you leave me alone."

Snyder responded, "I don't think that statement is a good idea. Sounds like a threat or a challenge. Grace can't afford to lay down the gauntlet, so to speak."

Grace said, "How about, I know that I've been followed since leaving the orphanage. I want nothing and I hope, now, that they leave me alone."

Wallnik said, "A little less challenging. I like it. I've gotten calls from the editors at Seattle papers. The Prosecutor's Office is not happy about losing their first big case to go public and the papers are looking for a statement. If it's okay with you, I'll give them that quote."

Grace looked at Snyder who nodded agreement. Grace said, "Okay."

Wallnik asked, "What's next for you?"

"I start Seattle Central this afternoon. I have my first visit with a psychiatrist on Wednesday."

"Grace," Wallnik said, "let me know if you find out anything and feel free to call me if you need something." Wallnik shook his head and continued, "Damndest case I've ever had."

Grace circled Wallnik's desk and gave him a hug. He noted, "Not too many defendants in drug cases give me a hug, even if they win. Thanks, we need that every so often."

Grace added, "I won't let you down."

Wallnik said, "I suspect you won't."

Once in the hallway outside the judge's chambers, Grace gave Snyder a hug too. As they separated, Grace said, "Paul, I lied during my testimony"

"You what?"

"Mrs. Watkins tried to stab her husband, but she had such bad arthritis, she couldn't grip the knife very strongly. After she pierced his skin, the knife dropped and Mr. Watkins got off of me, kicked the knife away and started pummeling Mrs. Watkins."

"And then."

"I got off the bed, found the knife and stabbed Mr. Watkins. Mrs. Watkins didn't even know that I had done it. Of course, he knew. Anyway, she figured her feeble attempt was adequate. After I stabbed him, I ran out of the room. My stab wound was the one that hurt him. He never said anything to me about it and no one ever questioned me or suggested that I had hurt him. I've let it lie dormant until now."

Snyder was stunned, "I don't know what to say, Grace."

"Neither do I. In some ways, I wished I had killed him," Grace said without a trace of remorse. "Maybe my nightmares wouldn't be so bad knowing he is dead and can't hurt me anymore."

"Shit, you might want to keep that to yourself."

Grace then turned and walked out of the courthouse to start her new life as a student.

* * * *

Cully Harris dialed Henry Farley at home at 6:00 am, New York time, on Tuesday.

"Farley here."

Harris said, "Get your ass out of bed. Did you read what Pine said to the judge?" Did you?"

Farley, already in 'I fucked up mode', said, "No boss. I heard from Rico that the judge set her free. Apparently, she is allergic to marijuana and they proved it, so they didn't think she was the perp. Is there more?"

Harris could hardly contain his emotions as he exploded over the phone, "She said she knows she's been followed for some time. She hopes we'll leave her alone. That's what she told the judge, God dammit."

"No way, Cully. I had our best men following her. We'd only tail her for a day or two once a year, that's it. We lost her when she left Missoula for a couple of years. When we located her in Seattle through Senator Hopkin's guy at the IRS, we checked on her once or twice. I don't buy her statement. She couldn't have known. I think she and her boyfriend or her lawyer figured out we'd been following her because they had no other leads on the marijuana drop. They were just fishing."

"Farley, this is bad."

"Not really, Cully. She has no idea who you are and never will. I'd stake my reputation on it."

"Right now, your reputation is shit."

"Boss, I told you that if this didn't work she would figure she was being followed. I told you this was a risk. No one could have guessed she couldn't tolerate being around marijuana. Either way, she's not gonna find us, ever."

Harris, a little calmer, said, "So now what?"

284

"Easy. We do nothing. At least not for a while, a year or two. She'll be easy to track. The paper said she's going to school and I'm betting she's still living with that doctor. Cully, you're as safe as a fifty dollar bill in a hooker's crotch."

Harris said, "That's comforting. One more fuck-up and I find another go-to guy."

"They'll be no more fuck-ups, Cully, this was a hiccup, that's all."

"I'll be brief. If you get even an inkling that's she's one fucking inch closer to me, I want something done."

"I get it."

"If I'm the one that gets the inkling she's closer, you're going to be looking for a job in Tijuana shoveling shit."

Chapter 14

Grace had found her first day at Seattle Central Community College not uniquely frustrating. She had elected to take German III, French III, and beginning Japanese. The random language courses she had taken in Missoula and Spokane were difficult to transfer for credit. The registration clerk was reluctant to let Grace take the advanced German and French classes without proof of prior education. After spending an hour waiting to speak to the Registrar, Grace took it upon herself to track down the French and German professors in their offices. Five minutes with each professor and a phone call was all Grace needed to enroll in the classes she wanted.

On Wednesday, Grace had her first appointment with Marilyn Crayman, M.D., the psychiatrist classmate of Aaron Gordon. If meeting Alex had been good fortune for Grace, Marilyn Crayman was a winning lottery ticket. From the first minute of their first meeting, Grace knew she was safe.

At the end of their first session, Crayman said, "Grace, before you go, we have a little housekeeping to do. Aaron Gordon is going to help defray the costs of these sessions, but that does not give him any right to know what we talk about. I don't even have to send a letter thanking him for sending you to me. How would you like me to handle it?"

Without hesitation, Grace replied, "Dr. Crayman, I've tried to keep no secrets from Alex and I don't see any reason to do differently with Dr. and Mrs. Gordon. They've been kind and so helpful, but, also, they've put their trust in me by helping me with school."

"Grace, you spent two weeks nursing Beverly, who I haven't seen in twenty years. Heck, that's at least a couple of years of tuition right there. You don't have to...."

Grace held her hand up and interrupted, "Dr. Crayman, let them know whatever they want. I know them well enough to realize they're not going to ask for real personal stuff. Just use your judgment. I trust you and I trust them."

"Grace, I can tell that we're going to get along fine."

Grace saw Dr. Crayman weekly for six months. Crayman left no stone unturned and dwelt on her 'marijuana' rapes and emotional problems with abandonment by her unknown parents, the friends made at the orphanage and the Ostergards. Crayman, with Grace's renewed permission called Aaron Gordon once, at the six-month mark.

After the usual pleasantries, Crayman got down to business.

"Aaron, Grace said I could call you. She is so thankful that you and Beverly made her visits possible. She is a remarkable young woman and I know she will accomplish great things. Her story is replete with one hardship after another, as you know. Many people, in fact, most, would have disappeared into the woodwork, but not Grace. She has incredibly deep resilience that allowed her to bounce back. I believe that it's something she was born with. I've seen it both ways, either you have resilience or you sink. She, without help or assistance, was able to sublimate her issues and keep going. Remarkable. Just remarkable. I'm going to see her less frequently for a while, and then, maybe in a year or so, only as needed. I'll keep in touch with you, if need be. Thanks again for letting me see her. Aaron, Grace is simply remarkable."

By the middle of summer session the following year, and with the help of her junior college language professor's letters and phone calls, The University of Washington accepted Grace as a transfer student into her sophomore year.

Giddy with the excitement of her acceptance to a major four-year university, Grace planned a surprise dinner for Alex. She had hoped to hold off the news until the middle of the meal, but didn't get past the busboys bringing water. She now knew that she didn't want Perrier or Pellegrino.

Alex, just as excited, said, "Grace Pine, I am so proud of you. So incredibly proud."

Grace said, "Thank you. Thank you for changing my life and believing in me."

"Grace, I think it's time that you consider changing names. I mean I can tell you're going to be some big academic language specialist."

"Alex, that is so sweet, but you have no idea what I will be."

"I do, and Pine was given to you arbitrarily. I can't see you using that name professionally."

"Alex, what are you talking about? I'm okay with Pine, arbitrary or not. What did you have in mind?"

"I was thinking more in the line of Gordon. Grace Gordon. It sounds so professional."

"Alex, that's your name."

"Exactly," Alex reached into his coat pocket, pulled out a small blue felt box, took a knee, and asked.

The wedding was held in San Francisco five days before Christmas. Anthony Wallnik, the judge from her trial, flew down from Seattle to preside.

Chapter 15

Seattle – years later

Dr. Grace Pine Gordon, Associate Professor of Linguistics, at the University of Washington, sat in her den watching Elizabeth Gordon, age 4 ½, and her brother, Mark, age 3, look through photographs taken after a family retreat in the Napa Valley with the entire Gordon clan.

Elizabeth, or Ellie, as she was called, had a small bone to pick with her mother.

Ellie was looking at pictures of Aaron and Beverly Gordon and said, "Mommy, who was your mommy and daddy? I know Grandpa Aaron and Grandma Bev were daddy's mommy and daddy but we never talk about your mommy and daddy, and we never see any pictures of them. All the kids, well mostly all the kids, in pre-school have four grandmas and grandpas. Even cousin Kevin has four grandmas and grandpas." Arms crossed, Elizabeth awaited an answer.

Grace said, "Come here and sit with me, Ellie." On the couch in the family room, Grace twirled and straightened her own hair with the left hand and put her right arm around her daughter and kissed her on the forehead. "The truth is I don't know who my mommy and daddy were. If a child doesn't have or know who their mommy and daddy are, they are called 'orphans.' When I was young, orphans lived in special homes called orphanages. So I grew up in an orphanage not knowing who my mommy and daddy were, and I still don't know. That was a long time ago."

While Ellie mused over the explanation, Grace added, "Today, orphans are given out to special kinds of people called foster parents. Foster parents help raise the children until they become the real parents or find others to be real parents."

Ellie sat for a while. "Are you sad because you don't know your mommy and daddy? I'd be sad if I didn't know you and daddy. Really, really sad."

Grace said, "I was sad for a long time. But when I met your daddy he made me so happy that I wasn't as sad. Then, when I had you and Mark, I was so, so happy, that I forgot that I was ever sad. That's how happy I am."

Ellie thought a bit, "Still, I'd be sad not knowing. Did you ever look for them? Maybe they are hiding close by?"

"The police and the orphanage, where I lived, searched for a year, but they never found anybody who was my mommy or daddy. That's why we don't have any pictures like we do for Grandma Bev or Grandpa Aaron. Aunt Samantha and Uncle Brett know who their mommies and daddies were, so that's why your cousin, Kevin, has four grandparents."

Ellie said, "Mommy, maybe when I'm a little bigger, I'll find them for you. Then, I'll have four grandparents like Kevin."

Grace was tearing but didn't want to show Ellie so she kept hugging her until the crying stopped.

Ellie, all seeing, said, "It's okay, Mommy. You and me, we'll find them."

Grace hadn't seen Marilyn Crayman for fourteen months. She called Crayman's office to make an appointment.

Four months later, Grace came downstairs after seven a.m. to find Ellie and Mark playing in the family room. Alex had already left for the hospital. She flipped on the TV and clicked 52 to get CNN. Actress Lena Loman, on probation for drunk driving and disorderly conduct, had been on the Jay Leno show when she went into the audience to punch a heckling spectator during an ad break. Loman's cuffing and subsequent arrest would fill the airways and sell an extra million copies of People, The National Enquirer and Star magazines. The almost comedic event for the trailer trash star would fill the airways when nothing else newsworthy was available. Grace wouldn't have time to read the NY Times that morning, so leaving the TV on CNN, Grace walked into the kitchen to make breakfast when the phone rang.

"Hey Grace. What's up?" was the typical start of Samantha's three-time a week phone call to her sister-in-law. Samantha had been married for six years to Brett Adamson, a San Francisco stockbroker. Their son, Kevin, was a few months younger than Ellie.

"Hi, Sam. Getting Ellie and Mark breakfast and then Ellie's off to school and the nanny comes in for Mark and I head off to work. Same old, same old."

"Ain't it the truth? Kevin's still wetting his bed every three nights or so. Doing the sheets again this morning. Alex tells me it will go away and not to worry. Mom told me Alex wet his bed until he was seven. I'm thinking you're lucky having a girl."

"Sam, you don't know drama the way I do. Every day. Alex, Mark, Brett and Kevin are easy, you can see what their thinking a day before and a mile ahead. Ellie is in a whole other league. Didja see the crap on TV, Lena Loman popped a spectator on Leno last night?"

"Yep. God, I love talking to you. Because we love the same crap." Both laughed.

Little Kevin Adamson walked into his mother's kitchen and said, "Mommy. Mommy. I saw Aunt Grace on TV."

Sam said, "Did you hear that. Kevin said he saw you on TV. What did you do?"

Grace chuckled, "Hardly. Unless it's a felony to watch worthless TV. Did you get the house rented for Christmas break in Cabo?"

Sam replied, "Yep. December nineteenth to January second. Make sure you get your flights booked."

Ellie then walked into the kitchen and said, "Mommy, I'm hungry. When are we having breakfast? Did you know you were on TV this morning?"

Grace said, "I wasn't on TV."

Ellie said, "Yes. I saw you."

Talking back into the phone, Grace said, "Sam, did you hear that, Ellie says she saw me on TV, too."

Sam responded, "Now I'm going to have to watch until we see what they saw. You off to work?"

"Yeah, I've got to meet with my post docs at eight fifty, then two classes. I'll be home at two thirty in time for Ellie."

"I'm free this morning. After Kevin leaves for school, I'll watch."

Grace called Samantha at lunch. "Did you find my face? Please tell me I'm having an affair with Brad Pitt and they caught me."

Sam said, "I watched for an hour and didn't see anything. Kevin was certain it was you."

"So was Ellie. What do we do?"

"I think you can buy CNN stories. I know someone at CNN here in San Francisco. I'll find out."

That evening, Samantha called Grace back. "I just got off the phone with my friend at CNN. We can download footage on the web. Since Kevin and Ellie both saw it at the same time, he's sure what the kids' saw was a national feed through Atlanta or New York. Go to www.imagesource.cnn.com and look at seven a.m. to seven thirty, Pacific Time. I'll do the same after dinner."

While preparing dinner, Grace watched the half-hour of CNN and saw nothing. She called Samantha after dinner.

"Sam, I watched the footage and saw nada."

"Me, neither. I'm having Kevin watch it on my computer screen. I had to bribe him with a mini-box of Fruit Loops. I'm a bad mom. I'll call you back."

Grace asked Ellie if she'd watch the footage. "No. I don't want to watch that," Ellie replied.

"How about if I give you some Gummy Bears while you watch?" Grace bargained, comforted that Samantha had done the same.

Ellie, arms crossed, "No, I don't want to watch."

The phone rang. "Grace, Kevin found it again. I had missed it. Go to seven thirteen a.m. It's a twenty second spot showing the governor of Michigan signing gun control legislation. Forget the governor, watch to his left, a woman standing behind him. I missed it when I watched earlier. Grace, I would have sworn it was you."

Grace, grabbing Ellie, ran back to her computer, put Ellie on her lap, and moved the time bar to seven twelve a.m.

"Ellie, tell me what you see."

"There you are mommy, right there. That's you. You're twirling your hair like you always do."

"Sweetie. That's not me, just someone who looks a little like me, maybe older. I don't know who it is, but we'll find out."

Grace called Sam back. "Sam, who is that? I'm guessing twenty years older, maybe twenty-five. Do you think you could find out? I don't think I could do it emotionally."

"Grace, I will have a name for you in a couple of days, even if I have to fly to Michigan. Hey, I'm an old Wolverine. Go Blue."

Grace, smiled at her sister-in-law's undying love for the U of M, said, "I'm guessing that woman either works for the governor, is a legislator, or some gun control lobby person."

Sam said, "Grace, I'm on it."

"Sam, I've got to get in to see my therapist."

"I'd tell her it's a bone-crunching emergency. You know, Grace, this is likely to be a wild goose chase. Although you have to admit, she looks a bit like you and that hair twirling deal. We'll see. Let me know what my brother thinks. Call me back tonight."

Alex called his sister that evening.

"Hey, Sam. How's everybody?"

"Fine, Alex. Did you see the footage?"

"Yeah, unbelievable. She's older than Grace but the resemblance is striking and then there's that hair deal. Kevin and Ellie split the finder's fee on this one, eh?"

Samantha opined, "Bro, Grace has been in such a good place for so long. I'm not sure this is going to go well, whether we find something or not. If we don't find anything, it'll rekindle some old bad memories. If we find something, we may not like what we find. Be prepared."

"Sam, you find the lady's name. We'll go from there."

Two days passed and Samantha called Grace.

"Grace, you sitting?"

"Sam, tell me what you found, sitting or not."

Samantha explained, "Her name is Melissa Friedman. She's a Michigan State senator. Her maiden name was Kaplan. She grew up in the Detroit area, or the northern suburbs. Graduated from Michigan in 1994, BA in sociology. Law school at Wayne State. Practiced trusts and estate law for four years, then ran for the Michigan House of Representatives, won and served three terms. This is her second term as a state senator. She's maxed out in the Michigan House and Senate because of term limits. She's a socially liberal Democrat, but fiscally conservative, which is why she's been elected and re-elected. She's had a bug about increasing gun registration her entire career. Depending on who's elected next year, she's likely to get a judgeship."

"How do we do this, Sam? I can't call and say, 'you look like me and twirl your hair like me, are you my missing sister?'"

"Grace, why not. I mean you're a professor of linguistics at a prestigious university. You've published papers, gotten scholarships, helped out the US government. Shit, that ought to get you in the front door."

"You think?"

Sam giggled and said, "Hey, you're not the floozy you were before the Gordon family met you."

"Sam, you're not helping."

"Grace, first, we've got to keep this light. Let's see if anyone in your department, or someone Alex knows, has some traction at one of the Michigan colleges, U of M, Michigan State, Wayne. That might be a good lead-in. Option two is call her office, make an appointment and see what happens."

Grace said, "Maybe that's the best. Getting someone else involved could weird them out."

Sam said, "How about you and Ellie go there. After all, Ellie and Kevin found her. Or all four of you."

Grace thought for a second and said, "Might take the edge off....no, I need to do this myself."

Sam said, "I did the all the leg work, the ball's in your court. Senator Friedman's office number is 517-737-1000. Try to get an appointment, maybe her last one of the day. Send her your CV first. That'll get her curious."

"Senator Friedman's office. Ruth speaking. How may I assist you?"

"Hello, Ruth. My name is Dr. Grace Gordon. I am a associate professor of Linguistics at the University of Washington in Seattle, and I'd appreciate an appointment to see the senator."

"The senator has open hours for constituents every Thursday from one to four p.m., fifteen minute slots. But you said you're from Washington State, right?"

"Yes, Seattle, Washington, to be exact. I've never been in Michigan."

"What's this about?"

"It's so bizarre and complicated, I could never explain it over the phone."

"Try me. I've been with the Senator for fifteen years."

"Tell you what, Ruth. Let me send you my CV, read it, call the Department of Linguistics at the University of Washington to confirm who I am, then I'll tell you. Otherwise, you'll hang up on me."

"Have it your way. Fax number is 517-737-1001."

"Got it. It'll be there in five minutes. My home number is on the bottom, call that."

Fifteen minutes later, Grace's phone rang. "Dr. Gordon, this is Senator Melissa Friedman. How can I help you?"

"Senator Friedman, I didn't expect you to call."

"My long time assistant, Ruth, took your call and then read your CV, and then I read your CV. Impressive. Bachelor of Arts, Magna. A special scholarship from the US Department of State to study translational linguistics. PhD. Tenured position at the University of Washington. But again, how can I help you?"

Grace said, "I was hoping to come to Michigan to meet you."

"I take it you're not in Michigan now?"

"Senator, I've never been to Michigan."

Friedman, skipping issues, asked, "I also see from your CV that you helped translate for the President at the G8 conference last July."

"Yes, I did. Were you there?"

"Actually I was. Someone from the University of Washington was translating four languages at a roundtable. I remember a colleague saying you looked like me."

"That was me, Senator."

"Astonishing, to me at least. I'm terrible with languages, for some people it's easy, I guess."

Grace said, "I've always had an ear for it."

Friedman said, "Some people are born with it, good gene pool."

"I wouldn't know that. Senator. *She has no idea what I meant by that.* I'd like to send you a DVD taken of me at that same conference. I'll send you only a three-minute segment. My husband, Alex, an Associate Professor of Urology at Seattle Med, took it of me while I was waiting to translate. Please look at the video and call me back."

"Professor Gordon, this doesn't make any sense at all. What possibly am I going to learn watching you wait to translate?"

Grace continued, "You'll see. You might want to watch this with your family, if possible. I'll send it out this afternoon, Fedex overnight. I'll include my contact information, so you can call me. I have your office address in Lansing, that okay?"

Friedman said, "That'll work fine. This doesn't make any sense."

Grace said, "It will."

300

* * * * *

"Cully, Farley here."

"What's up."

"I took care of the Louisiana deal for you. Ran money through a new bank in Atlanta to the Caymans. Won't be any trouble. The guy will eat shit for you if you ask."

"Good. Anything else?"

"Naw. Seattle's been dead for seven years. She's an associate professor and some big muckety-muck academic type. She's not looking and she's got nowhere to look."

* * * * *

Grace dropped the DVD at a Fedex box in the University district at two p.m. The delivery time to Lansing, Michigan, would be the next morning before eleven a.m.

Grace slept poorly and ignored Alex's pleadings. "Grace, no matter what happens, your life, your family, the ones who love you, your accomplishments aren't going to change."

Grace had two classes to teach the next morning but her mind was two thousand miles to the east. She rushed back to her office at noon, three p.m. eastern time, to see if any calls had come from Melissa Friedman. They hadn't.

Grace picked up the phone three times to call Melissa Friedman, getting as far as six numbers before hanging up. *I've gotta stop fixating on this. It's probably nothing.*

At three p.m., Pacific Time, Grace's office line rang.

"Dr. Gordon, this is Melissa Friedman calling. I saw the DVD segment with my daughter, Joan, who's a senior at Michigan. We both think the coincidences are remarkable, but just that, remarkable. You and I twirl our hair, as did my maternal grandmother, Rose Cohen. We know of no one else who did. Anyway, there's no way, we can think of that we're related. How did you find me?"

Grace told Melissa about the CNN footage seen by her daughter, Ellie, and nephew, Kevin.

Melissa said, "Such a coincidence. Have you talked to your family about this? They must think it's remarkable as well."

Grace wasn't sure where to start and said nothing.

Melissa said, "Dr. Gordon, you there?"

Grace said, "Senator, there's more to this story. Would you allow me to come to Michigan to talk to you? I promise not to try to make a big deal about this, but I need to talk to you in person."

The senator said, "Hold on a second while I check my schedule..." "How's Thursday or Friday next week at four p.m."

Grace said, "I'll be there. Friday at four."

Ruth, the senator's assistant vetted Grace as much as she could through the State of Michigan's information system and came up with no more information than was on Grace's CV.

* * * *

When Grace walked into the office of Senator Friedman, her long-time assistant, Ruth did a double take. "Wow, you two do look like sisters."

Dr. Grace Helena Pine Gordon and Senator Melissa Kaplan Friedman sat opposite each other in the senator's office.

"Dr. Gordon, please call me Melissa, if I can call you Grace."

Grace nodded, "Of course."

Melissa said, "Okay, you're here, what more is there to this remarkable coincidence?"

Grace said, "During our phone call last week, you asked me to check with my family. There's the rub, I have no family that I've ever known. At the age of two or so, a night nurse discovered me in an orphanage in Missoula, Montana. Despite a ten state search, the orphanage and the Montana police found no record of my existence, or family. Of course, that doesn't mean I come from Michigan but it is as likely as any place, other than Mars or Jupiter."

"I'm listening," said Melissa.

"Finding you on CNN is the first clue of any kind, anywhere, of my possible origin. I know it's crazy and I realize that it may be a cruel coincidence, but I had to follow the lead. I have to tell you that the family that dumped me so unceremoniously at the orphanage has kept tabs on where I've been and what I'm doing."

Melissa, confused, asked, "How is it possible that they know you and you don't know them?"

Grace then quickly explained the unsubstantiated followings she suspected and the bogus marijuana drop.

Grace added, "I want to let you know that I have no interest in any inheritance from your family. I will sign any document that relinquishes any claims. I am so fortunate to have a successful career and a successful husband. Money is not, nor will ever be, an issue."

Melissa nodded, "That's good. The first thing my dad and uncle would say is, "She's looking for *gelt*."

"I don't need the money."

"You speak Yiddish."

"I speak German and learned a good deal of Yiddish to impress my in-laws, who are Jewish. They needed to know they couldn't speak Yiddish around me, expecting me not to understand."

Melissa laughed and said, "That's funny, Grace. What do we do next?"

"Family tree. Starting with your grandmother, I believe you said, Rose Cohen. We'd need to trace her lineage."

"Rose Cohen is the only member of her family to have survived the flu epidemic of 1917. She died in 1977. She was raised by an unrelated aunt. She met my grandfather, Abe Kaplan, in Detroit, in the '30s. They had two sons, my dad, Max, and my uncle, Jerome. I am an only child, as far as I know. I've had only one pregnancy and haven't stored any eggs. My uncle Jerome had two sons, Ben and Phillip. Ben, a few months older than me, died in a motor vehicle accident driving home from his first year at Harvard. He was nineteen and he had no children. Phillip, three years older, is gay, and lives with his partner in San Francisco. Other than me, and my grandmother, no one had the habit of twirling and straightening their hair."

"Not such a big family," said Grace.

"Right. Of course, Rose Cohen could have had relatives in Europe that lived through the Holocaust, and came to the US. I don't know of any and neither did my grandmother."

"Melissa, do you think your family would undergo DNA testing to see if we're related, at my expense?"

"Good question. I don't know. All we can do is ask. If no one knows of an illegitimate child, they should say 'yes' and put this absurdity behind you."

Grace said, "Where do we start?"

Melissa thought for a moment, "I know where we don't start. My uncle, Jerome, and my aunt, Helen, have never gotten over the loss of Ben. They're accepting of Phillip's lifestyle. He was always different. When Phillip came out, no one was surprised, except Phillip. Everyone already knew. Not having any grandchildren to carry on the name, so to speak, hurts. I don't know what they'd do if asked, so I'd start with me and my father."

Grace said, "I'm embarrassed to ask you this. You'll need to ask your dad if there's any chance he has a child you don't know of, and if he ever did any sperm donations. If I'm in the family, in any way, testing your dad should be adequate."

Melissa chuckled, "No problem. I can ask dad anything. My mom, Celeste, that's another story, but you're lucky you're not looking at their family."

"I'm here until Sunday morning. If your dad wants to meet me before I head back to Seattle, let me know. I'll be staying in Detroit at the Westin, downtown, on Washington. I checked facilities that are certified and are able to do DNA evaluations here in the Detroit area. DNA Detections seems to be the best and they are certified. They have an office in Southfield and one downtown on Woodward. The downtown office has walk-in hours on Saturday from eleven a.m. to three p.m. The one in Southfield needs an appointment. Here are the numbers and addresses."

Melissa said, "I'm guessing my dad is not likely he'll ask to meet you, but we'll see."

A hour later Grace's cell phone rang.

"Grace, Melissa Friedman here. My dad wants to meet you. He thinks this is all crazy but his curiosity got the best of him. He says there is no way in hell that he's had another child other than me. How about we pick you up at your hotel at 1 p.m."

"Thank you so much for doing this. To be honest, I'm not sure what I'm hoping for."

306

"Grace, I'm hoping that this is a coincidence. I don't need any drama in my life now. Sorry, if that's not what you want, but I don't see anyone in my family being related to you."

Grace was sitting in the lobby of the Westin Book Cadillac hotel at twelve forty-five p.m. Subconsciously twirling her hair, she was re-reading a paper she was writing for the Journal of Linguistics on *Musical Interlude Variabilities in the Evolution of European Languages.* The paper was ready for submission, but she wanted one more run through. Turning pages and twirling hair, Grace didn't notice Melissa Friedman and her father, Max Kaplan, standing less than twenty feet from her.

Grace heard a faint voice, "Dad, do you need to sit down." Grace looked up to find Melissa Friedman leading an elderly man to a chair across from the couch she was sitting on.

Grace put her paper down and rushed to help Melissa. Grace said, "Are you okay. Can I do something? Melissa, if he feels faint, then let's move him to the couch and elevate his legs. If anything I've learned from my husband, it's that."

Grace and Melissa led Max Kaplan to the couch and had him lie down. Grace put a pillow under his legs. A bellhop ran over, but Melissa said, "I think he'll be fine, he just needed to lie down."

Melissa held her father's hand while Grace returned with a wet paper towel.

Melissa whispered to Grace, "On the way here, he was joking about what a waste of time this was. He said to me, "I figure this girl is a total *meshugana."* I told him you may be a bunch of things, but crazy, you're not. I told him a little about me seeing you work at the G-8 Summit. He said, "Obviously from the other side." He laughed, and then said to me, "I don't, nor does she know the first side, so how can we know what the 'other' side is like." He thought this was all comical."

"Anyway, he saw you on the couch as we walked in. I didn't need to point you out. Dad said, "Oh my living God. I can't believe what I'm seeing. That could be my mother or daughter." He grabbed my arm, tightly, for support and I asked him if he needed to sit. That's when you saw me."

Max Kaplan's forehead was moist with sweat but his eyes were open and he said, "I'd like a drink of water."

Grace found the bellhop and she returned with a bottle of water. Max was sitting up, alert and talking to his daughter.

"Thank you for the water, Miss uh..."

Grace said, "It's Grace, Grace Gordon."

Max took a big swig from the bottle and recapped it. "I'm sorry for scaring you."

Grace said, "Actually, I think it was me that scared you."

Max said, "You can say that again."

Grace said, "I think it was me that scared you."

"I was kidding about saying it again."

Grace was smiling, "I know, I was kidding saying it again. My husband's family goes through that routine every time they hear, *you can say that again.*"

"You looked like the pictures of my mother as a younger woman. I wasn't prepared. And then you were twirling your hair, just like she did."

"Dad," Melissa said, "Are you feeling better, we have an appointment at the DNA clinic."

Max nodded and the two women helped him to his feet. He walked steadily and without assistance to Melissa's car, but said nothing.

Max pleaded to sit in the back, despite Grace and Melissa suggesting he'd be more comfortable in the front passenger's seat. Grace and Melissa traded stories, mostly with laughing, about their daughters. Max sat quietly, looking out the window. Every so often, the girls in the front would hear him say, "What does this mean?"

* * * *

The DNA clinic intake person was knowledgeable and efficient. Max, Melissa and Grace filled out family histories. Grace's page was largely blank. The intake person then gave a full discussion of the breadth of the DNA testing limitations. The only sure outcomes were paternity, maternity, full-siblingship, or half-siblingship. DNA testing would not be able to guarantee any other relationship. In Grace's case, since neither parent was known, the results would be even more sketchy. After signing disclaimers, Grace Gordon, Melissa Kaplan Friedman and Max Kaplan had the inside of their mouths swabbed to collect cells for DNA analysis. Grace and Melissa would receive the results in the mail in about seven days. Grace had web searched DNA Detections and knew they required prepayment for any services whether covered by insurance or not. After Melissa's call the day before, Grace had visited a local Detroit branch of Wells Fargo, withdrew funds and paid for the DNA Detection services with cash.

After the testing, the three, subdued and quiet, walked out to Melissa's car.

Melissa said, "Dad, Grace, are you two hungry?"

Max said, "A little, maybe."

Grace had seen the same relationship between Alex, Samantha and their parents. When in doubt, ask if someone wants to eat. She answered, "Alex, that's my husband, told me that Detroit has great Jewish delis. Seattle has *bubkes*, nothing."

Max started to laugh at Grace's perfect intonation and use of Yiddish. He said, "Melissa, let's go to the Star."

Grace continued, "If it's not *glatt kosher*, I'm not going."

Max continued to howl. "Grace, Melissa told me you were raised in a Catholic orphanage in where, Montana, Idaho, whatever? How do you know all this stuff?"

"The sisters of St. Joseph's Orphanage were all Jewish girls, in hiding. Their parents wanted them to marry doctors or dentists, the sisters wanted cowboys, so they snuck off to Montana."

At the deli, Max asked Grace to re-tell him her story. "I know Melissa knows all this, and she's told me what she remembers, but I'd like it from the horse's mouth."

Grace told them everything she thought they needed to hear, other than the abuse and the marijuana portions. They were particularly interested in her wanderings until she met Alex.

Melissa drove Grace back to her hotel. Grace shook hands with Max, now sitting in the front.

Melissa got out of the car and gave Grace a hug and whispered, "Grace, I'm still doubtful that we have any relationship, but, nonetheless, I'd like to stay close."

Grace nodded assent, "That's a promise."

Melissa drove away and looked over to her dad and said, "Well."

Max, looking forward, said, "She's Ben's daughter. I didn't need the testing."

Melissa yanked the car over to the curb. "Dad, what are you talking about?"

"I took one look at her, watched her move, her facial expressions. Whatever. She is Jerry and Helen's granddaughter. I didn't need the testing, but we'd better have proof before we approach your aunt and uncle."

"Why are you so certain? Why didn't I know about this before?"

"We were never certain. Ben had called Jerry and Helen to tell them he had something important to tell them that night he died. They needed to talk whatever time he got home. He, of course, never arrived. His roommate, I can't remember his name, told me that he had received a call just before leaving Harvard from a girl he had met at prep school the summer before. She had never returned his calls, so he gave up and then, as he's leaving school, she telephones him, collect, and Ben accepted the charge. The roommate, Brad or Brent or something with a B, told me all this at the funeral. He said Ben was acting as if he was in semi-shock after the call, telephoned Helen, barely said good-bye, and left."

Melissa, mind whirring, said, "That doesn't mean he had a child."

Max continued, "He did hear Ben give the girl his home number and told her to call him the next day. Jerry and Helen never received a call that I know of and I'm sure they would have told me. The roommate sent me the number from their phone bill. I called it once or twice. It rang and rang and I threw it in a folder somewhere."

"Dad, I still don't get it. Why do you think Ben had a child?"

"I'm guessing but I don't think he knew anything about it until the call. Not Ben. He would have talked to Jerry and Helen. The dates are perfect, within a few months here or there. He met the girl at the end of the summer and then found out about it ten months later."

"Dad, this is all supposition."

312

"Melissa, at this point, yes. But if Grace Gordon has our gene pool, it fits. Remember, Grace doesn't know her exact birth date. But I can do the math. To be safe, we may need to get your cousin, Phillip, to get DNA tested too, unless you can think of some way we can find something with Ben's DNA on it."

Melissa said, "I don't think we're exhuming any bodies."

Max said, "Let's see where we are with the DNA. Not a word to your mom, yet."

Grace flew back to Seattle, resumed teaching and mothering and tried not to think about the Kaplans.

* * * * *

One week later, a Friday at 4:00 p.m., she received a Fedex envelope from DNA Detections. Grace opened the envelope the way a gambler would look at his cards, drawing to an inside straight.

Analysis #1

Grace Gordon, female. Max Kaplan, male

Paternity – <0.001%

Sibling - <0.001%

Grandparent – 12.5 %

Uncle – 18%

Grand Uncle – 32.5%

First or Second Cousin – 14.5 %

Conclusion: These data suggest that some relationship between Grace Gordon and Max Kaplan may exist.

Analysis #2

Grace Gordon, female. Melissa Kaplan Friedman, female

Paternity – <0.001%

Sibling - <0.001%

Grandparent – 10.5 %

Grand Aunt – 8.5%

First or Second Cousin – 16%

Conclusion: These data suggest that some relationship between Grace Gordon and Melissa Friedman may exist.

Given her father's premonition about Ben Kaplan and Grace Gordon, Melissa spent 4 hours in her parent's garage searching though boxes. On Friday, the same day that the envelopes arrived, Melissa had found the item she needed to answer questions – she hoped.

When she and Ben were nine and a half, they both lost their first molar on the same day. July 4th. The tooth fairy made the appropriate visit to both that night. Jerry and Helen Kaplan decided the coincidence was significant and had the teeth placed in a Lucite cube and inscribed *Ben Kaplan / Melissa Kaplan - First Molar - July 4, 1958*. Ben received the cube at Hanukah later that year. Ben was disgusted at the thought of the tooth on his shelf and gave the cube to Melissa. The cube stayed on her shelf until she was thirteen when Melissa scrapped everything from childhood and replaced them with Rolling Stone posters. Placed in a box and forgotten, until now, was the Lucite cube.

Not waiting for permission from her father, or her aunt or uncle, Melissa took the cube to DNA Detections. She didn't know which tooth was hers and which was Ben's, but she paid to have both analyzed. Teeth, being harder to analyze, would take ten to fourteen days, if DNA analysis was possible at all. She told her father about leaving the teeth a week later, so he couldn't talk her out of it.

Melissa called Grace, "Grace, I don't know how to analyze these numbers. It suggests we have some common genes and that's about it."

Melissa did not tell Grace that she had taken the baby molars in for testing.

Grace asked, "Could you arrange to have your aunt, uncle and cousin, Phillip, tested?"

Melissa hesitated, "That's probably the next step, but one fraught with angst on my part. My aunt and uncle have spent the past three decades trying to get over the death of Ben. They've accepted the reality of their situation. I'd say that they are in a good place right now after going through all the stages of grief. If we bring this up, the whole cycle could start again. I don't know what they'll do. I doubt that Phillip would go along with it anyway. He and the rest of the family, despite being accepting of his lifestyle, haven't gotten along. Said another way, his partner of the past twenty years is a flaming asshole who makes life difficult. Give me some time to work on this. I'll need my dad's input."

"Melissa, thank you, for everything. I'm sorry to put you through all this."

"Grace, you're welcome. To be honest, I'm still not sure how I want this to turn out."

"I understand. Please keep in touch."

* * * * *

"What do you want, Henry, dammit?" Farely rarely had news that would cheer Harris up.

"Well, it's probably nothing, but I know that you like to be kept in the loop. Our Seattle deal flew to Detroit ten days ago, stayed two nights in downtown Detroit, and returned to Seattle. I know you want to know if she comes anywhere near New York, Boston or Detroit."

"Are you worried?"

"Not usually, but yes, because I don't know why she went. Our sources send me her credit card bills and bank statements every month. I peruse them personally. There's nothing that gives me any clues. Car, some food and the hotel and then she returned to Seattle. Strangely, her bank statement did include a withdrawal of sixteen hundred dollars from a local Wells Fargo made out to cash. None of this makes sense. She didn't buy a car."

"What are you guessing?"

"I would have guessed she was interviewing for an academic job or maybe doing some high level translating for GM or Ford. I couldn't find any postings that Michigan or Wayne State are looking for someone with her background. I can't imagine what the cash was for."

"You watch her real good until you have more information. I want some plan B options."

"I understand. The only comfort is that I'm certain no one in Detroit knew she existed. The only way they could know is from us."

"Farley, I want some plan B options."

"Got it."

* * * *

Melissa met with her father twice trying to plan the approach to Ben's parents if the DNA confirmed Max's suspicions. After an hour of discussion, they decided on playing no games, no subterfuges, no piecemealing it, just come out with the whole story. Max and Melissa would sit Ben's parents down in their living room and tell them Grace's story. Max, with Melissa's agreement, decided against telling his brother and sister-in-law about Max's conversations at the time of the funeral with Ben's roommate. That could wait.

Melissa made one call to the Attorney General of the State of Michigan, Harry Short, a former member of the Michigan house. Harry and Melissa were on opposite ends of the spectrum when it came to gun control, in fact, most issues. Politics aside, both respected the other. Melissa explained the arrival of Grace and wondered if Harry could find out anything about Grace, particularly about her stay in the orphanage and anything he could find from her last seven years in Seattle.

Harry said, "Shit, Mel, talk about coincidence, she just shows up one day. I'll do what I can."

Eleven days after Melissa brought in the teeth, she received an envelope, similar to the one received earlier from DNA Detections.

Analysis #3

Grace Gordon, female. Tooth #2 ?Melissa Kaplan Friedman, female (based on tooth pulp specimen)

The DNA matches the DNA previously supplied by Melissa Kaplan Friedman.

Analysis #4

Grace Gordon, female. Tooth #2 ?Ben Kaplan?, male (based on tooth pulp specimen)

Paternity – >99.995%

Conclusion: These data confirm that Grace Gordon and Ben Kaplan are daughter and father.

Melissa caught her breath, shut the door to her office and called her father.

"Dad, the test came back. Grace Gordon is Ben's daughter. No equivocation."

Max said, "I knew it. *Oy.* I'm dreading the discussion we're going to have with Jerry and Helen."

Melissa said, "Dad, is there any chance that Ben could have done some sperm donations while he was at school."

Max said, "I doubt it but after Grace Gordon appeared, anything is possible."

Melissa added, "Dad, the dates of Grace's birth suggest that the pregnancy occurred before, or just after, he got to Harvard. It's doubtful that he would have donated sperm while still in high school. We'll have to ask."

Max asked, "When are you free to come down to Bloomfield Hills?"

Melissa said, "I'll come tonight. There's another issue."

"What's that?"

"We've got to call Grace and let her know."

Max thought for a moment, "Better we talk to Jerry and Helen first. They may have no interest in seeing Grace or they may want to fly to Seattle the next day or anything in the middle."

Melissa said, "I agree. We can then tell Grace what to expect. I'll pick you up at six p.m. Call Helen and make sure they'll both be home."

* * * *

Jerome Kaplan met his brother and niece at the door. "Max, Melissa, what the hell is going on? All this secrecy and Melissa had to schlep down from Lansing. This better be good. Is anyone sick?"

Melissa said, "Uncle Jerry, no one is sick, no one is getting divorced, no one is leaving Detroit. But what we're about to tell you is beyond anything in your imagination. Please, you and Aunt Helen take a seat on the couch."

The four sat around the spacious living room. Helen and Jerry sat on a large Louis XIV sofa. Melissa and Max sat in matching chairs on either side.

Helen Kaplan said, "I'm all ears, let's hear it. This better be good."

Melissa said, "I have to tell it as a story exactly as it happened to me. Five weeks ago, I was sitting in my office and received a call from a woman named Grace Gordon, a Professor of Linguistics at the University of Washington in Seattle. Her daughter and nephew, both four and a half years old......,

".... Grace was raised in an orphanage in Montana. She has no clue as to who her parents were, nor did the orphanage."

Jerome Kaplan interrupted, "Melissa get to the point, where is this going?"

Melissa, hesitant said, "Uncle Jerry, Aunt Helen, Grace Gordon is Ben's daughter, your granddaughter."

Helen, looked at her husband, sneered, and then looked back and forth between Max and Melissa, "Shame on you two for joking around with us. How dare you. Haven't we suffered enough? What's gotten into you two?"

320

Max said, "Jerry, Helen, We wouldn't joke with you about Ben. You should know that. What Melissa said is true. We have the DNA testing to prove it. There is no question. None."

After a minute of silence, Melissa said, "Let me continue with the story. Grace came to Lansing a month ago. We did DNA testing on her, my dad and me. The DNA strongly suggested that we were related. I then took those teeth of Ben and mine that you put into a Lucite cube when we were nine or ten years old. DNA analysis was conclusive that Ben was the father."

Jerome Kaplan, teeth clenched, spittle jumping from his mouth, "You did this without our consent."

Melisa thought *I've got to keep Dad out of this*. "Yes, I did. I didn't believe that Grace Gordon was related to anyone in our family. I didn't believe that she was real and I didn't want to burden you with possibilities that I thought impossible. I was wrong not to include you, but I did it with the best intentions. Uncle Jerry, you'll have to believe me. I did not discuss having Ben's tooth analyzed with my dad. I did that by myself."

Helen Kaplan, clenching her husband's hand, cried, "When did this happen? He's dead, why are we bringing him back to life?"

"Helen," Max said, "the girl became pregnant while Ben was at summer prep school, just before he went to Harvard."

"What girl, Max," Helen said.

Melissa moved to sit next to her aunt, "Auntie Helen, we don't know the girl's name. But we're going to look for her. We're guessing that Ben didn't know about the pregnancy or the child."

Jerome, still seething, said, "No you're not. No. No. I don't give a fuck about the mother and I certainly don't give a fuck about some illegitimate child that's probably looking for money. How do we know that Ben, in youthful stupidity, didn't have random sex with a hooker or just some girl? How do we know that Ben didn't donate sperm to some bank? He didn't need the *gelt*, he had plenty of money, but you know kids. The mother and the bastard aren't getting anything, except shit, from us. I swear I'll fight it to the Supreme Court."

Melissa looked at her father, and he nodded back.

Max spoke up, "Jerry, the girl is a professor at a major university. Her husband, who happens to be Jewish, is a professor of urology at the medical school in Seattle. Grace Gordon told me she's not interested in money and will sign anything you want that excludes her from receiving a penny."

Melissa said, "Dad's right. She's not interested in money. However, I think we've talked enough for tonight. I need to call Grace and tell her what we know. She'll find out anyway, but it's better coming from me. I will not force you to meet her and I will not have her come back to Detroit, unless you want her to come."

Jerome said, "Never. I don't want to see her, I don't want to talk to her, and I don't want you to see her or talk to her either," pointing a shaking finger at his niece and brother.

Max pleaded to Jerome, "Jerry, stop acting like this. We didn't bring this on; we didn't go looking for it. We thought it would be bogus. But it wasn't."

Melissa realized that her uncle was immovable. She turned to her aunt, "Auntie Helen, I am going to send you a three minute DVD of her, her resume...."

Helen, hands clenched, interrupted, "Melissa, what are you trying to do? Jerry has spoken for us. I don't want any information. I think it's time for you to leave and let Jerry and I talk."

Melissa said, "Do you want me to call Phillip and tell him that he has a niece?"

Jerome's face and forehead turned crimson and his forehead veins were pulsating with each heartbeat. Jerome stood and walked behind the couch to peer through the curtains, as if he was looking for intruders. The room quieted until Jerome spun around and said, "You two aren't listening. Stay out of our lives. Don't tell anyone. Nobody. Do you understand? If anyone is to tell Phillip, it will be me and that's not likely, ever. Am I making myself perfectly, one hundred percent clear?"

Max looked at his daughter, her face sagged and tears were running down both cheeks, "Melissa, we should go and let them be." He turned to his brother, "Don't take this out on Melissa. What did you want her to do, not tell you? What were we to do with the information? Anyway, it's done."

Max stood, asked for his daughter's hand, and they walked out.

In the car back to Max's house, the two sat silent for a full minute.

Melissa, death-gripping the steering wheel, started, "Dad, I thought that went well."

Max grabbed his daughter's hand and shook his head. He said, "I hope they'll speak to us again."

"Give it time, Dad. Maybe after it sinks in, they'll become curious."

Max said, "What do we do now?"

Melissa said, "We need to find Ben's roommate. Maybe he can shed some light about Ben's relationship with the mother. Hell, as crazy as this is, we still don't have a clue that the girl Ben was crazy about is the mother."

"Melissa, I didn't even consider that tidbit."

"Also, I have the AG of Michigan, Harry Short, looking into Grace's time in Montana. Maybe there's stuff she doesn't know about."

After another moment of silence and contemplation, Melissa said, "I've still got to call Grace and let her know. The one thing we do know for sure is that the Kaplan family didn't dump Grace in an orphanage."

* * * *

"Grace, Melissa here."

"Any news?"

"Yes. Grace, Ben Kaplan, my first cousin, is your biological father. I had an old tooth of Ben's analyzed and the certainty is like ninety-nine-point-nine-nine-nine-nine-nine-nine-nine-nine percent positive. Your biologic paternal grandparents are Jerome and Helen Kaplan of Bloomfield Hills, Michigan. My dad is your great uncle, and I am your first cousin, once removed."

Grace screamed, "Oh my God. Oh my God. What do I say now?"

Melissa followed, "Grace, the good news ends there. My dad and I went to my aunt and uncle's house and told them about you. The shit hit the proverbial fan. I'm sorry. My aunt and uncle have expressed no interest in seeing, meeting or talking to you, now or ever. They are sure you were interested in their money, although we told them that you'd sign away any rights to their estate."

Grace said, "Absolutely, Melissa, I have no interest in their money."

Melissa responded, "Grace, I know that and my dad and I told them so. However, after meeting with them, I can say with a certain amount of knowledge, that if you try to contact them, they will issue a restraining order."

Grace said, "I can't believe this. You don't think me talking to them would work."

Melissa said, "Grace, one hundred percent absolutely not, at least, not now. Trust me, under no circumstances are you to reach out."

Grace said, "Melissa, I merely would like to find out about my father. After knowing nothing for thirty years, don't you think I am entitled to know."

"Grace, I don't know the answer to that. Since we don't know the origin of the pregnancy, or the mother or her family, I'm not sure you have any rights. It's not out of the realm of possibility that Ben had random sex or donated sperm to a bank and legally, he, or his estate, or his family's estate, have no obligations to you. All I know for sure is, at this moment, Jerome and Helen Kaplan want nothing to do with you."

"Melissa, this is terrible. I didn't want to ruin the relationship with your aunt and uncle."

"Grace, we need to give this time. I don't know how much time. Whatever it takes, I guess. You'll have to trust me. I promise that I'll get back to you every so often to let you know what I've found or heard. Let's say I'll call you in a couple of weeks."

Grace said, "I'm so sorry I've jeopardized your family relationships. Please forgive me."

Melissa said, "Forgiven. I'll call you in a couple of weeks."

* * * * *

Two days later, Melissa was back at her desk in Lansing.

"Senator, your uncle is on line 3."

"Hi, Uncle Jerry. Are you okay?"

"Helen and I are fine. I am sorry that we jumped all over you and Max. We, perhaps, overreacted."

"Uncle Jerry, I'm not mad at you or Aunt Helen. I didn't find and wasn't looking for Grace, she found us."

Jerome said, "I know. I know."

Melissa asked, "Have you and Aunt Helen changed your mind about finding more about her?"

"That's why I called. You are my favorite niece."

"Uncle Jerry, I am your only niece."

Both laughed, as this routine had been played out countless times over four and a half decades.

Jerome Kaplan continued, "But here's the thing. Helen and I have talked and we haven't changed our position. We have no interest in this Grace person. None at all. Ben never mentioned her, nor did anyone else that knew Ben ever tell us about a serious girl friend. I've talked to our attorneys to find out what our legal position might be. We can't say for certain that Ben didn't sleep with a prostitute or some random girl or donate sperm to a bank. You know as well as I that calling all the Boston or Detroit sperm banks for privileged information isn't going to help us. They won't tell us a thing."

"I understand."

"Helen and I agree on one other point, and I'd like you to respect our wishes on this. I do not want you or my brother to call this interloper for any reason, no matter what you know or find. We do not want her in our life, period. Can you promise this for me?"

"Yes, of course, Uncle Jerry. However, I did promise her that I would call her back in a couple of weeks to let her know the family's position. I think I owe her that, to let her know we won't be communicating. If I don't call, she'll pester me. Is that okay?"

Jerome said, "I'll think about it."

Melissa said, "One other thing, she is not an interloper. She has no interest in anyone's money. She is an accomplished academician, well published and respected. She is married to a physician and has two darling children. She wants from nothing, other than to know where she comes from."

"Okay, call her once. That's it. Can you promise me that?"

"Yes. One call. Are you going to talk to my dad or do you want me to?"

"I'll talk to him. He's my brother and in seventy plus years, we've never had a fight. I'm not going to start now. As you said, you and he didn't go looking for this, it just ended up in your lap."

"Thanks, Uncle Jerry. I love you. Tell Aunt Helen I love her too."

That evening, Melissa called her father. "Dad, did Uncle Jerry talk to you yet?"

"No. I've been playing golf all day."

"He's going to call to apologize for how they acted."

Max said, "Good. He should."

"He also will demand that we stop all communication with Grace. He said I could call her once to tell her, and I quote, 'We do not want her in our lives.'"

"We'll have to listen to his wishes on this, Melissa. Grace is their biologic granddaughter, not ours."

"I know dad, but you've met her. She's not... Oh, what am I trying to say?"

Max said, "I know what you're thinking, but Jerry and Helen get to have their wishes on this one."

"Yeah, but I have one call. Were you able to find the folder on Ben that had his roommate's name and number and anything else?"

"No, but I don't think you should be giving out any information."

Melissa said, "Dad, she has the right to be able to find her mother. How do we know the mother is not looking for Grace? Ben's roommate may be the only one who can add some insight."

Max said, "Okay, I'll look again. But say nothing to anyone, particularly your mother."

"Want me to help look?"

"No. No. I'll do it. It's in the garage if it's anywhere. Besides, if you start opening boxes, you may find out things about your mother and I that you don't know."

"Like what? Tell me I have a brother living in France?"

"I was kidding. I have no secrets from you. But, I'll look. If you help, Mom is going to want to know what's up."

Max called back the next morning, "Melissa, I found it. But it's not much."

Melissa said, "What exactly is 'not much.'"

"I have his name, Brad Hahn and his family's phone number in Spokane, which I think is in Oregon or Washington."

"It's in Washington."

"I also have a copy of Brad and Ben's last phone bill. He sent that to me a few weeks after the funeral. He circled a phone number, which was a collect call to them. I remember trying the number several times thirty years ago and it rang and rang and no one ever answered."

Melissa said, "Dad, mail me the bill."

* * * *

"Grace, Melissa Friedman here."

"Oh, hello. I was worried I'd never hear from you."

Melissa said, "How are you holding up?"

Grace said, "Not so well. My nightmares have come back a bit. I think the stress of the trip to Detroit, rekindled some fears and hopes. I've started back seeing a therapist who helped me a few years ago. The nightmares will stop, in time. They always have in the past. I guess I'm so disappointed. My daughter is almost five and she is almost as upset as I am. My husband told her why I was going to Detroit, in general terms, and when I returned without a father she was crushed. She wants me to have parents as much as I do."

"Wow. I'm sorry, Grace."

Grace said, "I'm so sorry for going on. My therapist is paid to listen, you're not."

Melissa said, "I'm not sure my call is going to make you feel any better. Your biologic grandparents, Jerome and Helen Kaplan, are adamant that you not contact them, nor will they contact you. They've sought legal counsel about any obligations and...."

"Melissa, I don't want their money."

"Grace, I know that. I've told them exactly that a few times. It's just that your existence was a total surprise. They don't know that Ben didn't go to a sperm bank, or whatever."

Grace said, "I understand."

Melissa said, "However, there is one piece of news that I have. The last person to see Ben was his roommate at Harvard. His name is Brad Hahn and was from Spokane. I have no recollection where he is now but I think he went to law school. I do have an old Spokane phone number. I also have the last phone bill to Brad and Ben. Earlier, on the day of Ben's accident, he accepted a collect phone call from a girl. Brad told my dad at the funeral that the phone call was upsetting to Ben. My dad called the number a few times, but never got anyone to answer. He left it at that, Ben was dead."

Grace said, "Do you think that the call came from my mother?"

Melissa said, "I have no idea. But Brad Hahn, if you can locate him, might know something. I will send you this information today. After that, and following the wishes of my aunt and uncle, I won't be calling you again. I'm sorry."

Grace said nothing. A tear meandered its way to her upper lip and hung there.

Melissa said again, "I'm sorry." When she heard no response, Melissa hung up.

Grace sat at the kitchen counter and stared out the window. She twirled her hair with her left hand until she developed a cramp in her wrist and stopped.

Chapter 16

Three days later Grace received an envelope addressed from Melissa Friedman, State Senator. In it was a phone bill dated thirty years earlier to Mr. Bradley Hahn at an address in Spokane, Washington. Circled was the last phone number on the bill, a collect call, for four minutes and thirty-eight seconds, costing three dollars and eighty-four cents. Written in pencil, and faded, was the word 'katy?.'"

Grace called the collect call number from the bill.

The voice said, "Roberto's Pizzeria."

Grace said, "I might have the wrong number. How long have you been at this number?"

"Couple of years, lady. You want to order or not?"

Grace hung up.

Grace next called the phone number for Brad Hahn. The area code, 509, was Spokane, Washington. The recorded voice returned immediately, *"The phone number you dialed is out of service. Check the number and call again."*

Grace thought, *how hard could it be to find Brad Hahn, a graduate of Harvard and maybe a lawyer?*

Grace subscribed to an internet white page service for $14.95 a month and paid with a credit card. A national search lead to eleven hundred B., Brad or Bradley Hahns. *This could take forever. I need a little luck.* Twenty-one were in Washington state. Grace thought, *he's as likely to have ended up in Washington as anywhere else.* There were twelve B Hahns worth trying after discarding Barry, Brandon, three Bills, and four Bobs. Grace started dialing from the top of the list. On the fourth call she reached a law firm in Bellevue, Washington.

A pleasant voice answered, "Osgood Hahn. Jenny speaking. How may I help you?"

Grace jotted the name, Jenny, on a pad and said, "Jenny, I'd like to speak to Mr. Hahn, Brad Hahn, if I may."

"Mr. Hahn has meetings scheduled all day. Are you a client of Osgood Hahn?"

"No, not yet." *A little white lie....so far.*

"May I have your name please?"

"Grace Gordon. I'm a professor at the UW. Jenny, I'll tell you why I'm calling. I am doing some research on Harvard graduates here in Washington state." *A big white lie.*

Jenny said, "Professor Gordon, you might want to call Zachary Strasser at King Strasser and Minkove in Redmond. Mr. Hahn was past president of the Harvard alumni, but hasn't been active for a few years. Mr. Strasser would have more knowledge of Harvard graduates."

Grace said, "Jenny, I need to be sure that I have my information correct on Mr. Hahn. I am only interested in graduates of the undergraduate school, not law school." *Another lie, after the first, it's easy.*

"Mr. Hahn's law degree is from Boalt Hall at Berkeley, but he was a Harvard undergraduate."

"Exactly as I had it. I would appreciate an appointment to see Mr. Hahn."

"Professor, I would have to get Mr. Hahn's approval first."

"Of course, I understand. Will you tell him that I am a member of Ben Kaplan's family, from Detroit. That's K-A-P-L-A-N, first name is Ben. It would mean a great deal if I could get in to see Mr. Hahn. He can reach me at the UW Department of Linguistics. 206-543-1919 extension 2343."

Seven minutes later, Grace's phone rang.

"Professor Gordon."

Grace said, "Yes, this is Grace Gordon."

"Professor, I am Brad Hahn. You called earlier about doing some research on Harvard graduates and told my secretary that you are related to Ben Kaplan of Detroit. Just so we have no misunderstandings, how do you know Ben?"

"Mr. Hahn, I didn't say I knew Ben. He was killed in a motor vehicle accident in Canada after his freshman year at Harvard. I am related."

"How so, Ben had a gay brother, no sisters and one first cousin whose name was, uh.. Melissa."

"Mr. Hahn. I don't believe we should talk about my predicament over the phone. Is there a chance that I could come and talk to you, personally, about something serious? At least, serious to me."

"How much time do you need? If this is a legal problem, I bill out at six hundred dollars an hour. Are you okay with that?"

"I'll let you be the judge of whether it's a legal problem. I can pay if need be. The time, well that depends more on you. It might be an hour or two."

"Hold on......tomorrow my last appointment ends at three thirty. Can you be here then?"

"I have a linguistics class to teach that ends at three thirty, I could be there at four p.m., assuming the 520 bridge eastbound isn't a parking lot."

"I'll see you at four fifteen, you'll never make it at four."

* * * *

"Have a seat," Brad Hahn said, as Jenny lead Grace into his office, "Uh.. Do you go by Doctor, Professor, Mrs., or Grace?"

"Grace is fine."

"Please tell me, Grace, what's on your mind? Ben was my roommate and closest friend my first year at Harvard. His death haunts me to this day. I tried to keep in touch with his parents, but in time I think I reminded them of his mortality."

Grace said, "I may need to tell you a long story after I tell you the ending."

"And what is the ending?"

"I am Ben Kaplan's daughter."

Hahn quickly shut his eyes, shook his head 'no no', and said, "Impossible. No way."

After his quick dismissal, Grace pulled out a folder from her briefcase and extracted a single sheet of paper, and said, "Way. Ben did not have a twin and here is the DNA paternity test proving that I am his daughter, at least biologically. Moreover, the tests of Ben's uncle, Max Kaplan and his first cousin, Melissa Kaplan Friedman, confirm that we are related. You are welcome to call Senator Friedman if you want to confirm what I am saying."

"This makes no sense. None at all. Explain everything."

"Mr. Hahn, this could take a while. I need to know if you are going to bill me."

"Grace. No. Not unless something legal comes of this. You've shaken me to the core and I have to hear the rest of your story. Hold on one second." Hahn pressed a button on his phone, "Helen, call my wife and tell her I will likely not be home until after six or later. Tell her I'm sorry and that I'll explain a most incredible happening."

Grace started, "I was deposited in an orphanage in Missoula, Montana, at around age two......."

Two hours and four bottles of water later, Grace was coming to the end of her saga.

"... In the end, I think Melissa and Max were disappointed in Ben's parents but went along with their wishes to have nothing to do with me. Since

Ben's parents had no knowledge that I existed, their first assumption, and possibly the truth, was that Ben Kaplan had random sex with some girl or a prostitute or made donations to a sperm bank. The problem I have with the bank scenario is that if someone wanted to get pregnant bad enough to pay for sperm, why would they give the baby, me, away. Anyway, Melissa thought that you knew of some connection that Ben could have had with a girl before he got to Harvard. By the dates, I was likely born before you finished your first year, which means I was conceived the summer before or early in the fall at Harvard. I got incredibly lucky finding my father, or biologic father. I need to find my mother to make sense of all this."

Hahn said, "This is the most incredible turn of events. If nothing else, you ought to write a book. Except no one would believe you."

Grace said, "Mr. Hahn, Melissa did forward to me a copy of the last phone bill sent to you, which you subsequently sent to Max Kaplan. You circled a number. The area code is Westchester County, north of New York. The number connects to a pizzeria that's a couple of years old. Below the collect number, someone wrote the word 'katy', enclosed with question marks. I assume that you wrote it. I have nothing else to go on. Mr. Hahn, I am hoping that whomever Ben talked to before starting his drive home would have knowledge about me."

Hahn tugged on his left earlobe and then ran a hand through his hair. "I 'm thinking....I do know some information. However, from what you've told me, I'm not sure that Ben's parents would want me to help you. I may need to call them for permission."

"I can't stop you, but you will likely cause a major riff in the family between Melissa and Max and Ben's parents. Melissa told me that she and her dad had made a solemn pledge to Ben's parents not to help me. Nonetheless, Melissa sent me this phone bill and your name with the caveat to do with it as I pleased. But, under no circumstances, was I to contact them."

"Go on."

"If you call Ben's parents and tell them you've met with me, they'll know that I got your name from Melissa or Max, against their wishes. Ben's parents may never speak to Max and Melissa again. If I find nothing from your help, I'm done and I'll stop looking."

"Grace, let me give this some thought. If nothing else, I need to talk to my wife. She knows the Kaplan family and has a great sense of what's right and what's not. I'll call you."

Grace said, "I guess I don't have a choice."

Hahn said, "Please, let me talk to my wife. I'll call you either way."

Grace gave Hahn her card and wrote her home number on the back. "I hope I hear from you."

By the time Grace crossed the I-520 bridge back into Seattle, Alex was home and the kids were clamoring for dinner. Kraft Macaroni and Cheese was on the stove and the table was set for four. Alex was not a cook.

"Mommy, you look sad," said Ellie.

"I'm fine, sweetie. Just a long day."

Alex softly asked, "What'd the guy say?"

Whispering, Grace said, "He'd have to think about helping. He may call the parents for permission."

Alex said, "You know if he calls them, he'll never say another word."

Grace said, "I know. I know. Oh, Alex. This has been so hard. On you, and the kids too. I'm sorry."

"Are you kidding? Ellie promised she'd deliver you parents. Whatever happens, it's all been worth it. Honest. Glad you're home. After dinner, I have to go back in to see a patient I operated on today. I'll be gone an hour at most."

Before the Gordon family could sit down to eat, the phone rang.

Ellie jumped to the phone first. She loved answering and put the phone on speaker. Elle knew the house rules when she picked up the phone. "Hello, I'm Ellie, who's this?" she said, except the Ls sounded like Ws.

The voice said, "Is your mommy home?"

Ellie answered, "Sure." Ellie walked around the table to Grace "Here mommy, it's for you. I don't know who *is it?*"

Grace took the phone, kissed Ellie on the forehead and said, "You're the best. I think it's 'who it is', not 'who is it.' Okay?"

Ellie smiled and nodded.

Grace took the phone off speaker and put the phone cradle to her ear as she was dishing Mac and Cheese into a pink Cinderella bowl for Ellie and a blue Spiderman bowl for Mark. "Hello, who's this?"

"Is this Grace?"

"Yes."

"I'm Didi Hahn, Brad Hahn's wife. Do you have a second?"

"Really..., sure, I have time." Grace handed the bowls to Alex and walked out of the room.

"Brad told me your story. Men are so *effing* dense. Excuse my language. You're looking for your mother, who may be looking for you, and he's playing lawyer. He'll help you all he can. Your story is surreal. If you want to come over here tonight, I've got to meet you and I want to hear everything."

"Uhh. Sure. My husband is going back to the hospital and I don't have a sitter so..."

"Grace, I've got three grandchildren. Bring your kids. You've got to hear what Brad knows."

"Thank you, so much. It'll take me an hour to get the kids fed, into PJs and drive back to Bellevue."

"We live on Mercer Island, first exit off the I-90 bridge coming east from Seattle. Our address is...."

Grace arrived at the Hahn home at seven forty-five p.m.

Didi Hahn greeted Grace at the door and then ushered Ellie into a large playroom filled with toys. Three American Girl dolls, with varying outfits, assured that Ellie would be busy for a long time. Mark was already asleep. Didi led Grace into Brad's study.

Brad Hahn said, "Grace, I'm sorry about putting you off. I needed to have counsel with my senior advisor," looking at Didi.

Grace responded, "I understand. Thank you for having me back. I don't think I would have slept if I had to make another appointment."

Brad said, "I'll cut to the chase and let you know what I know. It's not everything you may have hoped for."

"Mr. Hahn, anything is more than I have. The entire Kaplan family knows nothing other than the tidbits you told Max Kaplan at the funeral.

Didi interrupted, "Brad, if you're going to have Grace calling you Mr. Hahn, then you should be calling her Professor or Doctor."

"Oh, of course. You can call me Brad."

Didi Hahn and Grace looked at each other and collectively rolled their eyes.

Brad started, "Ben and I hadn't met until the first week of school. Within days, we became close. Ben had been to a prep school, Phillips Academy in Andover, Massachusetts, during the summer before starting Harvard. He didn't need it, but his mom and dad wanted him uber-prepared. Anyway, academically, his first three months at Harvard were relatively easy. Ben was so smart, he rarely needed

342

to study. Much of his free time for those first three months, and a significant amount of my free time, was involved in trying to locate a girl, Katy, Ben had met at summer school. He was obsessed, and since I had nothing to do of importance, I became semi-obsessed with him."

Grace chuckled. Didi said, "He does get obsessive at times, even now."

"Ben was certain that this Katy was to start at Smith College. She never showed up. Ben had a home address and a phone number. He wrote and he called, and got no responses. Finally some guy got on the phone and threatened Ben and told him that Katy wanted nothing to do with him. Her last name escapes me; it's been too long. I don't even remember whether Katy was a nickname for Katherine. Next, Ben and I drove to Westchester County, north of New York City to check out her home address. I told Ben it was a bad idea, but he was unrelenting.

"Anyway, I was right. This girl lived in a large gated estate in the middle of nowhere. The first attempt to see Katy was at the estate's outside gate. One of the guards made a call and we then received an aggressive 'get lost' attitude. We stayed overnight in a nearby town and then tried the front gate again the next day. The same guard made a phone call and then told us he had notified the local police. The guard told us that if we stayed anywhere near the estate, we'd be arrested for stalking.

"We left Westchester and drove back to Cambridge. Ben was sad for another month, but then started dating and seemed to forget about Katy. He'd bring her up occasionally, but then was dismissive of what he thought had been love. Hey, we were only eighteen. What did we know? However, he could never understand why she hadn't contacted him in some way to say she didn't want to see him. He was certain that someone was controlling her actions.

"I am almost certain that Ben didn't make any contributions to sperm banks, at least around Boston. He would have told me. He didn't need money. But I did, so I'm sure he would have given me heads up about making some bucks. Random sex, I don't think so. He'd have told me about that too.

"Anyway, as we're packing to go home at the end of the school year, Ben gets a collect call from 'Katy', which he accepts.

"The conversation was unusual. I wasn't listening that hard, as it was none of my business, and the call lasted only a few minutes. She must have hung up quickly, as I remember him yelling *'Katy, Katy'* into the phone. After the call, he dropped the receiver and fell back onto his bed. He looked terrible. He then asked me if I would give him a few minutes of privacy so he could call his parents. As I left the room, Ben confirmed that it was the 'Katy' we'd looked for in the fall. When I returned he was subdued and distracted, which was rare for him. We said our good-byes thirty minutes later and he drove off for Detroit. That was the last I talked to him.

"I told most of this to Ben's uncle Max at the funeral. Max felt that getting an unknown girl involved wouldn't bring Ben back and why complicate issues. He did ask me to send him a copy of the telephone bill, which I did. He sent me money for Ben's portion. I think Max was handling all Ben's affairs for a while after the funeral.

"For the first four or five years, I would talk to the Kaplans every so often. I did enjoy meeting his first cousin, Melissa, who was a student at Michigan. I thought she was attractive and smart, but it would have been beyond weird to have taken her out. As time went on, I think I was a reminder to their families that Ben was dead. Anyway, I stopped contacting Ben's parents, although I did send a congratulatory note to Melissa after her election to the Michigan House. She didn't write back. That's it. That's all I know."

Grace sat quietly, biting her lower lip with her hands folded neatly in her lap as she twirled and straightened her hair.

Didi sat watching Grace. *I wish I could hug her.*

Brad then said, "Grace, if anyone is your mother, it would almost have to be this Katy. Good luck trying to find her. I would probably start with Phillips Academy in Andover. You'll have to think of some subterfuge to get the class rosters. I'd be flabbergasted if they released names and they're not going to release addresses or phone numbers."

Grace perked up and said, "I'll think of something. I did get your secretary to confirm that you went to Harvard by saying I was doing research."

"Touché. You need to contact whatever phone company handled Westchester and see if the phone number on the bill gives you a location. As I said, we went to her estate. It was in the middle of nowhere, maybe a mile from the nearest hamlet. I can't tell you anymore than that. The nearest city had at most four stores total and had a weird Indian-like name."

Grace stood and thanked Brad and Didi. "I'll get the kids and let you two get some rest."

Brad then added, "One more thing. If this Katy turns out to be your mother, then you were conceived in love. Ben was madly in love with Katy, that I know. How she felt, I don't know? But if she is the mother, then Ben's parents are mistaken that this was a random event. She may have been younger than Ben, but not much, so I'm guessing she is anywhere from forty-eight to fifty years old now."

Didi came over to her husband, gave him a big hug, and whispered in his ear, "Thank you for saying that."

Grace said, "I'll try to keep you in the loop." She hoisted the still sleeping Mark and the almost sleeping Ellie and returned home.

Grace put her *mother-hunt* aside for a few weeks. Consumed by the search, she had fallen behind in some of her academic writing, most of her mothering and all of her relationship with Alex.

She told Alex, "I'm exhausted. Physically fine, but mentally in shambles. I need to rest, gain strength and then look."

Alex agreed, "But, be prepared, your biologic father's side had no ax to grind, they didn't even know you existed. If you find your mother's family, it may get ugly, really, really ugly."

Grace had returned to weekly appointments with Dr. Crayman.

Crayman's position with Grace's endeavors was clear.

As she left her second appointment after the revelations from Brad Hahn, Crayman said, "You've past the point of no-return. If you stop looking, the pressure, the uncertainty and the nightmares will never go away. You will never understand what happened to you or why. In my opinion, you need to know. Finish your search. Then, you and I will deal with the consequences

Chapter 17

Summer came and Grace was renewed. Starting with the collect call phone number, she dialed 914-238-8888.

"Roberto's Pizzeria, Roberto speaking."

Grace asked, "Hello, I was given this number. I'm looking for a girl named Katy who might have lived nearby many years ago."

"What's many, honey?"

"Maybe twenty-five or thirty years ago. It's important that I find her."

"You're funny. What town you looking for?"

"That's it, I don't know, I was only given this number?"

"We're north of Pleasantville on Bedford Road, Route 117, if that helps. We're south of Chappaqua. We've had this number for two, three years and ain't nobody named Katy here or ever worked here that I can remember. Every so often we get a phone call that's dialed wrong."

"Oh, that's too bad."

"Who's this Katy? Never know, maybe she'll walk in one day and ask if anyone's called for her." Roberto laughed at his own humor.

Grace said, "I don't know Katy. My name is Grace Gordon. I live in Seattle, Washington. I am

348

looking for my mother. She used this number to call my father thirty years ago."

Roberto said, "Oh, I'm sorry. But I can't help you."

Grace asked, "Will you take my number anyway and call me if you ever find out any more information."

Roberto said, "Sure, but don't count on hearing from me."

"I understand. Thanks. Maybe I'll stop in for a pizza some day. You never know. In my craziness, I may call you again. Is that okay?"

"You come all the way from Seattle for a pizza, it's on me, lady. Call anytime."

Next Grace tried the phone company. Over the years, phone service to Westchester had changed from New York Telephone, an AT&T subsidiary, to NYNEX, to Bell Atlantic, to GTE, and finally to Verizon.

Grace called Verizon trying to track the number 914-238-8888 from thirty years earlier. Finding a location from Verizon was impossible for three reasons, they didn't know, they weren't sure how or where to look for it, and they didn't care.

Three days of holding, waiting, talking, holding, holding, waiting ended with "I'm sorry, Miss. We can't provide that information."

Grace tried calling the Phillips Academy in Andover, Massachusetts. Professionals staffed the registrar's office. Four more calls, using different names, different phone lines, and a host of friends calling in her stead, gave her no more information. The last phone call to the Academy ended with, "Dr. Gordon, we don't give out information on any registered student or class. We sign a contract with the attendees of the school. If the President of the United States called, we'd give him, or her, the same information."

Grace was desperate enough to call Melissa Friedman.

"Melissa, I know you're not supposed to talk to me, so I'll do the talking. I am hopeful that a girl that Ben went to summer school with at the Phillips Academy outside Boston may be my mother. But I don't have her name. I'm not sure they would give it to you, but as Ben's cousin, they might."

"Grace, this conversation didn't occur."

"I understand."

Melissa said, "If I call Phillips, under any guise, they may turn around and call Ben's parents. If that happens, our family falls apart. My aunt and uncle have warned us a few times since you left. My dad and I can't afford to have that happen. The next time I'm at their house, I will look to see if they have an annual or yearbook from the school. Since it was only a summer program, I'd doubt it. But I'll look. If I ask, they'll know I'm snooping. That's all I can do."

Grace said, "Thank you."

Two weeks later, Melissa called back.

"Grace, I did what I could. My aunt and uncle went out of town for a week and I offered to have my daughter go over and feed their miserable cat every day. Anyway, I went back to Bloomfield Hills and told my daughter, I'd feed the cat that day. I searched everywhere and could find nothing left of my cousin's belongings. I'm not going to be able to help you."

Grace said, "Melissa, you've gone out of your way already for me. Thanks."

* * * *

"Cully, nothing makes sense. She's not gone back to Detroit. I can't figure it out. The large cash withdrawal in Detroit is a total mystery. I did a little checking into the parents of the father. They're old and haven't travelled anywhere."

"You keep watching."

"Yeah, yeah. I know we're okay."

* * * *

Three months went by and Grace had returned to her normal routines. She had been tempted to go the Westchester County on a blind search, but thought better of it. She had only a name, Katy, and a probable age of around fifty, to go on.

Grace's luck changed on the day before Labor Day. Grace was making chicken salad for a Labor Day potluck when the phone rang.

"Hello," a thick New England accent said, "is Grace Gordon around."

"Speaking."

"I'm Roberto, of Roberto's Pizzeria near Pleasantville."

Grace said, "Yes, Roberto, I remember you. I get a pizza if I show up."

"Right. Anyway, dis guy walks into the restaurant with his three grandchildren. He called in a couple of large pies to go. As I'm ringing up da sale, he tells me dat my phone number is easy and he'll remember it, if da pizzas taste okay. I tell him dey're da best in a hundred miles."

Grace said, "I'm sure they are."

"They are. Anyway, 'dis guy then tells me my Roberto's phone number used to be a payphone on da outside of Chappaqua. He remembers because his high school girlfriend would call him to dat phone number. Apparently, dis guy's folks didn't like her, too low class for their boy. Anyway, he'd park near da phone booth waiting for her to call. He's still married to her and he asked that if I ever gave up the number, he wanted it."

"I remembered your call, looking for your mother and all. So I ask him exactly where dis phone was. He says it was on da northwest corner of Orchard Ridge Road and Bedford Road, same side as da church."

Grace said, "And then you called me."

Roberto said, "I couldn't believe it. I found your number in my desk drawer under a pile of shit..excuse me."

"No problem. I swear some, too."

"Anyway, dat's alls I know. Sorry I didn't get the guys name and he paid with cash."

"Thanks. Thanks so much. Roberto, I may have to take you up on that pizza, but I pay."

* * * *

Melissa Friedman, received a called from her friend, Michigan's Attorney General, Harry Short.

"Melissa, remember you asked me to look into Grace Pine from Montana a while ago."

Melissa said, "What did you find?"

Short continued, "The AG of Montana just provided us a full copy of Grace Pine's orphanage records. She did not have an easy life. In fact, it was a horror show. How she ends up a professor, I'll never know. The human spirit, I guess. Attached to the file was an addendum that Montana had forwarded the records to Seattle in 1995 for a trial. State of Washington versus Pine. The Seattle PD arrested Grace Pine for dealing two pounds of marijuana. The judge found her innocent. I talked to the current Seattle Prosecutor, Chris Callo, and a former public defender, Paul Snyder, who defended Ms. Pine. Callo provided transcripts of the entire case. The whole thing reads like a novel. Someone, according to Snyder, tried to set up Miss Pine by planting drugs in her workspace at the med school library. Snyder was a rookie defender and, yet, he beat Callo. Callo's still pissed, although he did agree that she was probably innocent. He didn't enjoy losing to a rookie. Anyway, the trial testimony corroborated the orphanage records. Grace Pine had a shit life."

Melissa said, "She told me that her life wasn't easy but didn't go into details about the rough spots."

Short added, "There were plenty of those. Snyder, her attorney, said that he couldn't say more without Ms. Pine's permission about who they believed tried to get her arrested."

"Thanks, Harry. I owe you."

"Another thing, Mel. I had a long chat with the Montana AG about Grace. He said that if the family that left her could have afforded to care for her, the Great State of Montana wants their money back."

Melissa said, "Interesting."

Harry Short, with a lilt in his voice, said, "I'll tell you what, Mel, when they make the movie of her life, I wanna be in it."

"Don't think they'll make a movie, Harry. Nobody'd believe it."

Short said, "Let me know how this all turns out. I'll have a courier deliver the stuff later today."

Melissa Friedman spent 6 hours reading Grace's Montana and Seattle files. She became ill reading the testimony about Grace's ordeal as a pre-teen with Ezekiel Watkins and vomited her dinner, then cried for an hour.

She called Brad Hahn in Seattle and then Fedexed him copies of what she had read.

Chapter 18

Grace, Alex, Ellie and Mark landed in Newark, rented a car and drove to Armonk, New York, and found adjoining rooms at the La Quinta Inn. Grace slept poorly and let Alex drive the next morning as the four mother-seekers drove to Chappaqua. They began at the corner of Bedford Road and Orchard Ridge Road and found the large First Congregational Church. On the northwest corner was a four-foot by four-foot cement pad, which was the likely spot for the payphone.

Grace said softly to Alex, "It is very likely that my mother stood here. Gives me goosebumps."

Alex gave Grace a hug, "I hope she did." Alex suggested trying the local pharmacy. The pharmacists, both younger than thirty, were children of Vietnamese refugees and knew no one named Katy. A small cafe, a barber, a florist, a real estate office and a hardware store were no more helpful.

Grace said to Alex, as they departed the hardware store, "I'm not sure that anyone in this town knows or doesn't know anybody named Katy, who might be wealthy and lived here thirty years ago. I do know that, so far, people don't like strangers asking questions."

By day's end, Grace's spirits were at low ebb. The kids were hungry and tired. The family had planned to go to Roberto's Pizzeria, a few miles in the opposite direction, but Grace was too depressed to face Roberto. Back at the hotel, a note was waiting for Grace at the front desk. "Call Chief Charles, 914-238-1000."

"Chappaqua Police. How can I help you?"

Grace said, "I'd like to speak to Chief Charles."

"Whatcha want with Lyle..uh, the chief?"

"He told me to call."

"Hold on..."

"Chief Charles, here."

"My name is Grace Gordon and there was a message on my door at the La Quinta in Armonk to call you."

The chief said, "Thank you for calling. I'll get down to business Miss."

"It's actually Mrs. Gordon."

Correcting the chief didn't help his mood. He said, "Whatever, lady. I had two calls that you've been asking a bunch of questions in town today. Something I ought to know?"

Grace said, "We're trying to find a person named Katy who lived near Chappaqua thirty years ago and made a phone call to my father from a pay phone just north of town."

"You kidding? Now there's a long shot. One thing about these parts, people like their privacy. Another way of putting it is that people don't like strangers nosing around."

"Am I breaking a law?"

356

The police chief said, "Since I'm the law in town, you're breaking my law. What do you want with this person who called your father thirty years ago?"

"She may be my mother."

"You're joking with me. Most times, it's the mother looking for the father. Where you from?"

"Seattle."

The police chief guffawed, "What, in Seattle, the father's have the baby while the mom's playing golf."

"Not funny."

"I thought it was funny, knee-slapping funny. Too bad you Seattle folks don't have a sense of humor. End of this conversation is that I don't like people snooping around our sleepy little town for no good reason. Yours sounds like no good reason."

"Chief, are you going to arrest me?"

"Don't try me, lady. You might win but don't try me. That's a warning and a fair warning. I'm going to go now and I suggest you do too."

Alex and Grace decided that night that leaving seemed to be the best option. They thought they'd need to hire a private detective who had a better way of going under the radar.

They packed in the morning but Grace insisted on driving through Chappaqua, and the phone booth remnant, on the way back to Newark.

On the windshield of their rental car was a note, 'Stay away, or else' and someone had driven a nail through the right front tire.

While Alex changed the tire, Grace called Police Chief Charles and asked if the Chappaqua police had put the note on the car or slashed the tire.

"Lady, you're shitting me." Charles was indignant and said, "Police don't leave notes on cars or slash tires. Someone, or, in your case, many, don't want you nosing around. You're leaving, right?"

"Yes, we're going to get breakfast and head back to Newark."

"Good. None too soon."

They found a little diner, The Yankee Grill, south of Chappaqua on South Greeley Ave. The waiter was a young boy, maybe eighteen or nineteen.

Alex said, "Don't even ask. He probably doesn't know who the president is, or even cares."

When the young man brought their water, Grace asked, "Hello. We're visiting the area. It's so nice around here."

The young man responded with a smile and a teenage eye roll, "Yeah, it's okay. Unless you live here."

Grace said, "That's funny. I'm Grace, this is my husband, Alex, and Ellie and Mark. What's your name?"

"People round here call me Dud."

"Dud, I've got a trivia question for you."

Dud was confused and said, "Are you gonna order something to eat?"

Grace said, "Sure. You're from around these parts, right."

"Yeah."

"So who's the richest person for ten miles around here?"

Dud said, "Shoot. That's easy. Cully Harris, owns most of the land north of town starting from the church near Orchard and Bedford. Maybe two hundred, three hundred acres. There's a joke in town that he wrote a check once and the Chappaqua National Bank bounced."

Grace and Alex laughed as genuinely as they could muster.

Grace said, "Anybody else really rich?"

Dud shook his head as he said, "Not in that ballpark. Cully Harris don't come into town, never has, and no one from his family comes here. All the help lives on the estate. If you're fixing to visit, he ain't gonna see you unless you're invited. The Harris people, they drive through in those big black limos, but they ain't ever stopped here that I know of."

Grace said, "Dud, I don't want to see him."

"There's others with some money, but they'd see you if you knocked on the door or rung the bell. People here are kind of private but the Harris people, they're *mean* private, if you get my drift. They're so private that no one knows nothing about them 'cept they're rich."

Grace said, "What's good to eat here for us and for the kids."

Dud said, "Pancakes ain't bad, I eat'em all the time and the kids that comes in here love'em, 'specially with powdered sugar and syrup."

Ellie said, "Pancakes for me."

Dud nodded, writing on his pad, "And the omelets are real good."

Alex said, "We'll have, two kids pancakes, two cheese and mushroom omelets with wheat toast. Milk for the kids and two black coffees."

Dud said, "Got it," and turned and walked back towards the kitchen.

Grace, once Dud was out of earshot, said, "Got it, too. Thank you, Dud."

Alex said, "I've got one smart wife."

Grace said, "Now we have to see if Katy Harris ever existed."

Alex said, "I agree, but not around here."

Grace called Samantha from the hotel that night outside the Newark Airport. "Sam, we've got a name, Katy Harris. I don't know if Katy is a nickname but the last name is almost certainly Harris. Her dad is Cully Harris and I assume that Cully is also a nickname. Harris is apparently incredibly rich and extremely private and guarded. The Chappaqua police told us we weren't welcome and to stop snooping. They did everything they could to frighten us."

Sam said, "Shit, Grace. You'd think you were in Iran or China."

Grace said, There's more. As we're leaving the hotel this morning, we found a note on our windshield with the same non-welcoming message and somebody put a nail into one of our tires. Friendly town, eh? We're flying back to Seattle in the morning."

Sam said, "The rest of the research can be done as easily from Seattle as it can there. I'd get out of Dodge. Do you think the police told this Harris guy who you were looking for?"

"I don't know, Sam. Wouldn't surprise me. Take it back; I'd be surprised if Harris didn't know."

"If these are the same people that planted the drugs in the library, no telling what they could do."

Grace said, "We'll be careful."

"Grace, if this guy is that big, then no way he stays out of the New York Times social pages. I can't imagine that if this Katy, or her brothers and sisters, ever got married, that it wasn't the highlight of the social season in Westchester. You guys have a safe flight and I'm going to do some research for you."

Grace, Alex and the kids left their Newark hotel the next morning for an 11:00 a.m. flight to Seattle. After they checked their baggage and headed towards their gate, Grace's cell phone rang, 'Samantha Adamson.'

Grace answered, "Sam, what's up. We're on our way to the gate. I can't talk long."

Sam said, "I'll talk quickly. I learned a ton. A classmate at Michigan, Jerry Mangold, is a Business section reporter for the New York Times. H. Culver Harris is big. Huge. He's one of the richest men in the US. But the kind you never hear about. He owns steel mills, bottling companies, trucking companies, food companies, high rises and more. You were right that his family is extremely private. His two sons and one son-in-law work for him and they're as tight lipped as the old man. They don't expose themselves, give interviews and rarely get photographed. He's a major donor to Catholic charities and to conservative politicians and causes. Word is that he owns a few judges, senators and representatives, on both sides of the aisle.

However, their marriages made the social pages in the Times and the Washington Post. His oldest daughter, Katherine 'Katy' Carter Harris was married in July, 1976, at the family estate in Chappaqua, NY, to Robert Ralston, M.D. of Portland, Maine. Twelve hundred people attended. No pictures were published. The bridesmaids included her sister and the groomsmen included her two brothers. Ralston was a resident in pediatrics at Tufts Medical Center in Boston. Katy Harris graduated from Colby College in Maine and was studying for her Master's degree at the School of Fine Arts in Boston.

Katy Harris Ralston was a bridesmaid at her brother's wedding a year later, also in Chappaqua. Then it's a bit crazy. Katy's name did not appear three years later in the wedding party for her last brother or in the wedding party seven years later for her sister, Holly, who married a man named Kerry Vernon. No mention of Katy Harris Ralston at all."

"Did you find out anything about Dr. Ralston?"

"He didn't show up in New York, so I took a hunch that he went back to Maine. Apparently, he's practicing pediatrics in Portland, Maine. I called his office this morning and asked if he was taking new patients because we're moving to Maine. *Not.* He is accepting new patients and could see me whenever we get to town. Hell, I can't get into Kevin's pediatrician for two weeks. Anyway, I took a chance and asked if Dr. Ralston is still married to Katy. The receptionist said, "Katy, I have no idea what you're talking about. You must have the wrong doctor. Dr. Ralston has been married to Gwen for more than twenty years." I don't think she suspected I was snooping. I told them I'd make an appointment when we moved. And that was it."

"Sam, I'm tired from these past few days. I want to come home, forget about this and let things settle down a bit. I didn't like the police chief's threats."

Sam said, "I understand. How's Alex holding up?"

Grace said, "Your brother's been great. He takes care of the kids, while I fret and worry. Sam, you don't think that Harris could get to Dr. Ralston, if he doesn't already own him."

"It's possible. What you thinking?"

Grace said, "I'm in this deep enough. I'm thinking that I let Alex take the kids home and I drive to Maine. If Ralston doesn't know I'm coming, and Culver Harris hasn't gotten to him, I'll have a better chance of getting information about Katy Harris."

Alex, listening to one end of the conversation said, "What? Grace, you're coming home. You're exhausted and you look like shit."

Grace, talking back to the phone, "Sam, I'll call you later. I'll need an address in Portland, Maine. Bye."

Grace turned to Alex, "We've come so far. Bear with me. Katy Harris married a pediatrician in Maine but isn't married to him now. I'm guessing that they're divorced, which means that Katy Harris is living somewhere else. I need to get to him before anyone else does."

Alex, now perturbed, said, "You're getting crazy. You're also putting yourself in harm's way. Maybe the kids, too. It's not fair."

"I'll be fine. At most, it might be a day. I could drive or take a commuter flight."

At the airport counter, Grace cancelled her ticket. The drive to Portland, Maine, was six hours. The one direct flight of ninety minutes was sold out for two days. Grace kissed Alex goodbye as she left her family and returned to the Avis counter.

* * * *

Grace arrived in Portland, Maine, before three p.m. and called Samantha.

"Sam, any more info?"

Sam said, "Ralston's office address is 707 Congress Street. Phone number is 207-772-7272. Good luck."

At three fifteen p.m., Grace parked her car across the street from Northeast Pediatric Associates and walked into a small waiting room. The aging placard on the front said Peter Ralston, M.D. and Robert Ralston, M.D., Pediatrics.

The smallish waiting room had two children playing with blocks in a corner, while two mothers chatted.

Grace went to the front desk and the receptionist, wearing a colorful smock with Winnie the Pooh characters, smiled and looked around for a child that she assumed would be with Grace.

"How can I help you? Dr. Ralston doesn't see sales reps."

"I'm not selling anything. My name is Dr. Grace Gordon. I'd like to speak to Dr. Ralston for a moment."

"Can I ask what you're here to sell?"

Grace smiled, "I'm not selling." Grace handed her a business card.

The receptionist said, "Says here you're a doctor of linguistics from Seattle. This really you? You're a long, long way from home."

"That I am. Dr. Ralston and I have something in common and I'd like a few words. I promise I'm not selling anything."

"He's got a few patients here now and if no one else walks in you could probably see him in twenty to thirty minutes. You could go out for a walk and return."

"If you don't mind, I've come twenty-five hundred miles. I'll wait here until he can see me."

"Suit yourself."

The receptionist turned and walked into the back of the office as Grace took a seat. Her two seat choices both had tears in the cushion.

A moment later, the receptionist returned and sat. Behind her, a man about fifty, slim, half-glasses over his nose, bowtie, suspenders and a pink shirt, peered over the receptionist's head at Grace. Grace looked directly at the man and smiled. He returned the look, blinked twice, and then appeared startled. He whispered something to the receptionist and disappeared back into his office.

At once, the receptionist called both children and their mothers back into the exam area. Within five minutes, both mothers and children exited the office. Grace was alone.

The bowtied man came into the waiting room, turned a chair around and sat across from Grace. The receptionist opened her window, not hiding the fact that she intended to listen to every word.

"I am Dr. Robert Ralston, and you are?"

"My name is Grace Gordon. I am a Professor of Linguistics at the University of Washington in Seattle. If I may ask, who is Peter Ralston?"

"That's my father, he started the practice. He's been retired for seven years now but comes by the office and likes to see his name on the plaque. So what can I do for you, Dr. Gordon from Seattle."

"I'm sure your time is busy," *which obviously it is not,* "so I'll come to the point. I believe that I am the daughter of Katy Harris of Chappaqua, New York."

The receptionist had no idea what Grace was talking about and wrinkled her nose.

Ralston, hesitated, then said, "Oh...my...God. I thought so. You look much like her. I've been waiting for you."

Grace, now surprised, said, "Did someone tell you I was coming today?"

"No, no, no. I've been waiting twenty-five years for you to come. I didn't know for sure that you existed. But somewhere in the back of my head, I thought you might walk in the door sometime."

"Did Mr. Harris call you?"

"No. I assume you mean Cully Harris, Katy's father? Haven't spoken to him since Katy died."

Grace's eyes opened, and her hand went up to her mouth, "Katy is dead?"

"You didn't know?"

"I didn't know she existed until this morning. I couldn't find out any information. I went to Chappaqua with my husband and children this past week looking for a missing phone booth. We weren't treated nicely in the town, but I did learn that Culver Harris was likely the father of my biologic mother."

Ralston said, "Oh, I'm so sorry for you."

Grace said, "Only then did my sister-in-law, Samantha, find that you and Katy had been married. I assumed you were divorced from her."

"How so?"

"Samantha called here and asked about Katy. Your receptionist didn't know what my sister-in-law was talking about, and that your wife's name is Gwen."

Ralston and Grace turned to the receptionist who nodded.

Ralston said, "I was married to Katy before I came back to Portland. She died giving birth to our first child. She died unnecessarily because the doctors and I didn't know that Katy had been pregnant before our marriage. She had delivered her baby, which I suppose is you, with a C-section. We had been told that her abdominal scar was from a twisted ovarian cyst. Had we known the truth, Katy would have had another C-section or, at least, wouldn't have been given drugs to stimulate labor."

Grace was crying softly. Ralston stood and went to the receptionist's desk and returned with a box of Kleenex, giving a few to Grace and handing her the box.

Ralston sat and continued, "Katy didn't tell anyone about the C-section either. She must have known but was under the thumb of her father. It's strange. She was so damn smart and must have known the dangers, but said nothing. I have no idea how she repressed the memory of the pregnancy. Anyway, she and my son died, and a little of me died with them. Culver Harris and the rest of the Harris family dissociated themselves from me the moment she died. They came to the funeral, said nothing to me or my family and left immediately after the ·ceremony. I've never seen or heard from them, any of them, again."

The two sat for a bit. The receptionist opened a new box of Kleenex for herself and dabbed her eyes.

After while, Grace spoke, "I suspect he will now, I mean talk to you."

Ralston said, "Why would he talk to me? Besides, I have nothing to say to him. He'd probably have a lawyer talk to me anyway. Cully Harris doesn't do anything personally unless he's forced to."

"I don't think he ever intended for me to find him. In fact, he's gone out of his way to make sure that I wouldn't. But I did and that's why I think Cully Harris might talk to you."

"Miss Gordon or Dr. Gordon, he's not a nice man. He's not someone you want mad at you. I can attest to that."

"I know, I've felt his wrath. By the way, I'm married. My husband is a urologist in Seattle. Alex Gordon. My maiden name was Pine, although the orphanage in Missoula gave me that name. And the name Grace is fine."

"Oh my. An orphanage?"

"Dr. Ralston, my life has been unusual."

"Dr. Gordon. Do you have an attorney?"

Grace, surprised, said, "No. I'm not trying to sue you."

Ralston, calm, said, "Of course. I don't know why you'd sue me, but you should have someone counseling you about Mr. Harris. He is powerful, well connected, and doesn't play nice."

"I hadn't even thought about having an attorney. I have some attorney friends in Seattle, especially one who helped me find my biologic father."

"Where's he, the father."

"He died in a car crash about the time I was born. I'm not entirely sure that he even knew I existed. His family did not know, of that I'm certain."

"How long are you going to be in town?"

"I didn't know what I'd find here. I was planning to return to Seattle tomorrow, if I could."

"Grace, if it's not too late. I think you need to talk to my attorney here in Portland. His name is Harry Fields. He's a longstanding family friend and was present when Cully Harris had me sign a pre-nuptial agreement before I married Katy. Harry always said that something was amiss but never went further. I'll demand that he give you time. Then I'd like you to come to our house for dinner and meet my wife. Both kids are off at school, one at Dartmouth, the other at Ohio State."

Grace left, Kleenex in hand, and drove to the law offices of Hearn Fields Barrett of Portland, Maine.

As soon as Grace left his office, Ralston called Harry Fields to warn him of Grace's impending visit and not to leave for home despite the late hour. Fields had time to pull and review Ralston's file. At their meeting, Grace told Fields what she had told Ralston.

"Grace, the pre-nuptial between Katy and Robert was strange. I had the first one revised before I'd let Robert sign it. I have copies of both. I remember the scene as if it were yesterday. The first pre-nup had a clause in it about only legal natural-born children having a claim on her estate. I questioned his lawyer and Culver Harris about it. I asked specifically if there had been any 'illegal' children. The lawyer seemed flustered, but Culver Harris had the word legal removed immediately. And, *ta da*, here you are. I assume that Katy Harris was not married to whoever was your biologic father?"

"Oh, no. They were not married. As I said, I'm not sure that my biologic father even knew that I existed. What exactly does that mean about being a natural born child?"

"You may have some entitlement to Katy Harris's estate, which had been withdrawn back into the Harris fortunes after her death."

"Oh?"

"Grace, when Robert married Katy, the trust had forty some million dollars in it."

"I don't want his money. I'd like to find out why. What did I do to I deserve placement in an orphanage when I had a mother and a father with families that could afford to raise me? I'd also like to find out where I was the first two years of my life? That's still a mystery."

"Grace, I think you will need a lawyer of your own. I still represent Robert. Given your appearance, we may have some dealings that involve Dr. Ralston. We can't have a conflict of interest."

Grace said, "I understand."

Fields said, "Another thing, men like Cully Harris know only two things, money and the power that comes with money. The only thing that will get Cully Harris's attention is if someone wants to take some of his money. Even a dime. He's wired that way. You go after his money, he'll take notice. In addition, somehow, someway, you'll need absolute proof that you are Katy's daughter. Harris will do everything in his power to prevent you from finding out. I'll talk to Robert about that."

"Understood."

"Anyway, Robert and Gwen are expecting you. We'll be in touch."

Grace arrived at the Ralston house at seven p.m. The modest split-level 1950s style rambler needed work. The walkway up to the house was badly cracked and paint was peeling around all the window frames. Gwen Ralston received Grace at the front door with a hug and a big smile.

"Grace, I've known about Katy from the time I met Robert. He was hurting and I helped him through some rough times. We've been happy for twenty-two years and have two adoring boys. Still, I know I wasn't his first love."

Grace talked for four hours about her life. She showed the paternity tests from Ben Kaplan from DNA Detections of Detroit. Ralston made a copy of the report proving paternity. After Gwen excused herself, Robert, spoke for an hour about his life with Katy Harris. Gwen didn't enjoy listening to her husband of twenty plus years talking about some other woman he loved. While Grace and Robert talked, Gwen made a motel reservation for Grace to spend the night.

Ralston added, "Not surprising about you being a linguist. Languages came so easily to Katy. It seemed like she'd hear four words of a language and could then speak it fluently. There's more to tell, good stuff. Someday, we'll sit and I'll tell all I know of Katy."

Grace laughed, "I'd love that. Languages do come easily to me, too. Now I know where it comes from."

Ralston said, "Katy was cremated. I know that I have little of hers anymore. Gwen made sure of that early in our marriage. I'll think on it."

At eleven thirty p.m., as Grace was about to get into her car to drive away, Robert Ralston came to the car with two large cardboard boxes and a sheet of paper.

"Grace, these are all the memories I have of Katy. I loved her as much as I love Gwen now. She was special. If you have questions about anything you find, let me know. Probably best to call at the office. Gwen doesn't always handle the Katy stuff well."

Grace gave Ralston a hug, and said, "Under different circumstances, you could have been my step-father."

"You're right. Wouldn't have been so bad."

Grace stayed in a motel outside of Hartford, Connecticut, off I-84, and drove back to the Newark airport the following morning, returned the car and arrived into Seattle at eight p.m.

* * * *

Robert Ralston took the next day off and drove to Boston at the same time Grace was flying west to Seattle. He went to see Dana Richie, Katy's OB doctor, now Chairman of Obstetrics and Gynecology at Brigham and *Women's Hospital* Medical Center.

Chapter 19

"Farley, you fucked me over. Some woman, towing a husband and two kids, was traipsing through Chappaqua two days ago trying to find a girl named Katy who made a phone call to someone thirty years ago. I don't have to tell you what I think is happening. The bastard is looking for us and she's close. Real close, and I don't like it."

"How'd they find you?"

"I have no fucking clue how they got to Chappaqua and I don't know what they know."

Farley said, in jargon mode, "How do we know that it's Seattle?"

"Who the hell else would be walking around Chappaqua with a husband and two small children asking about Katy, you idiot."

Farley said, "Hold on, Cully. Hold on. I was trying to be thorough. It doesn't make any sense that they'd find you. Unless, for some stroke of luck, they found the father."

Harris said, "The father didn't know he had a child, which means his family didn't know either. If they did know, we'd have heard from them decades ago. They'd want money, I know those kinds. Those Jews can smell it. I don't think they know anything."

Farley mused to himself. *There's the proverbial pot calling the kettle black.* "Cully, how are they going to prove your cremated daughter was the mother? That's not going to be easy. I can't see you offering DNA for them. Shit, this whole business with DNA scares me. Didn't exist when this all started. Cully, the only person that they can get information from is Robert Ralston. You want me to approach him and make sure he's on our side?"

"You have any other ideas?"

"Not really, because I don't know what Seattle knows."

Harris said, "We didn't leave Ralston on the best of terms. I walked out on him and took away all the perks he had from being my temporary son-in-law. He had no spine. I think you can quiet him with a little pocket change and a threat, if you know what I mean."

Farley said, "I'm thinking fifty thou a year, sound okay to you?"

"Seventy-five, if he plays hardball."

"Okay, Cully. I'll have it so he's not going to talk to himself."

Harris said, "Also, check in on the bastard and make sure she's back in Seattle. Can't see her calling Ralston on the telephone. I'm guessing she'll be making another trip to the east coast."

"I'd agree, Cully. I'll find out where she is."

"Henry, if this bastard finds Ralston and learns about the trust that was in Katy's name, we could have some big trouble. I won't let that happen, do you understand?"

376

"Cully, I understand. What would you like me to do?"

"If we get wind that she's onto something, I want it taken care of. She's not getting a cent from me, the fucking bitch," Cully said, voice rising with each sentence. "I want it taken care of. I've left her alone and she was supposed to leave our family alone. She's not getting one fucking dime from me."

"Cully, none of this makes sense. I can't see that there's a chance in hell that she knows anything. If we threaten her, in any way, she'll know for sure that she's being watched and we've got something to hide. She now has the resources to hire people to start looking if she thinks there's something to look for. I wouldn't do anything until we see if Ralston's gonna play ball. I think he'll fold for us like a cheap lawn chair."

"I don't know why I listen to you. You've been wrong so many times. I want her scared. Something that'll make her stop searching. I want her scared. I want her out of my life."

Farley hung up and then asked his secretary to find Rico Carpetti.

The next morning Farley and Rico met at his office.

"What's up Henry?"

"Remember that girl in Seattle that we tried to jam with some marijuana?"

Rico said, "Sure. I did everything right. Fuck. Who'd ever have guessed she was allergic to weed.

Never heard of such crap. Please don't tell me you want me to go back to Seattle. I can't stand that place. The weather and my bones don't do well together."

Farley said, "Not yet. But we may have to play hardball. Big, bad, ouch hardball. You can do this?"

Rico hesitated, "I can find someone. I can use the same contact from the last job. He'll do anything for money. This is going to cost more than the weed."

"I know, Rico. But I want you doin' it, nobody else. But don't do anything yet. Thirty-five thou up front plus expenses and fifty more if we need her to go away."

Rico said, "Sure. I'll look into it. It ain't gonna be me going. Took me six months to get over Seattle the last time. I'd kill myself before going back there."

"Rico, you'll go if I tell you to go. I want things in place. I've got one small wrinkle to work out. If it goes well, we don't need to do anything and you've made an easy twenty."

* * * *

Grace taught her morning classes the day after she arrived home, then visited Brad Hahn to bring him up to date. She brought some of the things from Ralston's box of memorabilia.

Brad Hahn called Harry Fields in Portland, Maine, the next day. They talked four times that day, sharing what they knew and planning the next steps. On a hunch, Brad also emailed Melissa Friedman an update.

Harry Fields called Robert Ralston to deliver a plan.

At the same time, Henry Farley called Cully Harris to tell him that Grace Gordon was in Seattle, taught her classes and then visited an attorney in Bellevue and returned home.

That night at home, Grace sat down after dinner with Ellie.

"I have some bad news. Some very sad news."

"What mommy?" Ellie said, already frowning.

"With all this running back and forth around the country, I have learned who my mommy and daddy were. You and I have been looking for them, so I could be like daddy and have my own mommy and daddy."

"Mommy, I know all that."

"It turns out that both my mommy and daddy died when I was young. I was unlucky not having a mommy and daddy like daddy did. I made up for it by having you and Mark. You will always know that daddy and I will be here for you. At least now, you and I know that I did have a mommy and daddy, but they couldn't raise me."

Ellie, in her five-year-old wisdom, gave Grace a hug and said, "Don't worry, mommy. I'll pretend that you're my little girl sometimes when we play."

Grace said, "Really. Really. That would be terrific, Ellie. Can I keep my name, Grace?"

Ellie said, "Of course, silly. Why wouldn't you have the same name? You can call me 'mommy' when we play, just like Raggedy Ann and Pooh call me mommy."

"Ellie, you are incredible. You should become a psychologist when you grow up."

"What's a 'psychologist'?"

"Someone who helps people who are scared. It's more than that. I'll explain later. You need to get on your PJs for bed."

"Mommy, I love you. I'll love you so much that you won't feel so bad about not having a mommy and daddy."

"I know I will. Now get ready for bed."

Chapter 20

"Dr. Ralston. This is Henry Farley. I'm Culver Harris's attorney. I was present when you came in for a prenup agreement."

Ralston, prepared for the call, said, "Sure. How is my ex father-in-law? I took an oath to help people when I graduated medical school. But, honestly, I hope Cully rots in hell and suffers from a host of painful illnesses. Now what would you like? Cully need a loan?"

Farley said, "Play nice, Doctor. Sarcasm won't get us anywhere."

"Or, what? Where are we going?"

"Dr. Ralston, I'm trying to be civil. I would like to come and talk to you about something that affects you and Mr. Harris. I'd be glad to come to Portland at a time that's a convenient for you. You name the date, time and place."

"Mr. Farley, I lost a wife and a child because of secrets hidden from me by the Harris family. I have to give this some thought. Can you call me back in forty-eight hours?"

"I'd appreciate coming sooner."

"I'd like to discuss this with my wife."

"I wouldn't do that, Doctor. What we have to talk about is between you and Mr. Harris and not for the ears of anyone else. If you discuss my coming with your wife, or anyone else, they'll want to know what we discussed, and that won't work."

"Okay, I'll keep it to myself. Still, I need forty-eight hours. Can I call you?"

Farley, annoyed, said, "No, no. I'll call you."

"Okay, give me a couple of days. Call after four thirty in the afternoon, I'll be done with patients."

Robert Ralston hung up and dialed his friend and attorney, Harry Fields.

Harry Fields called Grace Gordon and Brad Hahn.

Brad Hahn called the Attorney General of the State of Montana.

* * * *

"Dr. Ralston, this is Henry Farley."

"I was expecting your call."

"Did you talk to anyone?"

"I told my receptionist that I would be getting a call, that's all."

"Good. As I said a couple of days ago, I'd like to meet with you, and you alone, to discuss some important matters that could be beneficial to you."

"Only me? Not Culver Harris?"

"To both of you."

"I see. Anyway, I decided it couldn't hurt to talk. I'm under no obligation to do as Mr. Harris wants. Right?"

Farley said, "You're right, no obligations, unless, of course, you agree with our proposal."

"Fine. We'll meet. You can pick the place and time, here in Portland. But I do have one requirement."

"And that is?" said Farley.

Ralston said, "I want Cully Harris to be here for the proposal."

Farley, surprised, said, "Oh, I don't think so. Mr. Harris is a busy man."

"Farley, I'm busy, too. If this meeting is so important, let him come. If it's not so important, then I'm not interested. You call me when he's willing to leave his busy schedule and come to Portland."

"I'll have to check with Mr. Harris."

"You do that."

Thirty minutes later, Henry Farley called back. "Mr. Harris will come. How does next Monday at four thirty p.m. at the Portland Harbor Hotel on Fore Street. You know where that is?"

"Of course I know where it is. I live here. Five p.m. would be better. My office closes at four thirty and that should give me plenty of time to get there, even if I have a walk-in just before we close."

"Okay, five p.m. Mr. Harris will take a suite and we'll have you up to his room. When you get to the front desk, they'll connect you and someone will come down to escort you."

Ralston said, "I'll be there."

Farley spoke slowly and clear, "Alone. No one comes with you. Understood?"

Robert Ralston said, "I got it."

Farley then called Rico, already in Seattle.

"Rico, I'll make this quick. I have a meeting, Monday, at five p.m. here, or two p.m. in Seattle. I'll be done in an hour or less. If this meeting doesn't go like I want it to, you need to fill the contract."

"She don't come home until five o'clock. I ain't doin' nuttin' while she's at the university."

"Fine. I'll call you when I know. Be ready. If you don't hear from me by four thirty, assume my meeting didn't go well. Get it."

"I got it. She lives seventy-five yards from a park with a shitload of trees. We can see her garage and back door, clear as day."

"Who are 'we', Rico? I didn't want you to get anybody else involved in this."

"Same guy I worked with on the last job in Seattle and he helps me out. He don't know nothing."

"Yeah. The last job didn't turn out the way my people wanted it to."

"That ain't our fault. We did everything you asked."

Farley ended the conversation with, "I want you to do this. I'm paying you to do it."

Rico called Jaime Montez.

"Be ready Monday. If you don't hear from me by four thirty-five, it's a go as soon as she gets home."

Jaime said, "Clear. Just to be certain, you've given me five big ones already. Twenty more if four thirty-five isn't her lucky time. I'm going back to Mexico as soon as I'm paid ."

"Exactly. I'm not calling you again until Monday."

"Where you gonna be?"

"None of your business, but nowhere near you."

* * * *

The digital clock on his desk said Monday, 4:37 p.m. Ralston got into his 2008 Prius and drove east on Congress towards the Portland Harbor Hotel on Fore Street. He self-parked a block and a half away. He'd been at the Harbor Hotel before and the valet parking was ridiculously expensive. He walked into the hotel lobby, went to the front desk, and approached the clerk behind the counter.

"Hello. I'm Dr. Robert Ralston. A Mr. Culver Harris is expecting me."

The clerk said, "Yes. Yes, Doctor. We were expecting you. Have a seat and I'll ring his room."

Ralston sat facing the desk. The clerk, a young female, smiling and nodding, talked for thirty seconds and hung up. She eyed Ralston and said, "They'll be down in a minute to get you."

A moment later, a man, in a silk suit and tie, exited the elevator and approached Ralston. He was no taller than Ralston but comparisons ended at height. The man's neck looked bigger than Ralston's chest.

"Dr. Ralston. My name is Ralph. You're to follow me up to Mr. Harris's suite."

Ralston stood and followed the man, he renamed Thug #1, into the elevator, up to the fourth floor, and down a broad hallway. The man knocked on Room 402's door, swiped a keycard and opened the door. Ralston walked into a huge multi-roomed suite.

Henry Farley stood in the entryway and stopped Ralston from entering. "I'm sorry Dr. Ralston, but I'll need my friend here to search you for recording devices."

Ralston pulled a pen out of his coat and said, "This is my only recording device."

The muscular man chuckled as he patted Ralston down, "This guy's funny....he's clean."

Farley told the escort, "Ralph, thank you. That'll be all. You and Vince check the stairs and hallways. If clear, one of you stays at the elevator, the other at the stairwell. No one comes in unless we say it's okay."

"Got it, Mr. Farley." The man turned and knocked on the door to the suite next door. "Vince, c'mon."

Farley shut the door and turned to Ralston. "Dr. Ralston, it's nice to see you again."

Ralston thought *the bullshit has started.* "That remains to be seen. You've gotten older."

Farley smiled, "You're no spring chicken either."

"Touché. Where's Mr. Harris?"

"He'll be here in a moment. We wanted to make sure no one's following you."

"Who'd follow me? Is there something illegal going on here? If so, I'm leaving now."

Farley said, "Calm down, Doctor. Nothing's illegal. Mr. Harris likes to take precautions. I've been doing this for forty some years and I continue to do it, because I'm careful. Have a seat and we'll wait a few minutes and then call Mr. Harris."

"Call him. He's here, isn't he?"

"Yes, he's nearby."

Ralston shook his head and took a seat.

Farley asked, "Want something to drink?"

"Sure. A glass of water. I have a scratchy throat. I see sick kids all day."

"I hope nothing contagious?"

Ralston said, "No. I was yelling at a neighbor's dog digging in our yard last night."

Farley gave Ralston a bottle of water. Farley then opened the door to the outside hallway and looked right and left. He saluted okay to one of the men, Ralph or Vince, closed the door and then went into the adjoining bedroom. Ralston could hear a muffled phone conversation. Ralston re-appeared into the main room and said, "Mr. Harris will be here shortly."

A moment later, the door opened and in walked H. Culver Harris.

Ralston stood and approached Cully Harris. "Hello, Mr. Harris." Ralston had never called him anything but Mr. Harris. Never Cully, Culver, C.H, and certainly never, dad.

"Hello, Robert. You look well. I understand you remarried and have two children in college?"

"Yes, Gwen is my wife and I have two sons in college."

"Nice. Expensive?"

Robert thought *Expensive. He's always thinking of the money.* "Yes, colleges are expensive, and I've taken out some loans and so have the boys, but I am hopeful that the investment will be worthwhile. Mrs. Harris is well?"

Cully said, "She's fine. She has her gardens at Chappaqua, and her bridge and book groups in the city that keep her busy. Robert, have a seat. Your practice is going well?"

Ralston said, "It's okay. Makes ends meet. Maine is in somewhat of a financial slump, so young families don't always bring their kids in when they should. I'm fine."

Harris nodded. Ralston thought, *As if he gives a shit.*

Ralston then said, "Mr. Harris, I told Mr. Farley here that I had a scratchy throat. I was yelling at our neighbor's dog last night and early this morning. The mutt was trying to kill my cat. Do you think we could order up a pot of hot tea with honey?"

Harris looked at Farley who went to the phone and dialed the operator who connected him to the kitchen.

Farley asked, "Any kind of tea?"

"Green tea or any herbal tea will do."

Farley talked and hung up. It'll be here in ten minutes.

Ralston said, "Thank you very much," and turned back to Harris.

Harris was fidgeting in his seat, not happy about the delay, "Is that all you need?"

Ralston said, "Yes, I'll be fine."

Harris put his hands in his lap and sat back. "I have a little potential problem and I'd like your help."

"Help you with a problem? I can't see how?"

"Robert, here's the issue. I know you know that Katy had a child before meeting you. We did our best to put it behind her with extensive therapy and all."

Ralston said, "Did 'all' include threats if she told anyone."

Harris, ignoring the remark, said, "This child that Katy never saw, not for one second, has surfaced and is asking questions about Katy and our family. How she found us, I don't know. Moreover, I don't care. I don't want her getting any more information than she already has."

Ralston, frowned, and lied, "How would she find me?"

Harris said, "I don't know. She found us, so I suspect that without too much research, she'll find out that you were married to Katy and then seek you out."

Ralston countered quickly, "I wouldn't know that and what possible information could I give her that she doesn't already know. I'm not this girl's father and have no financial obligations to her. Personally, I don't want to be reminded of Katy and her unnecessary death any more than I have to. I am happy with my current wife and children and I'd like to keep it that way."

Harris said, "Good. I'm glad to hear that. Still, we don't want you communicating with her, in any way."

Ralston said, "So what's this girl's name?"

Farley interjected, "You don't need to know the name. She can tell you if she calls."

Ralston, looking only at Cully, replied, "If she calls me or shows up on my doorstep, what am I supposed to do?"

Harris said, "Tell her you have nothing to say and not to bother you ever again. You could add that if she continues trying to make contact, you will have a restraining order issued. We can help with that, if need be."

Ralston said, "I'm sure you will, however I'm not sure how I benefit by not talking to her. She already knows she's Katy's child, right?"

Farley said, "We think she suspects that Katy was her mother but we're sure she has no proof. We don't want to take any chances that she'll find out."

"I see," said Ralston. *These two in for a surprise.* Ralston suppressed a smile and said, "I'll say again, I'm still not sure how I benefit by not talking to her."

Farley sat next to Ralston and put a briefcase on the table. Harris got up and walked away, but stayed in the room.

Farley said, "We'd like to make it worth your while," as he opened up a briefcase filled with twenty-dollar bills. "There's fifty thousand dollars here, all in twenties. We'd like to help you with your kid's educational expenses. We are prepared to offer this same amount, yearly, as long as Mr. Harris is alive."

The doorbell to the suite rang. Vince knocked and then opened the door from the outside. Ralston noted that Vince, Thug #2, was taller than Ralph, Thug #1, and had an even bigger neck. Vince stood in the doorway and said, "Room Service's here, Mr. Farley."

Harris nodded to Farley, "Take care of that would you." It was not a question and Farley jumped up.

Farley walked quickly to the door. The room service trolley had pot of tea, a jar of honey and various sugars, milk, two cups and stirrers. The server was handsome, tall and athletic. He wore slacks, a white shirt and tie.

Farley said, "Okay buddy, where do I sign?"

The server said, "Are you Mr. Harris?"

"No, I'm Mr. Farley and I take care of Mr. Harris's business."

"I'm sorry Mr. Farley. I'm new and my boss told me that the only person allowed to sign is the person listed on the register. It says here, Mr. Culver Harris."

Farley's voice raised a full decibel, "This is bullshit. You ain't getting a tip. I'm going to call the manager and get your ass fired."

The server said, "I'm sorry, sir. I have to follow hotel policy. I just started and don't want to lose my job. The only person that can sign is the registered guest, or it comes out of my salary."

Harris shook his head and stormed to the door. "Get out of my way you idiots. Where do I sign?"

The server said, "Are you Mr. Culver Harris?"

Cully said, "Yes. I am Culver Harris and I don't expect that you'll be working here too much longer."

The server picked up a black leather case that would usually hold a restaurant bill and held it out. Cully Harris grabbed the unusually thick bill holder and opened it.

The server was, in fact, William Conklin, a local private investigator. Conklin said, "Mr. Harris, you have been served. My name is William Conklin and I am a private detective here in Portland. There are two notices. One from a Mrs. Grace Pine Gordon of Seattle, Washington and another from the Attorney General of the State of Montana. All the instructions are enclosed."

Harris and Farley screamed almost in unison, "What the fuck?"

Harris turned to Farley and continued screaming, "Farley, you lead me into an ambush. I'll have your neck for this."

Farley grabbed the service notices and threw them at Conklin, now surrounded by Ralph and Vince, the two large-necked thug twins. The notices fell to the ground.

Conklin said, "Farley, you're the lawyer. Your client has been served and there is nothing anyone can do. You know that and I'd seriously consider telling Mr. Harris what the law is. Also, if either one of these goons lays a finger on me or even messes up my hair, I'll have all of you, including Harris, thrown into the Portland City jail for assault. You know the rules. Have these guys back off so I can leave."

As Conklin spoke, the elevator doors opened and out stepped Harry Fields and two Portland City police officers. Fields spoke quickly, "Conklin, you okay?"

Conklin said, "Sure, Harry. Mr. Harris has been served. I'm going with you if it's okay."

Fields said, "Sure." Fields turned to Henry Farley and said, "Long time, no see."

Farley said, "Fuck you. You're in trouble."

Fields said, "I don't think so. Grace Gordon is suing Mr. Harris to reclaim Katy Harris Ralston's estate. She's the natural born daughter and the pre nuptial agreement was quite clear that any natural born child could claim the estate. I have both copies, the one that says 'legally born' and the final one that deletes the word 'legally.' You're not going to win this case and you know it."

"Fuck you, Fields. You don't have shit."

Fields, calm, replied, "We'll see, won't we. The other papers are from the State of Montana for the cost to raise Grace Gordon in the Montana Orphanage system. Mr. Harris owns several mines in Montana worth gazillions of dollars, and he pays Montana taxes. He has to appear or he'll lose the mines. Either way Montana gets their money."

Harris had gone to sit down. Farley's face was bright crimson and he kept repeating, "How the fuck did this happen. How the fuck...."

Fields continued, "I might add, Henry, that a grand jury panel will be called in New York State to question you about your dealings with Mr. Harris in regard to Grace Gordon. I would strongly suggest

394

you hire a lawyer, and a good one, to represent you. Attorney-client privilege cannot be waived if the communication was made for the purpose of committing a crime. Kidnapping Grace and transporting her across state lines to Montana certainly sounds like a federal crime. You'll be lucky to lose only your license to practice law. Both of you could easily go to jail."

Farley, unused to being pushed around, said, "Fuck you. You got nothing."

Fields laughed and continued, "Also, I have contacted the FBI in Seattle, the Seattle Police Department and security at the University of Washington and Seattle Med. If Grace Gordon, or anyone in her family, is threatened, or worse yet, hurt, you and Mr. Harris will be guilty until proven innocent. I swear if Grace Gordon so much as burns her hands making pancakes for her kids, it'll be your fault. Leave her the fuck alone."

Robert Ralston had quietly slipped out of the door and was standing next to his attorney. Ralston said, "Sorry about the tea going to waste. I'll gladly pay for it."

Farley started towards Ralston. Fields, smaller than both Ralston and Farley, and half the size of Vince and Ralph, stepped between Farley and Ralston.

Fields thought to himself, *the presence of two Portland City officers, who happen to be on your side, makes anyone brave.* Fields said, "I think we're done here. Robert, I believe you should walk out with us."

Ralston, smiling, said, "I agree. I don't think Mr. Harris and Mr. Farley are going to feel well. I'm guessing that they won't be closest best friends anymore."

Fields said, as he turned to the elevator, "I'd agree."

After a few steps, Fields turned back and approached Farley. Vince and Ralph guarded the door preventing Fields from seeing or talking to Culver Harris.

Fields, reaching into his coat pocket, said, "By the way, you said I had nothing. Here's a report from DNA Detections of Detroit, Michigan. In it is proof that Grace Gordon's mother was Katy Harris Ralston. They had plenty of tissue from her hysterectomy slides and tissue blocks to run a DNA maternity test. I threw in the paternity reports, too. Her father was Ben Kaplan of Detroit, now deceased, but I assume you knew that."

Fields turned again, put his arm around his old friend, Robert Ralston, M.D., and walked into the elevator. Fields left a terse message on Grace's office voice mail . "Mission accomplished."

* * * *

Defeat hung in the air. Farley opened the DNA report and went immediately to the bottom of the page.

Conclusion: These data confirm that Grace Gordon and Katy Harris Ralston are daughter and mother.

Farley read the report twice, backed up against the door, and mumbled. "Fuck, fuck."

Cully Harris was slumped on the sofa, the color drained from his face. He had removed his glasses and was slowly shaking his head. "This can't be happening.... I did everything....This can't be...."

Farley left the DNA report on the coffee table, picked up his briefcase that contained fifty thousand dollars in twenties that had been intended for Ralston's payoff, walked out of the hotel room and took the elevator down to the main floor. On the way to the Portland airport, Farley called Rico Carpetti in Seattle.

"Back off, Rico. Nothing's to happen. Nothing. Don't touch the girl."

"That's it. Nothing."

"Everything's turned to shit. They're onto us. Get out of Seattle."

"Fuck. My guy's in place outside her house waiting for her."

"What guy? You weren't gonna get anyone else involved. Get him outta there. The cops might be there any minute for all I know."

"Fuck. I want my money. And I gotta pay this guy too."

"You got paid some already. You'll get the rest, someway. Get your guy outta there, now." Farley hit the 'END' button on his cell phone. *No way I'm around when he returns.*

Rico immediately tried to call Farley back. *What did **someway** mean?* Farley didn't answer after three additional attempts. *I'm fucked and I'll never see the money. Fuck.*

Rico then called Jaime Montez's cell phone. He had spoken to him an hour earlier. After four rings, the call went to voice mail which was full. Rico called twice more, each time getting the same non-existent response. Rico's cell phone said four fifteen p.m. Jaime's instructions were clear. Rico sped north on I-5 towards Grace's house twenty-five minutes away. Halfway there his phone read four twenty nine.

Rico hollered at the phone, "Answer you fucking asshole. Answer the goddamn phone."

South of downtown, opposite the Boeing Access Road, traffic slowed to a stop.

I'll never get there.

Rico reached into his shirt pocket and swallowed a handful of Tums. He exited the freeway and reentered I-5 south towards SeaTac Airport. As he drove, he kept redialing Jaime's number over and over.

* * * *

Waiting for his plane, Farley called his private banker and told him to move all of his savings into an established account in the Cayman Islands. When he got to New York, Farley went directly to his office and stayed there until four thirty a.m.

* * * *

Jaime Montez sat in a forested area seventy-five yards from Grace's back door and the separated garage entrance. Rico Carpetti had supplied him

with an untraceable Heckler and Koch MSG90
sniper rifle with five 7.62 x 51 mm NATO rounds in
the cartridge. Jaime was familiar with the rifle.

They don't make nothing better than this.

The gun lay in its case by his side as he waited
for Grace to return. A slight drizzle and dark sky
had no effect on his excellent vantage point. He
could see everything he needed to see. His watch
said 4:36 p.m. He unzipped the gun case, hefted the
rifle, then assembled and focused the Hensoldt ZF6x
telescopic sight on the garage door handle. Grace
hadn't returned, so he replaced the gun and sight in
the case but left it unzipped. His watch said 4:47
p.m. when he heard the garage door open. Jaime
removed the gun from the unzipped bag and sited
Grace's SUV as she drove into the garage.

What the fuck did she do to deserve this?

Grace exited the car and stood to the left rear
side as Jaime searched for her in his sights and put
his finger on the trigger waiting for her to stand still.
Graced pushed the key fob and the tail gate door
opened, blocking his view of Grace above the waist.
Jaime waited. As the tail gate opened, a bag of
groceries fell to the ground, shattering a jar.

Grace yelled, "Dammit, dammit. I need some
help here."

Immediately, little Ellie exited the back door of
the house and stood on the stoop.

"What happened, mommy?"

"A jar of pasta sauce fell out the back and broke. I need a plastic bag. Can you get it for me from the kitchen pantry?"

"Sure, mommy."

Grace reentered the garage picked up a broom and came back to the rear of the car to take a look at the mess. Jaime elevated the rifle again, finger on the trigger, but Grace got down on her knees and crawled back into the garage to sweep glass from under the car towards the back.

Jaime was sweating, despite the cool Seattle evening air. *Shit.* A drop of perspiration, unabsorbed by his ski hat, trickled down his forehead and settled outside his right eye. Two blinks and a quick sleeve-swipe cleared his vision. He rolled to his side and felt a soft vibration in his rear pocket. Keeping an eye in the scope as Grace tried to push broken glass onto the driveway, he reached into his back pocket and removed his cell phone. He had silenced the phone when he entered the forested area. He quickly turned to the phone screen which flashed 14 call attempts and one text message from Rico. He opened the text message box "It's off. I'm at SeaTac."

Jaime looked back at the garage. Grace was standing still, straight up, waiting the for tail gate to close. *I could have hit her from a thousand yards.* He quickly disassembled the scope, packed the rifle and walked away from the house deeper into the wooded area and called Rico.

"Fuck, man. I had the phone silenced and didn't get your message. I came a half-second from taking her out."

Rico said, "It's over. My guy back east hung up on me and won't answer. Sounds bad. He owes me money. I'm on a American flight in thirty-five minutes. I'll call you with a mailing slip for the rifle."

"No way. You owe me money, too. That was our deal. No way your fucking me."

"Fuck you. I didn't get paid either."

"I don't believe you. You never work without the scratch up front. You musta brought my money with you."

"Fuck you, man. Mail the gun. When I get it and when I get paid, you get paid. That's the end of this conversation." Rico disconnected the call.

Jaime sat down against a tree. *I'll never see the asshole again. I needed the money. Shit, this rifle's got to be worth ten thou. Bodyguards are making more money in Culiacán than I am making here. Why do I always get fucked? I knows what I gots to do.*

Jaime walked back to his car and locked the sniper rifle in his trunk. He drove around the block and parked in front of Grace's house. He sat motionless for a few moments and then, by habit, he popped the trunk with the lever by his seat. He exited the car and opened the trunk. He unzipped the rifle case and stared at the sniper rifle.

The best.

Jaime rezipped the case and slammed the trunk shut, hard enough that someone might have mistaken the sound for a gunshot. Jaime walked slowly up to Grace's front door and knocked.

Rico was arrested in New York the following morning at Kennedy Airport exiting from his American Airlines flight. His briefcase contained twenty thousand dollars.

* * * *

The United States Attorney presented evidence to a grand jury in New York City forty-eight hours later. With Rico Carpetti's plea bargained testimony, The Attorney General of the State of New York recommended proceeding with prosecution of Farely. Not surprisingly, Farley's whereabouts were unknown and his office contents and computers were missing or had been destroyed. His staff had no idea where he had gone.

Absent Henry Farley or his records, the federal prosecutors believed that criminal charges against Cully Harris would be difficult, if not impossible, to prove. Rico Carpetti did not know of Cully Harris. Additionally, Grace was adamant that she would not participate in a prolonged criminal court battle against her biologic grandparents. With Fields and Hahn's encouragement, Grace had no hesitation trying to recapture her mother's estate.

Chapter 21

May 2007

The State of Montana settled with Culver Harris for the expenses incurred raising Grace Helena Pine. Sixteen years at twenty-five thousand dollars per year plus four percent interest and expenses. The total came to five hundred ten thousand dollars. The Attorney General of the State of Montana did not pursue the kidnapping charges. The AG had no absolute proof that Harris or Farley had transported Grace across state lines to the orphanage in Missoula. The statute of limitations, according to Montana State law was five years for kidnapping, and the clock started when the AG learned of Cully Harris's involvement. The case remained open.

Brad Hahn, of Seattle, and Harry Fields, of Portland, met with Cully Harris's new attorneys over Grace's entitlement to Katy Harris Ralston's estate. At the time of Katy's death, the fund had a net worth of forty-three point seven million dollars. As proof, Robert Ralston provided Fields with copies of the statements from Paine Webber dated the month before Katy's death. Culver Harris worst fears of a prolonged court battle, with the attendant negative publicity, led to a quick settlement for Grace Gordon of two hundred eleven million dollars, about one-quarter of Culver's net worth. Even though the case contained a gag clause and a promise of no further civil actions, the New York Times, Wall Street Journal and Washington Post ran articles the following day. The sources of the leak were never determined. Grace's story, to which she refused comment to the press as part of the settlement, ran nationally for a week in print, radio, and web based news media. Jay Leno's comment in his monologue, "This week, babysitting rates jumped from seven dollars an hour to eleven million dollars per hour. I'd like to tell Cully Harris that I am available to sit, anytime, any day that he wants."

Grace set up trust funds to ensure the education of her two children, her nephew and the two children of Robert and Gwen Ralston. Grace endowed the Grace Gordon Chair of Linguistics and Speech at the University of Washington. In addition, she and Alex endowed the Gordon Chair of Urology at Seattle Med and made a ten million dollar grant to renovate the medical library and a ten million dollar grant to Child Protective Services of the State of Montana.

Two weeks later, Grace Gordon received a call from Brad Hahn.

"Grace, sit down. I just got off the phone with a woman named Mary Lipson. She had worked at the Lost Souls Orphanage in Mt. Nazareth, Virginia, about the time you were born, and is certain that you were there for the first two years of your life."

"Brad, how can you be certain? We've had a dozen calls already saying the same thing."

"I think this is the real deal. Listen to the story. You appeared at the Lost Souls Orphanage in the middle of the night, with no contact information. Richard LeVite, the director of the orphanage at the time, seemed not to care about contacting the authorities, which in itself was unusual, and not standard procedure. The name given to you, by this Mary Lipson, was Sophia Rose Richmond. Mr. LeVite had specifically placed Mary in charge of 'Sophie Rose', as the staff called her. Mary grew quite attached to little Sophie Rose. Mary and her husband, Jerry, had two children of their own, and had adequate finances, but Richard LeVite blocked every attempt by the Lipsons to adopt Sophie Rose. As mysteriously as she appeared, Sophia Rose Richmond disappeared before her second birthday. LeVite told Mary that her parents reappeared and he took it upon himself to return Sophie to their graces. A five hundred dollar bonus to Mary Lipson purchased her acquiescence. Mary thought it strange that Sophie's parents took none of her belongings, including a small pink leopard stuffed animal, 'Leppy' that Sophie Rose would sleep with every night. Mary kept the stuffed animal as well as Sophie's blankets, hoping that she'd return. Curiously, a week after Sophie's unexpected disappearance, her chart remained in the file cabinet. The chart contained no notes of her return to her parents. Mary took the records and has them, including a footprint ID. So distraught over Sophie's, or your, departure, Mary Lipson quit the orphanage six months later."

"Brad, that still doesn't prove it's me she's talking about. I suppose we can have the prints checked."

"Grace, there's more. Mary Lipson's most endearing memory was little Sophie's habit of twirling and straightening her hair with her left hand as she sat and watched other children or when looking at picture books."

Grace remained silent.

Brad said, "Grace, how are you doing? I know you have to be sad that, in the end, both your parents died before having any benefit of knowing you. What a shame. I know you have money, more than you'll ever need, but that wasn't what you were looking for. I am sorry."

Grace said, "Curiously, I wanted to do it for my daughter as much as for me. She's not yet eight years old, but feels a strange sadness because I didn't have a mother or father. She started this whole thing by finding Melissa Friedman on TV and, in some way, takes responsibility that it didn't turn out quite the way she, or I, hoped."

* * * *

Alex lay next to Grace as her thirty-seventh birthday approached. He said, "Your birthday is around the corner. Anything special you want to do?"

Grace thought a second. "No, not really. In the orphanage, one's birthday was a short announcement at the beginning of each month. So every November 1st, one of the nuns would read out all the November birthdays. That's it. Since we found Mary Lipson, I know that my birthday was around May 1st. Which one are we celebrating?"

Alex kissed Grace on the lips and said, "We've missed the May date, but from now on, we'll celebrate both. Ellie and Mark will be so jealous. They'll each want a second birthday."

Grace said, "I don't want a party. Just family would be fine for me."

"Family it is. I've already talked to Ellie, you know, the one that when she's not your daughter, is your surrogate mother."

"And."

Smiling, Alex continued, "She wants to plan a surprise party for you on Thursday, November 8th. I'll take off work early and you have no late classes that day, I checked. Ellie thought I should send you out for a massage and when you come back, we'll be hiding in the living room. Ellie and I will get a cake from Brown's Bakery. I told her that thirty-eight candles was dangerous and she said, 'That's a big number.' She then proceeded to count to thirty-eight."

Grace laughed. "God, how I love you and my kids."

Alex said, "You'll need to walk in and be surprised."

Grace said, "The massage sounds great. Ellie is so special. I'll scream and jump up and down."

Alex said, "No screaming tonight. Just oohs and aahs," as he started on Grace's buttons.

* * * *

At three thirty p.m. on November eighth, Grace headed to the Heavenly Bliss Spa for a massage, facial and pedicure. She would be done at six thirty p.m. and home by six forty-five p.m.

Grace walked into a dark and seemingly empty house with the lights turned off. Playing the game, she yelled, "Hello. Hello. Anyone home?" She waited for a second and yelled again, "Alex...Ellie...Mark. Anyone home?" She waited another second and yelled, "It's my birthday and nobody is here. Alex...Ellie...Mark."

Smiling, Grace walked towards the living room and opened the double sliders that separated the living room from the kitchen. The dimly lit room was empty save an older couple sitting on the couch. The couple looked familiar, but not.

Grace, now surprised, said, "Excuse me. What's going on? Who are you? Where is my family?"

The older couple stood and the man, in his early seventies, said, "Hello, Grace. I am Jerome Kaplan and this is my wife, Helen. We are your grandparents. We are Ben Kaplan's father and mother."

Grace stood in the doorway, unable to move. She had planned to scream and jump up and down for Ellie, but dumbstruck, all she could mutter was, "This is my birthday. Why are you here?"

Helen Kaplan said, "Alex told us that you wanted a birthday party for family. We're family. We're family now."

Grace, disoriented, stumbled to a chair across from the couch where the Kaplans stood and sat down. She regained her composure enough to say, "I thought you never wanted to see me. I had stopped hoping that we'd ever meet. Why are you here?"

At that moment a side door to the living room opened, the lights went on and Ellie Gordon led a parade of people into the living room singing the 'Happy Birthday' song. Alex followed, holding a large cake with thirty-eight burning candles. Cousin, Senator Melissa Kaplan Friedman and her husband and daughter, Uncle Max and Celeste Kaplan, Phillip Kaplan, Ben Kaplan's brother, and his partner Barry Smith, walked in finishing the song.

The only non-family members were Brad and Didi Hahn, but Grace considered them family.

When the hullaballoo died down, Grace sat with her grandparents and asked, "How did this happen? I thought you wanted nothing to do with me, ever."

Jerome Kaplan explained, "You're right. We did want nothing to do with you. Ben's loss to us cannot be measured. It lives with us each and every day. We believed your existence was an aberration. We knew nothing of Katy Harris and what she meant to Ben or what Ben meant to her. Not a clue. If you were created of an unloved relationship, we wanted nothing to do with you. Your existence would have made our loss even worse."

Grace said, "That's what Melissa had told me."

Helen Kaplan, holding her husband's hand, said, "Then a month ago, Brad Hahn and Melissa came to our house. We were angry. No, we were beyond angry, but Melissa refused to leave until she could say what she wanted to say. Brad Hahn's presence stopped us from going berserk. Together they sat us down. Brad told us the story of Ben and Katy. He told us how Ben pined for her and talked about her, incessantly, for the first three months of the school year. Calls, letters, but nothing. How the two *nudniks* drove to New York so Ben could try to talk to her. When they were threatened, Ben finally gave up but then she called him the day that Ben died. Ben never told us that he and Katy had a child, but we can only surmise that she was able to get free for those few telephone moments she told him. He told us that he'd need to speak to us as soon as he got home, no matter how late, but he wouldn't tell us why. I am certain it was to tell us that he and Katy had a child. You."

As for Katy Harris, from what we've learned, her father is a piece of work and manipulated his daughter to the point that we're sure she didn't even believe her own memory. Did she even remember Ben? Did she even love him? We'll never know for sure but we think so."

Helen said, "After that, Melissa made us read the orphanage records and the trial testimony of your life in the orphanage. A life that you did not want, or deserve."

Grace nodded and said, "No one deserves that kind of life."

Helen continued, "We have decided that if Katy's father had stayed out of the way, she would have been able to love Ben the way we did. So many ifs. At the least, if we knew you existed, and Katy's family didn't want you, we would have raised you. You are Ben's daughter, we are your grandparents and we will try to spend the rest of our lives making up for lost time."

The three sat quietly, weeping on the sofa, until Ellie came and sat next to her mother.

Grace put her arm around Ellie and said, "Ellie, these are your great grandparents. Great Grandpa Jerome and Great Grandma Helen. They are the mommy and daddy to my daddy. They are going to tell us all about who my daddy was."

Ellie said, "Oh, mommy. You're silly. I know who they are. I told you that we would find your family and we did." Ellie moved across and sat between an astounded Jerome and Helen, folded her arms and smiled at a bawling Grace.

Chapter 22

The New York Times and The Wall Street Journal reported that the Cyclical Systems IPO of 28 million shares closed at $56 by the end of trading yesterday, up from an opening price of $28 in heavy trading. The widely awaited IPO was the most successful first day release in three years on the big board. Analysts feel that Cyclical Systems (CSCS), headquartered in Durham, NC, will likely reach one hundred thirty dollars per share within the next two months. Kerry Vernon, the founder and CEO of Cyclical Systems remains the majority stockholder with eighteen million shares. Participating in the IPO were Madrona Investments and Ranier Baker Partners from Seattle and Gold and Blue Partners from Berkeley, CA.

The sale netted Mr. Vernon $500M and pushed his net worth to just under$1B. Mr. Vernon is the son-in-law of H. Culver Harris and married to his daughter, Holly. Mr. Vernon left The Harris Company three years ago to start Cyclical Systems. Mr. Harris, as usual, had no comments about Mr. Vernon leaving but insiders believed that Vernon's departure was less than friendly. The Harris Company held no stake in Cyclical Systems. Harris had no comment about the IPO.

* * * *

"Dr. Gordon, a Mrs. Holly Vernon called twice this morning and is on line #3 saying that she needs to speak to you. I told her you were very busy. She says she has information on Katy Harris, whoever that is, but she said you'd know. The phone number is from 919, which is North Carolina. She's holding on line three, and said she would wait."

Grace looked at the clock. She had twenty-seven minutes before her two p.m. class began. She held her breath and punched #3.

Grace said, "Hello, Mrs. Vernon. I am Dr. Grace Gordon at the University of Washington. Are you who I think you are?"

Holly said, "Yes, I believe I am. I am Katy Harris's sister, your aunt. I've been waiting to talk to you for almost forty years and I have something for you."

Grace said, "As part of the settlement with your father, I agreed not to approach anyone in your family."

Holly said, "I know, but I approached you and will send you a letter certifying that I did so."

Grace said, "Thank you, but I probably should talk to my attorney first."

Holly said, "Of course. I would too. However, I checked with our attorney and she said that you'd be fine as long as I am the one initiating the contact. In addition, I've already let my father's attorneys know that I was going to make contact. They had no comment. I haven't spoken to my father in almost two years. I'm guessing that you know he's not the most forgiving of people. I'm sorry that I didn't seek you out sooner, but Kerry, my husband, didn't want me to start anything until after our company went public. Anyway, check with your lawyer and then call me. I'll give you a number to call."

"Thank you. You said you had something to give me."

Holly said, "Yes, I did. I have Katy's diary. She wrote in her diary every day until she came home from Phillips Academy. She gave me the diary later that day, knowing that our father would take it. I've kept it all these years. She didn't know she was pregnant at the time."

The line remained silent for a moment. Holly said, "Are you still there?"

Grace said, "Yes, I'm here. I was looking for some tissue."

* * * *

Grace received her mother's diary from Holly Vernon three days later. Grace opened the brown wrapping slowly, somehow hoping that her mother might actually reside under the layers of twine and paper. The diary was red leather that had faded to a maroon hue. Faded yellow stitching outlined the outside cover with oiled bronze rivets at the corners. A stitched yellow outline of a heart at an angle filled much of the front. Within the heart were rows of small embroidered roses and a leather bow. Two oiled bronze hinges and an oiled bronze clasp finished the front. Grace held the book to her cheek, hoping it would tell her secrets without opening the cover. She smelled the diary hoping she might learn of her mother's favorite fragrance.

Grace went to her bedroom, closed the door, and placed the diary on her bed. She called Alex at work.

"What's up?"

Grace said, "When are you coming home?"

"It's 4:00 o'clock now and I have some letters to dictate and then stop by the hospital on the way out to see a post-op. I should be home by 5:30 at the latest. Why?"

"Remember Holly Vernon was going to send my mother's diary. It came today."

"And?"

"I'm afraid to open it. I don't want to be disappointed. Holly said she never opened it, even once. That was the deal Holly struck with her sister when Katy had Holly take it. I don't know what I'm going to find."

"Grace, what do you want me to do?"

"I'd like to be alone in my room. I need you to watch Ellie and Mark, maybe take them out to dinner. I'd like to be alone."

"Are you sure you don't want me to be around."

"No, I'm not sure of anything. It's as if I'm going to meet her for the first time. I think I'd just like to do it alone."

"I understand. Your call. I'll be home at 5:30 and I'll take the kids out for pizza."

Alex took the kids out ninety minutes later and Grace went into her bedroom, got in bed and opened the book.

My Diary

KATY

HARRIS

JUNE 1970

Grace ran her hands over the red broad stroked letters, pleading for them to come alive. She wasn't sure why, but she opened to the middle of the diary.

July 12, 1970

It's late and I'm exhausted. But I had to write this note because it could have been the best day of my life. No. It WAS the best day of my life. Ben took me to a dorm party. Someone had Johnny Mathis' Greatest Hits. Chances Are. Wonderful! Wonderful!. I hoped he'd kiss me. He danced me over to a darker section of the rec room and at the end of It's Not For Me To Say and he took my face in both his hands and said, "I love you - in French. Je t'aime." He kissed me so sweetly, my first. My lips, my nose, my eyes and back to my lips. I know I am naive, but I can't imagine anything better than tonight.

I didn't know that boys could be funny, sensitive and handsome. École Sacré Marie would have dances for us. I had a debutante ball. My family had social friends, not many, but some with sons my age. I saw few redeeming qualities in any of the boys I met, other than they were rich. I didn't enjoy their company and never looked forward to seeing most of them again. Now, I wake up in the morning and all I can think about is Ben. Ben. Ben. Ben.

Grace closed the diary and turned off the light.

Grace thought nothing of the orphanage, Sarah or Jodie, or Ezekiel Watkins.

Chapter 00

July 1969

Ben Kaplan met Katy Harris in the library on the first day of summer school at Phillips Academy in Andover, Massachusetts. Welcoming parties attracted every summer student, except Ben and Katy. As the two sat in the cavernous hall, six desks apart from each other, both couldn't help noting that they were the only two people in the library.

Harvard University accepted Ben Kaplan, largely on the strength of his science grades at Bloomfield Hills High School. Ben struggled with foreign languages and knew he'd face three semesters of foreign language, probably French, at Harvard. He decided to enroll for the summer in non-credit French at Phillips.

Katy Harris was fluent in three languages. She struggled with advanced math. She was set to start Smith College. For the same reasons as Ben, she was taking calculus.

Ben got up to look for a water fountain, only to run into Katy.

Ben started, "I assume that you know that we're the only two crazies here tonight. Everyone else is partying." Now closer to Katy than six large library tables, he got a better look. Light auburn hair, large expressive blue eyes, unblemished skin, and a strong chin with a small cleft. This has to be the most enchanting creature in the world.

Katy said, "Hard not to notice. I'm having trouble with calculus, so I thought I'd get a leg up. I've been looking at pre-calculus stuff for two hours and I still haven't a clue."

Ben nodded, "I can't learn foreign languages. I think, eat, sleep, and dream in English. I don't get the point of learning another tongue that I'll never use. I'm from Detroit. I'd have to go two thousand miles to find another language that I need to speak. Calculus, math anal, trig, all come so easy to me."

Katy shook her head, "I speak three languages besides English, including French. I hear it after a few sentences. Obviously, we're from different gene pools."

Ben laughed, "You loan me some of those French genes, the real tight ones, and I'll give you all the math help you'd ever need."

Katy, laughing at the play on the word, genes-jeans, said, "That's a deal. Can you help me with linear functions?"

Ben said, "Sure. Let's walk a straight, or linear function, back to your table and I'll see what you're up against. If I help you, you've got to get me through French."

Katy said, "Pourquoi pas. J'aimerais aider"

Ben said, "What's that?"

Katy, giggled, and said, "Why not. I'd love to help."

By the end of the first night, the two were enamored with each other. For six solid, uninterrupted weeks, Ben and Katy saw each other every day. She spoke French and he taught advanced math. Privacy was close to impossible on the small campus but Ben or Katy would steal a kiss, or longer, at any moment when they thought no one was watching.

As the summer drew to a close, Katy said, "Ben, you are so special. How am I going to live, me at Smith and you at Harvard?"

Ben said, "Je ne sais pas. Worcester is half way between Harvard and Smith. An hour drive for each of us. We'll meet for breakfast, hurry back for class and do that three times a day."

Katy laughed.

Ben, smiling, said, "Odd, you're like every girl I grew up with in Detroit, other than you're not Jewish."

Katy gave him a quick elbow to the ribs.

Ben turned Katy towards him, and held her face gently between his hands. "Katy Harris, I can say that you are the most stunning creature ever created, if that counts for anything. I never knew exactly what the 'it' factor is, but for me, you've got 'it.' I've never had the feelings for anyone like I have for you." Ben kissed her gently on the lips.

"Ben, not here," as she scanned the busy hallway between classes, "but I love when you speak French."

Ben whispered, "You promised that we could sneak out one night and go into Boston for a dinner and a movie. Neither of us has seen *Easy Rider* and it's supposed to be an incredible movie. We've got to do it, before summer session ends."

Katy said, "Next Thursday is perfect. I have finals on Wednesday, as do you. Thursday is a dead day and then we're only a few days from going home. What are they going to do if we come home late? Expel us?"

Ben said, "Thursday it is. After lunch, we sign out twenty minutes apart, walk into town and take the bus to Boston, dinner and a movie."

"Deal."

Ben and Katy arrived in Boston at 2 p.m. The heat and humidity of Boston's August seemed almost light and airy to the two freedom seekers. Ben took Katy's hand, and for the most part of the next five hours, didn't let go. They both understood that each would be going home in few days to the other ordered worlds from which they were raised. Katy, to a cold cloistered existence, run by rules, boarding schools and nannies. Ben, to the intense, smothering and overwhelming attention that his parents, one generation from the Holocaust, applied.

Walking past the Old State House on Washington Street, Katy said, "I don't want to go home. I want you to never let go of my hand. These past six weeks have been more fulfilling than any time in my life. I feel so free, so full of *life, so excited for every day and every adventure."*

Ben turned and enveloped her into his arms. "How do you do it? How do you say things that I only wish I could say? You are the most amazing person on earth, and, yes, I will never let go of your hand."

By 8 p.m., the two had forgotten completely about dinner or the movie. As the sun set, Katy and Ben found themselves walking through the Boston Public Garden. A brief shower caught both unaware, followed by a strong evening breeze off the harbor.

Katy said, "I'm chilled. Hard to believe I'd be cold with the temperature above 80°."

Ben said, "I'm too tired to be cold. Do you think they've missed us?"

"Doubtful, All the testing is done and the good-bye parties have started."

As they started to walk back to the bus station, Katy again complained, "I'm so cold."

Ben wrapped her in his wet sleeves as they headed up Charles Street. Ben looked at her blue lips and shaking. "Katy, we have two options. You and I can tough it out and catch the bus back to Phillips. Or we're in front of this hotel and I can get us a room. We can take hot showers, dry our clothes, and go back to school later tonight, or in the morning. It's your choice."

Clinging to Ben, she whispered, "I can't go another step. I'm so cold."

Ben said, "Are you sure, Katy?"

"I'm so cold."

Ben took charge. He walked Katy into the foyer of the hotel and sat her down. The air-conditioning and fans made Katy even colder.

Ben went to the desk. "I need a room. My wife and I were caught out in the rain. We're three hours from the Cape and our hotel and she's freezing. We've decided to stay the night. Nothing fancy."

The desk clerk looked over at Katy, arms wrapped around her chest, blue lips, shivering. He said, "I have a double room, third floor, for eighty-five dollars."

Ben put ninety dollars on the counter, filled out room forms with bogus names and got a key and five dollars back. He escorted Katy up to 312. The room was cool and Ben turned on the heat. He started filling the tub with hot water from the showerhead to create a steam. He then pulled one of two terry cloth robes from the closet.

"Katy, I'll give you some privacy. Go into the bathroom, get your clothes off and get into the robe. The steam should warm you up quickly. When the bathtub is full enough, switch it to the tub faucet and keep the hot water dripping after the tub is full. Give me your clothes and I'll hang them up as soon as you get them off.

Katy, despite feeling and looking like an iceberg in an earthquake, smiled, and whispered in his ear, "You are so sweet."

After Katy handed her clothes off through the partly opened bathroom door and got into the tub, Ben yelled through the door, "I'll be back in 5 minutes." He went down to the men's bathroom in the foyer. With five quarters, he bought a condom from a vending machine and returned to the room.

When he returned he announced to the bathroom door, "I'm back. You feel better?"

"Much. Almost toasty. I unlocked the door. You need to get warm too."

Ben hadn't given the cold much thought. He looked at his bare arms and saw goosebumps. He said, "Are you sure?"

Katy said, "Ben, I'm sure. I've never been so sure."

Ben entered to find Katy in the hotel robe and combing her wet hair as the tub emptied.

Ben said, "I like showers."

Katy replied, "I usually do too. Can't remember the last bath I took, but this one was awesome."

Ben turned on the shower, undressed, stepped into the tub and pulled the curtain. He peeked to find her still combing her hair. He had been erect since getting into the shower.

Ben put shampoo on his hair, worked up a lather and stood facing the showerhead letting the suds run down his face. He felt hands on his shoulders and turned around to find Katy sliding her hands down his chest. She looked down and said, "Oh. Oh, my God. I never...."

Ben, taller by nine inches than the five-foot, four-inch Katy, pushed his firm penis to the side, so he could hold her close. He said, "Me never, either. Are you sure you want to be here?"

"I'm sure. I've never been so sure. I'm sure it's not right. But, I've never been so sure that I wanted something so much."

Ben said, "God, I love you."

Katy said, "Ben, most of the girls who talk about 'it', say that the first time is a huge letdown. I can't see that happening. Don't let it happen, Ben. Don't make it forgettable."

As the water poured over both faces, he kissed her face, her eyes, her nose, her ears, her lips and chin.

"Are you warm now?"

"Yes."

Ben turned off the water, helped Katy out of the tub and put her robe back on. They went into the hotel room and he removed the covers from the bed. Before he could return, she dropped the robe on the floor and got into bed, on top of the sheets.

Ben said, "Katy, are you sure you're okay?"

A small tear hung on both her eyelids. The tear drops hesitated, then fell slowly down her cheek to her upper lip. Ben hesitated, then followed the tears slowly down her cheeks with kisses, but didn't stop.

Katy's breasts were small, perfectly proportioned for her thin and athletic figure. The nipples were erect and pointed arrows through Ben's chest. As Ben went lower, Katy was gripping the sheets, "I've never been this excited."

Ben didn't know how long he could last. He got up, walked towards the chest of drawers in the room, and opened the top drawer.

Katy said, "Don't stop. Don't go away."

Ben smiled, "Just a sec. I need to put this on," holding up the condom.

Katy sat up, "Let me do it. We couldn't talk about condoms at school in health class. We couldn't stop talking about them after class when the nuns had left."

Katy had Ben lie on the bed and she opened the foil package and unrolled the condom.

"Katy, I am so excited. I don't know how much more I can..."

Before he could finish the thought, Katy had gotten on the bed on both knees and then got on top of Ben, guiding him. "I don't want you to think that you forced me. I know this will hurt me for a moment."

Ben said, "I love you with all my heart."

Katy relaxed and as she descended onto him, "Ah..ah." Then she said nothing but rose and descended again.

Ben rolled Katy over and sat up.

She begged, "Don't stop."

He started kissing her belly button as he twirled both of Katy's erect nipples with his fingertips. He moved his head lower and Katy let her legs separate. Using his tongue as a probe, he searched everywhere.

Katy was moving rhythmically up and down and pleaded, "Ben, now. Ben."

Ben looked to make sure the condom was still in place, and descended into heaven.

Later, Ben said, "I didn't know I could feel the way I do. There's no way to describe it. Katy, I love you beyond reason."

Katy said, "Quoting someone very dear to me, 'How do you do it? How do you say things that I only wish I could say? You are the most amazing person on earth.'"

"Can we use this thing again?" Ben smiled, looking at the condom. "It looks okay."

Unknowingly, to Ben and Katy, that decision was flawed. Katy and Ben returned to Andover the following morning in time for breakfast. No one said a word to either. Ben told Katy as they were leaving for home. "I love you more than you could possibly know. I will call and write every day, I promise."

Katy, crying, nodded, and said, "Me, too," as she got into a large black limousine.

* * * *

Ben and Katy never saw each other again, and, according to the ATT bill, spoke only once for four minutes and thirty-eight seconds, ten months later, from a phone booth in Chappaqua, New York to a dorm room in Cambridge, Massachusetts.

James Gottesman M.D. is a Urological Oncologist who has been writing most of his adult life. He has authored more that a 100 scientific papers, medical book chapters, research grants, operative consent forms, and computer programs written in BASIC and HTML. *The Search of Grace* is his second novel. His first book, *The Road Back Isn't Straight* was published in 2013.

He graduated from UC Berkeley and UC San Francisco Medical Center and did his Urology training at UCLA. He is a Clinical Professor of Urology at the University of Washington. He lives on Mercer Island, Washington, with his wife and dog, Biscuit. He plays golf and has travelled much of the world.

8-10-02

Made in the USA
San Bernardino, CA
04 May 2014